THE BRI... ER

Katherine's ... d up at Lachlan. A dee... and the temptation to ki... grew with each passing moment.

'Twas impossible to ignore.

He was enthralling. Being this close did strange things to her. A spark of recklessness kindled inside her and Katherine felt her body lean forward. Boldly, she tilted her chin upward, encouraging him to do what they both wanted.

He understood her invitation. She trembled as he framed her face with his hands. Then his head dipped and his mouth found hers, locking it in a tender kiss. . . .

Books by Adrienne Basso

HIS WICKED EMBRACE

HIS NOBLE PROMISE

TO WED A VISCOUNT

TO PROTECT AN HEIRESS

TO TEMPT A ROGUE

THE WEDDING DECEPTION

THE CHRISTMAS HEIRESS

HIGHLAND VAMPIRE

HOW TO ENJOY A SCANDAL

NATURE OF THE BEAST

THE CHRISTMAS COUNTESS

HOW TO SEDUCE A SINNER

A LITTLE BIT SINFUL

'TIS THE SEASON TO BE SINFUL

INTIMATE BETRAYAL

NOTORIOUS DECEPTION

SWEET SENSATIONS

A NIGHT TO REMEMBER

HOW TO BE A SCOTTISH MISTRESS

BRIDE OF A SCOTTISH WARRIOR

THE HIGHLANDER WHO LOVED ME

NO OTHER HIGHLANDER

THE BRIDE CHOOSES A HIGHLANDER

Published by Kensington Publishing Corporation

The Bride Chooses A HIGHLANDER

ADRIENNE BASSO

ZEBRA BOOKS
KENSINGTON PUBLISHING CORP.
www.kensingtonbooks.com

ZEBRA BOOKS are published by

Kensington Publishing Corp.
119 West 40th Street
New York, NY 10018

All Kensington titles, imprints, and distributed lines are available at special quantity discounts for bulk purchases for sales promotion, premiums, fund-raising, educational, or institutional use.

Special book excerpts or customized printings can also be created to fit specific needs. For details, write or phone the office of the Kensington Sales Manager: Attn.: Sales Department. Kensington Publishing Corp., 119 West 40th Street, New York, NY 10018. Phone: 1-800-221-2647.

Zebra and the Z logo Reg. U.S. Pat. & TM Off.

First Printing: January 2019
ISBN-13: 978-1-4201-4620-2
ISBN-10: 1-4201-4620-3

ISBN-13: 978-1-4201-4621-9 (eBook)
ISBN-10: 1-4201-4621-1 (eBook)

10 9 8 7 6 5 4 3 2 1

Printed in the United States of America

*To my dear friend Barb Batlan-Massabrook,
a courageous lass who loves all things Scottish—
especially plaids, brogues, and handsome,
sexy Highlanders in kilts*

Chapter One

Highlands of Scotland, Winter, 1335

"I'll marry him," Katherine McKenna declared in a quiet, somber voice. "I'll take Laird Drummond's eldest son, Sir Hamish, as my husband."

"At last!" Sir Brian McKenna, fearsome warrior and powerful laird of Clan McKenna, slapped his hand on the wooden table in obvious delight. The lines at the corners of his eyes deepened as he smiled broadly at his daughter. "I'll send a servant to tell Laird Drummond the good news. With luck, the first banns can be read before the snows start to melt."

Katherine sighed inwardly. Her father's smile of approval gave her confidence a much needed lift, helping to quash the sudden flush of panic that gripped her belly.

Yet before the McKenna could open the chamber door to summon one of his retainers, a female voice echoed through the room.

"Hold!" Lady Aileen McKenna's mouth twisted in

skepticism as she cast a piercing look at Katherine. "Are ye entirely certain that it should be Hamish?"

"Aye, Mother." Though she kept her expression steady, apprehension nibbled at Katherine. Nay, she wasn't *entirely* certain, but the business of choosing a husband had been all consuming, plaguing her for years. Being unmarried at her advanced age of twenty-two had become an embarrassment to herself and her clan. She needed to be done with it and Hamish seemed a reasonable choice.

"Sir Hamish is but a few years older than I and has much to recommend him," Katherine continued. "Most important, Father insists the alliance with the Drummond clan will be of benefit to us."

"If all we sought was a political alliance, I would have allowed ye to be married at sixteen," Lady Aileen said dryly.

The McKenna's head snapped up, his eyes burning into his wife. "Damnation, Aileen, dinnae be putting doubts into the lass's head. I've waited far too long to hear these words pass from her lips."

"Och, ye always were an impatient man, Brian McKenna," Lady Aileen retorted crisply. "I'll not have my only daughter marry unless she is ready."

"Ready? Ready?" The McKenna's voice rose as his famous temper reared. "Most females her age have a parcel of bairns clinging to their skirts. Others who have suffered the loss of their husbands have been blessed with a second marriage. 'Tis past time fer Katherine to be *ready*."

The truth of her father's word made Katherine cringe. 'Twas highly unusual for a woman of her station and age to be unmarried, unless she had committed herself to the church. From the time of Katherine's birth there had been countless offers from men young and old to contract the McKenna's daughter in marriage and all had been refused, thanks to a promise Lady Aileen had somehow extracted from her husband.

Katherine would not be married unless she agreed to the match. In essence, she had been gifted with the rare power of being able to select her husband. Many of the Highland lairds thought the McKenna must be going soft in the head, allowing such an unheard of arrangement—though none dared to voice the sentiment within his hearing.

Being given a choice had made the selection of a husband a far more daunting task than Katherine could ever have imagined. Raised with three brothers, she was used to the roughness and directness of males, but she quickly learned that men could be duplicitous as well as charming when they wanted something.

Some who came courting declared their undying love within minutes of meeting her, claiming to be struck by her luminous beauty and charm. Others appeared more interested in her breeding capabilities than her feelings, while a few were clearly enamored of the size of her dowry.

Yet all became peevish and annoyed when she refused them, leaving Katherine to wonder if this choice her mother had fought so hard to give her was more burden than gift.

Her parents continued arguing. The louder the McKenna bellowed, the quieter and more tightly controlled her mother spoke. Their squabbling barely registered in Katherine's mind. 'Twas a common occurrence for her parents to bicker—and even more common for them to hastily retreat to the privacy of their bedchamber once the matter had been resolved.

Once she was old enough to be aware of it, this unrelenting passion between the pair had fascinated

Katherine. She had witnessed it time and again, along with the joy, laughter, love, and respect that somehow never wavered between the couple. Her eldest brother, Malcolm, always said that their parents were bound together by a thread so strong that no matter how hard it was pulled, it never seemed to break.

Malcolm and her second eldest brother, James, appeared to be on the road to achieving a similar relationship with their own wives, furthering Katherine's dreams of one day creating this type of marriage for herself. All she needed was the right husband.

Was it Sir Hamish? Katherine lifted her gaze to the heavens and whispered a prayer of hope, then felt a stab of guilt for such a selfish request. There were far more serious matters in this world for the Almighty to be troubled with than her happiness.

The squabbling between her parents abruptly ceased. The McKenna paced restlessly about the chamber while Lady Aileen pinned her husband with a scathing look. He stilled suddenly, signaling that he had succeeded in bringing his agitation under control.

Her mother relaxed her stare and turned toward Katherine. Smiling, Lady Aileen reached over and stroked the stray wisps on her daughter's temple that had escaped her braid. Katherine's tresses were one of her most striking features; streaks of red, the same shade as her mother's, mixed in with the darker brown hues of her father.

Katherine was in truth a combination of both her parents, physically and emotionally. She hoped she carried the best of each, yet was honest enough to admit she possessed her mother's strong, vibrant spirit and her father's unrepentant desire to have his own way in all matters.

"'Tis settled?" Katherine asked, her voice unusually timid. She glanced anxiously from one parent to the other. "I'll marry Sir Hamish?"

The McKenna nodded firmly, yet waited for her mother to announce the decision.

"Aye," Lady Aileen proclaimed. "We'll send a message to Laird Drummond this very afternoon."

Katherine bit back the urge to sigh. If her mother sensed any hesitation, she would pounce and the business of a husband would remain unsettled until the spring—or longer.

Nay, 'twas past time that she move forward with her life. Being a wife—and hopefully, God willing—a mother one day, was what Katherine desired. If all went according to plan, then it appeared she was finally going to have a chance to fulfill those dreams.

Two days later an impressive contingent of McKenna retainers set out for Drummond Castle. Katherine and her mother, along with several female servants, rode in the center of the long column, surrounded by the fiercest of the McKenna warriors. Her father rode at the front, leading his men, her youngest brother, Graham, at his side.

At her father's insistence, they had gotten an early start, leaving before the sun rose, thus ensuring they would arrive at their destination before darkness prevailed. The McKenna set a grueling pace, yet Katherine and her mother, as well as their female servants, had no difficulty keeping up with the McKenna warriors.

Their mounts were among the finest horseflesh in Scotland, bred for speed and endurance. Lady Aileen had chosen her female companions wisely, taking those who had skill with hair, clothing, and riding. She had always relished the opportunity to show her husband—and her clansmen—that women were as capable as men in many areas of life.

Despite the fast pace and cold temperature, Katherine found the journey enjoyable. They rode beneath a cloudless blue sky and her fur-lined cloak protected her from the biting wind. Her eyes glinted with pleasure at the sight of the snowcapped mountains in the distance. The ethereal beauty of the stark landscape intrigued her and she drank in her surroundings with interest.

She had been raised with far more freedom than many other females of her class, leaving the confines of McKenna Castle often throughout her childhood. Yet this journey felt different, for it was going to change the course of her life.

Once the marriage contracts were negotiated and signed, Katherine would return home to prepare for her wedding. Her mother had hoped to wait until the spring, but her father had already declared that the best way to break the confines and boredom of winter was to have a celebration.

While hardly the ideal season to host a large feast, Lady Aileen had concurred that the fall harvest had been bountiful and there was enough food and drink in the storerooms to provide a proper meal for their guests. Katherine knew that meant in all likelihood she would be married by the end of the month.

They stopped only twice during the journey, to water the horses, hastily eat some brown bread, oatcakes, cheese, and dried fruit, drink some ale, and attend to personal needs.

Just as the sun began its descent, Drummond Castle came into view. Katherine's heart skipped as she gazed ahead. *My future home.* Strategically set on the edge of a bluff, the four-story stone fortress blocked the view of anything beyond it. Though not as large as McKenna Castle, 'twas an impressive structure, boasting a tall, square watchtower surrounded by a thick curtain wall.

Even from a distance, Katherine could clearly see both soldiers and archers atop the parapets, pacing to and fro, alert to any potential threats. The drawbridge was open, yet well guarded, with several heavily armed men positioned around it.

As they descended into the valley, the clang of a warning bell rang throughout the land.

"Raise our clan banner higher," the McKenna shouted. "I want to make certain those archers know who we are or else we'll be starting a feud instead of negotiating a marriage contract."

The circle of warriors around Katherine and her mother closed ranks. They rode for a few tense moments until they received several friendly waves from the guards on the wall. Katherine felt the stiffness in the men surrounding her ease. She smiled in relief, took a deep breath, and settled back in her saddle.

Word of their arrival spread quickly through the village that was nestled at the base of the castle. Men, women, and children stood in the lane and peered at her with open curiosity. Katherine could feel even more sets of eyes fastening upon her as they crossed the drawbridge and entered the bailey. She offered a gracious smile to a gathering of women; a small wave to two children. They returned the gestures eagerly and Katherine's nerves began to calm.

Still, she felt a surprising jab of uncertainty when she spied Laird Drummond standing at the end of the bailey, surrounded by a gaggle of clansmen. There would be no turning back now. The laird's eager smile made it clear he was very pleased to see them and no doubt anxious to negotiate the terms of her marriage contract. Once signed, her fate would be sealed.

Katherine's eyes searched the men who stood beside their laird, looking for Sir Hamish. She had only met him three times, spending no more than an hour in his company on each occasion. She had found him to be a pleasant companion with a biting wit and a charming manner.

At last she spotted him in the crowd. There were four other clansmen between him and Laird Drummond and she wondered why he wasn't standing beside his father. The men around Sir Hamish were talking to him, but he didn't appear to be listening. Nay, he was gazing up at her with a thoughtful expression on his face.

The deep blue cloak he wore reflected the blue of his eyes and highlighted the golden streaks in his hair. His features were plain, nondescript, but his smile had the ability to transform his face, giving it an almost handsome countenance.

He smiled often—a trait that Katherine found most appealing. His jovial temperament was what had drawn her to him initially, had given her cause to seriously consider his suit.

Disappointingly, he was not smiling now.

The McKenna party came to a halt and dismounted a few feet from the entrance to the great hall. Her parents greeted the widowed Laird Drummond, speaking for a few moments in quiet tones, their words undistinguishable.

Katherine curtsied when Laird Drummond raised his head and glanced at her, his eyes bright with interest.

"Welcome, welcome!" Laird Drummond said with a beaming smile.

"We thank ye fer yer gracious invitation," Lady Aileen replied.

"'Tis an honor. We are pleased to have ye here to discuss such an important matter," Laird Drummond declared, rubbing his hands together vigorously. "Hamish, after ye've greeted our guests, ye must show Lady Katherine yer mother's private garden."

Sir Hamish weaved his way through the crowd. Frowning, he looked at his father. "There's naught to see. The plants and bushes are bare and there's three inches of snow covering everything."

Laird Drummond narrowed his brow in annoyance, glaring pointedly at his eldest son. "Lady Katherine has been in the saddle fer hours. A walk in the garden will be a welcome relief to her cramped limbs."

Katherine cleared her throat. Her limbs were not at all cramped; truthfully, she could ride for several more hours. She lowered her eyes modestly. Did Sir Hamish not realize his father's intent was to give them time alone?

"Lady Katherine." Sir Hamish gave her a surprisingly elegant bow at the same moment Katherine's father gave her a nudge.

With a startled cry, Katherine pitched forward. Sir Hamish bolted upright, catching her before she tumbled to the ground.

"Fergive my clumsiness, Sir Hamish," she mumbled, feeling the heat rising in her cheeks.

"Ye are not clumsy, Lady Katherine. The ground here is rough and uneven," he replied gallantly, casting a scolding eye on those around them who had broken into delighted chuckles.

Katherine righted herself and Sir Hamish promptly removed the arm he had wrapped around her midriff.

"Where is the garden?" she asked.

"This way," he replied.

There were too many pairs of eyes to count trained upon them as they left. Nervously, Katherine knotted her fingers into fists at her side, hoping she looked dignified. Literally falling into Sir Hamish's arms was hardly the impression she was hoping to make to him and his clan.

Sir Hamish remained silent, leading her around the main keep to a half-walled plot that extended beyond the kitchen door. The ground was indeed covered with a layer of snow; the trees planted along the south side stark and barren.

"I can assure ye, it looks far more impressive in the spring and summer," he said. "Even in the fall there is beauty to be found here."

"Laird Drummond said this was yer mother's garden?"

"Aye, 'twas her pride and joy. She supervised the planting of every tree and bush, deciding which herbs and flowers would be included."

Katherine ran her fingers over the branch of a snow-covered bush. "Naught is in bloom, yet I can see she did a fine job with the design."

Sir Hamish nodded. "She loved seeing things grow. Though all lies dormant now, I feel her presence most strongly when I am here," he added, his voice tinged with sadness.

"Ye miss her," Katherine said quietly.

The pensive look in Sir Hamish's eyes deepened. "I do. Her death was so sudden. She complained of a headache one afternoon and took to her bed, asking fer quiet so she could rest. Her maidservant found her a few hours later, prostrate on the floor, her body cold with death."

"How dreadful!"

His expression was laced with sorrow. "'Twas more

than three years ago. At times it seems so long ago, at others, like it was yesterday," he said, his voice quivering.

"I'm sorry fer yer pain," Katherine said sympathetically.

Sir Hamish turned his head abruptly, avoiding her gaze. "Fergive me. I should be welcoming ye to Drummond Castle, not regaling ye with maudlin tales."

Katherine rested her hand upon his arm. She didn't mind the awkward conversation, for it gave her a glimpse into his emotions and she liked what she saw.

"Grieving the loss of someone we love is hardly maudlin, Sir Hamish. 'Tis noble."

He released a quiet sigh. "I believe my mother would have liked ye, Lady Katherine. Very much."

"Och, but would she have approved of me marrying her son?" Katherine said, squeezing his arm playfully.

"Aye, she would. 'Tis a good match that will forge a strong bond between our two clans." His smile faded and his expression grew solemn. "Are ye certain?"

Katherine could feel the heat of a blush rise in her face. "I know 'tis said that I am a fickle woman, changing my mind like the ever-moving direction of the wind. But once decided, I stand firm. And I have decided."

Sir Hamish placed his hand gently upon her cheek. His fingertips were cold, but Katherine knew that was not the reason she shivered. Boldly, she took a step closer.

Sir Hamish's eyes widened in surprise. He hesitated a moment before snaking his other hand around her waist. Katherine sighed and willingly pressed herself closer, gasping at the feel of his hard, muscular body pressed against the softness of her breast, the feel of his warm breath on her cheek.

She raised her hands, her fingers gripping the blue

wool of his cloak, anticipating with nervous excitement the kiss she knew was forthcoming.

He tilted, then lowered his head, but instead of claiming her lips, he placed a kiss on her cheek before rubbing his jaw across it. There was a softness, a gentleness to his movements that she found pleasant. Eagerly, Katherine angled her head, hoping their lips would meet. Instead, he pulled back, ending the contact.

Katherine sighed with regret and shut her eyes, needing a moment to compose herself. When she was ready, she took a deep breath and raised her eyelids.

He favored her with an uneven smile. She held her eyes steady on him, trying to read his expression. Did he think she would have rejected his kiss? Or even worse, disliked it? The proper custom was for a couple to wait until their official betrothal ceremony to kiss. Was that the reason he had hesitated? Or was it something else?

"I'm certain yer parents are wondering why we have not returned. We must go back before someone is sent to fetch us. 'Tis important fer me to make a favorable impression upon them, especially yer father." Sir Hamish gave her a slight bow and extended his arm. "Shall we join the others?"

After a moment, Katherine nodded. She was relieved to discover his reason for forgoing a kiss, though truthfully she would have been happier if he had been bolder and taken the risk. And she would have liked to have more time alone together.

He is being proper and respectful, she told herself as they walked away, tamping down the twinge of disappointment that washed over her. When they reached the entrance to the garden, Sir Hamish paused. He placed his hand over Katherine's and gave it a reassuring squeeze.

"I will care fer ye and protect ye, Katherine. Ye shall want fer nothing as my wife."

Sir Hamish's tone was earnest and sincere, his expression kind and agreeable. It pleased her that he had already dropped the formalities and no longer addressed her as "lady."

Katherine's heart swelled with relief. She had chosen well. They were making a good start toward feeling at ease with each other. The rest would come with time.

By all accounts, their marriage should be a happy one.

Chapter Two

"Word has reached us that Robbie is being held prisoner by the McKennas," Lady Morag said, her voice laced with hope. "'Tis but a four-day ride to the McKenna border. If ye negotiate a ransom, he could be returned to us in a week's time."

Laird Lachlan MacTavish straightened in his chair, glancing over at his stepmother. Lady Morag was an attractive woman, yet she appeared much older than her forty-two years. Her dark hair was streaked with swaths of gray, her shoulders slightly stooped by weariness, her figure far too thin and fragile.

She had worked tirelessly to aid Lachlan when he became laird of the MacTavish clan at the death of her husband—Lachlan's father—a little more than a year ago. He was grateful for her support and well aware of all that he owed her.

Last spring, Lachlan's half brother, Robbie, had been lured south by the glittering prize money offered at the tournaments in the Lowlands. He was expected to return in a month, two at most. 'Twas now nine months later and each day Lady Morag's pain over the mysterious absence of her youngest son visibly grew.

It brought Lachlan no small measure of grief to witness her decline and tore at his heart to see her suffering. It further needled his pride knowing he couldn't answer the wide, hopeful expression that now glowed in her eyes. How he wished there was something he could do to bring her the relief she so richly deserved!

"Every few weeks there is another rumor about Robbie," Lachlan said gently. "Last month we heard that he had been taken by the English and the month before that he was off to sea."

"This time 'tis different," Lady Morag insisted. Hope dampened her eyes and she grasped his arm tightly. "Old Angus heard it from his grandson's wife. She was an Armstrong before she married and came here. She went to visit her kin and heard that our Robbie was a prisoner, sentenced to hard labor working in the McKenna quarry. Angus shared the information with me the moment he discovered it."

Lachlan scrubbed his hand across his chin. "The Armstrongs and the McKennas do share blood ties," he conceded. "There's a possibility that this information could have merit."

"It does! I feel it in my bones." Lady Morag hastily crossed herself. "Oh, Lachlan, at long last my prayers have been answered."

Looking away guiltily, Lachlan let out a heavy sigh. "I share yer deep concern fer the fate of my missing brother, but if the McKennas have him, there is naught we can do."

"Truly?" Lady Morag brought a trembling hand to her mouth to muffle her cry. "There must be something. Can ye send a messenger to see if they will ransom him?"

Lachlan frowned into his bitter, watery ale. "We have

nothing to offer in exchange—no coin or plate, no grain, no livestock, no fine goods."

The words were a sour reminder of how far the MacTavish clan had fallen, how his father's efforts—and now Lachlan's—had failed to significantly improve their lives.

Once a wealthy and powerful clan, generations ago they had chosen the wrong side in the Scottish war for independence, a conflict that had thrown the country into turmoil, breaking long-held alliances and dividing loyalties among the fierce Highland clans.

When he finally secured his regal power, Robert the Bruce had not forgotten the MacTavish clan's misguided allegiance. If not for Lady Morag's blood ties to the Campbells—an ally of King Robert—the Mac-Tavish clansmen might have all been put to death.

Though their lives had been spared, the clan had paid a heavy price. The king had stripped them of their most fertile land, gold plate, coins, livestock, and other wealth.

In the ensuing years, they had proven their loyalty time and again to the Scottish king and his son, fighting to keep Scotland free. Yet many of the Highland clans still remembered that generations ago the Mac-Tavish had paid homage to the hated English.

The land on which they now lived was mountainous and rocky, the soil of poor quality. The planting of crops was a futile endeavor, though many of his clansmen and women persisted in trying. A thin yield of barley, oats, scrawny turnips, cabbages, and carrots was preferable to starving.

For the past few years Lachlan worked tirelessly training himself and his men to be skilled fighters. Each spring, summer, and fall he had taken his best soldiers south, offering their services to the clans in the

Lowlands who were struggling in the fight to keep the borders secured from the English.

Lachlan's reputation as an excellent leader, a clever tactician, and a talented swordsman quickly grew and the Lowland lairds aggressively bid for the services of the MacTavish soldiers. The coin he and his men earned had kept the clan alive, but it was only a temporary solution.

As laird, Lachlan's goal was to petition the crown for the return of some of the MacTavish fertile lands. This year, two of the Lowland lairds he had fought for had agreed to support his request and speak on his behalf. Yet this plan was most certainly doomed to failure if a man as powerful as Brian McKenna opposed it.

"I could write to my cousin," Lady Morag suggested, wringing her hands. "He might intercede on Robbie's behalf."

"The Campbells and the McKennas have a long-standing rivalry. Even if yer cousin is willing to help, the McKennas willnae be inclined to grant a Campbell any favors." Lachlan drained his tankard before pushing it aside. "In truth, it could make matters worse."

"There must be something we can do," Lady Morag cried, her voice rising with emotions.

Lachlan tightened his fingers on the well-worn wooden arms of his chair. Justice was serious business in the Highlands and the clans were fiercely protective of their right to dispense it as they saw fit.

"If the McKennas have indeed imprisoned Robbie, they must believe they had good cause," Lachlan said slowly. "Even if we had the means to negotiate his release, I doubt the McKenna would consider it."

"We need to try," Lady Morag insisted.

"Aye, Mother. We do," chimed another male voice.

"And if our laird will not organize a rescue party, then I will."

Lachlan's half brother Aiden strode into the hall, surrounded by several younger clansmen. He was the elder of Lady Morag's two natural sons and though they shared the same father, Lachlan and Aiden bore little resemblance to each other.

Lachlan was dark; Aiden fair. They were both considered handsome men, yet their features were stark contrasts. Lachlan's face possessed a sharp, rugged edge while Aiden's was chiseled and pretty in an almost feminine manner.

Aiden sported a beard; Lachlan preferred to be clean-shaven. Both were tall, with wide shoulders and well-defined muscles, earned from hours of swordplay on the practice field. Women swooned equally over the pair and each had his pick of willing females, though out of respect for Lady Morag they exercised restraint and discretion.

Each man was stubborn in his own way, and they disagreed on everything from the number of men that were needed to guard the gates of the keep to the time the evening meal should be served. 'Twas no surprise that the fate of their third brother, Robbie, would be discussed any differently.

Lady Morag turned her full attention to Aiden. "Ye've heard the news about Robbie?" she asked.

Aiden nodded. "Old Angus told me. As soon as we can gather supplies, my men and I will ride to the McKenna border," he proclaimed. "I will bring him home to ye, Mother."

"We dinnae even know if they are holding Robbie prisoner," Lachlan protested.

"I intend to find out."

"Then what?"

"I shall free my brother."

Lachlan frowned in exasperation. "How? We've nothing of value to offer in exchange fer his freedom."

Aiden moved his hand to the hilt of his sword. "If necessary, we'll take him by force."

Lachlan took hold of his brother's arm, forcing Aiden to face him. "I forbid it."

A glint of anger invaded Aiden's eyes. "Ye've no right to give me such an order!"

"I am yer laird." Lachlan stood, tension knotting his limbs. Frustration coursed through his veins, but he tamped down his emotions. Getting angry would change nothing, though he suspected his stepmother would appreciate a show of outrage and indignation from him.

"The McKennas are not known fer their mercy," Lachlan continued. "If we dare to interfere in their clan business, none of us would walk away."

"'Tis exactly why we must save Robbie!" Aiden insisted, gritting his teeth.

Lachlan slowly shook his head. "If the information old Angus received is true, then the McKennas have spared Robbie's life. He will return to us once he has paid his debt to them fer whatever crime he committed."

"Crime? Our Robbie is not a criminal," Lady Morag protested.

"The McKennas are not so heartless as to hold a man fer no reason," Lachlan said, hoping a gentle tone would soften the blow. "We must believe they have just cause."

Truth be told, hearing of this circumstance was not a complete surprise. Robbie had a wild, impulsive streak that reminded Lachlan too much of the undisciplined, reckless Englishmen he sometimes faced in combat.

"And what if Robbie does not survive his imprisonment, Lachlan?" Aiden asked. "Will ye sleep well at night knowing ye could have saved yer brother, yet ye chose the easier path?"

Lady Morag turned a desperate eye to him. "Lachlan?"

Lachlan felt a hot flush of anger crawl up his neck. *Damn, Aiden!* This was not an easy choice, yet 'twas the only sane choice in these circumstances. How could Aiden not see it?

"Dinnae fret so, Mother," Aiden said sharply. "Lachlan might not have a care fer Robbie, but I do."

Lady Morag wiped her eyes. "I'm grateful, Aiden."

His stepmother's words surprised Lachlan. She was not one to show overt favoritism; 'twas rare for her to pit one sibling against the other. These uncharacteristic actions indicated the extent of her distress and desperation and it wounded him deeply that he could not oblige her and do as she bid.

Though Lachlan was not her natural son, he had never been made to feel that way. His own mother had died in childbirth and his father had married Lady Morag the following year, when times were still good and the new Scottish king had not yet exacted his revenge on the clan. Lady Morag had lovingly cared for Lachlan and that devotion never waned, even when she had given birth to two sons of her own.

The heated discussion between Lachlan and Aiden had attracted an audience—many eyes in the great hall were upon him. Lachlan knew he needed to tread carefully. Only his fighting soldiers knew him well; the rest of the clan were curious and cautious around him, uncertain of his mood, temperament, and motives.

Lachlan knew the importance of being a respected,

strong leader. This situation was a prime test of his will to put the needs of the clan above his personal desires and he was determined not to waver in his decision or attitude. 'Twas the only path he deemed honorable to win the support he needed from his clansmen.

He looked meaningfully at his brother. "My order stands."

A glint of defiance clouded Aiden's eyes. "I willnae let my brother suffer and die at the hands of the McKennas."

Lachlan's stony expression yielded. "Our best swordsmen are no match for the might and strength of the McKennas. Ye will quickly fall prey to slaughter."

"The MacTavish are Highlanders—we fight with skill and honor," Aiden declared proudly.

"Ye'll die with it too." Sighing, Lachlan rubbed his hand over his face. He understood Aiden's passion—hell, he shared it. But he had to be practical and act on what was best for the safety of the entire clan. As laird, he didn't have the luxury of pursuing a personal vendetta. Especially now.

He had not told anyone of his plans to regain some of their property, fearing to raise hopes that could be dashed. And he dare not breathe a word of it to Aiden, for if it failed it would be held as a mark against Lachlan's leadership.

"Yer wild talk is upsetting our lady mother." Lachlan placed his arm around Aiden's shoulders, bent his head, and whispered in his ear, "We dinnae even know if this information about Robbie is true."

Aiden's mouth turned down in a mulish frown as he batted Lachlan's arm away. "'Tis the first solid lead we've had about Robbie's whereabouts fer months. We owe it to him to bring him home."

Lachlan held up his hand. "Dinnae be a fool! If it is

true, then there is a chance that Robbie will be released once he has settled his debt with the McKennas. But if ye persist in this madness, our mother will most assuredly be burying two sons."

Aiden whirled and slammed his fist against the table. "Aye, I'm a fool," he said bitterly. "A fool to think ye would act with courage."

Lachlan clamped his teeth together so hard his jaw began to ache. "Ye go too far, Aiden."

"Do I?" Aiden ran his gaze scornfully over his brother.

Lachlan shifted on his feet, feeling the tension of his brother's bitterness. He was not surprised by Aiden's arrogance, but he was annoyed by it. Dissension in the clan was dangerous and arguing would accomplish little except further upsetting his stepmother. He summoned control, revealing no expression.

"We are all concerned about Robbie, but I cannae afford to let my emotions rule my head," Lachlan said. "What happens if the McKennas decide to retaliate? What of our women and bairns? Who will protect them when the full wrath of the vengeful McKennas rains down upon us?"

"That willnae happen," Aiden declared, though his voice had lost some of its conviction.

"Lachlan is right." Lady Morag's shoulders sagged. "Ye cannae place Robbie's life above others."

While Lachlan appreciated his stepmother's support and understanding, the victory felt hollow. The sadness in her eyes haunted him and prompted him to take some action.

"To be fair, we should discover if this information about Robbie's whereabouts is indeed true. It will set our minds at ease," Lachlan decided. "Aiden, I give ye leave to travel south and seek the truth. But ye must not approach the McKenna nor any of his sons. Be stealth and discreet and return quickly."

His brother's nostrils flared. He hesitated, then bowed his head in what appeared to be reluctant acceptance, but his hands were clenched into tight fists. Three of Aiden's loyal men stood in fierce resolve at his side. At Aiden's tense nod, they too bowed their heads respectfully before storming out of the great hall.

Lady Morag broke into noisy sobs. Lachlan folded her into his arms, feeling helpless. The solace he offered her today was fleeting. No matter what Aiden discovered, he feared his stepmother was destined to shed many more tears.

Chapter Three

Laughter rang out at the feast in the Drummond great hall, celebrating the upcoming nuptials of Katherine and Hamish. The newly betrothed couple sat side by side on the dais, smiling and graciously accepting the good wishes and bawdy comments of the crowd.

Katherine was pleased that her father and Laird Drummond were also in good spirits, for they had each looked a tad sour earlier when the marriage contracts had been signed. Their attitudes had worried Katherine, but her mother assured her that a show of temperament was the result of a good negotiation. Each had gotten some of what he had wanted, while relinquishing something he would have preferred to hold.

Katherine had made the most of her time while waiting for the settlement to be reached. There had been two private meetings with Sir Hamish—Hamish, as he insisted she address him—filled with lively conversation but regretfully no kisses, even on the cheek or forehead.

However, there was much to like about her future husband. The time she had spent with him—both alone and in the company of others—served to reassure

Katherine that she had made the right decision about her marriage.

From the women in the castle, Katherine had learned the history of the Drummond clan and the current workings of the household. Her mother was often with her, but had stayed in the background, allowing Katherine to take the lead. She had maintained her composure under the cautious, appraising stares and pointed questions the women had posed to her, understanding their keen interest.

When she married Hamish, Katherine would become chatelaine of the castle and the highest-ranking woman in the clan. 'Twas natural that these women wished to learn more about her.

"More venison stew, Katherine?"

Turning at the sound of the familiar voice, Katherine abandoned her thoughts and smiled at her betrothed. She was feeling more at ease with him each day. Hamish had been considerate, but not overbearing during the meal, ensuring the choicest bits of meat were on her side of the trencher they shared. He had introduced her to more clan members than she could name and told her amusing stories about many of them.

"Thank ye, Hamish, but I cannae swallow another morsel."

He refilled her wine goblet, then stood. "Excuse me. I must . . . uhm . . . that is, I need to . . . uhm . . ."

Having seen how much ale Hamish consumed with the meal, Katherine knew exactly what he needed. Saving him further embarrassment, she nodded and he gratefully departed.

Sipping from her wine goblet, Katherine admired her surroundings. The great hall was smaller than the one at McKenna Castle, but 'twas well-appointed and comfortable. Two large fireplaces gave off enough heat to warm the chamber, and the tapestries depicting the history of the clan that hung on the stone walls added color and warmth.

The rushes were fresh; the dried herbs scattered among them gave off a pleasant scent. The ale and wine served were of good quality and so was the whiskey, judging by how many times her father had refilled his goblet.

Of course, there were improvements to be made. Katherine noted that many of the servants' garments were mended in places and the food, though plentiful, lacked the proper seasoning. She had already decided that these would be among the first changes she would undertake when she became mistress; no doubt others would soon follow.

The remains of the meal were cleared and the tables pushed back to allow for entertainment and dancing. In the midst of the chaos and laughter, Katherine seized the moment to venture from the great hall. A few minutes respite from the noise and intensity of the celebration would be welcome, as she was unused to being the center of attention for such a long period of time.

Hamish had not yet returned, making it easier for her to slip away unnoticed. Embroiled in the excitement of the feast, the energetic pages and giggling maidservants paid her no heed when she passed them. Katherine stood for a few minutes beneath an arrow-slit window, breathing in the fresh, crisp air, realizing for the first time how stuffy it had become in the great hall, which had been nearly filled to the rafters with clanspeople.

Intent on extending her solitude, Katherine started following one of the passages. Spirits high, she allowed her mind to wander as she made her way through a maze of winding corridors, eventually finding herself in a deserted hallway, deep inside the castle.

It was dark, with only a few lit torches fastened to the walls. They cast eerie shadows in front of her, giving off a sinister glow. Shaking off the sudden chill that ran down her spine, Katherine turned, intending to retrace her steps. But the corridors all looked the same and she soon found herself back where she started.

A sudden noise made her jump. Startled, she turned, but saw only dancing shadows in the distance. Heart thumping in an erratic rhythm, she waited, nearly crying out when she heard it a second time. Animal sounds—or human? 'Twas impossible to tell.

Taking slow, measured steps, Katherine moved toward the sounds. She rounded a corner, coming to a halt when she discovered a couple locked in an embrace. Shaking her head, Katherine smiled at her foolish imagination. 'Twas not the growling of a monster or beast hidden in this darkened hallway that had frightened her. 'Twas the moans of passion and delight from a pair of enthusiastic lovers.

Katherine's cheeks heated at the sight and she glanced away. In any other circumstance she would have discreetly taken her leave, but she needed assistance in finding her way back to the great hall and these two were the only people she had seen.

Raising her chin, Katherine loudly cleared her throat. Oblivious to her presence, the couple deepened their kiss. Red-faced, Katherine glanced down at her feet, pondering her next move.

'Twould take a far louder noise to get their attention. Her lips curled into a smile when she recalled seeing the McKenna cook tossing a bucket of water on a pair of amorous hounds who had taken up residence at the open kitchen door. They had yelped and separated with nary a moment to spare.

Unfortunately, Katherine possessed neither a bucket nor a source to obtain water, nor the nerve to douse two adults with it. She was considering backing away and then stomping toward the couple when a flicker of torchlight revealed the deep blue wool tunic of the male lover.

Katherine blinked. *I know that garment.*

Blood rushed in her ears and her heart pounded as she drew closer.

"Hamish?"

The man lifted his head and she caught sight of his profile, confirming her worst fears. A high-pitched keening sound escaped from the back of her throat.

Katherine's breath came out in a short gasp and for an instant she thought she was going to throw up. Bending forward, she wiped her mouth with the back of her sleeve, then straightened her shoulders and pulled herself to her full height.

What are ye doing? 'Twas the first thought that sprang into her mind, and Katherine was relieved she had retained enough of her wits not to say it, as it was more than obvious what he was doing. "Hamish! Who is this woman?"

At the sound of her loud voice, Hamish turned. His jaw slacked and his brows rose in surprise. The girl moved beyond him, gazing at Katherine in wide-eyed horror while clutching her hand to her breast.

"Katherine!" Hamish looked nervously between the two females. "How did ye find yer way to this part of the castle? Are ye lost?"

"Lost?" Katherine felt her face color. She stared unseeing into the distance, trying to understand the impossibility of what she had just witnessed. "Who is this woman?"

Hamish's eyes remained on Katherine's face, yet he said nothing.

"I am Fe . . . Fe . . . Fenella," the young woman finally stammered, averting her eyes.

"And what is yer relationship with my betrothed?" Katherine asked frostily.

"She is a friend." Hamish cleared his throat. "A boon companion. We've known each other since we were children."

Katherine raised her eyebrows. "I, too, have many childhood friends and I can assure ye, I dinnae bestow that kind of affection upon them."

Hamish rubbed his neck in discomfort. "We were saying farewell. Fenella is leaving in the morning to visit her mother's people in the Lowlands."

"Why?" Katherine asked.

"My father thought it best."

Katherine gasped. There was only one obvious reason a lass would be sent from her home. Katherine's eyes fell to Fenella's belly, but it appeared flat beneath her gown. "Does she carry yer babe? Is she yer leman?"

"She is not!" Hamish's brow contorted in offense. "Fenella is an honorable and chaste maiden. Her father was the captain of the Drummond guard fer many years."

"A soldier's daughter." Katherine gave them both a long, penetrating look. "Respectable, but not nearly high born enough to wed the laird's heir. God's teeth, Hamish, why did ye ever agree to our marriage when ye were in love with another woman?"

Katherine clutched her clasped hands to her breasts as if this shield could somehow protect her from the hurt and betrayal that coursed through her veins.

Hamish's expression crumbled with misery. "I never

believed ye would choose me. And when ye did, well, everyone was so pleased, especially my father. I know my duty to him and my clan and I'll not selfishly forsake it fer my own happiness."

"Ye'll sacrifice yerself and marry me?" Katherine's voice rose as anger replaced surprise and hurt. "Aye, ye are truly a noble Highlander."

"I deserve yer contempt—and more. I've made a great mess of it all, Katherine. Fergive me." Hamish bowed his head, looking so guilty and remorseful Katherine's anger began to ease.

She had long been told that love was an unpredictable and uncontrollable feeling. 'Twas not entirely Hamish's fault that he felt such a strong emotion for Fenella. Though Katherine could—and did—blame him for being deceitful about it.

She rubbed her hand vigorously across her eyes, then took several deep breaths to compose herself. Somehow she had to accept that fate had granted them a reprieve from a marriage that would strain to be pleasant and in all likelihood would lack trust, passion, and fulfillment.

Judging by the way they clung to each other, Katherine felt certain Fenella would one day return from the Lowlands. And she knew she would not be a wife who simply turned a blind eye to her husband's infidelity. That would be unbearable.

Katherine told herself she should be grateful to have made this discovery now, while there was still time to rectify the situation. Her father would be angry and disappointed; her mother supportive, but also disappointed at the failure of an arrangement that had seemed so promising. The clan, too, would feel the sting of this failure, for it would be gossiped about throughout the Highlands in a most unflattering way.

"In the morning we must inform our families that we have decided not to wed," Katherine declared, her heart sinking as she uttered the words.

"Nay!" Hamish's face twisted with panic. "The contracts have been signed, the terms agreed upon. We shall be married at the end of the month, as planned."

Katherine shook her head vehemently. "The contracts can be torn up—or better still, burned. We both know that our union will bring us naught but misery."

"I had not realized that ye were such a romantic," Hamish blurted out. "Few couples of our station marry fer love. The more practical elements of property, alliance, and advancement are considered."

"Aye," Katherine agreed. "I dinnae expect to be gifted with yer love on our wedding day. But I had hoped fer the chance to someday be blessed with it."

"That remains a distinct possibility," he insisted, taking a step closer.

Fenella let out a gasp of pain and Hamish's face instantly filled with contrition. His reaction was only more proof to Katherine that his heart was already taken and a marriage between them would never be more than a duty to him.

"If ye lack the courage to break the contracts, then I will do it," Katherine declared, swallowing hard to push back the sourness in her stomach. "One of us needs to be practical."

"I willnae break the contract. It will create a feud between the clans," Hamish warned. "I'll not be responsible fer the consequences."

Katherine's confidence faltered. Clan wars had been started over less. Still, she would not sentence herself to a life of misery just to avoid the possibility of a conflict between their families.

"My father will understand and thus in turn make

certain yer father agrees with this decision," she replied. "Ye know in yer heart this is what must be done."

A muscle ticked in his jaw. Hamish reached out and slowly dragged his knuckle down Katherine's cheek. "I am sorry," he said. "I hope one day ye will be able to fergive me."

Tears stung her eyes, but Katherine refused to let them fall. Her pride demanded that she remain dignified. She would not allow any man—least of all one who had played her false—to witness her pain and disappointment.

"I bear ye no ill will, Hamish Drummond," she said, forcing her voice to remain steady and even. "My only hope is that one day ye will have the courage to hold fast to the love that is within yer grasp. 'Tis a precious gift that should not be squandered."

She bowed her head gracefully before turning away. Hamish called to her. She ignored him, clinging fiercely to her self-respect. She was a McKenna; tenacious to the end when facing adversity.

She mastered the strong urge to run, moving slowly down the corridor. Miraculously, she found her way to the staircase that led to her bedchamber. Her feet flew on the stone stairs and with a heavy sigh she pushed open the chamber door. There was a low fire burning in the grate, casting a soft glow of light on a section of the room.

Her maidservant, Mary, rose from her pallet and approached, valiantly stifling a yawn.

"Go back to sleep," Katherine murmured. "I can attend myself."

After a slight hesitation, the maid obeyed. Katherine sat on the edge of the bed, staring ahead, yet seeing nothing. The sounds of music reached her ears and she realized her betrothal celebration was still going on. She covered her face with her hands, nearly laughing at the irony.

As her confused emotions gradually receded, Katherine's mind replayed the encounter with Hamish once, twice, and then a third time. Had she overreacted? He claimed to be ending the relationship, insisting it would not affect their marriage.

Had she been too hasty, too impulsive in her decision? Were her expectations of Hamish too unreasonable? Few men came to their marriage beds as virgins, even while it was demanded of women. Was she asking too much of the man she had agreed to marry?

Not going through with the wedding was going to create a difficult, unpleasant situation for her family; it could even affect future alliances for clan McKenna. Searching her heart, Katherine tried to find a less severe solution than rejecting Hamish outright.

Alas, none was forthcoming.

Groaning, she crossed the chamber and pulled aside the thick leather window covering. A gust of cold night air struck her full in the face and she breathed deeply.

What an awful mess! She gazed at the silvery, moonlit horizon, trying to make sense of it all.

"Perhaps I should consider taking the veil," she muttered, taking small solace in believing such an act would at least save her family from ridicule and humiliation. Even if it would condemn her to a life she neither desired nor was suited to live.

Hamish had made it very clear he considered their marriage contract binding—he would not ask for it to be dissolved.

Nay, that burden—and blame—would fall to her.

Katherine rubbed her hands up and down her arms, trying to warm herself, but the coldness she felt so keenly was buried deep in her heart. Drained, she plodded over to her bed. Not bothering to even loosen her gown, she lay on her back, staring up at the ceiling, as if somehow the answers to this dilemma could be found in the rough wooden planks overhead.

Hours passed. Resolutely, she shut her eyes, yet sleep was impossible. No matter which way she thought of it, her future looked bleak. And pitying herself over it only made her more frustrated.

Katherine tugged at the bodice of her gown. The air in the chamber seemed to be closing in on her. Impulsively, she jumped from the bed, grabbed her cloak, and flung it over her shoulders.

The music had stopped; the celebration was finally over. Deeming it safe to leave the confines of her chamber, Katherine cautiously found her way down the staircase and into the great hall.

The embers glowed softly from the fireplaces, the snores of the servants asleep on the pallets in front of it echoed through the vast chamber. Slowly, carefully, she crept across the expanse, quietly opening the heavy oak door.

The bailey was empty as Katherine made her way to the stables. The dark shadows of the night were beginning to fade, the soft light of the dawn appearing on the eastern horizon.

"Is something amiss, Lady Katherine?" came a deep, male voice from the shadows.

Katherine reeled in surprise, reaching for the dirk she kept hidden in the depths of her cloak pocket. The speaker stepped from the darkness and she breathed a sigh of relief when she recognized one of the McKenna retainers.

"My goodness, Brochan, ye nearly frightened the breath out of me," she said.

"I beg yer fergivness, milady, and confess to being equally startled. I dinnae expect to find ye here, alone, at this very early hour," Brochan replied. His eyes narrowed, as though a sudden thought entered his head. "By chance are ye meeting Sir Hamish?"

Katherine snorted back a most unladylike squeak. "Nay! That indeed is the very last thing I would be doing. I needed someplace to think and be alone."

"There's a fine chapel on the other side of the bailey. I'd be honored to escort ye there, if ye wish."

Katherine shook her head. "My mood and temper are not fit company fer such a holy place."

The corners of Brochan's eyes crinkled with compassion. He was a pleasant-looking man, with a bonny wife and three young bairns. "Is there aught I can do to ease yer distress?"

Take me home!

The thought brought her the first small slice of comfort since she had discovered Hamish embracing Fenella. If she left now—right now—she could avoid facing the entire Drummond clan, avoid the scene she was convinced Hamish would enact when she insisted their marriage contract be broken.

"I need to return to McKenna Castle immediately," Katherine exclaimed. "Will ye gather some of yer most trusted men and lead my escort?"

She saw the flash of surprise in Brochan's eyes, followed by puzzlement and uncertainty. "The celebration of yer betrothal will continue fer the next three days. I heard the servants speaking of it last night."

Katherine dropped her chin into her palms. "I willnae be marrying Hamish," she confessed. "I cannae."

"Lady Katherine! Has that cur done something—"

"Please," she interrupted, grasping Brochan's arm. "Dinnae ask me fer any details."

"Does the McKenna know ye want to leave?"

"Not yet." She tightened her grip. "I shall write a letter, explaining all to him and my mother. My maid-servant will give it to them several hours after we have departed."

"Need I remind ye that the McKenna hold fast and stand sure," Brochan said, proudly reciting the clan motto.

"Aye, we have more mettle than to flee in the face of adversity." Katherine lifted her chin and stared morosely into the empty stall in front of her. "But not always."

"Running away will solve nothing," he said gently.

"True. 'Tis cowardly to flee and I know I'll be bringing this problem with me when I leave." Her disillusioned spirits sank further. "But at least I'll avoid being subjected to public humiliation when my betrothal is broken."

"The McKenna willnae approve," Brochan said.

"Aye, his bellows of anger will rattle the rafters of our great hall. But we both know he'll be more distressed to discover that his daughter made the journey home on her own, without any protection or escort," Katherine countered, holding his eyes until she was certain he fully understood her meaning.

Brochan shot Katherine a concerned glance. "I could foil yer plan and send one of the men to rouse yer father right now," he threatened.

"Aye," Katherine agreed. "But ye willnae. Ye've too kind a heart. Please, Brochan, take pity on me and grant me aid in my hour of greatest need."

Brochan threw his head back and groaned. "Och, Lady Katherine, it saddens me to see ye in such distress. And I know the McKenna will skin me alive if I allowed ye to leave on yer own."

"Then yer path is clear. Ye must ensure that I am

properly guarded." Sensing a weakening, Katherine pressed further. "I shall bear the brunt of my father's anger, I promise."

Brochan groaned again and Katherine knew she had found the means to escape. "Ye'd best hurry, before my senses return and I change my mind," he finally replied.

Katherine sighed with relief and hugged the retainer. "Thank ye. I shall forever be in yer debt."

"I'll try to remember that when I'm staring into the darkness from the curtain wall, shivering in the cold night air instead of lying in my warm bed next to my wife," Brochan grumbled. "Fer once my part in this is discovered, I will most certainly be assigned the worst hours of guard duty for the rest of the winter."

"Och, Brochan."

His lips quirked. "Aye, I'm addled to agree, but 'tis my choice. Dawn is breaking. Hurry now."

Katherine hastened to her bedchamber. Without waking her maid, she prepared for the journey, changing into her warmest traveling gown and leather boots. Then she swiftly scribbled a brief note to her parents, praying they would understand her need to remove herself from here with all due haste.

Shaking her maid's arm, Katherine gently woke her. "Ye must put this letter in my mother's hand when the castle gathers fer the morning meal. Can ye do that fer me, Mary?"

"What has happened, Lady Katherine?" Mary asked, rubbing the sleep from her eyes.

"I'm going home," Katherine admitted. "And I dinnae want my parents to know of my departure fer at least a few hours."

"But Lady Katherine—"

"I've no time to explain," Katherine insisted. "My escort awaits."

"I should accompany ye," Mary exclaimed, rising from her pallet.

"Nay." Katherine squeezed the maid's hand. "Delivering my missive is far more important."

Looking uncomfortable, Mary accepted the parchment. "If that is what ye wish."

"It is." Katherine leaned down and gave Mary a brief hug. "Thank ye."

Brochan and four other McKenna retainers were gathered in the stables when Katherine arrived. She nodded her thanks to each man before mounting her horse. The Drummond soldiers milling around the bailey gave them only a cursory glance as they approached the front gate.

"Open the portcullis fer the McKenna guard," Brochan commanded.

His tone of confidence and authority produced immediate results. The iron gates were lifted without question or challenge. Katherine kept her head down and the hood of her cloak up as they rode over the drawbridge.

She was surprised that none of the Drummond guard questioned their identities or business until she realized they were leaving the castle, not trying to gain entrance.

They rode through the quiet village streets, spurring their horses when they reached the open fields. A sense of freedom enveloped Katherine and some of the distress that weighed so heavily on her heart began to lift.

It had been cowardly to sneak away, leaving only a brief message for her parents. After their initial annoyance, she hoped they would understand and forgive her rash actions. Hoped, too, they would forgive Brochan and the men who accompanied her, as they all knew how obstinate she could be when her mind was set.

'Twas too foolish by half for a young woman to travel such a distance alone, even though it could be accomplished in a day. Katherine was relieved she did not have to test her courage and undertake the journey on her own. She glanced at the men of her escort, grateful for their help.

They were far younger than most of her father's retainers, but fierce, honorable, and loyal to a fault. She felt a sharp pang of guilt; her father would be angry with them when he learned the truth. Yet her need to remove herself from Hamish and his clan was too strong to do anything else.

McKenna Castle would afford her the privacy she so desperately needed to decide on her future. She sincerely hoped that in time, her parents would understand and forgive her rash actions. Only then would she be fully able to find the strength to forget and put this unhappy nightmare behind her.

Chapter Four

"They say the McKenna is not here," the young MacTavish soldier reported as he rejoined the group of MacTavish men gathered in the village square. "And he willnae be returning fer at least a week."

Aiden let loose a string of curses. His horse pranced excitedly and he had to pull hard on the reins to keep the animal from rearing.

"What of his son Malcolm?" Aiden asked. "Did ye request an audience with him?"

The soldier shook his head. "He's not here either and they dinnae tell me when he'll return."

"Is there anyone in authority that I can speak with?" Aiden's voice was getting louder, but he couldn't control it. To have come this far to be denied was maddening.

"Nay. I asked three different men and they each told me there's no one in the castle who is able to negotiate the release of any prisoners."

Aiden's next string of curses was louder and more colorful than the first. This unexpected, unwanted news made him want to pound his fists in frustration. The rage pulsed through him, but when he noticed that his men were looking at him expectantly, he sought to control his temper.

"Both the laird and his eldest son are away," one of the MacTavish men muttered. "It could work to our advantage having such a plum property left unguarded."

Aiden's arm swung wide and he cuffed the man on the head. "Dinnae be daft, Jamie. Look up at the ramparts and the curtain wall. There are nearly sixty men on patrol. And that's only those we can easily see."

Jamie shot Aiden a resentful look as he rubbed his bruised scalp. "I dinnae mean the castle. I was speaking of the quarry where Robbie is being held."

"'Tis equally well guarded," Aiden replied dryly. "Rest assured, we willnae be storming the quarry. Any attempt to free my brother would fail."

The men's indistinguishable grumbling let Aiden know they were not in accord with his decision, but his opinion was not swayed. He had formulated a plan for his brother's release—a good plan—and he had no intention of deviating from it.

"If our business here is done, shall we start fer home?" one of the men asked. "Or wait until morning?"

Aiden gritted his teeth. He would brave the fiery pits of hell before returning to the MacTavish Keep without Robbie. Nay, he had promised his mother, had an obligation to his imprisoned brother and reasons of his own for sticking to this plan.

Freeing his brother and pleasing his mother were only two of the benefits Aiden planned to achieve. The best reward of all would be the looks of awe and admiration on the faces of every clansman and woman when he entered the great hall with Robbie at his side. Their mother would weep tears of joy and Lachlan, aye, Lachlan would be proved wrong.

That alone made any risk Aiden took worth it. He

would do whatever was needed to show everyone that he was the worthier brother, the man who should have been named laird upon their father's death.

Aiden was convinced that Lachlan had been chosen merely because he was the eldest son, a tradition that was not always upheld in the Highland clans. Younger sons had been named laird ahead of their older siblings. 'Twas what Aiden had expected since he was the better known man among his people, and he had been sorely disappointed when it did not come to pass.

He was the one who had struggled and suffered alongside them while Lachlan had spent the last few years in the Lowlands, a hired sword to any clan that could pay him and his men.

True, the coin Lachlan and his men had earned had been used to keep the clan from starving during the long, bleak, cold winters. That, along with the legends of Lachlan's prowess as a fighter and unmatched skill with a sword, had influenced their clansmen enough to agree that Lachlan should be laird.

However, Aiden too was a fine swordsman and he intended to use his talents to free Robbie—and gain the position he had long coveted. The McKennas were a bloodthirsty lot. He fully expected when he issued his challenge to fight any McKenna warrior for Robbie's freedom, it would be accepted.

"We are not leaving McKenna land until my brother rides at our side," Aiden announced, chafing at the delay in executing his plan.

"If we're not to return home, what shall we do, Aiden?" Jamie asked.

"We wait fer the McKenna to return," Aiden replied, pushing his disappointment aside.

"Here?" Jamie exclaimed, glancing around the square.

"Nay." Aiden frowned. "The McKenna guard will be

asking questions if we linger fer more than an hour in their village. We'll retreat into the woods and stay out of sight."

Jamie squeezed the cloth pouch hanging from his saddle. "We dinnae have enough food to last more than a day or two."

"Then we shall live off the land," Aiden proclaimed, swallowing the bitter taste in his mouth. "Or have ye all gone soft on me?"

Jamie scratched his head. "The McKennas willnae like us hunting in their forest."

"Aye, that's why we shall make certain we are not caught," Aiden replied with false cheer. "We'll retreat to the edges of their borders where we are less likely to be found."

Aiden waited while a few of his men grumbled amongst themselves, wondering if any would challenge his decision. He almost wished one of them would test his resolve, as the excuse to fight would alleviate some of his pent-up tension and anger. However, none were so rash.

When they quieted, Aiden slowly turned his horse and they obediently fell in line behind him.

Katherine urged her mount forward as they galloped toward the McKenna/Drummond border. The air was dry and crisp with cold, the wind biting, the horses still fresh and primed for exercise. She wryly observed that when they rode this exact route a few days ago, she had thought the land rich with beauty and promise. Now as she left, it seemed barren and stark, a reflection of her mood and future.

Katherine drew in a breath and mentally shook herself. With considerable effort, she cleared her mind of the distressing events of last night, focusing instead on the safety—and warmth—awaiting her at McKenna Castle.

She glanced over and found Brochan's gaze fixed upon her, his brow furrowed. "If we keep to this pace, we should arrive home well before darkness," he said.

"I'll not slow us down," Katherine assured him.

"I'm not questioning yer horsemanship," he replied. "Or yer stamina. However, when nature calls . . ." Brochan's voice trailed off, revealing his discomfort.

"I'll be sure to tell ye when I need to take a respite," Katherine answered, wondering if that was truly a blush she saw on his face or a result of the howling wind.

Brochan was a good man. Loyal, considerate, and kind. The guilt Katherine harbored over the way she had all but blackmailed him into leading her escort rose to the surface. They both knew that no matter what she said to the McKenna to defend her actions, her father's anger would be fierce and spread among all those who aided her.

'Twould not be easy to make amends to these gallant men who risked much for her. Yet Katherine vowed that she would find a way.

A distant rumbling drew her from her thoughts. Rain? Nay, the sky was cloudless and blue. Katherine turned to Brochan and immediately noticed his shoulders tensing as he stared intently at the horizon.

Concerned, Katherine followed his gaze. The sight made the fine hairs on the back of her neck rise. Ahead were a dozen men on horseback, swords drawn, riding hard and fast—directly toward them.

"How far are we from McKenna land?" Katherine asked.

"Too far," Brochan muttered. "And much too far from the castle to cry out fer help."

"Should we take shelter in the forest?" she suggested.

A taut line of worry settled between Brochan's brows. He shook his head. "They will be upon us before we reach the tree line. If we run, they can separate us. We've a better chance if we make a stand together, here in the open."

Katherine's throat tightened. "Forgive me, Brochan," she whispered. "If I had not insisted on such a small escort, our chances would be much improved."

"We are not defeated yet," Brochan replied heartily. "Stay close to yer guard, milady."

Katherine nodded. The alarming sound of crashing hooves and panting beasts grew louder. The breaths of the charging men and their horses mingled together, creating a frosty, eerie mist surrounding them as they drew closer.

'Tis what it must look like in hell, she thought with a shudder, unable to tear her eyes away from the charging horde.

"McKenna, to arms!" Brochan shouted.

His deep roar vibrated through the air, followed closely by the ringing sound of steel being pulled from leather sheaths. The five men drew their swords and formed a tight circle around her. Katherine reached for the dirk she carried in her cloak. It looked puny and ineffective compared to the warriors' weapons, but it could inflict some damage to her enemies.

Time seemed to hold still as they waited, and then suddenly the attack began. There was a brutal clash of swords as the two groups met. Outnumbered nearly three to one, the McKenna warriors fought bravely, their brows thick with sweat, their breaths puffing clouds of steam into the cold air.

Katherine saw two of the attackers fall from their horses, but the men soon rebounded, swords in hand.

One of them reached for the bridle of her horse. She kicked at him and he grabbed for her boot.

Shrieking, Katherine pulled hard on her reins, jerking her horse away. Searching for a safe haven now that she was separated from her guard, she turned her mount toward the trees. She had gone but a few feet when thundering hooves behind her told Katherine that she was being chased.

Anxiously, she glanced over her shoulder and saw her pursuer gaining ground. Crouching lower, she urged her horse to an even faster gallop.

It did no good. Within minutes she was plucked neatly from her saddle and pinned against her captor's broad chest. Fearing she would fall and be trampled, Katherine didn't struggle when she was taken, but the moment she was settled on his horse, she squirmed and arched her back, assessing her chances of breaking free.

The arm thrust around her waist tightened until the breath was nearly squeezed out of her lungs.

"I've got ye now, my little dove," he cackled, reaching down and twisting the dirk out of her hand.

Powerless, she continued struggling, with little effect. Using the muscles in his legs, the warrior turned his horse around and returned to the battle. The moment they came into view, Brochan and several other McKenna retainers surged forward.

Katherine's captor swiftly drew the dirk he had taken from her across her throat.

"McKenna, hold!" Brochan shouted.

The sound of metal clashing with metal abruptly ceased as the McKenna warriors slowly lowered their swords.

"Call off yer men," the brigand cried. "If ye surrender, we shall grant ye mercy."

"McKennas dinnae accept defeat," Brochan replied, holding out his claymore, the blood on the blade starkly visible.

"Yield or else the lass loses her life," the man snarled.

"Only a dishonorable swine would threaten a lady in such a crude manner," Brochan said in a tight, hard tone, his eyes never leaving the blade that was held against Katherine's throat.

The man let out a menacing chuckle. "Yer words are as limp as yer sword. Throw yer weapons to the ground and slowly dismount. Now!"

The brute gave a twist to the dirk and Katherine felt a trickle of warm liquid cascade down her neck. Brandishing their weapons, the McKenna men began shouting furiously at her rough treatment.

"I told ye to drop yer weapons and get off yer mounts," her captor repeated as he casually wiped the blood from her neck.

Her heart thumped wildly and for a moment nearly stopped, but Katherine quickly gathered her wits. "I'll be of no value to ye if I'm dead."

The brigand laughed, once again pressing the knife to her throat. "Order yer men to stand down."

Katherine flexed her fingers. "We are prepared to make concessions if ye release me at once," she stated in a carefully modulated tone.

A chorus of male laughter echoed through the glen. "We have no need to make *concessions*, as we've already taken what we want, Lady Katherine."

Katherine stiffened. *He knows who I am.* This was no random attack; 'twas a planned assault. Who were they? They spoke with a Highland accent, yet wore no plaid.

Katherine's mind raced. She could see the bloodied forehead of one of the McKenna soldiers, the torn sleeve and red sheen of blood on the arm of another. In that moment she knew she must do all that she could to ensure the survival of her escort.

"Ye promised my men mercy," she said. "Will ye keep yer word?"

"Aye, but the offer willnae stand forever."

Katherine's eyes sought Brochan's and the determination she saw in them gave her a jolt of angst. She had complete faith in the skill of her men, but they were outnumbered and at a distinct disadvantage.

She looked at the brigands, noting the wild swirl of desperation in their eyes. These men would fight to the death, if the McKennas did not yield. The result would be carnage on both sides, an unacceptable circumstance.

Nay. 'Twas obvious that she was the prize they wanted. Being taken by these men was a terrifying thought. Her stomach roiled at the vulnerability of her position as their hostage. Yet she would never forgive herself if any of her escort were maimed or killed—not when she had the chance to save them.

"Who are ye?" she asked, trying to twist her body to an angle where she could see her captor. His arms tightened around her, preventing any movement.

"I grow impatient, milady," the brigand replied, ignoring her question.

"'Tis best if ye do as he asks, Brochan," Katherine finally said. "This brute may be lacking in honor and courtesy, but he appears intelligent enough to know that if I come to any harm, his days on this earth are numbered."

Her captor chuckled. "Ye wound me, fair lady, with yer low opinion of my character."

"My father will do far more than wound ye with words when he finds ye," Katherine promised.

She felt her captor stiffen, his fingers biting into her

tender flesh like a hawk's talons. "Take their weapons and horses," he commanded.

Biting back oaths, the McKenna retainers reluctantly surrendered their swords and dirks. After handing over his weapons, Brochan looked up at her captor. "Ye'll never be more sorry fer anything ye've ever done in yer miserable life if ye dare to mistreat her in any way."

The brigand snorted. "Tell the McKenna I'll send word when I've decided exactly what I want fer the return of his daughter."

He turned his mount with a flourish and rode off. Katherine looked over her shoulder at the group of dejected McKenna men and said a prayer for their safe deliverance.

And her own.

They rode for hours. Katherine's back was stiff and aching, for she refused to lean against the chest of her captor. Instead, she pulled herself forward, held her back straight, her shoulders high, her chin lifted.

At one point she thought they had crossed onto McKenna land, but there was little to distinguish one copse of trees from another. Though frightened, Katherine calmed herself imaging her father reading the note she had left, bursting into a rage, and storming after her.

If that had occurred, he would soon discover the abandoned men of her escort. And once they were found, McKenna warriors would be combing the countryside searching for her. 'Twas only a matter of time until she was rescued.

Those thoughts comforted and sustained her. The hours dragged until finally, as the sun began to sink, they stopped. Katherine's captor lowered her from his horse, then slid down behind her. Her legs were so weak she nearly crumbled to the ground. Gripping her arm more tightly than necessary, the brigand held her upright.

She swayed and when she was steady, he signaled to one of the other men, who promptly handed him a length of rope. Katherine's wrists were bound behind her back and she winced as the rough cord bit into her tender flesh. She raised her chin, preparing to unleash her displeasure at this treatment when she got her first good look at the man who had captured her.

It took a tremendous effort to keep her jaw from dropping. Quite simply, he was the most beautiful man Katherine had ever seen. Aye, beautiful, for there was no other way to describe the perfection of his features, the splendor of his physique, the compelling combination of blond hair and striking blue eyes.

"I think the lass has taken a fancy to ye, Aiden," one of the men teased.

"She willnae be the first," another man declared. "Nor the last."

The brigands all chortled. Katherine could feel the heat creep up to her cheeks. Mortified at being caught staring, she averted her gaze. She was led to a fallen log and ordered to sit, which she managed awkwardly with her hands bound.

No one spoke to her as they set up camp. A hare and several fish were roasted over an open flame. Katherine's stomach growled persistently at the tempting smells of food. Eventually, her hands were untied and she was given a portion, which she quickly ate.

A blanket was spread near the fire for her. Shivering, she pulled the blanket around her shoulders. The night air had a biting chill that no wool or flame could easily conquer.

Aiden squatted down beside her and she was struck anew at his handsome features. "Rest while ye can," he instructed. "We'll be riding again in a few hours."

Apprehension rolled through her. How could she possibly fall asleep in a camp full of unknown men?

"Who are ye? What do ye want?" she queried.

"I've yet to fully decide," he replied.

"My father willnae react well to a demand fer ransom," she muttered.

"He will negotiate if he wishes to see his only daughter again." At her gasp, Aiden modulated his tone. "Ye have my word that as long as yer father cooperates, ye willnae be harmed."

Katherine's brow lifted. "What good is the word of a scoundrel and kidnapper who willnae reveal his full name?"

She saw the flash of his white teeth as he smiled. "'Tis the best ye've got, milady."

Tense and uneasy, Katherine tried to settle herself on the rough and uneven ground. Aiden placed himself at a respectful distance, yet he was near enough to watch her every move.

The sound of gentle snoring soon filled her ears. Amazed that anyone could fall asleep so quickly and deeply on such a hard, unforgiving surface, Katherine attempted to do the same.

For come morning, she knew she would need as much strength as she could muster.

Chapter Five

At the sound of footsteps, Katherine's eyes flew open. She rolled over, reaching for her dirk. Hand empty, she groaned, remembering her capture.

"Did ye sleep well, lass?" Aiden inquired.

"Like a queen," she replied tartly. Brushing the hair from her eyes, she sat upright and noticed a soft shaft of light hovered on the horizon. Dawn was nearly upon them.

The men broke camp quickly. She was allowed a scant bit of privacy to see to her personal needs, given a dry bannock hard enough to break a tooth to eat, and then hoisted onto her horse. She turned a questioning eye toward Aiden and he smiled.

"We'll travel faster with ye on yer own mount," he said, taking her horse's reins and tying them to his. "Though if ye miss being in my arms that much, I can sleep beside ye tonight."

Katherine's answering growl stuck in her throat and she began coughing. Their journey today was a mirror of yesterday, though they rode even faster and much farther. Katherine gave up trying to recognize her surroundings, though she paid close attention to any landmarks she could identify, committing them to memory.

'Twas how she then realized that they were going in a circular path, establishing a false trail. Her heart sank. She was certain that by now there were parties of McKenna retainers searching for her. This trickery could explain why there had been no sound of following riders.

At night she once again was placed close to the fire and despite his threat, Aiden slept several feet away. The next morning Katherine awoke with a pounding headache and a dry throat, though she refused to express any of her discomfort to Aiden or his men.

This day was a repeat of the previous one. The one glimmer of excitement had been overhearing the clan name of her captors—MacTavish. It eased some of her fears, as they were not sworn enemies of the McKennas, though clearly they weren't allies.

Today there was still at least an hour of daylight, but for some reason they had decided to stop and make camp. Katherine suspected it was because they were getting closer to wherever they intended to keep her until her ransom could be paid.

The thought depressed her. She had hoped to be rescued by now and returned home to the safety of McKenna Castle. Resentfully, Katherine glared at her captors, who were conversing amongst themselves as they gathered kindling, brought out a cooking pot, and started simmering their evening meal. 'Twas at that moment she suddenly realized that none of them were paying any attention to her.

Escape! Did she dare? Her mind racing, Katherine slowly, casually strolled farther from the fire, toward the outer boundaries of the camp. Her hand itched to grab the reins of one of the horses, but she resisted, knowing it would instantly draw their eyes.

If she did manage to escape, 'twould not be easy to find her way home. In all likelihood she would be recaptured, as it was impossible to outrun anyone pursuing her on horseback. But the commotion would disrupt the journey, perhaps long enough for a McKenna search party to find her.

No matter what the result, Katherine knew she needed to try; this was the one way to atone for her foolishness in leaving Drummond Castle so hastily.

Careful not to make a sound, she crept farther away. Nervously biting her lip, she peered anxiously into the forest, laying out an escape route in her mind. If she could make it to the thickest section of the trees, they would be unable to follow her on horseback.

She glanced again at the men, muttered a quiet prayer, then made her move. 'Twas almost too easy— one moment she was standing at the edge of the camp and the next she had slipped away and disappeared into the forest. She walked quickly at first, then broke into a run. Her heart shuddered and sweat beaded on her forehead, yet she never broke stride.

Faster and faster she ran, leaping over fallen branches, pushing her way beyond prickly brambles, moving into the thickest part of the forest. Her breath came in great, panting gulps, her chest heaved from exhaustion, her heart felt near to bursting, yet she kept moving. Only one thought consumed her, drove her, pushed her—escape. This was her best chance and Katherine intended to give it her full effort.

Any second she expected to hear shouts of alarm and the sound of pursuit. None came, but Katherine didn't slow her pace. Veering to the right, she tried to double back to the stream they had passed earlier in the day, since that was the direction she needed to travel.

Suddenly, a deep male voice echoed through the trees. Katherine stopped dead in her tracks, for an instant ceasing to breathe. Had she imagined it? Nay! She heard it a second time, faint and distant. Knowing the third time would bring it closer, she lengthened her stride.

Resolutely, Katherine wound her way deeper into the densest area of the forest. She could hear the heavy footsteps on the frozen ground behind her. Her heart sank, knowing that she couldn't outrun these men— but perhaps she could outwit them. Her eyes darted anxiously about her as she ran, searching for a place to hide, to conceal herself.

She vaulted over a thick tree root, biting back a grunt of pain when the bottom of her boot scraped against the rough bark. Then mercifully she saw her best opportunity lay several yards to the left. Never breaking stride, Katherine changed direction, desperately heading toward possible salvation.

Breathless, she squeezed herself under a fallen tree trunk. Lying on her back, she hastily pulled a pile of dead leaves to cover herself. Her nose twitched with the smell of damp earth and decaying vegetation as she burrowed farther into the soil.

All went silent for a moment and for an instant it felt like a strange, ethereal dream. Then suddenly, the sounds of gruff, guttural male voices drew nearer and her chest tightened with fear.

"Lady Katherine! Lady Katherine!"

They shouted her name as they tromped through the forest, their lilting Highland accents a mockery to her ears. They called to her, promising no retribution if she surrendered, yet she dare not trust them.

Panic and hysteria bubbled within her. The reality of her own vulnerability swept through her and she began trembling. She had no weapon, no means to defend herself. If she were discovered . . .

Katherine gave her head a shake, resolutely thrusting those thoughts aside, quelling her quivers of dread.

The situation was dire—there was no need to allow her imagination to make it even worse.

After what felt like an eternity, the voices faded, along with their footsteps. Katherine felt a surge of hope. Impatient to flee, she tamped down the urge, forcing herself to remain still. These men were clever—and desperate. They could easily be lying in wait, hoping she would reveal herself.

With Herculean effort she stifled the cough that rose in her throat, her entire body shivering with the struggle. The tightness she had first felt when she had been captured had intensified each day. 'Twas now raw and painful, but succumbing to the impulse would surely reveal her hiding place.

Choking back the tickle, Katherine pressed her fist against her mouth, willing herself to remain quiet. Her head spun and her body trembled, yet the small hope that she might escape enabled her to command her body to do her bidding.

Minutes passed. Dare she move? Nay, she would wait longer, just to be certain they were gone. Her head began to ache and she was thirsty, yet she remained in her hiding place. Her eyelids grew heavy and she had difficulty keeping her eyes focused.

She had barely slept since she had been taken. She was so tired. Tired.

Rest. A short rest and then I shall flee. If I am very lucky, I shall find someone to aid me. The promise of a handsome reward will make it easier. If not, I shall make my way on my own and seek sanctuary at the nearest nunnery. The holy sisters will send word to my family.

Katherine had always been a woman of action and having a plan drove away the darkness. The tension in her shoulders gradually eased, the tight bands of fear around her heart lessened, and her eyes closed.

In moments she was fast asleep.

"What do ye mean ye lost her?" Lachlan said through gritted teeth.

In the evening darkness of the MacTavish great hall, Aiden stood before his older brother, his cloak wet, his boots muddy, his face streaked with dirt. Aiden and his men had been gone from the keep for nearly a fortnight, giving Lachlan just cause for concern. Yet the last thing he expected to hear when his brother returned was that Aiden had taken Lady Katherine McKenna hostage—and that she was no longer in his custody.

Aiden licked his lips. "I dinnae say that we lost her. I said that she ran from us and we have not yet been able to find her."

"God's blood, Aiden, why the hell did ye take her in the first place?" Lachlan stormed. "I expressly forbid ye to meddle with the McKennas. Ye were supposed to discover if Robbie was in truth being held prisoner. Nothing more."

"Aye, ye made yer feelings well known to one and all. Yet my conscience would not allow me to sit idly by and do nothing while my brother suffered," Aiden shot back, his expression revealing no remorse. "We stumbled upon a small party of McKenna retainers and noticed a well-dressed female among them. I dinnae know fer certain 'twas Lady Katherine until we had taken her. I knew then that her father would be eager to exchange her fer Robbie."

"It will be rather difficult to ransom the lass if ye dinnae have her," Lachlan replied sarcastically. "All ye have succeeded in doing is raising the wrath of the

McKennas, which will most likely put Robbie in further danger. Yer daft actions can easily start a feud that will hurt us far more than it will benefit the clan."

Aiden's gaze slid away. "She has no horse, no supplies, and no knowledge of the area. She cannae have gotten far. We've returned fer fresh mounts and more men to widen our search. Lady Katherine will be found and a ransom, as well as the demand fer Robbie's release, will be sent to the McKennas the moment she is once again in our hands."

"I've little faith in yer ability to achieve that lofty goal, given the way ye've handled yerself thus far," Lachlan said grimly. He walked slowly around his brother, his hands clasped behind his back. "Ye've risked the clan's future fer naught. I will organize the search fer Lady Katherine. Ye will stay here!"

"Nay!" Aiden sputtered.

"Ye will do as I command," Lachlan insisted, his fierce expression brooking no argument, his eyes giving no quarter. "Under my direction, teams of men will depart at first light tomorrow. I, too, will join the search and ye will stay inside the walls of this keep. Do I make myself clear?"

Aiden grumbled again. In no mood to listen to any more excuses, Lachlan loomed over his brother, his fist clenched, his face set in stone.

Aiden understood. He wisely refrained from making any further comments, though his stomping boots as he left the great hall spoke loudly of his displeasure.

Lachlan made a harsh noise in the back of his throat and slowly unclenched his fist. Wrestling away his frustration, he turned his mind toward organizing the search for the missing woman. He had much to prepare if they were to leave at first light.

Whatever it took, he would find Lady Katherine,

return her to her father, and somehow make amends to the McKennas.

Lachlan looked around the clearing, then glanced up at the darkening sky. The light snow that had started at dawn was becoming thicker, the flakes larger. He glanced behind him, not surprised to see the snow was rapidly covering his tracks, erasing all trace of them.

'Twas barely past noon, too early to end his search. He had been out here for hours and was loath to admit that this task was proving to be far more daunting than he had anticipated. Alone and on foot, he assumed the McKenna lass would not have strayed too far off MacTavish land. Yet thus far, there had been no sign of her.

Lachlan steered his horse to the edge of the forest, dismounted, and knelt. Carefully, he examined the ground, brushing away the newly fallen snow, hunting for tracks. Finding none, he shook his head in disgust, cursing beneath his breath.

Mayhap some of the other MacTavish search parties were having better luck, yet somehow he doubted it. 'Twas like trying to find a single blade in a meadow filled with grass. Impossible.

Resolutely, he stood, determined not to give up. He would continue to search until darkness prevented it. Then he would set up camp, try to stay warm and dry throughout the night, and start again at first light.

He traversed a stream, guiding his mount over chunks of ice floating through the swift current. He moved at a slow trot, surveying all around him, looking for any natural shelter that might be concealing the lass.

His keen eyes scanned the drifts of snow-covered bushes and leaves—stopped—then looked again. *Hold.*

A dot of vibrant blue stood like a beacon against the white of the snow. *Have I found her?*

Tamping down the burst of excitement, Lachlan eased his horse forward. Surrounding the spot of blue beneath a fallen tree trunk was an oddly shaped pile of snow-covered leaves—the form of a woman?

Senses on tense alert, conscious of the slightest movement from the mound, Lachlan dismounted and approached cautiously. Squinting through the white haze of falling snow, he could tell it was indeed a body, curled into a ball, huddled beneath the leaves and snow.

The blue he had seen was part of a larger garment, most likely a cloak. It had to be the McKenna lass! Lachlan moved softly, fearful of startling her. Fearful, too, of having a dirk or any other weapon pressed against his throat.

"Lady Katherine," he called softly. "I've come to aid ye."

The body shifted slightly, revealing the top of a shoulder and one leather-clad boot. A dainty woman's boot. Encouraged, Lachlan knelt at her side, brushing back the snow, small twigs, and rotting vegetation, freeing her face and upper torso from its leafy cocoon.

She lay motionless, save for the occasional trembling of her gloved hands. Her eyes were shut, her complexion unnaturally flushed. Yet he could not help but notice the feminine perfection of her features; the high cheekbones, pert, straight nose, delicate arched brows, and sweet, crescent mouth.

Her breathing was labored, her eyes ringed with purple shadows. Gingerly, he touched her forehead, startled by the warmth—he had expected her to be chilled.

"Christ's blood," Lachlan muttered beneath his breath. "Ye're ill."

He pushed back the hair that had fallen over his

eyes and stared down at her. The edges of her lips were blue and she shivered visibly. Almost as though sensing his presence, she suddenly bolted upright, her eyes flying open. Brilliant blue, they were bright with fever and confusion.

"I must escape," she whispered hoarsely, before slumping back, limp and exhausted.

Lachlan lifted her securely in his arms. She stirred again and instinctively pulled herself closer to his warmth. He felt an odd twist of emotion in his chest at her vulnerable, trusting gesture.

If ye only knew who I am, lass.

When he stood, the remainder of the leaves she had buried herself beneath fell off her like raindrops, showering them both. Her body hung lifeless in his arms, indicating that she was no longer conscious.

'Tis fer the best, Lachlan decided. Given the tenacity of her actions, he suspected she would not have come quietly and could have been further injured if a struggle between them occurred.

He hoisted her over his saddle, then vaulted up behind her. Steadying her upright in his arms, he wheeled his horse around, following the path that had led him into the forest. The snow continued falling and occasionally a larger portion would tumble down from a heavily laden branch.

He bent over Katherine, protecting her from the worst of it and by the time they reached the clearing, Lachlan's head and shoulders were covered with snow. He scanned the terrain, trying to decide the best way to the Convent of the Sacred Heart.

The northern route would be the most direct, but the path was slick with ice in many spots and dotted with deep ruts. His mount was sure-footed and strong, but if he went that way, they would need to move at a snail's pace.

He elected instead to sweep around to the south, hoping to find more hospitable road conditions. Holding her tightly in his arms to keep her warm, Lachlan fought the elements and plodded ahead.

Their progress was far slower than he had hoped. He glanced down at the silent woman huddled in his arms. She had not made a sound for the last hour; not even a cough. He had tried to limit the amount of jostling she had to endure, but that had been impossible. Yet it appeared at this stage not to make much difference.

Darkness fell quickly on this moonless night. Lachlan crested the hill and glanced at the sky, dismayed to find no stars. The air was heavy with cold and dampness. The snow that had plagued him most of the day was now pelting icy droplets. He had tried his best to keep the moisture off her, but he could smell the wet wool of her cloak.

His plan to ask the sisters of the convent to shelter and care for her was quickly unraveling. The journey was taking far too long and the darkness increased the risk of injury to his horse. Accepting that he had no other choice, Lachlan directed his mount off the narrow path, through the thickest section of the forest.

Miraculously, his memory was correct for he soon came upon an abandoned crofter's hut. 'Twas in deplorable condition, but it offered some protection from the harsh weather. He carried Katherine to the threshold and kicked open the door.

There was little difference in the temperatures inside the hut and outside in the elements. When he moved, Lachlan's breath formed visible puffs of air from the cold. He gently propped Katherine against the wall while he made a bed for her from the pieces of straw and dried leaves that covered the earthen floor. He removed her cloak and shook off the bits of snow and ice that clung to the wool.

'Twas then he noticed that the inside was lined with fur, which was dry. Absently, he rubbed a section between his thumb and forefinger, marveling at the quality. The McKennas truly were a wealthy clan if they could afford to put fur this costly *inside* a cloak.

Katherine coughed. With the back of his dry sleeve, Lachlan wiped the ice from her face, then remembering that his childhood nurse had always said that wet hair was the surest way to catch the sweating sickness, Lachlan unbraided her hair.

The gleaming tresses spread over the ground like a blanket of silk. Even in the darkened hut he could see them shine. He placed her cloak over her, tucking it tight to her body before going back outside to search for kindling dry enough to catch fire and burn.

After leaving a sizable pile of wood next to Katherine, he fetched his horse, tying the mount on the far side of the hut. 'Twould be cruel to keep the animal exposed to the harsh elements, and its body heat would be welcome in the enclosed space.

She began moaning and moving her head back and forth. Lachlan touched her brow, concerned at the heat he felt. Her fever had intensified and being exposed to the cold, icy snow had not helped.

As he gazed down at her, a peculiar feeling invaded his chest. She looked so helpless. The desire to cure her, protect her, save her, ran deep inside him. Not only because he felt partially responsible for her current state—though he had expressly instructed Aiden to have very little contact with the McKennas—but there was more.

He had always felt concern for those smaller and weaker, an impulse that sometimes placed him in harm's way. It was thus with this woman, yet somehow the emotions stirring inside him were stronger than usual. Which seemed utterly ridiculous, since he didn't know the lass at all.

There would be no taking back what Aiden had done, but if she were returned unharmed to her family, the McKenna's anger might be appeased and his retribution lenient. Especially if his daughter pleaded their case.

Sitting close, Lachlan leaned his head against the wall. He looked down at Katherine with renewed apprehension. She was warm and dry, away from the biting cold and harsh elements. Her sleep appeared peaceful, though her chest rattled with each breath. She was young and apparently strong, for she had weathered the days of hard riding since she had been taken with enough stamina to enact a successful escape.

The best Lachlan could hope for now was that she had the strength to recover from this illness.

If she did not, well, that was simply too dire to consider.

Chapter Six

A male voice penetrated her mind, calling to her. Deep, smooth, and kind, Katherine struggled to make sense of the words, but could not. *Papa? Nay, Papa's voice would not have been so soothing, 'twould be bellowing with anger.*

The thought made Katherine briefly smile. Her mirth soon brought on a fit of coughing. Her legs flayed involuntarily as she fought for breath, her body shivered and shook.

Hurts. Everything hurts.

Her limbs ached; her lips were dry and cracked, her throat scratchy and parched. She could feel herself being lifted and carried and then a sudden blast of warmth. *He must have placed me beside the fire.*

A strong hand elevated her head, a metal cup was raised to her lips. She tried to swallow, but her throat was too tight. The cup disappeared and she moaned, then miraculously droplets of water bathed her lips. Katherine thrust her tongue out to catch them, ignoring the pain they caused when she swallowed.

Exhausted by the efforts, she collapsed, a wave of

chills running through her. A damp tendril of hair was brushed from her eyes; strong arms cradled her, wrapping her in comfort and security.

A male spoke to her in a low, gentle voice. Who was this shadowy figure of a man who showed her such tenderness and consideration? A man of God, she thought, skilled in aiding those in need.

He must have found her, rescued her. *Bless ye, fer delivering me from my fate. Ye are truly one of the good Lord's angels.* She must thank him properly for his kindness. Katherine struggled to open her eyes, but they were weighed down with fever and would not do as she commanded. She could feel herself sinking, losing control. She drifted into a bleary fog, soothed by the warmth of the fire, the unfamiliar voice and his gentle touch.

Sleep, I must sleep. No longer resisting, Katherine blissfully sank into the darkness.

An angel? Had she just called him an angel? Lachlan's face broke into a rare grin. He knew well that a strong fever could cause a person's mind to wander from reality. She must be very ill indeed to believe him to be an angel.

He looked down at the woman lying so still on the pallet. A sheen of sweat glistened on her upper lip. Her cheeks and brow felt hot to the touch. Putting one hand under her shoulder blades, Lachlan again lifted her into a sitting position, cradling her against his chest.

"Drink, milady," he said coaxingly, holding another cup of fresh water to her lips.

Once again, she moaned and turned her head. Determined, Lachlan placed the cup on the floor, dipped his fingers in the water, and brought the droplets to her lips.

He repeated the motions until her tongue darted out to catch them.

Encouraged, he picked up the cup and once again placed the vessel at her mouth. This time she sipped greedily until it was gone, then collapsed against him, clearly exhausted.

He brushed his fingers through her hair, then softly caressed her cheek. She sighed. He continued trying to soothe her, moving his hand over the smooth, bare flesh of her slender throat, down to her chest.

He watched her breasts rise and fall with utter fascination, like a green lad catching his first glimpse of a woman. Her tight-fitting gown displayed the curves and contours of her generous form, causing an ache to blossom inside him. A jolt of heat struck him and Lachlan realized that his body was starting to respond to her nearness.

Disgusted with himself for having carnal thoughts for a senseless woman, Lachlan abruptly pulled his hand away. She was an innocent victim caught in a situation that was not of her choosing.

Just as he was.

He was well aware of the harshness of fate and one's inability to control it, but perhaps this time he could change its course. For her sake, as well as the Mac-Tavish clan's. If the unthinkable occurred, the blame would fall on their heads and the retribution that the McKennas would extract for her death would be swift and harsh.

Yet when he once again stared into her lovely, pale face, that worry gave way to a true concern for her well-being. Lachlan had no great healing knowledge, but he was a practical man possessing a fair amount of common sense. She must be kept dry and warm and fed a hearty broth. Honey would be best for her throat, but there was none to be found at this time of year.

Crushed mint leaves steeped in hot water would have to suffice. The woods were covered in snow, but mint grew like a weed and since the storm had finally eased, Lachlan planned to search for some at first light. He would also lay some rabbit traps—they would provide a rich broth that could help Katherine regain her strength.

She will recover, he told himself. And the moment she was strong enough to travel, he would bring her home to her kin and pray to the good Lord that would be the last time he had any dealings with the McKenna clan.

Katherine awoke with a start, blinking her eyes against the weak ray of sunlight that danced across her legs. Lifting her head, she saw that she was inside a small, crude dwelling, lying on a lumpy floor pallet that even through her clogged nose gave off a distinctly musty odor. Two cloaks covered her—one she recognized as her own, the other a larger, plain, well-worn garment.

Anxiously, she gazed about the chamber, yet puzzlingly saw no one. The room was barren of furniture, indicating the hut was uninhabited, yet a substantial fire blazed in the hearth. Hanging from a hook over the fire was a black kettle. The contents boiled and bubbled vigorously, wisps of vapor escaping and rising to the low, thatched roof.

Katherine sniffed, but the cauldron was too far away for her stuffed nose to catch any aromas. Her stomach growled and she hoped it was broth or stew simmering in the pot, not laundry or soap.

Her throat was sore, her head ached, but her chest

didn't feel as tight and her cough had loosened. 'Twas a hopeful sign that she would soon recover, and sooner still return home.

The door opened. Tensing, she looked up expectantly, her breath coming in short, shallow pants. A stranger entered the hut, stomping snow from his boots. It soaked into the hardened earth floor, creating a pattern of dark spots.

He wore no cloak and she realized that she was snuggled beneath the garment. 'Twas no small sacrifice to brave this cold winter weather without the protection of a cloak. Did she dare to assume that this considerate gesture was proof of his good character?

She didn't recognize him as one of her captors. He was tall and broad, with hair dark as night that hung nearly to the top of his shoulders. The muscles in his arms and chest looked solid and well-defined. Dark stubble shadowed a strong jaw while deep-set eyes brimmed with curiosity and intelligence.

His handsome face was ruggedly sculpted and his impressive stature gave him an air of authority. Katherine wondered who he was and how he had come to find her.

His eyebrows lifted in surprise when he realized that she was awake, and his dark blue eyes lightened with interest. Nervously, Katherine ran her tongue over her dry lips. She had been raised among powerful men, both in stature and temperament, and learned 'twas always wise to be cautious when dealing with them.

"Good day to ye, sir." Her voice sounded strange to her ears, low and husky.

He nodded in greeting. "Fair maiden."

She raised her head, which oddly caused the aches in her body to intensify. A frisson of fear shot through her, as her weakened condition only emphasized how much she was truly at his mercy. Katherine's mind suddenly danced with all manner of dire possibilities and she struggled to push these disturbing images away.

"I believe that I owe ye my thanks fer caring fer me," she rasped.

"Alas, I lack the healing skills to do much to ease yer discomfort," he replied apologetically. "I swear that ye have improved in spite of my care, not because of it."

He lowered his head as though uncomfortable with her gratitude and Katherine felt the sharper edges of her fear begin to soften.

"I'm Katherine," she said, deliberately omitting her clan name. "And ye are?"

"Lachlan."

She waited expectantly, but he followed her lead, revealing no more than his given name. Though frustrating, Katherine knew she had no right to fault his lack of candor. "Where am I?"

"An old crofter's hut, long since abandoned. 'Twas the nearest shelter I could find."

"Ye found me?" she whispered.

"I did. Buried under a pile of rotting leaves, dirt, and snow." He walked to the kettle and dropped a handful of leaves into the boiling cauldron. "Tell me, lass, how did ye come to be out in the woods all alone in this foul weather?"

Indecision plagued her. *What do I say?* Katherine fidgeted with the edge of the cloak that covered her, then forced her hands to still. Obviously, he did not recognize the McKenna plaid of the garment, which was a stroke of good luck. 'Twas dangerous and foolish to reveal anything about herself and her circumstances until she knew more about him.

"I'm uncertain why I was alone in the woods," she lied.

His handsome face clouded with concern. "Ye dinnae remember? I knew a soldier once who suffered the same malaise after being struck in battle on the side of the head with a broadsword. Did I miss such a wound on ye?"

Nervously, Katherine fingered a section of her hair. "Is that why ye unbraided my hair? To search fer injuries?"

He shook his head. "'Twas wet. Loosening it was the fastest way to dry it and prevent yer illness from worsening."

Carefully, she moved her hand through her scalp, threading the hair through her fingers, hoping to appease his concern by making a show of checking for additional wounds. "I'm fairly certain I wasn't struck by a sword. In any event, there are no bumps or cuts on my head."

"'Tis good to hear."

His worry seemed genuine, causing her anxiety to drop another notch. "How long have I been here?"

"Two days." He crouched by her side, locking his gaze upon her. "Do ye recall none of it?"

"Only bits and pieces that make little sense."

He nodded. "Yer fever raged at times. That can cloud the mind and disorder yer memories. Dinnae push yerself too hard to remember. With luck it will all come back to ye once ye regain yer full strength."

A pang of guilt rushed through her. Her memories of fleeing from Drummond Castle, being taken and escaping from her kidnappers were all too vivid. Though he modestly denied it, this man had in all likelihood saved her life. It seemed so uncharitable to deny him the full truth of how she came to be in this predicament. Yet she needed to make certain that she would be safe before revealing her identity.

"Was I too ill to travel any farther than this hut?" she asked, reaching up to brush the hair from her face.

"The snow was falling fast and hard and became too deep in sections fer my horse to make his way," Lachlan explained.

"I dreamt of a horse," she muttered. "Snorting and tossing his head, pawing at the ground. 'Twas strange and oddly vivid."

Lachlan's expression turned sheepish. "'Twas not a dream. The weather was too foul to abandon my mount to the elements. He stayed in the hut with us the first night."

Katherine's eyes widened. 'Twas common practice for peasants to sleep with their livestock during the coldest nights, a resourceful way to keep both man and beast warm. As a wealthy laird's daughter, she had never experienced the like. Wondering at his background, she studied Lachlan beneath lowered eyelids.

He spoke well, without the thick accent of the lower classes. His clothes were well-worn and simple, but the broadsword he carried was an expensive, finely crafted weapon.

Was he a mercenary? A sword for hire? That could explain why he was traveling alone and had not immediately recognized the McKenna plaid of her cloak.

"Where is yer horse now?" she asked.

"Outside, where he belongs." Lachlan tilted his head. "The snow has ceased falling and the sun shines. He is content and will be well rested when we start our journey. Will we have far to travel to bring ye home?"

Nerves of warning fluttered in her chest. Katherine turned her eyes away, willing herself to remain calm. The question was posed casually, but she refused to be so easily fooled into revealing her identity. She was not especially adept at lying and in her weakened condition it was a true struggle to keep her answers from divulging too much.

Distraction always worked well with her young niece, Lileas. It seemed a logical course to try now.

"May I please have a drink? My throat is parched and aching."

She held her breath and waited, sighing with relief when she heard him rise to comply with her request. To show her gratitude, Katherine attempted a timid smile when he returned.

She reached for the metal cup he held out to her, noticing it was dented on one side. Their hands touched—his was large and cold, with long, callused fingers, yet the contact sent a spark of heat through her. Startled, she eased herself back.

His brows rose. "Are ye afraid of me, Katherine?"

"Should I be, Lachlan?"

"Depends on what ye fear, lass."

Katherine took a big gulp of the hot water, then rolled her back against the wall to get a wider view of him. *Dinnae panic.* He had the right to question her, she told herself. Just as she had the right to refuse to answer.

She drained the rest of the minty liquid to give herself more time to compose a diplomatic response. "I fear being at the mercy of a stranger," she said, staring at his broad shoulders and thick, muscular arms.

Lachlan hunched forward, bracing his forearms on his thighs. "Why would I go through the bother of saving ye if I meant ye harm, lass?"

"Why indeed?"

His nearness caused her breath to catch. He was too close. His male strength surrounded her, consumed her. Though she was seated, her knees felt weak, her hands unsteady.

"Ye've no cause to be suspicious of a simple act of kindness and hospitality," he countered.

"Och, so this is yer home? Ye live a very simple life, Lachlan," she replied, glancing pointedly around the empty hut.

He grinned and they shared a quiet laugh, then his expression turned thoughtful. "Ye were buried under leaves and snow when I found ye. Who were ye hiding from, Katherine? An angry husband? A thwarted lover? A tyrannical father?"

"I have no husband or lover." She nearly smiled. "My father is a tyrant, though he can be reasonable—at times. What were ye doing riding out in such brutal weather?"

"Hunting."

"Fer me?"

"Fer fresh meat. Winters are harsh this far north and hunger more sharply felt."

Both his expression and tone seemed sincere. Tiring of the cat and mouse game, Katherine reasoned 'twas safe to reveal a small part of the truth.

"I ran from men who thought to profit from my capture," she said, keeping her voice firm and calm.

"And ye fear that I shall do the same?"

"Ye might." Yet even as she spoke the words, Katherine admitted she did not entirely believe them. Lachlan had cared for her, nursing her through her illness, relinquishing his cloak and enduring the cold so that she would stay warm. Her wariness lessened as she reminded herself of all he had done, gaining him another small measure of her trust. "The men who took me were from the MacTavish clan. Do ye know them?"

"Aye. Their holdings are north of here."

"Do ye count them as friend or foe?"

His head lifted and he met her eyes steadily. "If they are yer enemy, then so shall they be mine."

Katherine allowed herself a brief smile. His voice was proud and powerful, his words rang true. "Can I rely upon yer honor to aid me and bring me, unharmed, back to my clan?"

"Ye can, good lady. As soon as ye are well enough to sit upon my horse we shall depart." There was a slight pause. "Though ye'll need to tell me the name of yer kin."

The bands of tightness around her chest eased and Katherine felt a sense of calm. She believed him. There was goodness and benevolence in mankind, just as their family priest, Father John, had told her. All would be well.

Lachlan, her savior, a man who had exhibited such kindness and caring, would return her to her family as soon as she was strong enough to make the journey. The surge of relief was so great she almost felt giddy.

"My father will be most generous in his thanks to ye," she promised.

Lachlan frowned. "I dinnae do this fer a reward."

"I know." She grinned. "That is precisely why ye shall receive one."

Lachlan hastily checked the traps he had laid earlier, pleased to discover that he had snared three hares. Slowly boiled, they would make a rich broth and aid in Katherine's recovery.

When the weather had finally cleared the previous morning, he had debated riding home to MacTavish Keep and informing them that he had found her. He

could have replenished his provisions and asked the
clan healer for advice and medicines to hasten Katherine's recovery. But that journey would have taken him
away from her for nearly the entire day and he did not
wish to leave Katherine so long on her own.

The Convent of the Sacred Heart was a shorter distance away, but would still have kept him from her side
for a dangerously long time. What if she had weakened? Called out in need for him? Nay, the risk was far
greater than the reward, thus he had elected to provide
for her as best he could on his own. Thankfully, that
had proven to be the best course.

If one of the other search party had discovered
them, he would have ordered his men to bring the
needed supplies. Unfortunately, none had appeared.
He assumed some of his men had sensibly abandoned
the search during the worst of the storm and would
now be combing the woods again.

Perhaps they would find him and Katherine. Perhaps not. Life had taught Lachlan that self-sufficiency
was the only way to survive. Thus, he was set on taking
action instead of waiting for help.

The croft hut was barely intact. A second fierce storm
could see it splintered into pieces. Katherine's illness
had abated, but Lachlan knew a relapse could quickly
occur if she were exposed too long to the elements.

The Convent of the Sacred Heart was the answer.
Katherine would soon be well enough to reach the
sanctuary, even if they traveled at a slow pace. He would
leave her in the care of the good sisters and return
when she was strong enough to journey all the way to
McKenna Castle.

The other possibility that could disrupt that plan was
if one of her family's search parties found them first. If
that occurred, his best chance of making amends for

Aiden's reckless action would be gone, leaving him vulnerable to the McKenna's wrath and judgment. That unsavory thought had caused Lachlan an endless amount of worry these past few days—and nights.

Lachlan dismounted and slung the brace of hares over his shoulder, this time remembering to stomp the snow from his boots before entering the hut. Katherine was sitting up, her back pressed against the wall. Thankfully, she was slight of weight or else the fragile structure might collapse, enforcing again the need for them to depart soon. Her face was pale, her cheeks hollow, yet she was still a comely sight.

"Yer breathing is better," Lachlan observed. "How do ye feel?"

She turned her head and a lock of hair fell over her face. "The tightness in my chest has eased and I grow tired of sleeping." She wrinkled her brow, as though suddenly realizing how strange that sounded.

"Will ye eat some broth once it's ready?"

She sighed. "I'll try, though my throat still hurts when I swallow."

"Ye need nourishment to get well."

"I am hungry," she admitted.

"I believe I have the perfect remedy fer yer aching throat." Lachlan grabbed the metal cup and left the hut, returning quickly. "I was going to bring ye some earlier, but feared you'd be offended at such a poor offering."

Katherine looked at him suspiciously, then smiled when she saw what he had brought her.

"Och, I wish I had thought to ask ye fer some of this sooner," she said, reaching for the cup. She daintily extended her tongue, catching some of the white flakes on the tip. "I always liked eating snow when I was a lass, though my mother lamented that I was most likely chewing on dirt and pebbles and the good Lord only knew what else."

Lachlan shook his head. "Ye cannae stop a head-strong lass when she is hell-bent on doing something."

"Even as it was falling from the sky, my brothers and I would pile a bowl with fresh snow and then drizzle honey over it that we had snuck out of the storeroom. I remember it always tasted like heaven." Her lips curved into a gentle smile of remembrance. "Did ye ever do such a thing as a child?"

"Nay. There was never any honey to pinch when I was a lad," he replied offhandedly. "Though we, too, enjoyed eating snow. Sometimes there was rocks and dirt in it, yet we were wise enough to avoid any that was yellow in color."

Katherine's laughter pealed through the dreariness of the dank hut and Lachlan found himself joining her. Despite the fact that she was no young maiden, there was a fresh innocence about her demeanor that managed to melt something inside him as quickly as the snow in her cup.

His gaze moved to her lips and his body tensed. More than anything, he wanted to steal a kiss. The feeling surprised and alarmed him. She was a bonny lass, but he had no right to have any feelings toward this woman. She had been wronged by his clan and he needed to tread carefully so he could fix the situation before it escalated into something far more serious.

There would be no kisses. Feeling the muscles in his shoulders tighten, Lachlan abruptly turned away.

Chapter Seven

"Yellow snow?" she repeated.

Katherine's second round of laughter brought on a coughing fit that abruptly ended her mirth. She rose to her feet, hunched her shoulders, and braced her hand against the wall. Lachlan came closer, rubbing her back vigorously, speaking in a gentle, reassuring tone. His touch was calm, soothing. The fit soon ended, leaving Katherine with the ridiculous impulse to press her head against the solid expanse of his chest.

Her stomach filled with fluttering butterflies. She was alone with a strong, virile man, but it was not fear churning in her stomach, nor the remnant of her illness. It was an attraction that seemed to hold a power over her usual common sense.

He was near enough that his strength and warmth surrounded her. The exhilaration of being so close made her feel every inch a woman. An engaging, desirable woman. The pain and betrayal she had felt when discovering Hamish's love for another dulled.

She noticed the vein in Lachlan's neck was beating with a rapid pulse, matching the thumping of her heart. He inched ever so much closer and she shut her eyes in delight as the warmth of his breath grazed her cheek. The sound of her own breathing seemed overly loud in the quiet room. Hearing it sent a shiver through her body.

Katherine's eyelids flew open and she stared up at Lachlan. A deep, powerful yearning filled her and the temptation to kiss him grew with each passing moment. 'Twas impossible to ignore.

He was enthralling. Being this close did strange things to her. A spark of recklessness kindled inside her and Katherine felt her body lean forward. Boldly, she tilted her chin upward, encouraging him to do what they both wanted.

He understood her invitation. She trembled as he framed her face with his hands. Then his head dipped and his mouth found hers, locking it in a tender kiss.

In spite of his strength, his lips were soft. Katherine's breath caught and her body shivered as his lips moved over hers. She answered the kiss with hesitant pressure and he responded enthusiastically, nibbling on her lower lip.

He moved his hand and pressed it against the small of her back, bringing her against him. A fiery trembling shook her. She felt his tongue slide between her teeth and she moved, arching herself closer, molding her softness to his hardness.

Mimicking his movements, Katherine tangled her tongue with Lachlan's, heightening the desire that coursed through her limbs. His mouth, warm, moist, and insistent, stirred her as no other kisses had. He spread his fingers through her hair, cupping the back of her head.

Breaking the kiss, Lachlan trailed his lips down the side of her throat, moving his teeth and tongue over the most sensitive places on her neck.

Her mind went hazy with longing and all thoughts of propriety fled. Katherine heard her breath now coming in short gasps as the pleasure churned deep inside her. Clutching her arms around his broad shoulders, she nuzzled her face down toward his, whimpering with the need to feel his lips again.

She boldly sought his mouth, urging him to kiss her harder, longer, deeper. Low sounds of pleasure escaped from her throat. She was shivering with a hunger she couldn't identify, didn't know how to assuage. Yet instinctively she knew that Lachlan would.

He kissed her once more, then turned away. Katherine swayed and he dug his fingers into her shoulders to keep her from falling. They were both gasping for breath. When hers steadied, he loosened his hold on her.

Katherine allowed her gaze to travel slowly up his powerfully muscled legs to his broad chest and finally his handsome face. Something hot and glittering sparkled in the depths of his eyes. Something she couldn't completely explain, yet could never ignore.

His smoldering kisses had awakened a passion that she had hoped existed within her, yet feared she might never find. The desire to keep kissing him, touching him, *feeling* him, nearly overcame her. How had he so easily beguiled her?

She had felt no need to withdraw from his kisses—quite the contrary, she had encouraged the contact. Why? Aye, she was comfortable with him, her guard was lowered, her curiosity raised. Was that all it took to allow a stranger such liberties?

Katherine carefully banked the fire inside her, needing time to examine and understand it. The kisses had been extraordinary, yet they were but a small part of what drew her to him.

What little she knew of him she admired—his caring

nature, his forthright manner, his intelligence. Despite the odd circumstances that had brought them together, there was an ease she felt around him that had never existed with any other man. He had seen her at her worst, ill and unkempt, and yet somehow he still found her appealing.

Extraordinary.

"We cannae stay here alone together any longer," he announced, a visible pulse throbbing in his neck.

Katherine ran her tongue over her tingling lips. "Because of the kisses?" she asked softly, searching his eyes.

"Aye. Nay." Lachlan tossed his head, as if trying to clear a befuddled mind. "There are many reasons."

Warmth rose in her face, but she met his eyes straight on. Was he rejecting her? Nay, his kisses bespoke of his desire, his expression revealed his passion. "I dinnae think I am strong enough yet to make the journey to my home," she protested.

He moved a few steps away from her. "I know of a convent a day's ride from here. I'll take ye there so that ye may fully recover yer strength. When ye are fit, the nuns will send word to me and I'll arrange a proper guard to take ye home."

Katherine's heart began pounding at a quicker speed. The thought of being separated from him brought on an acute ache. She closed her hand over his and squeezed.

"When the time comes, will ye lead my escort?"

He released her hand, looked away, and shifted on his feet. "There's something I need to tell ye first."

Suspicion curled through her and her stomach dipped. From his tone Katherine knew that something was wrong. He refused to meet her gaze and his handsome face was lined with guilt. Over their kisses?

Nervously, she started rubbing the tightness in her

neck, her mind spinning in turmoil. *Married. He's married. That's why he looks so guilty.*

"Tell me," she whispered, exhaling slowly to hide her trepidation.

He compressed his lips into a tight line, his expression grim. She continued to stare at him until finally he blurted, "My full name is Lachlan Alexander James MacTavish. I'm laird of the MacTavish clan."

Katherine shook her head rapidly, her eyes filling with great confusion. "Truly?"

"Aye." Lachlan stepped forward, worried that her knees might give way and she would tumble to the ground. His instinct was to reach for her and prevent it, yet he dare not touch her until she revealed her full reaction to his confession.

A wave of guilt needled Lachlan's conscious. Deceit was difficult for him. Concealing his true identity from Katherine had made the situation easier for him, but he worried now if it had been the wisest course.

Trust, once broken, was difficult to regain. And he needed both her trust and cooperation if he was going to prevent her family from starting a feud with his clan.

For a moment it appeared that his betrayal had left her mute. He tried to read her eyes, but they skillfully concealed her thoughts.

"Are ye acquainted with the man who took me?" she finally asked, warily. "His men called him Aiden."

"Aye. He's my younger brother."

Katherine gasped and blanched white, covering her cry with her open palm. "Did ye order yer brother to kidnap me?"

Lachlan turned to hide his anger, strangely hurt that she would think him capable of such an act. "I knew nothing of his plans, for if I had, I would have forbidden it. Aiden claims when he unexpectedly saw the opportunity to take ye, he seized it and thus I believe he tells the truth. My brother has a real talent fer acting first and thinking second."

She took a cautious step back. "I must have seemed like a prized pig easily stolen when he and his men spied us. 'Twas foolish of me to be riding a long distance with such a small escort."

"Ye are many things, Lady Katherine, but a swine is not one of them."

He had hoped to elicit a small smile on her lovely face. When none appeared, he felt a strange tug in his chest and an almost overpowering urge to cradle her again in his arms and banish her fear and uncertainty.

"Ye know all, then? Who I am?"

"Aye."

"Will ye ransom me?"

"Nay. I have no quarrel with the McKenna clan and no wish to make an enemy of them."

She shivered. "It might already be too late to prevent it. One doesn't kidnap the kin of their friends or allies."

"All is not lost," he insisted. "Ye shall be returned unhurt. Will that not appease yer family?"

"Some of them, perhaps. However, my father willnae be fergiving when he learns what yer brother has done. It will be even worse when others hear of it. His fearsome reputation will suffer, his pride will be wounded, and retribution fer that will fall directly on the Mac-Tavish." Katherine's throat constricted as she swallowed. "Directly on ye."

"I shall convince him that no harm was intended and will pay whatever reparation he believes fair," Lachlan said, the confidence of his tone belying his inner doubts. "However, in order to do that, I'll need yer help."

Her brow rose in suspicion and he could not fault her mistrust.

"My father will want to know my fate since my capture and I shall tell him all. Even to keep the peace, I willnae lie to my family," she insisted.

"I would never ask that of ye," he replied. "All I require is the opportunity to plead my case. I believe that if ye ask yer father to listen to me, I'll get that chance."

Katherine sighed and anxiously bit her lower lip. "The joy of my safe return will quickly be replaced by anger at my foolish behavior. I cannae guarantee that my father will be inclined to do anything that I ask of him, including listening to ye."

Lachlan's gut roiled. 'Twas an impossible situation, yet at all costs, a feud between the clans had to be averted. Ironically, if Laird McKenna consented to hear Lachlan's explanation, there was little he could offer the wealthy and powerful McKennas in payment for Katherine's kidnapping.

Still, Lachlan remained determined to somehow find a way to settle things peacefully. "Will ye try?" he asked.

Katherine closed her eyes as though deep in prayer, and he was struck anew at her beauty. 'Twas so easy to fall prey to her charms and he cursed his lack of restraint, admitting that he was hardly indifferent to her. No man with sight would be able to resist her unaffected allure.

Yet he couldn't allow her feminine splendor to cloud his senses, to impede his judgment. He knew that he could not let this attraction interfere with what he needed to do—return her to her kin as quickly as possible.

As much as he had relished them, Lachlan was forced to admit the kisses had been a mistake. He had no right to kiss her with such passion and longing, yet her sweet, open manner had tempted him beyond reason.

He had always prided himself on his ability to exercise restraint with women, but the ability to control his desires had vanished when he began kissing Katherine. The feel of her in his arms, the passionate, honest response to his kisses had nearly driven him over the edge.

Was it the appeal of something that he knew was forbidden to him? She was the daughter of a rich and powerful man; he was the laird of a poor and disgraced clan. She was destined to belong to a man with considerably more coin, property, and power than Lachlan could ever hope to possess. That realization left a bitter taste on his tongue, but facing the truth was something he had trained himself to accept years ago.

Katherine's eyelids slowly raised and he clearly saw the indecision in her eyes. *God's teeth!* What then if she refused to help him? She certainly had the right. They looked at each other for a long while. Lachlan held his breath, trying not to reveal the anxiety he felt.

"If ye keep yer word and return me safely to my clan, I'll do all that I can to aid ye in explaining the truth of my capture to my father," she finally said.

"'Tis a bargain," he replied solemnly.

Katherine cast a glance at the doorway. "When do we leave fer the convent?"

Lachlan breathed a small sigh of relief. "Now."

It took but a few minutes to gather anything of value from the hut and pack it on Lachlan's horse. As Katherine readied herself for the journey, questions mingling with seeds of doubt plagued her. Had she escaped the clutches of one brother, only to land in the lap of another?

Was it true that Aiden's rash nature was responsible for this predicament? She desperately wanted to believe that Lachlan had no part in her abduction, yet she knew all too well the folly of trusting the wrong man.

He told her that he was the laird. In her experience, few Highlanders possessed the audacity to defy their leader, even if they were of the same blood. Still, he had insisted he had not ordered her kidnapping in a sincere and truthful voice. And there was no denying that he had shown her kindness and compassion during her illness.

Was she judging him too harshly?

"Ready to leave?"

Lachlan's simple question startled Katherine away from her inner thoughts. Though her mind and emotions were still in a hazy turmoil, she knew her choices were few. She could hardly stay in the hut alone. Mercy, even if she refused to leave, he could easily remove her by force.

"I'm ready." She pulled on her leather gloves and accepted his hand to assist her onto his mount. She slowly settled herself, then heard the saddle creak when he vaulted up behind her.

Reaching around her waist, Lachlan gathered the reins. 'Twas a necessary move, yet it sparked a feeling of intimacy. The desire to lean back and cuddle into his warmth and strength seized Katherine and she acknowledged the attraction she felt for him had not suffered from the doubts she had about his honesty and his motives.

Nay, her attraction was as strong as ever. Hell, if he pulled her shoulders back and turned her into his arms, she would willingly accept his kisses—then likely beg for more. Annoyed at her physical weakness, Katherine stiffened her spine.

I must remain cold, distant, and in control.

For the next few hours she sat in front of Lachlan atop his great beast of a horse with her shoulders squared and back stiff. Thankfully, the fabric of her cloak separated them. Yet she could hear him shifting restless in the saddle, moving close enough that she could feel the strong muscles of his chest whenever they glanced against her.

Her heartbeat quickened, a consequence she reluctantly conceded that was due to Lachlan's nearness. The man had a power over her that she fully intended to control, a task made all the more difficult by his ability to send ripples of emotion through her merely by being close.

Tattered clouds drifted across a gray sky and Katherine was grateful no rain, snow, or ice fell from them. They rode in silence, through a dense forest that Lachlan seemed to know well.

Katherine's eyelids grew heavy. Closing them, she dozed intermittently, until a rustle of noise sounded ahead, startling her completely awake. Lachlan slowed the horse, shifting his eyes in a wide circle around them.

"Riders ahead," he whispered. "To our left."

Katherine's heart thumped. She squinted through the boughs of pine trees, alarmed to see that Lachlan was right. "Yer men?" she asked hopefully.

"Nay. We left MacTavish land over an hour ago," Lachlan replied, still watching the trees ahead. "One of our search parties wouldn't have come this far south."

The pines soon gave way to stark branches of oak, giving them a clearer view. Eight mounted Highlanders approached. Two carried bows, arrows notched and ready to fly. A third man balanced a spear expertly across his saddle.

"Are they hunting?" she whispered.

"Aye." Lachlan mumbled an oath.

Katherine shrank closer to him, then stiffened the moment she saw the colors of the Highlander's plaid. "Frasers."

She uttered the name beneath her breath, but Lachlan heard her.

"'Tis the laird himself leading the men. Does he know ye?" Lachlan asked.

Katherine shook her head. "I've never met him. But 'tis no secret that the Frasers have little kindness fer the McKennas."

In truth, Laird Archibald Fraser was a bitter enemy of the McKennas—the feud between them ran deep, heightened by the fact that Katherine's brother had recently married Archibald's divorced wife. 'Twould be a boon indeed to the Fraser clan if she fell into their hands and a powerful weapon to use against her own kin.

Katherine watched with growing trepidation as the Fraser men spread out and came closer, effectively surrounding them.

"I dinnae think they have seen us yet," she whispered. "Can we outrun them?"

"If we bolt, they'll hear it and give chase, believing we have something to hide," Lachlan replied, steadying his horse. "'Tis best if we brazen it out."

Katherine wanted to argue, but she saw the wisdom in his plan. She nodded and tried to swallow the lump of fear that lingered in her throat, saying a silent prayer that Lachlan MacTavish was the honorable Highlander she hoped him to be.

Suddenly, the deadly hiss of an arrow whizzed over their heads, striking a tree.

"Ye are on Fraser land," shouted a harsh, authoritative voice. "Show yerselves at once or the next arrow shall strike far closer than that tree."

"Calm yer men," Lachlan cried. "I'm Lachlan Mac-Tavish. I pose no threat."

Lachlan kicked his heels against the horse's flanks, steering them forward. Katherine held her breath as an uneasy stillness filled the air. The men sat casually on their mounts, their hands loosely holding the reins. It should have brought her a sense of calm. But she knew those weapons so close at hand could be drawn in a heartbeat, yielding deadly consequences.

Though she had never met him, 'twas easy for Katherine to pick out Laird Fraser. Mounted on a large, white horse with a pack of fierce-looking warriors flanking him, Archibald was a formidable sight. He was as handsome as she had been told, with a strong brow, bold eyes, a squared jaw, and a winning smile of straight white teeth.

Yet Katherine knew better than to be taken in by his outward pleasing appearance. Her sister-in-law, Joan, rarely spoke of her years as Archibald's wife, but the few things she had said bespoke of his cold heart and barbarous cruelty.

"Are ye lost, MacTavish?" Archibald questioned in a mocking tone. "Or are ye looking fer a private spot to enjoy some bed sport with yon maiden?"

Katherine sucked in her breath as the Fraser laird's narrow glare fixated on her, his lecherous gaze traveling down the length of her body.

"I'm merely taking a shortened route to MacTavish Keep so that we may arrive before darkness," Lachlan said in a clipped, hard tone.

"Och, so ye're eager to do yer rutting beside a fire with a roof over yer head?" Laird Fraser let out a snide chuckle, but then his eyes suddenly narrowed with further suspicion. "Who is this wench? She wears a cloak with the McKenna plaid."

Katherine tried not to flinch as Archibald's heavy stare bore into her. The gaze unnerved her, far beyond the fear that he might discover her true identity. There was something feral and cruel lurking in the depths of Archibald's eyes.

"Yer thirst fer revenge against the McKennas is well-known," Lachlan said casually. "But I dinnae think ye'd find a former serving girl of much interest."

"A servant?" Archibald quirked a brow. "The quality of the cloak wrapped around her says otherwise."

Lachlan rubbed his jaw. "The garment was a parting gift from her former mistress."

"McKenna's shrew of a wife? Or his spoiled daughter?" Archibald cast them both a jaundiced eye. "'Tis unlikely that either of them would relinquish such a fine garment to a mere servant."

Lachlan leveled his gaze at Archibald. "I dinnae say the McKenna lass gave it to her, now did I?"

There was a chorus of laughter from the men surrounding their laird. Katherine experienced a twinge of indignity at the insults leveled against her and her mother, then silently chastised herself for being so foolish. The opinion of these men mattered not a whit.

She caught Archibald's skeptical look and struggled to appear unconcerned. Did he believe Lachlan's tale? The Fraser laird had eyes that seemed to peer directly into her soul. A feeling of foreboding took hold and she shivered. God help her if he somehow discovered that she was the McKenna's daughter.

"What's yer name, lass?" Archibald barked.

"Isabel, milord," Katherine answered. Fearing to reveal even an ounce of truth, she used her middle name.

"How did a McKenna servant come to be riding with the laird of the MacTavish clan?" Laird Fraser wanted to know.

"Former servant," Katherine corrected.

Archibald's mouth pressed into a grim line. "She's far too bold a lass to be in service," he declared, his cold gaze directly challenging Lachlan.

"Aye, now ye understand why the McKennas sent her away," Lachlan said.

A few of the men grinned. Archibald instantly silenced their mirth with a frosty stare.

"They should have put the strap to her back and taught her a proper humble attitude," Archibald insisted. "Ye'd best make sure ye beat her well so she understands her place."

"I dinnae need any advice from ye on how to discipline my household servants," Lachlan replied flatly.

The undercurrent of strain between the two lairds grew. Katherine bit her lip, cursing her tart tongue. It had served her well growing up as the only female with several tough, willful brothers, yet now it could prove to be her downfall.

She should have kept her mouth shut and her eyes lowered, remembering that was how most servants acted among their masters. Thanks to the kindness and compassion of her mother, those who worked at McKenna Castle were treated far better than most, though they quickly learned to stay out of her father's way when his temper flared.

"Well, if she becomes too much fer ye to handle, MacTavish, send her to Fraser Castle. I'm sure I can find something to do with her," Archibald proclaimed with a lewd smirk.

There was another chorus of laughter from his men. Katherine could feel the blood pounding in her head as Archibald's chilling words rang in her ears. Every instinct in her bones was screaming at her to kick her heels into the horse's belly and urge the animal to break into a gallop.

"Aye, ye'll be the first one I contact," Lachlan said with a laugh.

Katherine turned her head and caught a glimpse of Lachlan's smile. She sucked in a breath, her heart racing frantically.

He is only jesting, she told herself, knowing any other explanation was simply too terrifying to contemplate.

With a desperate sigh of relief, Katherine felt the horse pivot and move in the opposite direction, away from Fraser and his men. The tension around her heart gradually eased, though the flutters in her stomach would not leave.

"Archibald would have paid good coin fer me," Katherine finally said in a trembling voice.

"I dinnae want his money." Lachlan let out an exasperated sigh.

His voice sounded gruff, but she wasn't frightened. The encounter with Archibald had shown her the face of a real enemy.

"How far must we head in this direction before turning back?" she asked ten minutes later.

"They'll be no turning back. It's not safe. Fraser and his men will be watching us."

"How will we get to the convent?"

"We willnae be going to the convent."

Katherine frowned. "Shall we return to the hut?"

"Nay. We ride fer MacTavish Keep."

Katherine's brows knit together with worry. "Will Aiden be there?"

Lachlan shrugged. "'Tis his home."

Lachlan spurred his mount up a steep hill, leaving no chance for further conversation. Katherine found herself shaking when they reached the summit, uncertain if her distress was caused by the unpleasant encounter with Archibald Fraser or the prospect of once again coming face to face with Aiden MacTavish.

Chapter Eight

The sun was setting when they finally arrived, coloring the sky with streaks of red and gold, casting shadows on the looming structure ahead. It was a single, square stone tower of significant height, with an old-fashioned thatched roof. The outer curtain wall was constructed from both wood and stone, surrounded by a narrow moat filled with water.

The moat surface was frozen solid, indicating it didn't run very deep. As they drew closer, Katherine's eyes moved upward, noting that four men stood at the ramparts surrounding the front gate. They were a motley group, with gray beards and stooped shoulders, dressed in padded vests instead of proper protection and clan colors.

There were no archers in view, no eager young men patrolling the wall in hopes of impressing their laird. Even to Katherine's untrained eye, the defenses seemed insufficient.

As they entered the bailey, men, women, and children scrambled forward to greet their returning laird. A young lad took hold of Lachlan's horse while one of the soldiers came to Katherine's side and extended his hand to her.

The smile of thanks she readily offered immediately faded when she caught a glimpse of the man's features. Aiden! Pulling back as if scalded, Katherine pointedly refused his assistance and began dismounting on her own. Her legs felt unsteady once she reached the ground and she swayed slightly. A strong arm caught her by the waist. Peevishly, Katherine raised her hand to bat it away and then realized 'twas Lachlan who held her so securely.

"Thank ye." She nodded gratefully before stepping away.

A middle-aged woman pushed herself through the crowd. "Thanks be to God, ye've returned at last. I've been so worried."

She pulled Lachlan into a tight embrace, which he returned. Then, as if remembering he had not arrived alone, he gently disengaged himself and pushed Katherine forward.

"My mother, Lady Morag. This is Lady Katherine McKenna."

The older woman's face paled as her eyebrows arched in surprise, yet her expression remained calm. "Our men have been searching near and far fer ye, Lady Katherine. I'm pleased to see that ye are safe."

She gave Katherine's hand an awkward pat. Katherine forced a small smile, uncertain how to respond. Her upbringing would not allow her to be outwardly rude, yet what did one say to the mother of the man who had unceremoniously abducted her? Should she tell her to box Aiden's ears?

"Why have ye brought her here?" Aiden frowned and crossed his arms over his chest. "Have ye changed yer mind about a ransom?"

"Nay!" Lachlan pinned his brother with a hard look. "I had hoped to bring Lady Katherine to the Convent of the Sacred Heart, but we met Archibald Fraser on our journey and immediately had to change course."

Lady Morag stiffened. "How did ye manage to escape from him?"

"With cunning," Katherine replied sourly.

"I cannae believe Fraser willingly let her slip through his grasp," Aiden remarked, his frown deepening.

"I concealed her true identity," Lachlan explained. "And thus it must remain."

Heart pounding, Katherine wiped her damp hands down the sides of her cloak, her fear renewed at hearing Lachlan's words. Archibald Fraser posed a true threat to her and the defenses of MacTavish Keep did not appear to offer the protection she needed from such a brutal enemy.

"Gracious, what's wrong with ye, lass?" Lady Morag looked nervously from her son to Katherine. "Ye've turned white as a cloud."

"She's been ill with fever and a cough. Standing out here in the cold air must have weakened her and worsened her symptoms," Lachlan said, a scowl twisting his lips. "She needs to be indoors. Please show her to my chamber and find her some warmer garments."

"Lachlan!" Lady Morag's brows rose in scandalous shock and she cast an anxious eye toward Katherine. Those individuals close enough to hear his request also started muttering amongst themselves. "'Tis most unsuitable fer Lady Katherine to share yer bedchamber."

Lachlan's brows drew together and he gave his mother a disgruntled look. "Ye misunderstand. I'll sleep elsewhere. She'll be staying there alone."

"'Tis not necessary fer ye to relinquish yer chamber," Katherine protested. "I dinnae wish to be a nuisance."

"Ye need to fully recover from yer illness before ye can make the journey home," Lachlan reminded her.

Aiden snorted. "If ye hadn't run off, Lady Katherine, we wouldn't have to be making all these complicated arrangements," he said in a surly tone.

Katherine's back stiffened. How dare he blame her for all that had occurred when 'twas his decision to kidnap her that started this long line of unfortunate events?

"Shut up, Aiden," Lachlan growled. "'Twas ye who put us on this road with yer foolish, impulsive actions."

While she appreciated Lachlan's defense, she was surprised at his harsh tone and the undercurrent of aggression that existed between the two brothers. Her own brothers often had disagreements with each other but seemed to be able to resolve them without undue anger or open hostility.

Katherine searched Aiden's handsome features for a hint of remorse for her abduction, yet found none. Clearly, he had few regrets. Her mind started spinning. With Lachlan at her side she was in no immediate danger, however 'twas an important reminder that she needed to be on her guard whenever Aiden was near.

Lady Morag hesitated, then clasped Katherine's arm. "Come inside. I'll show ye where ye may rest."

Katherine dutifully followed Lady Morag, trying to control the tremors that shook her body, worried that her illness was returning. They climbed many steep stone steps and Katherine swore she could feel the cold and dampness leeching from the walls that surrounded them.

Weak light from the arrow slit windows did little to illuminate the way and she paid careful attention to every step to make certain she didn't lose her footing.

Katherine's breathing was winded by the time they

reached the landing, distressing proof that her illness still lingered. Unease etched on her face, Lady Morag opened the door to a bedchamber. Curious to learn more about Lachlan, Katherine stepped inside, and quickly realized that she would find no clues about him here.

The furnishings were simple, almost crude, and well-worn. 'Twas easy to spot the many sections that were mended on the bed curtains, the floor lacked rugs, and the walls were devoid of tapestries that could have provided decoration and warmth.

'Twas difficult to believe this was the laird's chamber, supposedly the best in the keep. With a bit of shock, Katherine realized that there were household servants at McKenna Castle living in greater luxury.

"I'm sure 'tis not as grand as yer chambers at home," the older woman said apologetically.

"The room is most inviting and comfortable," Katherine replied. She could feel Lady Morag watching her anxiously and she chose her words carefully, not wanting to cause any embarrassment. "'Twas kind of Lachlan to allow me the use of it."

Two servants entered the chamber. They filled the fireplace with peat and a few small pieces of wood, then struggled to start a fire.

"I could see about arranging a bath," Lady Morag said, tapping her finger nervously against her chin. "Though with yer recent illness, 'tis probably best not to get wet."

Katherine would have dearly loved the chance to soak in a hot tub and wash the grit and grim of the last few days from her body. However, she felt certain it would cause a great disruption to the household to have one prepared.

"A basin of hot water, some soap, and a clean cloth are all that I need, Lady Morag," Katherine said graciously.

The older woman's face relaxed. "We can manage that easily," she said. "Och, Beth, stand aside. Ye're never going to get wood that damp to catch."

Beth obediently moved away. The second servant, a tall, thin lad, took her place. He too struggled, but between the pair a meager fire was finally started. Katherine hoped when it burned brighter it would take some of the chill and dampness from the chamber.

"I pray that ye are not overly distressed over this misunderstanding with my son Aiden," Lady Morag said. "I fear yer kin will misjudge his actions, but ye must believe that he meant ye no harm."

Misunderstanding? Katherine opened her mouth to issue a sharp rebuke of that false assessment, but held her tongue when she glimpsed Lady Morag's uneasy eyes.

"Mayhap that is true, yet I cannae say how my father will react when he learns what Aiden did."

A shadow crossed Lady Morag's features. "The reputation of the McKennas is fierce."

"Only toward our enemies," Katherine replied.

"We aren't yer enemy," Lady Morag whispered, wringing her hands. "We wish ye no harm."

"We can only hope that my father will see it that way," Katherine replied, realizing that she meant it.

The blame rested squarely with Aiden and his men. The others were innocent and she felt uncomfortable at the notion that her father's wrath could fall upon them.

Upon Lachlan.

"There's something else I'd like to ask ye." Lady Morag's anxious eyes met hers. "We've heard that my youngest son—Robbie—is being held prisoner by the

McKennas. 'Tis said that he toils in the quarry. Can ye tell me anything of his fate?"

The question stunned Katherine. For a few moments she could only stare at the older woman in disbelief and then the pieces suddenly began falling into place. Aye, when the opportunity had presented itself, Aiden had snatched her, but he had done so with a specific plan in mind.

Her mind spun as the possible reasons for her abduction took on new meaning. Was it revenge that Aiden sought? A fine payment of ransom? Or had he taken her believing the McKenna would be forced to free Robbie in order to gain her freedom?

She racked her brain, trying to remember if she had ever heard of any MacTavish men being taken prisoner by her family. However, none came to mind.

"I know naught of such things," Katherine finally answered, as kindly as possible. "Prisoners are men's business."

The sadness in Lady Morag's eyes intensified and Katherine felt a twinge of pity for her. 'Twas clear that she loved her son and understandable that she worried about him.

"Forgive me fer asking." Lady Morag wet her lips nervously. "I should not have troubled ye with such a question, especially when ye are unwell. Ye must rest now. When it's time fer the evening meal, I'll have one of the maids bring ye clean garments so that ye can change and stay warm."

And before Katherine could think of anything else to say, Lady Morag was gone.

All eyes were upon Katherine when she entered the great hall. She felt awkward dressed in garments that were not her own. The soft wool gown stretched tightly across her breast and the hem exposed her ankles. It clung to her narrow waist and hips in an almost provocative manner.

In all likelihood it was one of the older woman's best gowns and Katherine felt strange wearing it. But the garment was indeed clean and warm and she would not insult Lady Morag by refusing her generosity.

Lachlan motioned to her and Katherine came to the dais and took the seat at his side, trying to ignore the whispers that followed her.

Lady Morag flanked Lachlan on the other side, and next to her sat Aiden. Katherine was pleased to have some distance from her kidnapper, as his presence made her uneasy. Each time he glanced at her, Katherine's flesh prickled uncomfortably with awareness.

Platters of food were placed in front of them. Lachlan courteously served her first. Eagerly, Katherine selected several large pieces of what she assumed was either beef or venison and placed them on the trencher they shared.

Using the sharp eating knife Lachlan offered, she stabbed a morsel and popped it into her mouth. The outside was charred to perfection, the inside tender and juicy. Savoring the taste, she reached for another, then sipped from her goblet.

Her face twisted in a grimace. Instead of wine, 'twas filled with a watery ale that had an unpleasant, bitter aftertaste. It caused her mouth to pucker and her eyes to water when she swallowed.

"Is our local brew not to yer liking, Lady Katherine?" Aiden asked with a sneer. "Shall we beg yer pardon fer not breaking out our best French wine to celebrate yer arrival?"

Katherine slowly placed her goblet on the table,

aware of the many pairs of avid eyes that were turned upon her. "The ale is unique. Alas, the soreness of my throat prevents me from drinking too much of it."

Aiden cast her a second glance; this one cold enough to chill her blood. Katherine tossed her head as though she had not a care in the world, and she flickered her eyes over the people gathered in the hall.

'Twas oddly quiet. Used to the loud merriment and comradery of the McKenna great hall, she was startled to discover that conversations were few. Indeed, most had their attention on the food that was rapidly disappearing.

Striving to be polite, Katherine left the remaining pieces of meat on the trencher for Lachlan. She looked with hungry interest at the other bowls and platters on the table, dismayed at the sparsity of the offerings.

There were some boiled turnips and cabbage, stewed onions that gave off a pungent odor, a few small pieces of fish, and slices of thick, hard brown bread. There was no roasted fowl, no thick stews, no cheese or dried fruit, no confections of any kind.

Stomach rumbling, Katherine ate another piece of the meat, then forced down a boiled turnip. She looked hopefully toward the servants standing near the entrance to the great hall, but disappointingly, no additional platters of food appeared.

A serving lad approached the dais and Katherine's chin lifted with interest. Alas, he held only a pitcher, which she assumed contained more of the bitter-tasting ale.

With a kind smile, Katherine refused a refill, then watched the lad carefully fill Lachlan's tankard. The laird nodded his thanks, then leaned back in his chair.

"I find that I am unable to eat another bite," he said, slowly pushing the trencher toward the child.

Katherine nearly reached out to snatch another

piece of meat, hesitating only when she took a close look at the lad. He had a gaunt appearance, his arms and legs visibly thin beneath the fraying tunic he wore. Her heart twisted with pity.

"Father Joseph says 'tis a sin to waste food," the lad said wistfully.

"Then ye best eat some of it, so we dinnae offend him—or the good Lord," Lachlan said gently.

There was no mistaking the excitement in the lad's eyes as he reached for the food and began eating. His eyes closed in bliss as he chewed. The moment he was gone, a second child took his place. This time 'twas a lass of no more than four or five years. At Lachlan's bidding, she took the remaining pieces of meat and stuffed them into her mouth so quickly Katherine feared she might choke.

A third child appeared and was given the meat-soaked trencher of bread. He held it in his hands as though it was the most precious gift in the world. Katherine bowed her head in silent thanks, realizing she had never truly appreciated the comfortable life with which she had been blessed. Due to their wealth, no man, woman, or child ever suffered from severe hunger in her clan.

"Why is there so little fresh meat tonight?" Lachlan asked Aiden, his voice tight.

"The hunting has been slim with so many of the men out searching fer Lady Katherine," Aiden said defensively.

"We'll hunt in two groups tomorrow," Lachlan replied. "I'll lead one and ye the other."

Lachlan took a swig of ale. He turned toward her and she noted that the expression in his eyes seemed far older than his years. 'Twas clear the poverty and want of his people weighed heavily upon him. So much so that he willingly gave them the food from his own table.

'Twas a depth of caring and sacrifice that touched her heart. More than anything, she wanted to reach out and take his hand, to offer him silent comfort and understanding. But she lacked the nerve, uncertain how he would interpret the gesture.

Instead, she waited for the music and storytelling to begin, hoping that would lighten the mood. Finally, the trestle tables were pushed to the edges of the great hall. Katherine wiggled in her chair, debating if she should offer a song.

At home, many praised her lyrical voice and she was often asked to sing. Perhaps the familiar verses of a ballad would help ease the feelings of loneliness that gripped her.

However, after all the tables had been moved from the center of the hall, everyone began to leave. Confused, Katherine sagged in her chair, clamping down her disappointment.

"Do ye need an escort to yer chamber?" Lachlan asked. "One of the maids can light the way."

Katherine nodded. Her stomach rumbled and her head began to ache. She was hardly tired after the nap she had taken, but there was no reason to stay. She bid the family good night and followed the maid from the great hall.

'Tis best if I go to bed, she told herself as she climbed the winding stairs. It had been a long, tiring, eventful day.

Things were bound to look better come morning.

"Now that she has been found, Aiden and I were hoping ye'd tell us yer plans fer Lady Katherine," Lady Morag said.

She placed a half-empty bottle of spirits in front of Lachlan, then nodded dismissively at the few servants lingering in the great hall. Lachlan sighed, knowing she wanted privacy so they could speak freely. He ached with fatigue and hunger and longed for sleep, but this conversation could not be avoided.

"As soon as Lady Katherine has fully recovered from her illness, I will lead an escort of my men to McKenna Castle and return her safely to her family," Lachlan replied, taking but a small sip of the potent whiskey. It slid smoothly down his throat, warming him from the inside.

Aiden scoffed. "Ye cannae mean to simply take her back to her family and demand nothing in return? What of our brother?"

"The McKenna laird might consider an exchange," his stepmother added hopefully. "'Twould be a benefit to us all."

Lachlan bit back a snort. "If I demanded anything from the McKennas, 'twould be sacks of grain and a few cattle to feed us through the rest of the winter," he replied, disgusted with himself for even considering the notion of accepting payment.

"Lady Katherine is a great prize. Ye hold her so easily in yer grasp and yet ye'd ask fer grain?" Aiden scowled at Lachlan, his disgust evident. "The McKenna would gladly give up Robbie fer his daughter along with a hefty pile of coins."

Lachlan shook his head. "I cannae risk further angering the man. Robbie's fate is foremost in my mind, but it willnae rule my actions. Laird McKenna respects the Highland honor. I will return his daughter— unharmed—and apologize fer her abduction. 'Tis our best chance, dare I say our only chance, of preventing him from riding to our gates with a band of his fiercest warriors and burning us out," Lachlan said wryly.

"Have ye no pride? There are no circumstances on earth that would have me grovel and cringe before any man, no matter how powerful!" Aiden pushed himself away from the table and began pacing, his angry strides crushing the rushes beneath his feet. "Ye are throwing away our best chance—nay, our *only* chance of rescuing our brother."

Lady Morag gave Lachlan a silent, frenzied look. He turned his head away, tired of having to justify his decisions, wishing he could simply give her and Aiden what they wanted. Yet as much as he would like to please his stepmother, his first consideration must be the welfare of the entire clan.

Suddenly, Aiden ceased his pacing. "We wouldn't be so vulnerable to the McKennas if we had a strong ally."

"I can think of no sane laird who would side with us against the McKenna," Lachlan replied, taking a final sip of his drink. Lady Morag lifted the bottle, but he slid his hand over the rim of his goblet, refusing another portion.

"Archibald Fraser might," she whispered.

Aiden flashed a triumphant grin and Lachlan had to admit, under different circumstances the suggestion might be something to consider.

"Fraser lacks honor," Lachlan stated bluntly. "We could never trust him."

"All the more reason not to make an enemy of him," Aiden insisted.

Lachlan shrugged. "He's never bothered with us in the past."

"Katherine McKenna has never before slept beneath our roof," Aiden countered.

"She will be gone before week's end," Lachlan replied.

He kept his voice calm, his manner relaxed, but Aiden's point had rattled him. Fraser was a complication he had not anticipated and could swiftly turn into a problem. He presented a real danger to Katherine and, in turn, to all of clan MacTavish.

"Lady Katherine's presence in our home places every one of us in jeopardy," Aiden said. "What if Fraser discovers that ye've lied to him about her? He'll be furious, bent on avenging the insult."

"We've all heard the terrible stories about him." Lady Morag's face looked stricken. "Could we withstand a feud with the Fraser laird and his clan?"

"If Archibald learns the truth, he'll most likely be angry, perhaps even vengeful, but we have nothing of value to pillage or plunder," Lachlan said in a tightly controlled voice. "'Tis one of the few benefits of being so poor."

"Katherine McKenna is a prize above all others in Fraser's eyes," Aiden said. "He would be in our debt if we gave her to him."

Never! A shudder coursed through Lachlan at the thought of Katherine in Fraser's clutches.

"Men like Fraser kill fer the joy of it." Lachlan scrubbed a hand wearily across his brow. "And ye are proposing an alliance with him."

Aiden turned his gaze to Lady Morag, then back to Lachlan. "I'm trying to do what is best fer the clan."

Lachlan made a derisive noise deep in his throat. "Ye are trying to justify yer poor judgment."

"That's a lie!"

"God's bones!" Lady Morag gasped and clutched her hand over her heart. "It distresses me to no end to witness my sons acting like combatants. If ye dinnae work together, how will we ever survive this upheaval?"

Lachlan reached out and put his hand on her shoulder. To his surprise, Aiden did the same.

"We are too much alike, my brother and I," Lachlan observed. "We both want to be in command and have others do our bidding without question or protest."

"Lachlan is our laird," Lady Morag said, determination filling her expression. "The final decision rests with him."

"Aye, Mother. Ye need not remind me." Aiden muttered an oath and stepped away, his footsteps echoing through the chamber.

An awkward silence settled between Lachlan and his stepmother.

"Aiden is passionate because he cares so deeply," she said quietly. "I hope that ye understand it."

Lachlan sighed. "I do."

Understand it, aye. Continue to tolerate it? Not much longer.

Chapter Nine

Katherine slowly drifted awake. She opened her eyes, pleased to discover her head was no longer throbbing. She swallowed, relieved to feel only a trace of soreness in her throat. Apparently, a thorough rest in a proper bed did have the power to heal.

Katherine stretched her arms above her head and rotated her shoulders. Most of the stiffness was gone from her limbs and she felt more refreshed than she had in days. Spirits lifted, Katherine glanced around the chamber.

It appeared even more plain and sparse in the morning light. The linens she had slept upon were threadbare, though clean and infused with the fresh scent of lavender. The mattress stuffed with straw was firm, the pillows soft and feather-filled. The wooden floor was swept free of dirt and there was no sign of vermin.

A chest was placed at the foot of the bed. Resisting the temptation to investigate, Katherine assumed it contained Lachlan's clothing. There was a table with a single chair and another smaller wooden stand with a pitcher and basin for washing. The tiny flame in the fireplace gave off the only light in the room, as the iron sconces in the walls were either empty or held candle nubs so small they would not hold a flame. Judging by the smell, they were made of tallow and not beeswax.

There were no personal items to be seen that revealed the character of the occupant. No armor or weaponry, no maps or a chessboard and finely carved pieces. It appeared that all Lachlan did in this chamber was sleep.

Katherine crossed the room to the largest of the three windows. Slowly opening the wooden shutters, Katherine pulled back the leather covering that provided protection from the wind and cold. They, too, were well worn and she feared that if she were not careful, she might tear them.

The resulting window view was surprising in its beauty—rugged, rolling hills, a dense forest of green pines, and a sparkling blue loch were spread before her. The lovely sight of the Highlands, even in the dead of winter, lifted her mood.

A soft knock at the door drew Katherine's attention. At her bid to enter, a young maid arrived, carrying Katherine's clothing. "We've cleaned yer gown and mended the small tears," the lass said nervously. "I'm to help ye dress and then take ye to the hall to break yer fast, milady."

"I am grateful fer yer assistance, . . . ?"

"Flora," the maid answered with a relieved expression, causing Katherine to wonder if the lass worried that she would turn the famous McKenna temper upon her. After all, Katherine had been brought here against her will. 'Twould be understandable if she was less than gracious toward those who held her captive.

"Let's start by untangling my hair, Flora," Katherine said with what she hoped was a reassuring smile.

The maid produced a hairbrush and comb. Katherine sat in the chair, trying not to wince as the knots were brushed away. When that was done, Flora expertly braided the long tresses and pinned them in a circle at the crown of Katherine's head.

"Lady Morag gave me a short veil fer ye," Flora said, holding out the headpiece.

"How thoughtful," Katherine replied. "I fear mine was lost days ago."

Flora's wide eyes grew even rounder. "Is it true that Sir Aiden gave chase and plucked ye right off yer galloping horse?" the maid asked in a trembling voice.

"Aye. 'Tis a miracle neither of us were injured," Katherine said in a biting tone, the memory a most unpleasant reminder of her current circumstances.

"Sir Aiden is such a skilled horseman and a brave fighter," Flora said, her expression filling with awe. "He is much admired by all."

"He may well possess an abundance of virtues," Katherine replied sourly. "Unfortunately, common sense is not among them."

"He was doing what he thought best fer the clan," Flora insisted. "'Tis awful how he has been chastised, his opinion disregarded. The laird shouldn't be so angry with him."

Katherine tilted her head. "Are there others who believe the same? That Sir Aiden has the right of it?"

Flustered, Flora turned away, no longer meeting Katherine's eye. "There are many who believe what Sir Aiden did was right, though they'll not show disrespect and defend him to the laird."

Katherine was uncertain how much credence to give

to this bit of news. Were there warriors in the clan who also supported Aiden or was it mainly impressionable females like Flora, who could easily be taken in by Aiden's handsome face and winning smile?

Highlanders could be a fickle lot. They admired strength, cunning, and loyalty. Though uncommon, 'twas not impossible for a laird to lose the respect of his people and be replaced. Was that a possibility? Katherine clenched her teeth. If Aiden replaced Lachlan as laird, she feared things could go badly for her.

Flora went silent. She was, however, efficient and Katherine was soon ready, feeling far more like herself dressed in her own clothing. The maid escorted her out and Katherine immediately took note of the two warriors standing guard in front of her door, wondering when they had arrived at their post—late last night? This morning?

"Two guards?" she muttered beneath her breath, wondering if they had been placed there to keep her in the chamber or others out. Either situation did not sit well in her mind, reminding her again of her vulnerability.

Saying no more, she followed the maid down the winding stone stairs into the great hall. It was nearly empty, causing Katherine to realize how late she had slept.

"I'll fetch ye some porridge," Flora volunteered.

The bowl the maid soon brought contained a thin, bland, unappetizing gruel, but Katherine relished the warmth it provided as it filled her belly. She was surprised to realize she could have eaten a second bowl, yet after the events of last evening knew better than to ask for another. Food, no matter how poor in quality, was scarce at MacTavish Keep.

Only a few servants cleaning off the wooden tables remained in the great hall when Katherine was finished with her meager meal. She swallowed the last of her bitter ale and headed for the door, half expecting a guard to materialize, perhaps even stop her—yet none appeared.

Though cold, the fresh air felt invigorating and the strong sunshine chased away an initial chill. Katherine toyed with the notion of returning to her chamber to retrieve her cloak, but decided she would simply return indoors if she became cold.

The noise and bustle in the bailey was a sharp contrast to the quiet of the hall. A group of women were drawing water from a well, while others stoked the fires of a row of laundry kettles. Two lads carrying baskets of dark brown bread plodded through the muddy ground while children of all ages and sizes darted around the buildings and between the carts, playing a lively game of tag.

Katherine received a few polite nods from those she walked past, but many averted their eyes. She turned the corner and hesitated, spying a large group of workers gathered around one of the outbuildings. The pleasant scent of freshly cut wood wafted from a cart positioned at the structure's doorway and she surmised they were engaged in some sort of construction project.

Curious, she paused to watch. Two lines of men carefully passed a large beam up the side of the building, handing it off to a smaller group at the top, the grunts and groans attesting to the weight of their burden. For a moment Katherine held her breath, half expecting to see it slip and crash to the ground, but somehow it managed to reach the crew on the roof.

Katherine moved her hand to her brow, shading her

eyes for a closer look, and was startled to realize that it was Lachlan on the roof, angling the heavy beam like a common laborer. He was directing the men's efforts, calling out commands as he worked alongside them.

He had stripped down to his shirt. Every line of his muscular form was defined through the thin fabric; his shoulders looked broader, his arms thicker. She could clearly see the array of flat muscles rippling down his stomach as he lifted the beam over his head.

It took three men on the opposite side to handle the beam that Lachlan moved by himself. His chest was damp with sweat causing his shirt to cling to his arms and torso, attesting to the effort that he was exerting.

Katherine found herself unable to look away. There was something almost mesmerizing about watching his muscles flex with each of his movements. 'Twas an undeniable exhibition of brute strength, yet there was grace, even elegance in it.

Katherine slowly, evenly released the breath she didn't realize she had been holding. With the beam secured in place, Lachlan ordered the men away and scrambled down the roof. He landed on the ground with a soft thud. Stepping back, he heaved a large sigh and pushed a lock of damp hair from his brow.

Her senses reeled. His eyes looked tired and she could see the shadow of a beard on the chiseled line of his jaw. Aiden might possess the perfectly sculpted features of a Greek god, but Lachlan had a strong, rough, masculine beauty that sent a shiver sweeping over her.

It seemed the more she learned about him and observed his behavior, the more she admired him, was attracted to him. It was evident in the way these men looked to him for instruction that he was a natural leader. She was impressed at his knowledge of building, but also his willingness to do the hard, physical work that any soldier she knew would think beneath him.

Katherine tried to imagine her father—or even one of her brothers—doing the same, but could not. They were Highland warriors to the bone, proud of their fighting prowess, strength, and cunning in battle. They protected those who tilled the soil, tended the live-stock, and repaired the buildings. They did not work beside them.

Lachlan's head turned and their gazes unexpec-tantly met. His brow rose and something sparkled in his eyes. Joy at seeing her? Nay! Inwardly, Katherine chastised herself for such vanity, deciding he was most likely glad that she was up and about and would soon be ready to make the journey home.

"The color has returned to yer face," Lachlan said as he came to stand beside her. "Or is it the cold weather and lack of a proper cloak that brings the redness to yer cheeks?"

Katherine flushed with embarrassment at the gentle rebuke. "I've only been outside fer a short time and the sun is warm."

"Ye can see yer breath in the air," Lachlan admon-ished, wrapping his own cloak around her shoulders. "'Tis foolish to tempt fate. If ye catch a chill, yer sick-ness will return."

Katherine drew the garment closer, enjoying its warmth. The masculine smell of wood and soap rose to tickle her nose and seize her senses—Lachlan's scent. With effort, she resisted the temptation to smother her entire face into the wool, knowing Lachlan would think she had lost her wits.

"I was surprised to see ye in the bailey," she said. "I thought ye'd be out hunting with yer men."

"We've already gone and returned with but a small

result." Lachlan kicked a stone out of his path. "One of the men saw boar droppings. 'Tis best to hunt those beasts at dusk, so we shall try again later this afternoon. We could eat well fer days if we kill one."

"'Twould be a good reason to celebrate." She studied him from under her lashes. "Once the hunt is completed, will ye make plans to bring me home?"

"Ye appear fit enough fer the journey."

"I believe that I am, but do ye have men to spare?" She shifted and kicked the same stone, reminding herself of the game she played as a child with her brothers. "I've learned the errors of my ways. I'll not travel again without a goodly number of swords surrounding me."

"I'll be taking my best, most experienced warriors as yer escort," Lachlan assured her. "To avoid trouble, we'll need to slip away before Archibald Fraser becomes a threat."

"Aye. I shall never again take my safety fer granted," Katherine admitted with a shudder. Falling into MacTavish hands had been trying. Being captured by the Fraser laird was unthinkable. "'Twas purely my fault that Aiden was able to kidnap me."

Lachlan lowered the corners of his mouth into a puzzled frown. "Aiden insists that when he saw ye, ye weren't on McKenna land. I'm surprised that yer father allowed ye to travel so far with so few men protecting ye."

"He dinnae know." Katherine blushed. "I was running away."

"From yer father?"

"From my betrothal celebration to Hamish Drummond, eldest son of Laird Drummond. 'Twas being held at their castle. I was trying to get home when Aiden and his men saw us."

Lachlan tilted his head. "Fie, I knew that it had to be

an exaggerated rumor that ye were going to choose the man ye would wed."

Katherine clenched her teeth. Why did nearly every man she encountered think this was such a daft notion? Did they truly regard all females as such pea-brained creatures?

"'Tis true," she said. "My mother fought hard to ensure that I would have the right to refuse any man I dinnae wish to wed."

"Then why did ye have to flee from Drummond? Did yer father go back on his word and force the match upon ye?"

"The McKenna never breaks his word!" Katherine replied hotly. "'Twas one of the reasons I had to get away, to give myself time to consider how I could dissolve the marriage contract without compromising my father's—and our clan's—honor."

A puzzled look crossed Lachlan's face. "If ye had the right to refuse the marriage before the contracts were signed, then why did ye agree to it?"

Katherine bit her lower lip. "I realized too late that I had made a mistake. A dreadful mistake."

Lachlan's puzzled expression deepened. "What could possibly have happened to make ye change yer mind about wedding Drummond?"

Katherine hesitated. She had struggled to push the incident from her mind and was hardly eager to remember the details. Yet she took responsibility for her actions and saw no reason to withhold the truth from Lachlan.

"I discovered that Hamish was in love with another woman. 'Twas obvious he had no intention of abandoning that relationship after we were wed, so I told him that I wouldn't be his wife. He refused to accept it, so I fled." Katherine lowered her chin. The unsettling feelings of disappointment and her own female inadequacy returned to plague her.

"That's it? That's why ye ran from him?"

Katherine's head shot up. "Dinnae I have the right to escape a marriage of misery?"

Lachlan lifted his brow. "Misery? 'Tis a rather dramatic statement. Women—and men—of yer rank marry fer many reasons. Love is seldom one of them."

"I know that—I even accept it. Yet I could not allow myself to become an obligation to be endured by my husband, to vie with another woman fer his attention and regard, to always be wondering and hoping that someday he might feel true affection fer me. Surely ye must understand—"

Katherine heard herself babbling and abruptly stopped. This was humiliating.

A kind smile touched Lachlan's lips. "Many men have a lusty appetite and an eye fer beauty. That doesn't disappear once they are wed."

Katherine rubbed her fingers against her temples. "Ye may believe that faithful husbands are a rarity, but I know of several. I will accept no less from the man that I marry. I want a man who is capable of love, who has the capacity fer kindness and affection."

"Dinnae Drummond possess any of those qualities?"

"I believed that he did when I agreed to the match, but had no inkling that he had already bestowed his love upon another."

Lachlan crossed his arms over his chest. "Are ye saying that a man can only love one woman in his lifetime?"

"One woman at a time," she clarified. "Preferably the one that is his wife. I had no wish to walk a long and tortuous road tied to a man who could never truly love me. I firmly believe that over time that disappointment would eventually turn to heartbreak."

He shot her a reproachful look. "How do ye know? Did ye give him a chance?"

Inwardly, Katherine cringed. Had she been too hasty in her decision to reject Hamish? She understood how her reasoning might seem trite and foolish to others, yet she had trusted the intensity of the emotions she had felt at the time to propel her actions. Was she wrong?

Nay! With a heavy sigh, Katherine shoved the lingering doubts away. Marrying Hamish Drummond would have been *wrong*. Though all had not turned out the way she could have ever anticipated, Katherine refused to abandon that decision.

"Have ye ever been in love?" she inquired, her heart suddenly pounding as she awaited his answer.

"Love? Nay." He paused, then smiled. "Though I'll confess to being infatuated a time or two when I was younger."

"I am speaking of something beyond a young man's curious fascination." Her heart lurched. "Love involves sacrifice and selflessness. Hamish claimed that he loved this other woman, yet he would not fight to have her, to keep their love whole and pure.

"A man must be the greatest protector and defender of the woman he loves. Hamish most definitely was not. Instead, he was being deceitful to her and to me and that I could not tolerate."

Katherine sucked in a sharp breath. "Tell me, Lachlan, would ye not have seized the chance to avoid such a costly mistake and done the same as I did, no matter the consequences?"

* * *

Lachlan felt her gaze burn into him and he struggled to formulate a reply. For the life of him, he didn't understand why he was pressing her so hard to defend her reasons for refusing to marry Hamish Drummond. Was he trying to test her resolve or prove her sincerity? Or was it something else entirely?

Some might think her spoiled, but Lachlan recognized that Katherine was a spirited woman with strong opinions, independent opinions, that she had been encouraged to express all her life. He could understand how no woman would appreciate being humiliated by her betrothed and he was fascinated by the fact that Katherine saw no reason to hide her displeasure at the prospect.

Many females would have unraveled under the strain of that discovery, fallen to their knees and prayed for deliverance, perhaps begun weeping at the unfairness of the situation. Instead, Katherine had exhibited an impressive display of strength and action and had taken steps to remove herself from what she felt was an intolerable circumstance.

Leaving with such a small escort had been most unwise—a critical lapse in judgment that had brought them all to this current predicament. Still, Lachlan felt he had no right to fault her decision.

"I dinnae know what I would have done had I been in yer position," he answered. "I only know that ye dinnae always get what ye wish fer in this life. Few are granted the luxury of choosing their own path and that holds true more fer women than men. They seldom have a say in their fate."

"Then it would have been foolish of me, indeed, to squander my chance to steer my life off of a rocky course," she concluded, her eyes sparkling with delight at proving her point.

Lachlan grinned. Aye, Katherine McKenna would make the most of her life, defying any who would dare to stand in her way. And from all accounts, Drummond did not sound like a man who was deserving of a woman like Katherine, nor one who valued her unique qualities.

"Perhaps ye did make the right decision," Lachlan mused. "Many men dinnae appreciate a woman with spirit. They want a wife who will be obedient and silent, who will never express an opinion or an original thought and do exactly as they are commanded."

"That sounds more like a well-trained horse." She notched her chin upward. "Is that the type of woman ye want to marry?"

Lachlan's mind churned. Nay. A weak, timid wife was not an ideal matrimonial situation for him. He preferred a woman with a ready wit and smile, whose eyes would light up with pleasure when she saw him, who had courage and convictions and could set his passion ablaze with a single sultry look.

Sadly, none of that was relevant in his current circumstances.

"I cannae afford a wife," he answered truthfully.

"Ye're a laird. Ye'll have to marry to produce an heir," she muttered.

"Aye, then any woman would do, as long as she is young and healthy," he said, hoping that would get a rise out of her. He liked it when Katherine's eyes flashed with defiance, her chin raised in challenge, and an edge of belligerence crept into her voice.

"Ye are teasing me, Lachlan MacTavish," she said with a saucy toss of her head, not taking the bait. "I dinnae believe a word ye said."

Katherine lifted her skirt and stepped over a pile of mud and dung. Lachlan found himself staring at her slender ankles. Her lavender scent surrounded him and he had difficulty concentrating. Long-dormant desire sparked within him, followed swiftly by guilt.

It felt wrong to hunger so strongly for a woman like Katherine unless he could offer her the honor of being his wife.

Shit! All this talk of marriage and husbands has put the most ridiculous thoughts into my head.

"I hope that one day ye find what ye so desperately seek, Katherine," he said quietly.

"Thank ye, Lachlan."

He looked deep into her eyes and felt something pass between them. A connection of grave significance that he couldn't define, much less understand. It sent his heart thumping louder than ever in his chest.

Bloody hell! Temptation rose to a poignant ache. He wanted—nay, needed—to kiss her. To once again taste her sweet lips, feel her lush body pressed against his.

Here. Now. In front of everyone gathered in the courtyard, especially those who were trying so hard not to appear that they were staring at their laird and the McKenna lass.

Yet he held back. For one simple reason. He had no right.

Few men would be able to resist her unaffected allure. Yet, Lachlan knew that he must. He could not let this attraction interfere with what he needed to do—save his clan and return her to her kin as quickly as possible.

Chapter Ten

Katherine stood on the ramparts and inhaled deeply, appreciating the fresh air. The afternoon clouds had drifted away, taking the misty rain with them. The moment the weather had cleared, Katherine had seized the opportunity to be outside.

She had intended to stay in the bailey, but Aiden had been training a group of men in the courtyard. She had given the handsome warrior a wide berth in the few days she had resided at MacTavish Keep, avoiding him whenever possible, suffering through his company only at the evening meal. His overt animosity toward her appeared to have softened, yet she was not foolish enough to take any chances.

Sword training was a normal part of a soldier's day and Aiden was not only supervising the men, he was also sparring with them. The riotous sounds of clattering swords drew the eyes of several females, including Katherine's, but alas Lachlan was not among the men practicing.

'Twas Aiden who was in command. Katherine could not help but notice how he held his heavy claymore with great ease. He faced a broader, more muscular warrior, but his superior skill was quickly evident. In just a few swift moves, Aiden was able to block a strong blow with his shield, sidestep another, and disarm his opponent with a single sword hit, sending the man's weapon skittering across the dirt.

Some of the men broke into cheers, while others grumbled. Katherine had taken advantage of the distraction to slip unseen past the group and find a peaceful spot on the ramparts.

Much to everyone's disappointment, the boar hunt had been unsuccessful yesterday and the day before. She had heard that Lachlan and his men were preparing to try again today. Like everyone else, Katherine would be pleased to enjoy a hearty meal, but a consequence of a fruitful hunt would mean the warriors needed for her escort home would be available.

Katherine felt a stab of reluctance each time she envisioned leaving. The strong emotion surprised her, yet she knew the cause. The time she had been spending with Lachlan had created an intimacy between them that she did not wish to lose.

Each evening when the meal had ended, they had fallen into easy conversation, sharing stories of their youth, discussing the politics of the day, even telling a joke or two. Beneath the strong, rough exterior, Katherine had been delighted to glimpse a playful lad, with a fine sense of humor and an honest interest in the welfare of others.

They had played numerous games of chess with an equally matched competitive fervor, trading good-natured barbs in the hopes of creating a distraction that would gain them an advantage. Katherine smiled at the memory of Lachlan's astonished expression the first time she had beaten him at the game, remembering with delight her sense of accomplishment.

With a wry laugh, he had congratulated her profusely, then proceeded to annihilate her in the next match. She had accepted her defeat as graciously as he had, determined to be victorious the following night. And when she succeeded, Katherine was unable to resist displaying just a hint of smug satisfaction, bringing them both to laughter.

Aye, there was no mistake that her heart beat faster whenever she was in Lachlan's company. An attraction to a handsome man, she told herself. Nothing more.

But she knew that was not entirely true. No man affected her quite the way Lachlan did. There was something very different about him, something unique about the way he made her feel.

Katherine sighed. It didn't matter. Once she returned home, she would never see him again.

MacTavish Keep was old, drafty, and lacking in many basic comforts; there wasn't enough good food for all, including the laird's family and his soldiers. Yet Katherine felt comfortable here. Every man and woman and many of the children worked hard and complained little. They were good, honest, hardworking folk and she admired their dedication to each other and the clan.

"I think I see a boar in the forest, Lady Katherine! Come and look!"

Katherine smiled at the gap-toothed lad who stood beside her. She had met young Cameron yesterday and he had quickly become her shadow. His widowed mother was the household cook, too busy with her daily chores to pay much attention to a curious and energetic boy. The six-year-old followed her around like an eager puppy and in truth Katherine was glad of the company.

Things were never dull when Cameron was by her side.

"I fear 'tis the wind that causes that movement in the trees, not an animal," Katherine replied as she playfully ruffled his hair, hoping to erase his disappointment.

"Are ye certain?"

"Fairly. Look, there, on the opposite side. Can ye see the dots of white among the brown grass?" she asked, pointing to the distant horizon.

"Aye. But Lady Morag said 'twas getting too warm fer snow," Cameron replied, scrunching his nose in puzzlement.

"If I'm not mistaken, the white ye see isn't snow, but the first snowdrop flowers getting ready to bloom."

Cameron's eyes lit with excitement. "We have to pick them fer Lady Morag. She loves flowers."

"'Tis a fine idea, but the guards willnae allow me to leave the keep," Katherine said, touched by the child's considerate gesture. No doubt Lady Morag—and others—would appreciate having something pretty to decorate the hall.

"Ye cannae leave? Are ye a prisoner?" Cameron asked, his eyes wide.

Katherine suppressed the urge to laugh at the disapproving expression on the lad's face. "Not exactly. But the moment they see me, they will stop me from venturing beyond the wall."

A mysterious grin pulled at Cameron's lips. "I know a way out that will hide ye from their eyes."

He took her hand and led her off the ramparts and through the bailey to a small door that was built into the outer curtain wall. Standing on the tips of his toes, Cameron struggled to reach the latch. His third try was met with success, and with a cry of delight the lad lifted the metal bar and slowly, cautiously opened the door.

"I can see that ye've done this before, Master Cameron," Katherine said, trying—and failing—to use a scolding tone. Cameron answered her with a giggle and an enthusiastic nod, then before she could stop him, the lad disappeared through the opening. Katherine cried out and reached to stop him, but he slipped beyond her grasp.

Anxiously, she looked about for a guard who might challenge her if she left, but there were no soldiers anywhere in the vicinity. Seized with the desire for a few minutes of freedom, Katherine hurried after the lad. For a child of his size, Cameron managed to cover a lot of ground in a short amount of time.

"Flowers!" he cried, bending low to run his arms over the tight white buds.

"Och, well, as long as we are here, there's no harm in gathering a few before we return," Katherine decided.

With a cry of delight, Cameron dropped to his knees and started yanking on the flower stems. Appreciating his excitement—if not his finesse—Katherine delicately snapped the stems of a few buds before spying a cluster of perfectly formed blooms several yards away.

"Ye start on yer way back to the keep," Katherine instructed the lad. "I'll follow in a moment."

Crouching low, Katherine picked a few more buds, shifting the bounty in her arms to hold it all. 'Twas then that she noticed an unusual quiet in the field, accompanied by an equally strong sense that someone was watching her.

The hair on the back of her neck rose and a tingle went up her spine. Her head turned swiftly, rapidly in several directions.

There was nothing.

Insisting to herself that she was being fanciful, Katherine attempted to shake off the odd feeling of foreboding. Yet it persisted, intensifying until a warning sounded in her head.

Run! Hurry!

Heart pounding, she squinted at the dense forest ahead. Suddenly, there was movement. Panic seized her.

Could it be a wild boar? Cameron had said that he had seen one.

Boars were unpredictable animals; if one charged her, there would be no place to run for cover here in this open field. The boar's large tusks and sharp teeth would easily tear through her flesh, causing her considerable, possibly fatal, injury.

Her eyes traveled anxiously along the tree line. There was movement again, this time accompanied by a rustling noise. She caught a glimpse of a shadowy figure among the pines and then astonishingly a lone rider on a magnificent white horse emerged from the trees.

Man and beast stood silently at the edge of the forest. Katherine blinked, uncertain if she could believe her eyes, wondering if she had somehow imagined such a splendid sight.

The horse and rider moved forward. A moment of confusion froze Katherine in place before she was able to catch a clear glimpse of the rider's features.

Archibald Fraser!

Knots of fear rose in her throat. She could see no other Fraser warriors in the woods, yet even if he rode alone, Archibald presented a huge threat. Dismay filled her as she glanced back at the keep and realized how far she had strayed from the protection of its gates. Her only comfort was that Cameron was no longer visible; the child had made it safely back inside.

Hoping the rider wouldn't immediately notice her,

Katherine slowly began inching her way backward. Her throat trembled with the need to call for help, but there were only a few guards stationed on the ramparts and none were currently looking in her direction.

Better to stay silent and move a few yards closer to safety. The horse whined, then stomped its hoof restlessly on the hard ground. Archibald's eyes caught hers and the menace and determination shining in their depths set Katherine's heart thundering in her ears.

He must know who I am. He must know that I'm the McKenna's daughter.

Her arms opened. She dropped the flowers she held, scattering them at her feet, turned, and ran. Archibald's cry of anger split the air. Within moments the pounding hooves of his horse sounded behind her, spurring Katherine to run as fast as her legs could carry her.

As the gates of MacTavish Keep loomed closer, Katherine began screaming for help, wasting precious breath on the hope that someone would hear her and sound the alarm.

I must reach the keep! Holding her skirts high to avoid tripping over them, Katherine sprinted across the open terrain. She could hear Archibald's angry blasphemy as he bore down on her, could imagine the feel of his horse's hot breath on her neck.

He reached for her, but Katherine twisted away at the last moment, miraculously avoiding his grasp. Terrified, she continued running, her lungs burning as she pushed her legs to move faster.

Suddenly, the gates opened and a warrior mounted on horseback came charging forward. Sword drawn and raised, his bloodthirsty war cry sent a chill down her spine.

Lachlan!

Katherine's relief was so great that she nearly stopped,

but then prudence prevailed and she ran past Lachlan. At the sound of clashing steel, she pivoted, watching in terror as the contact tilted each man sideways in his saddle.

Lachlan succeeded in knocking Archibald from his horse. The Fraser laird hit the ground hard, rolled, and quickly regained his feet. Sword in hand, he charged the mounted Lachlan, aiming for the horse's chest.

Somehow, Lachlan was able to turn the beast before a death blow was struck. However, the sudden movement caused the animal to rear up on its hind legs. Katherine watched in horror as Lachlan struggled to get the frightened horse under control.

Pressing his advantage, Archibald charged.

"Lachlan, watch out!" Katherine cried.

Lachlan jumped from the horse. He landed on his feet, gracefully ducking beneath Archibald's blow. Swords poised, the two combatants warily circled each other. Archibald struck first, the deadly sound of steel against steel reverberating through every nerve in Katherine's body. The pair were well matched, as every strike was met with a returning one.

"Ye spun a pretty tale about the lass, but I know 'twas a lie. She's the McKenna's daughter and I'll pay ye well if ye give her to me," Archibald proposed, his breath coming in rasping pants.

"She's not fer sale," Lachlan answered. "Now get off my land."

"I'm not leaving until I get what I came fer," Archibald shouted.

In a burst of strength, Archibald attacked with renewed vigor. With two hands tightly gripping the sword handle, he swung the heavy claymore in a deadly arc, bringing it down with savage force. Lachlan somehow managed to block the blow and counter with one of his own. A spark flared between the metal blades as they met and pressed against each other.

Standing above Lachlan, Archibald leveraged the advantage to slowly lower his sword until it inched closer to Lachlan's head. Gritting his teeth, Lachlan fought hard to keep the blade from his neck.

Katherine glanced frantically toward the keep. Why did no one else come?

Suddenly, Lachlan lowered his shoulder, dropped his sword, and fell to the ground, knocking Archibald off balance. Katherine screamed in alarm, but in a blur, Lachlan rose to his feet and lunged at Archibald, knife in hand. He raised his leg, kicking Archibald square in the stomach and sending him sprawling onto his back.

"It will give me no small pleasure to send ye to hell, Fraser," he snarled, placing his boot on the man's heaving chest and pressing the tip of his blade against his throat.

"Lachlan, hold!" Katherine screamed, frightened at the blood lust gleaming in his eyes. "If ye kill him, ye'll start a war with the Frasers."

"He deserves to die," Lachlan insisted, digging the tip of his knife into Archibald's windpipe until a trickle of blood cascaded down the Fraser laird's neck.

"Aye," Katherine agreed. "But not today. And not like this."

Lachlan shoved Archibald. Hard. "Ye live only by the mercy of Lady Katherine," he grunted, reluctantly standing, his blade still pointed at his enemy.

Placing a hand against his wounded neck, Archibald slowly gained his feet. He shook the dirt from his clothes, then lowered his hand and stared at the blood on his palm. "Ye'll rue this day, MacTavish," Archibald promised, glaring at him.

"Aye," Lachlan agreed. "I'll regret not killing ye. Go quickly, Fraser, before I change my mind."

"Fool!" Archibald bent and reached for his sword, but Lachlan swiftly placed his foot on the blade.

"Leave it."

"That sword has been in my family fer generations," Archibald protested. "My father carried it into battle at Bannockburn, alongside the Bruce."

Katherine gasped at the implied insult to Lachlan and his clan, as their family had unfortunately chosen to side against the king during that conflict.

Lachlan spit on the ground. "The sword is now mine. Be grateful that I'm allowing ye to take yer horse."

For a moment it appeared that Archibald would again challenge Lachlan, but the gates of the keep opened and a group of MacTavish warriors spilled out. Sniffing loudly, Archibald stormed toward his horse.

Katherine could hear him groan as he swung himself into the saddle, a testament to the force of Lachlan's blows. With a final growl of anger, the Fraser laird turned his mount and rode away, leaving a cloud of dust in his wake.

Sobbing with relief, Katherine threw herself into Lachlan's arms. His senses jolted, his pulse pounded, and he shockingly realized that his body was aching with pent-up desire. The heat of battle, so recently consuming him, had changed to a totally different sort of heat. One that was on the verge of exploding with a clawing need so strong it nearly overpowered his common sense.

"Ye're injured," Katherine cried, pulling away.

Lachlan glanced down at his side, surprised to see a streak of red blood spreading over his tunic. He hadn't known that Fraser's blade had struck so deep until Katherine mentioned the wound, which now stung like hellfire.

Lachlan paused and took a shallow breath, waiting for the pain to pass.

"Dinnae look so worried," he joked. "I'm not that easily killed."

"Oh, Lachlan." Her eyes clouded with concern.

He could not tear his gaze from her. She was so lovely, so appealing. Lachlan raised his arm, then quickly lowered it, resisting the urge to run his fingers over her quivering lower lip.

"What of ye, Katherine? Are ye injured?" he asked gruffly.

"Nay. I'm fine." She shuddered. "And grateful that ye saved me from that beast."

Swords drawn, Aiden and several other retainers arrived. Three of the men pressed forward to the edge of the forest, but Archibald had wisely disappeared.

"What happened?" Aiden asked. "The watch guards said that ye crossed swords with another."

"Aye." Lachlan pulled in a steadying breath. "Archibald Fraser. He tried to snatch Katherine. I ruined his plan."

"How the hell did he breach our defenses and take her away?" Aiden asked.

"He dinnae." Katherine's eyes lowered remorsefully. "I was beyond the wall."

"What? Why?" Aiden glared at Katherine with reproachful eyes.

She shrugged her shoulders helplessly. "I came to pick a few flowers. I dinnae realize that I had strayed so far from the gates."

"Flowers! Are ye daft, woman?" Features tense, Aiden turned away in disgust.

Katherine lowered her head. "Fergive me. I dinnae intend fer my impulsive action to put anyone in danger."

"Well, it did," Aiden retorted.

"Calm down, Aiden," Lachlan said wearily. "Katherine was in plain view from the ramparts of the keep. She should have been safe."

"Did ye give her permission to leave the bailey?" Aiden asked, his gaze darting from Lachlan to Katherine.

"She's not a prisoner," Lachlan replied curtly.

Katherine's cheeks bloomed with color. "Please, let's go inside. Lachlan's wound needs tending."

Lachlan nodded. The pain in his side hadn't dulled. If anything, it had grown stronger.

Several men and women rushed forward when they entered the bailey, wanting to assure themselves that the laird was not seriously wounded. Knowing how important it was to appear invincible, Lachlan kept insisting it was merely a scratch. Yet by the time they finally entered the great hall, his entire body was shaking with the effort to stand straight, walk with an unaffected stride, and smile.

With each step, he could feel the warm blood trickling down his side and he was relieved that his dark tunic managed to hide most of the stain. As they entered the great hall, Katherine beckoned a servant, calling for hot water, clean cloths, and a medicine basket.

"Dinnae fuss," Lachlan insisted, cautiously lowering himself into his chair.

"I need to bind yer wound before ye start dripping blood onto the rushes," she replied.

Lachlan flinched when she lifted his tunic and pressed a warm compress against the cut, sucking in a sharp breath between clenched teeth. Their gazes collided and she murmured an apology before bending closer. Lifting his eyes to the rafters, Lachlan took another deep breath.

Och, she is a bonny lass! He could feel the tension gripping his entire body and knew it wasn't from the stabbing, stinging pain in his side. Nay, it was caused by the throbbing in his loins, the direct result of Katherine's touch.

Sitting across from him, Aiden was oblivious to Lachlan's discomfort. Indeed, his brother had lapsed into a sullen silence, scrutinizing Katherine's every move.

"Will ye sear or stitch it closed?" Aiden asked.

"Stitch," she answered, her face paling.

"I'll fetch the whiskey," Aiden said.

When his brother returned, Lachlan took several long swallows, then nodded to Katherine. He drew in a sharp breath as the needle pierced his flesh, yet somehow Lachlan held himself steady.

A stitch, a swig, a stitch, a swig. 'Twas an inspired idea and Lachlan followed the pattern religiously twelve times, preferring the feel of the whiskey sliding down his throat far more than the sharp stabs of the needle and the pull of the thread through his bruised flesh.

Thankfully, Katherine made quick work of her task, knotting the thread when she was finished and snipping away the excess. She next gently cleansed the wound, placed a clean cloth over the gash, and wrapped a long binding tightly around his waist to hold it in place.

"I fear it will leave a rather nasty scar," she said regretfully.

"One that all the maidens shall admire," Aiden said with a laugh.

"Perhaps the bloodthirsty ones," Katherine replied dubiously.

Lachlan glanced down at his side. "Did yer mother teach ye the healing arts?" he asked, admiring her handiwork.

Katherine smiled. "I learned from my mother what *not* to do when tending the wounded and infirmed." She bent low and whispered in his ear. "Her healing potions are legendary among the McKennas and pointedly avoided by all she tries to heal. 'Tis bad enough when she makes a salve fer yer wounds—worse still when she conjures medicine ye have to drink."

"That hardly inspires my confidence in ye, lass."

"Aye, but it distracts ye from yer pain."

Lachlan grinned. She had succeeded in easing his discomfort—or mayhap 'twas the twelve shots of whiskey he had drunk. Either way, the sharp, stinging pain in his side had lessened to a dull throb.

Though he protested the attention, it had felt good to have a woman fuss over him with such gentleness and concern. For too long he had attended to his battle wounds himself or relied on the assistance of one of his men.

"I shudder to think what might have happened to ye if Fraser had succeeded in his abduction," Lachlan said, a ball of emotion tightening his chest.

Katherine blanched. "He is a cruel, brutal man. My sister-in-law, Joan, bears the scars of his abuse."

Aiden's eyes narrowed. "I heard that she was a willful, spoiled, disrespectful wife, unable to learn her proper place."

"'Tis true that Joan has a strong will and knows her own mind," Katherine said. "But that cannae excuse how she was treated by that brute."

"A man must be obeyed without question in his own household," Aiden countered.

"Och, so when a man cannae control and dominate a woman through logic and reason, he must resort to using his fists on her?" Katherine asked, her voice growing thick with emotion.

"Nay. A man who beats a woman is a swine." Lachlan's temper flared. "A man must be confident and decisive and do what he believes to be right. But physical abuse of someone ye have vowed to protect and cherish is disgusting."

"And dishonorable." Aiden bowed his head. "I beg yer pardon, Lady Katherine, fer speaking without considering my words."

Katherine appeared startled at the unexpected apology, but she recovered quickly and acknowledged Aiden with a cautious nod. Lachlan was equally surprised. Aiden's attitude toward Katherine had always bordered on belligerence. Why the sudden change?

Lachlan tried to make sense of it, but his head was swimming in whiskey. Nay, there was something, more pressing, more important that he needed to focus upon.

"We should give thanks Fraser's plan was thwarted, yet we must find the answer to the more important question." Lachlan coughed, then took a swig of the whiskey Aiden poured for him.

Katherine raised a brow. "More important?"

"Fraser knew who ye were, Katherine," Lachlan said quietly. "How? How did he come by that information?"

The three exchanged looks. Aiden scrubbed a hand across his face. Katherine shrugged.

"The answer is obvious." Lachlan slowly placed his empty goblet on the table. "Someone told him."

Chapter Eleven

The quiet in the chamber grew to an uncomfortable stillness. Katherine shivered, knowing that Lachlan was right. Archibald must have been informed of her true identity by a clan member. But who?

She glanced anxiously around the room, realizing it could have been anyone. A shiver of fear rumbled through her as those with whom she had felt so comfortable suddenly seemed threatening.

"This is not only a betrayal of Lady Katherine, but a betrayal of our clan," Lachlan said. He winced as he rearranged his position on the chair. "I want this person found, Aiden."

Aiden's head jerked toward his brother. "Ye want *me* to take charge of this problem?"

"Aye. Ye know our people better than I do. It should not take ye long to discover who committed this act of treachery."

Aiden sniffed in annoyance and took a swallow of whiskey, looking none too pleased at the prospect of routing out the informant.

"Are ye certain that Fraser knew she was Katherine McKenna?" he asked.

"I am." Lachlan's stare turned hard. "He called her by name when he offered to buy her from me."

Aiden's expression turned calm and Katherine eyed him with suspicion. Why was he not more surprised? Was it because he was the one responsible?

To her mind, he seemed a prime suspect. 'Twas no secret he held her in little regard and disagreed with his brother's plans to simply return her to her clan and receive nothing in return.

Had Aiden gone against his brother's orders and bargained with Archibald to receive what he felt he was owed? The two brothers were openly at odds over a variety of matters, which begged the question—what, precisely, was Aiden's level of loyalty to Lachlan?

Katherine felt a sudden chill. She rubbed her arms as panic began to steadily build inside her.

"It could be anyone," Aiden murmured offhandedly.

"Not anyone. Someone. I want a name. Or names."

Lachlan speared his brother with another hard glare. The expression on Aiden's face told Katherine he would protest no longer—yet he also gave no indication that he would do as his brother bid and investigate the matter.

Lady Morag bustled into the great hall, stopping suddenly when she caught sight of her sons and Katherine gathered around the table. A deep ridge furrowed her brow as she approached.

"Why are ye here at this hour of the day? Is something wrong?"

Lachlan's face tightened. "Sit down, Mother."

"Ye're hurt," she exclaimed, reaching out to touch

his bloodstained tunic. "I'll send one of the servants to fetch my medicine basket."

"Katherine has already dressed my wound."

Lady Morag turned to Katherine and she saw gratitude and relief in the older woman's eyes.

"Were ye injured on the practice field?" Lady Morag asked, her expression relaxing into a smile. "I'd like to know the name of the man who was able to best ye. Or was two? Three? All sparring with ye at the same time?"

Lachlan shook his head. "I fought Archibald Fraser. He struck a blow, but dinnae best me, getting far worse than he gave. I drove him from our land."

Lady Morag recoiled. "Why was Laird Fraser here? And why did ye cross swords with him?"

"He tried to abduct Lady Katherine," Aiden answered.

"In the bailey? I heard no commotion."

Katherine cleared her throat. "I was outside the walls gathering flowers when Archibald suddenly appeared. Lachlan saved me."

"Flowers?" Lady Morag's voice tightened. "Ye compromised yer safety fer some flowers?"

Katherine squirmed uncomfortably under Lady Morag's cutting glare. She was right to be angry with her. Katherine knew she never should have left the safety of the courtyard, even for such a short time. 'Twas a foolish mistake that could have had far worse consequences.

"Why Katherine ventured beyond the gates doesn't matter," Lachlan said as he let out a long, frustrated breath. "No one should be in such grave peril when they are that close to our keep."

"She would have remained out of danger if she had stayed within the protection of our walls," Lady Morag interjected curtly.

Aiden made a dismissive noise in the back of his throat and looked accusingly at Katherine, who felt a flush stain her cheek. A wave of guilt washed over her and she lowered her head.

"Ye had planned to bring Katherine back to her family. How can ye do that now? The Frasers will be watching fer ye." Lady Morag wrung her hands together. "Ye'll not get much beyond the gates before ye are assaulted. Ye both could be injured—or worse."

Katherine gripped the edge of the table. Lady Morag was right. Given the events of the afternoon, 'twould be impossible to leave without being seen and possibly captured by the Frasers.

"We must outwit Archibald," Lachlan said, his tone firm.

"How? Fraser will be suspicious of any travelers in the area," Aiden said. "If he's angry enough, he might even place men in our forest to watch our gates and report on yer movements."

"Och, he's angry enough," Lachlan said with certainty. "I took his sword."

Lachlan hoisted the weapon in the air. There were bits of grass and dirt on the blade, and a dark streak of dried blood. Lachlan's blood. Katherine shuddered at the memory of seeing him slashed during the fight. Thank God he had rebounded from the wound in time to save himself—and her.

"Christ's bones, Lachlan, ye've guaranteed Fraser's retribution by taking his sword," Aiden noted, sending a scowl at his brother.

"The action shall serve as a warning and a show of our strength," Lachlan insisted.

"Be that as it may, ye've now made yerself a prisoner in this keep," Aiden said.

"I dinnae fear Archibald Fraser," Lachlan proclaimed.

"Ye should," Katherine said softly. "He's a monster."

Lachlan's expression hardened. "All the more reason to get ye safely back home and beyond his reach."

"How?" she asked.

"If ye leave with only a small group of riders it would attract less attention," Aiden offered.

"True. Yet a small convoy would be easily overtaken if we are seen. We need to take a sizable escort." Lachlan scratched the back of his neck. "There has to be a better plan."

"A disguise," Lady Morag mused. "Ye must slip away without anyone knowing that ye have gone. Both of ye." She eyed Katherine up and down with a critical glare. "If the Frasers are indeed watching, the perfect ruse would be to dress Lady Katherine as a lad."

Lachlan scoffed. "Fraser will have to be very far away and half blind to believe that Katherine was a lad."

Katherine blushed and modestly lowered her gaze.

"Ye could both wear servants' clothes," Aiden suggested.

"Nay." Lachlan shook his head. "'Twould look too suspicious. Why would servants be in the company of so many soldiers?"

"Instead of bringing me home, ye could send a message to my father and ask him and his men to come and fetch me." Katherine glanced up at Lachlan. "Fraser willnae dare to attack a contingent of McKenna retainers, especially if my father is leading them."

"'Tis true that Fraser prefers to engage with smaller, weaker forces that he knows he can defeat." Lachlan bent his head, appearing to consider the matter.

"If ye contact them, do we not run the risk of the

McKennas attacking us?" Lady Morag asked, her hands still trembling.

"If the missive is carefully worded, my father will know that I have been treated well and that ye mean me no harm," Katherine replied, hoping her words rang true.

Her father's temper had been the cause of many a rash action, yet surely the days of travel it would take for him to arrive here would be sufficient time for it to have cooled.

"Which is it to be, Lachlan? A disguise or a message to the McKennas?" Aiden asked impatiently.

"I dinnae know yet. I need more time to consider the choices." Lachlan frowned. "In the meantime, find me that informant."

"Yer stitches are very neat and precise," Lady Morag remarked, admiring the cloth in Katherine's lap. "Thanks to yer diligence, this piece will be completed sooner than I had hoped."

Needle in hand, Katherine looked up and smiled at the older woman. After the commotion and excitement of the afternoon, she needed something to occupy her hands—and mind. She had asked for a basket of mending to work on and instead Lady Morag had given her a section of altar cloth.

Initially, Katherine had protested the choice, preferring the more useful task of hemming or repairing, but once she saw the beautiful silk piece, her spirits had lifted. 'Twas a privilege to be allowed to work on such fine fabric with such a complicated composition.

"Did ye design the piece yerself?" Katherine asked, running her finger over the small section of embroidery she had just completed, using the new stitch Lady Morag had taught her.

"From memory," Lady Morag replied. "A long time ago, I created a similar one with my mother. I was just a lass and so proud to be allowed to sew a section. My mother and I spent many peaceful hours working together on it. Though she has been gone fer many years, re-creating it somehow makes me feel closer to her."

Katherine understood. She, too, had many happy memories of working on projects with her own mother. A wave of guilt attacked as she thought of the worry her disappearance was certainly causing her mother. No doubt Lady Aileen was consumed with fear over the uncertainty of her daughter's fate, and Katherine regretted the unintended pain she felt certain her mother—and the rest of her family—was suffering.

It had to end. She knew there were difficulties—that in part were her fault—yet a way must be found for her to either return home or let her family know that she was alive and safe. She would speak with Lachlan at the first opportunity and express the importance of making that happen.

A collection of male voices interrupted the peace in the great hall. Katherine's muscles tensed at the distinct sound of Lachlan's voice. Earlier, she had told him to rest, insisting his wound would heal faster. He had thanked her for the unsolicited advice and promptly left with his men, citing important work that needed to be done.

His devotion to duty was admirable, yet like most men he was pigheaded when it came to matters of his own well-being. Her eyes scanned his form, noting that he was favoring the side where the blow had been struck. Foolish man! He would soon be abed with fever and chills if he did not take care.

"Ye'll not persuade him to be sensible and rest," Lady Morag said mildly. "He sees it as a weakness and Lachlan only shows his strength."

Startled that her thoughts could be so easily read, Katherine mumbled an unconvincing denial and hastily returned to her sewing. However, trying to concentrate on the intricate design was near impossible as Lachlan's presence proved too distracting.

After stabbing herself twice with the needle, Katherine sighed and gave up. She would ruin the lovely cloth if she pricked herself deep enough to draw blood.

She again looked over at the group of men, who were now gathered around a table, drinking. They were unusually quiet, appearing to listen intently to Lachlan before nodding in agreement and departing. Were they hatching a plan to outwit the Frasers? Or making plans for her departure?

The uncertainty unsettled Katherine. Yet there was more to the unease that she was suddenly feeling. Lachlan had not left with the others and was now staring at her with intense scrutiny.

It unnerved her. His countenance reminded her of a stable cat, sitting in watchful stillness near a mouse hole, waiting with unflinching patience for the rodent to emerge.

Katherine's first instinct was to avert her eyes modestly, but she ignored the impulse and instead she met his gaze boldly. He regarded her with unwavering steadiness and she returned it in kind.

She motioned that he should be resting. He raised his brow and shook his head. Bristling, she raised her own.

A smile slowly emerged from Lachlan's lips. She answered with one of her own.

Nodding, he lifted his tankard in a silent salute. She accepted his regard graciously, trying hard not to stare at his powerful hand. The sight of his strong fingers and sun-darkened skin, lightly dusted with hair, sent the most peculiar feeling fluttering through her.

Color heated and bloomed in her cheeks. Katherine lowered her gaze, needing a moment to compose herself. It took multiple deep breaths until she succeeded.

However, when she looked up again, Lachlan was gone.

Aiden entered the chapel alone, immediately spying his mother. She was kneeling at the altar, her hands clasped tightly together, her head piously bowed in prayer. Candlelight illuminated her profile and even in the dim light he could see the fine lines radiating from the corners of her eyes, a stark reminder that she was no longer a young woman.

"Mother." He called softly to her and she tensed. Aiden grimaced. 'Twas not a good sign.

"Aiden! Ye startled me."

She turned to meet his gaze, then quickly shifted it back to the altar, once again bowing her head. Aiden walked forward and stood beside her for several long, uncomfortable minutes.

"'Tis odd to see ye here at this time of the evening," he remarked. "Was there a specific reason ye felt the need to come here tonight?"

"These are very unsettled times," she answered. "Prayer brings me comfort."

"Ye can speak with God anywhere. Why was it necessary to come to the chapel?"

Lady Morag's face whitened. "I relish the quiet."

Aiden gently placed a hand on his mother's shoulder, startled at how fragile it felt. "I spoke with yer maid, Catrina, this evening."

Lady Morag sighed deeply and sat back on her heels. "Ye know?"

"Aye. 'Twas Catrina's husband who brought the news to Laird Fraser about Katherine McKenna. At yer behest."

Lady Morag's face fell. "Do ye brand me a traitor?" she asked, slowly unclasping her praying hands.

"Nay. But I need to understand why ye did it."

Her breath caught on a sob. "'Twas never my aim to put Katherine in any danger. How was I to know that she would venture beyond the walls, making herself an easy target? Or that Lachlan would come to harm defending her?"

His mother's voice cracked with emotion and Aiden could hear the genuine anguish and remorse in her voice.

"How could ye not realize the possible consequences of yer actions?" he asked. "Fraser is known to be a ruthless man."

Lady Morag would not meet his eyes. "'Tis exactly why I did it. I feared Fraser's reaction when he discovered Lachlan had lied to him about the lass."

"And what of the McKenna's wrath?" Aiden inquired.

Lady Morag's eyes narrowed. "Ye kidnapped his daughter. His anger is already assured. I thought an alliance with the Frasers could aid in protecting us against the McKennas. 'Twas ye who first suggested it."

"I did. And Lachlan rejected the notion in no uncertain terms." Aiden stroked his chin thoughtfully. "Ye've always shown great deference and loyalty to Lachlan's authority as laird. Has that changed?"

"Mayhap. I dinnae know." Lady Morag sniffled and turned toward the altar. "The McKennas hold Robbie prisoner. If they learn of yer role in Katherine's kidnapping, they might take ye next. And I believe that Lachlan would allow it."

"I'll not allow it, Mother."

Hearing his mother's doubts about Lachlan gave Aiden a brief sense of victory. She would support him, not Lachlan, if the choice were put to the clan.

Yet the triumph felt oddly hollow. In truth, Aiden realized that he did not wish his brother harmed. Removed as laird—aye. Brutally, savagely injured—nay.

Seeing Lachlan battle with Fraser today had brought forth emotions inside Aiden that had surprised, even shocked him. He thought he would have eagerly embraced Lachlan's defeat at Fraser's hand, for it would have all but assured Aiden's place as the clan's new laird.

Instead, he had prayed for his brother's victory. Afterward, Aiden had wanted to deny that strong sense of protection and concern that had stirred inside him. Yet it had remained.

It puzzled him. He knew that he still wanted Lachlan gone so that he could become laird, yet when faced with the reality of his brother's death, Aiden's feelings had been deeply conflicted.

"I've done something horrible, unforgivable, haven't I? I'm so regretful and ashamed." Lady Morag's face clouded with uneasiness. "Lachlan will be hurt, perhaps furious when he learns that truth. Must ye tell Lachlan? Can ye wait until the incident is not as new, as raw?"

She let the plea hang in the air.

Aiden hesitated. The loyalty that he knew he owed Lachlan as laird was not as easily ignored as he had hoped. But what of the loyalty he owed his mother? "I see no good that could come of revealing yer betrayal to Lachlan."

Relief flooded his mother's eyes. "Aye, 'twould only cause him more grief."

Grief. Aye, perhaps that was the key to ousting Lachlan as laird and leading the clan himself one day. Betrayal could break a man; turn him bitter and resentful. Mayhap even dishonorable. The MacTavish would never tolerate such a man as their laird. They had little to cling to except their pride and honor and they held tight and fast to both.

Aiden decided. He would say nothing to Lachlan. He would wait, remain watchful and vigilant and fuel the fires of dissension as they emerged.

My time will come and when it does, I will be ready.

Hands clasped behind his back, Lachlan walked through the bailey. The stitches in his side throbbed dully, a reminder of yesterday's encounter with Archibald Fraser. A reminder, too, of his need to get Katherine McKenna safely back to her family before Fraser could strike again.

Lachlan drew in deep breaths of air while he walked, hoping the scent of fresh rain would help to calm his mind and spirit. The conversation he had just had with his stepmother had been illuminating and painful and more than anything he wished he could forget it.

Lady Morag had looked like a hare caught in a trap, her eyes wide, her face pale and streaked with tears when he confronted her with the proof of her betrayal.

Lachlan shook his head vigorously, trying to erase

the memory from his mind, to block out the sounds of her sobbing and pleas for forgiveness. Yet, they lingered.

Lachlan turned a corner. Some of the men were gathered outside the barracks, polishing their swords and armor. Others were gambling with dice, boisterously shouting and laughing. They nodded respectfully as he strode past them and he silently returned the greeting.

Someone emerged from the chapel. Frowning, Lachlan altered his course to intercept them.

"Confessing yer sins, Brother?"

Aiden stiffened, then favored him with a teasing smirk. "Praying fer yer soul."

Lachlan bit back a retort. Nay, he would not give Aiden the perverse satisfaction provoking his temper. The years of fighting for hire and defeating the enemy had taught Lachlan the importance of being in control of his emotions.

"I thank ye heartily fer yer prayers. They are both needed and appreciated." Lachlan blocked Aiden's path, forcing his brother to face him. "I can remember when the brotherly affection between us ran deep and true. I would like fer it to once again be that way."

"We were lads," Aiden countered. "Much has changed."

Lachlan could decipher nothing in Aiden's words or tone to let him know if that bothered his brother. "We must stand together against our enemies or most assuredly we shall be defeated," Lachlan insisted.

"I'm loyal to the clan," Aiden insisted hotly.

"Aye, but not to yer laird," Lachlan said softly.

Aiden lifted his chin sharply. "Harsh words, Brother."

"Harsh truths."

Lachlan waited, hoping, yet not really expecting, a denial.

Aiden's eyes narrowed. "I'll not follow ye blindly, if that is what ye're asking of me."

"Aye, ye've shown me proof of that. I specifically ordered ye to stay away from the McKennas and instead ye brought me one."

Aiden pulled in a mocking breath. "Ye seem rather pleased with her."

Lachlan nearly growled as his anger spiked. His brother had spoken aloud the truth that Lachlan had been trying so hard not to acknowledge. He was very attracted to Katherine and frustrated because he knew there could never be anything of substance between them.

"What have ye discovered about Fraser's attack yesterday?" Lachlan asked, deftly shifting the conversation.

Aiden's eyes widened but a fraction, yet Lachlan swore a look of guilt momentarily darkened his brother's face. "I have unearthed some promising leads, but no definitive answers as of yet," Aiden hedged.

Lachlan fought to contain his disappointment. "Then, in the interest of family harmony, I'll not press ye fer the name of the woman who betrayed us."

There was no sense of satisfaction when he saw the glint of shock in Aiden's eyes. Only further disappointment that his brother had deliberately withheld the truth.

"Ye know?" Aiden croaked.

"I know." Lachlan sighed. "Secrets are impossible to keep, especially from the laird. 'Twas easy to get Mother's maid, Catrina, to confess that her husband had brought a message to Fraser. Though pressed, Catrina refused to admit that her mistress had ordered her to do it, not even when I threatened to have her whipped."

"Ye'd have a lass punished so severely?"

"'Tis my right."

Aiden gave him a long, disgusted look. "Christ's blood, Lachlan, have ye no mercy in yer soul? The lass was just doing as she was bid."

"I said I threatened," Lachlan clarified. "No matter what ye may think of me, I can assure ye that I dinnae brutalize women or children. I am sworn to protect them."

Aiden scrubbed his hand vigorously across his brow. "Mother thought she was helping our cause by placating the Frasers. She meant no harm to ye or Lady Katherine. 'Twas a mistake that has brought her a great deal of anguish and guilt."

"Aye, so Mother has said."

"Ye've spoken with her about this?" Aiden asked, frowning when Lachlan nodded. "Do ye believe her regret is sincere?"

"Should I?"

Aiden didn't bother to hide his skepticism. "Ye'd trust my word on this matter?"

"I would. Even though we both know I should not." Lachlan clasped Aiden's arm. "There's nothing wrong with wanting to rise in the world, Brother, but ye willnae do it at my expense.

"I want the MacTavish to be known as a respected, honorable clan. I want our people to have enough to eat, clothes that are not threadbare, land to live on that is fertile and provides fer us all. We need to be able to fend off our enemies, keep our people safe and secure, and hold what we own.

"I'm not so arrogant that I believe I'm the only one

qualified to make decisions fer the clan. But if our opinions differ, then my word is law. I will be obeyed. If ye cannae respect that, if ye cannae live with it, then ye had best take yer leave."

Lachlan spoke with force and command. If his brother did not yield to his authority and continued to openly defy him, Lachlan would have no choice but to banish him. Aiden remained silent and the strain between them surged as neither man spoke nor looked away.

"Ye must do as ye see fit," Aiden finally replied. "And so must I."

Then with a curt nod Aiden turned and walked away.

Chapter Twelve

The alarm bell sounded soon after the great hall had been cleared from the morning meal. Katherine swallowed her final bite of porridge and exchanged an anxious glance with the maid who had been brushing the few bits of food from the tables. The young girl's eyes widened and she dropped her rag. Wordlessly, the two women ran outside.

The courtyard was in complete disarray. Men were shouting, women screaming; everyone seemed to be running in a different direction. Katherine had never seen the like. McKenna Castle was a fortress, protected by great numbers of Highlanders known for their fighting skill. None had ever been so bold as to advance upon her father's holdings—not even the English.

Katherine waited anxiously for the portcullis to drop and the gates to shut, but instead they opened wider. 'Twas then she realized that the villagers would be at the mercy of the attackers, exposed without any protection. She had heard chilling tales of attacks where villages were burned and the innocent killed. Their best chance for survival lay within the walls of the keep.

If they could reach it in time.

Amidst all the chaos, Katherine spied Lachlan. He appeared calm, ordering the warriors who surrounded him with words and gestures. They hurried to do his bidding, arming themselves with axes, bows, maces, and swords and then positioning themselves strategically on the parapets and at posts throughout the courtyard.

The villagers began pouring into the bailey, carrying children and herding livestock, packs of their belongings hastily thrown on their backs. She could see the frantic fear in their eyes as they huddled together, uncertainty punctuating their movements.

One of the soldiers ordered them into the great hall. En masse they moved. Katherine was swept up in the tide and found herself being propelled along with them. Yet, just as she reached the doorway, Katherine caught a glimpse of Lady Morag bursting through the crowd.

The older woman grabbed a young soldier's arm to garner his attention. "Is it the Frasers?" Katherine heard her ask.

"They are too far away to see their colors, milady. Our lookout spied a cloud of dust on the distant horizon. We know only that there are a fair number of men, riding hard. They will be upon us soon."

"Too many of our people are still outside the walls," Lady Morag exclaimed. "We must see to them."

"I am ordered to prepare the archers, milady," the soldier answered, lowering his gaze. "I cannae help."

Lady Morag nodded in understanding and Katherine watched in astonishment as the older woman ran through the bailey and out the gates. Giving the matter little thought, Katherine charged after her. 'Twas clear that the other men were also too busy to help—thus the women must do their part.

"Katherine!"

She heard Lachlan shout her name, but she ignored

him, suspecting he would forbid her to leave. She di
not wish to openly defy him if he ordered her to th
great hall with the others. Yet she could not cower i
safety when she was fully able to aid those in such de
perate need.

Following on Lady Morag's heels, Katherine ra
through the gates into the winding lane, heading fo
the cottages at the farthest edge of the village. Ther
she found a mother in tears as she struggled to carr
her four young bairns.

"Bless ye," the woman sobbed, when Katherin
stopped.

She scooped a toddler under one arm and accepte
the babe who was gratefully thrust at her in the othe
The poor mite was shrieking in her ear, but there wa
no time to try to soothe him. Together, the two wome
fled toward the keep, their breaths coming in rapi
pants as they ran.

Katherine handed her precious burdens off to a la
standing a few feet from the gate, then turned and ra
back. She passed Lady Morag, who was holding th
hands of two crying children, pulling them along s
quickly their feet skipped off the ground. Behind the
a man carrying a goat and a woman balancing a larg
basket in her arms urged them to move faster, pani
evident in their voices.

Katherine noticed there were fewer people about a
she sprinted through the lanes. She helped five mor
women and their children and one very pregnant las
to safety and returned once more to the nearly empt
village.

Suddenly, the alarm bell rang again, causing her hear
to jump in fear. The riders must be getting closer! She
was preparing to turn back when a noise drew her atten
tion. She ran to the back of the cottage and discovered

n elderly couple trying to coax a thin, sickly looking cow
rom its pen. The animal's eyes were round with distress
s it loudly protested their prodding.

"Ye must get to the keep," she cried. "There's no time
o waste."

"If they steal our cow we'll have nothing," the old
man argued, wincing as he tried unsuccessfully to
move the beast.

"There's no time," Katherine protested.

"If we lose her, we'll starve," the old man insisted, his
ace flushed with his failed exertions.

"Go!" she ordered, deciding it was useless to waste
 any more time arguing. "I'll see to the animal."

The old man's brow curled in objection, but his wife
ugged urgently on his arm. Reluctantly, he handed
Katherine the switch. His wife dipped a hasty curtsy,
caught her husband's hand, and the two hurried away.

For a moment, Katherine was flummoxed as she
stared at the reluctant animal. She knew little about
livestock—except for horses—but she knew the old
man had spoken the truth. The couple would suffer
mightily without this beast. She had to at least try to
bring it to safety.

Seeing that the couple's method of switching the
cow from behind had failed, Katherine threw the stick
away and reached for a length of rope. She hastily tied
it around the cow's neck and attempted to lead it from
the pen.

The balking animal refused to budge. Katherine
wound the rope tightly around her arm and pulled,
leaning so far back her slippers dug into the hard dirt.
But the cow planted its feet, too, let out a mournful
sound, and wouldn't move.

Growling in frustration, Katherine tried again,
achieving the same result. She considered abandoning

the beast and somehow compensating the couple for the loss, yet knew that all possible sources of food would be needed if whoever was approaching laid siege to the keep.

Renewing her efforts, Katherine looped the rope around her arm and began tugging with all her strength. She swayed off balance, leaning to the right, and nearly tumbled to the ground when amazingly, the animal took a step. Only a single step, but it was progress.

"Aye, now ye understand," she said.

Encouraged, Katherine repeated the motion, this time leaning to the left, and the cow again took a step. She continued to alternate the lead until she managed to get the beast to move at a steady pace.

"Bless ye, milady, ye've done it!" the old man cried when Katherine reached the gate. With a relieved, exhausted smile, she handed off the rope and turned to go back into the village. 'Twas then she realized that she and the cow were the last ones to reach safety.

"Katherine!"

She lifted her head and met Lachlan's furious gaze. He was still on the ramparts with his men, preparing for their defense. Though she understood the reason for his anger, she felt a stab of disappointment over his lack of understanding. Did he believe her to be so unfeeling that she would sit idly in safety when she was fully able to help?

A soldier approached him and Lachlan turned away. Mouth tightening, Katherine took advantage of his distraction and followed the remaining villagers into the great hall. She accepted the tankard of ale thrust into her hand. Her thirst was so strong she drank it all at once, managing to ignore the constant burn of the bitter brew as she swallowed.

"Lady Katherine."

She spun around, nearly choking on the last of her drink. Aiden stood before her, his expression grim.

"What has happened?" she asked nervously, wiping her wet mouth with the back of her sleeve.

"My brother commands yer presence on the ramparts."

She tried to study his face, uncertain what to make of the request. However, Aiden turned away without waiting for her reply, clearly expecting her to follow. She watched his long, steady strides and for an instant felt shaken and afraid.

Was it the Frasers coming to exact revenge? Or coming for her? And what would Lachlan do? The warrior in him would want to fight. Yet given the poor condition of the keep's defenses and the relatively small number of soldiers at his side, the odds of victory would be against him.

Lachlan's first duty was to his clan—would he be forced to give her over in order to save his people?

Katherine shuddered. He had demonstrated that he was the sort of man who would not surrender easily. Yet could he in truth put so many innocents in such grave danger for her?

Katherine felt her cheeks burn as she climbed the steps. When she reached Lachlan's side, she followed his gaze and looked to the eastern horizon. Squinting, she lifted her hand to shield her eyes from the sun and scanned the long column of men riding hard toward them, counting at least seventy.

"They fly the McKenna banner," Lachlan observed.

"Aye!" Katherine replied excitedly, her heart accelerating its rhythm as she recognized the confident warrior leading the men. "'Tis my younger brother, Graham, in the lead."

"Why does he come with so many soldiers?"

"I assume that he is searching fer me and expects a battle to win my freedom." She could feel Lachlan's eyes upon her, watching her intently, as though assessing her thoughts. "Fear not. Once he sees that I am unharmed, Graham will act reasonably."

Lachlan grunted in reply. Katherine leaned forward, hoping to recognize some of the other riders. Lachlan placed a restraining hand on her arm. "Be careful. The last thing we need is fer ye to go tumbling over the wall."

She nodded, keeping her eyes on the column of men. She smiled when she saw two of her father's guardsmen, but her delight was short-lived when the features of another man became clear.

Nay! It cannae be!

Lachlan somehow sensed her distress and moved protectively closer. "Whatever ye aren't saying is causing me great concern, Katherine," he said softly, his expression quizzical.

For an instant, words failed her. She shivered with apprehension, then deliberately calmed her nerves. "Sir Hamish Drummond rides at my brother's side," she said.

"Yer betrothed?"

"Aye." Katherine swallowed, then shook her head vigorously. "Nay. No longer. He knows that I willnae marry him. I dinnae know why he has come."

Lachlan scoffed. "I do. Ye've placed too little value on yerself, Katherine. If ye were my intended, I'd not let ye get away from me so easily."

He was close enough that his warm breath feathered her cheek, causing a fluttering of excitement in her breast. Tentatively, she looked up into his eyes. They shone like fire and she felt her heart jump anew at his scrutiny.

There was something strangely hypnotic about Lachlan's stare, for it seemed to be reaching inside her to a deep, secret, hidden place. A place that only he could find.

The sound of hoofbeats broke the spell. Katherine turned away, once again looking beyond the wall. The McKenna contingent had arrived. Two men separated from the rest and rode across the moat bridge. Katherine didn't have to squint to identify them—'twas her brother and Hamish.

"I am Sir Graham McKenna. My sister, Lady Katherine, stands at yer side," he shouted with a menacing scowl. "I demand that ye release her at once."

"I'm not a captive, Graham," Katherine called out.

Her reply seemed to bewilder her brother. He looked hesitantly back at his men, most of whom still held their weapons aloft.

"I am Lachlan MacTavish, laird of my clan. There is much to tell, but I'll only open my gates fer ye, Sir Graham," Lachlan yelled. Despite its volume, his voice was calm, authoritative, but Katherine sensed the tension in him.

Graham's scowl deepened as he and Hamish exchanged a silent look of communication. The two men pointedly lowered their swords. Graham signaled one of his men to come forward. He and Hamish then made a great show of relinquishing their swords to the fellow.

"As a sign of good faith we two shall enter without our weapons," Graham conceded.

The MacTavish retainers on the wall went silent as they awaited their laird's decision. After a moment of contemplation, Lachlan spoke.

"Open the gate. Only these two men shall be allowed entrance."

Katherine lifted her skirts and started scampering down the stone steps. Lachlan grasped her elbow and drew her back.

"Nay, we'll wait until they have passed through the portcullis and dismounted before entering the bailey," Lachlan said.

His firm expression told her it would be most unwise to question his command. In truth, she did not mind the delay. She knew she should be feeling joy and relief at the sight of her brother's familiar face and instead her stomach was twisting in knots.

It took a few minutes for the men to arrive in the courtyard. Once they were off their horses, Lachlan and Katherine went to join them. As they gained the courtyard, she forced a smile to her lips. Graham returned it with a hard stare and she nearly stumbled when she felt the weight of his disapproval.

Hamish's eyes locked with hers and he began to make his way toward her. Panicked, Katherine veered away.

"Stay beside me," Lachlan commanded.

Katherine obeyed without hesitation, taking comfort from the calm power emanating from him. Hamish extended his arms as he drew closer.

"Dearest Katherine. 'Tis joyful to see that ye are unharmed," Hamish gushed.

Instinctively, Katherine pulled back, not allowing the embrace. Hamish's grin quickly vanished and his brow narrowed with displeasure.

Ignoring him, Katherine faced her brother with a broad smile. "I'm safe, Graham. The MacTavish have treated me well."

He gave her a puzzled stare. "How did ye come to be

here? Did one of the MacTavish men rescue ye from yer kidnappers?"

"Nay." Aiden stepped forward, planting himself in front of her brother. "We were the ones who took her."

Katherine nearly groaned. Did the man have no sense? Provoking her brother would merely serve to escalate a situation that had the potential to be most dangerous to the MacTavish clan.

"Ye dared to take my sister?" Graham growled.

"I'm fine," Katherine insisted.

"'Tis not yer place to defend yer kidnappers," Graham snapped.

"I'm offering ye the facts, Graham, nothing more."

She could feel the blush rising up from her neck and invading her face, yet Katherine's eyes blazed as she bristled under his chastisement. One would think her brother would express joy and relief at finding her safe and unharmed.

Instead he appeared angry with her! God's teeth, Hamish Drummond had demonstrated greater delight in laying eyes upon her than her own flesh and blood.

A calculating look crossed Graham's face as he turned a hard stare upon Lachlan. "My father was very specific in his instructions. Once I found my sister, I was ordered to dispense justice to the men who kidnapped her."

"What sort of justice?" Lachlan asked.

"Whatever I deem appropriate." Graham's face tightened. "Knowing my father that could easily mean having ye gutted, then castrated, drawn, quartered, and burned."

Katherine flinched, her stomach turning at the gruesome image. "I've said time and again that I have not been harmed," she insisted, hardly believing such brutal words sprang from her brother's lips.

Where had the sweet lad who used to follow her around and beg for cream cakes and buns gone? In his place was a stranger, a hard, shrewd warrior.

"'Twas not Lachlan who took Lady Katherine," Aiden interjected. "I did. Against his specific wishes."

Graham turned suspiciously toward Aiden. "Ye acted against yer laird's orders? Yet ye appear to be suffering no discomfort fer all the turmoil that ye have caused."

Aiden shrugged. "'Tis our business."

Graham grimaced in disgust. "Why did ye not send word and request a ransom? At least then we would have known she was alive."

"It was never my intention to demand payment fer Lady Katherine's return," Lachlan answered. "She was ill fer a short time. I was waiting fer her to fully recover before taking her home."

She could see that Lachlan was making a great effort to be civil, a fact that appeared to make no impression upon her brother.

"My father has no tolerance fer action taken against our clan," Graham informed them. "Nor fer those who defy his will. Including his kin."

The last comment was directed at her. Katherine could feel every muscle in her body seizing as she struggled to keep her expression impassive.

"Graham, it appears that no real harm has been done," Hamish interjected. "I fer one rejoice at being united with my betrothed and now that she is found, I fully intend to keep her." Hamish braced his feet apart and crossed his arms. "I've thought and prayed upon the matter and under these circumstances the best way to preserve Lady Katherine's reputation is to find a priest to marry us before we return to McKenna Castle."

Katherine fell silent, staring up at Hamish, trying to

remain calm, while inside her mind tumbled with dread. His features were harsh, his determination evident. A sense of unease swept through her. She had not come this far, endured so much, to once again be facing a marriage that she knew she could not accept.

"I've made my feelings about this matter well known to ye," she hissed at him. "I'll not wed ye, Hamish. Ever."

He uncrossed his arms and seized her hand, stroking her palm gently with his thumb. "Ye are too cruel, milady."

"Nay, too honest." Squirming, Katherine pulled her hand away and stepped back.

Hamish's expression hardened as his eyes raked over her. "I willnae insult either of us by asking ye to want me or care fer me," he said. "The betrothal contracts have been signed, we've pledged our intentions in front of our families and our clans. We will marry."

Tears threatened, but Katherine contained them. The situation was more intolerable than ever. Hamish's gaze was unnerving, filled with callous intent. Any kindness he might have felt toward her was clearly gone.

"Ye cannae force me," she insisted, her voice wavering.

"There will be retribution if ye dinnae honor the agreements," Hamish lashed out. "A Highlander doesn't tolerate betrayal."

"How dare ye!" Katherine gasped. "I wasn't the one who professed a great love fer another. Ye betrayed me and thus the bargain between us dissolved."

"Nay," Hamish retorted sharply. "It stands. Now stop acting like a spoiled brat."

He started toward her and she backed away, shaking her head. Katherine turned a nervous eye to her brother. "Graham! Do something."

Her brother let out an impatient oath. "Father has

ordered me to allow Hamish to decide what to do about the marriage. If he still wants ye, then ye must wed him."

Katherine felt as though her heart had stopped. "I dinnae believe it! What of my wishes?"

"Father wanted to marry ye by proxy to Hamish before the search began." Graham turned his head aside and mumbled beneath his breath. "Mother wouldn't hear of it."

Her father was willing to let the marriage take place? Even after she had explained in her letter why she fled to avoid the union? A wave of misery engulfed Katherine. She took a deep breath, seeking to hide her hurt and desperation.

She had badly miscalculated her father's reaction and would now suffer the consequences. But not without a fight. Shaking, Katherine pulled herself together. She still had her mother's support. All was not completely lost.

"A swift marriage is best fer all," Hamish declared. "In time ye shall thank me, Katherine."

Never! She compressed her lips in frustration. Even in her wildest imagination Katherine could not conceive of such a thing. She opened her mouth to tell him, but held her tongue when she caught sight of the malicious cast to Hamish's eyes.

Why had she never noticed it before?

Knowing that she could not let him best her, Katherine found her voice. "Despite what my father might wish, I'll not be shackled to ye by vows of marriage."

"Ye act as though it will be a terrible hardship to have me fer yer husband," Hamish said, moving toward her again.

Katherine returned his glare even as she scrambled

away, then suddenly ran into something solid. Startled, she turned and found herself staring up into Lachlan's eyes.

There was a sudden crack of thunder so loud it made Katherine's ears ring. In moments, large pellets of rain fell from the sky. Everyone scrambled in separate directions seeking shelter.

Katherine had taken only a few steps before someone grabbed her hand and pulled her toward the stables. Instinctively she shied away from her captor, feeling only a slight sense of relief when she saw it was her brother who held her hand so possessively. At least it wasn't the loathsome Hamish.

The horses paid them no mind as Graham dragged her to a protective corner of the stable. Clamping her jaw tightly, Katherine tried to leave by going around him, but he blocked her path.

"Let me pass," she said. "I wish to go into the great hall with the others."

"Hush, Katherine, we have but a few moments of privacy," Graham said sternly.

Katherine blinked. His voice sounded so much like their father's it made her shiver.

"How dare ye speak to me as though I were a dim-witted child," she cried, hurt edging her anger. "I've never been so humiliated in all my life."

"Sister." Graham reached out and pulled her into his arms, enveloping her in a wide hug, so tight it nearly crushed her ribs. "Saints be praised that ye are alive and unharmed," he whispered. "Fer days we feared the worst."

Relief surged through Katherine and for a moment she clung to her brother, then suspiciously drew back. What sort of game was Graham playing now? She opened her mouth to berate him. However, the sincerity in his eyes moved her, causing a bit of her pain to fade.

"All are well at home?" she asked.

Graham smiled. "They will be once they learn that ye are safe."

"What of the McKenna men who aided me when I fled from Drummond Castle?" Katherine asked. "A few were wounded in the scrimmage."

"They've recovered. Malcolm has assigned the lot of them to duties that will keep them out of Father's sight."

Katherine was relieved. She shared a smile with her brother and then unwittingly her anger resurfaced.

"Why have ye been acting like such an arse?" she demanded. "And why the hell does Hamish Drummond ride with ye?"

"Father thought it best. We scattered to the four winds once we learned that ye had been taken. Malcolm to the south, James to the west, Father to the east. I was sent north. Since it seemed least likely that ye'd be found here, I was given the task of bringing Hamish with me. The Drummonds are vexed and I was charged with making them believe that we agree they have been gravely wronged."

Katherine caught the flicker of distaste in her brother's eyes when he mentioned Hamish. Perhaps her cause was not as dire as it first appeared. "Do ye think I should wed him?"

"My opinion has no bearing on yer situation. If ye want to break the betrothal, then ye must convince Father." Graham's expression darkened. "And I warn ye, it willnae be easy."

"What about Mother?"

Graham smiled. "She'll forever be yer champion, but even her power has limits. Her hope was that ye'd be found unharmed, and Drummond would decide that he no longer wanted ye."

"Well, that hope is well and truly dashed." Katherine sighed bitterly. "Hamish appears more eager than ever, if fer no other reason than to spite me."

"Aye, that seems to be his way."

Katherine stared back at the sympathy in her brother's eyes. "There has to be some way to escape from him."

Graham slowly released his breath. "He might not want ye if he thought ye were unfit to be his wife."

"Unfit?" Katherine scoffed. "Isn't running away from him reason enough?"

"Hamish expects his bride to be pure. Ye were taken from us by a group of Highlanders and traveled with them without any female companionship fer days. If something happened, 'twould not be yer fault." Graham's face heated as he sent her a knowing look.

Katherine's eyes widened as she caught her brother's meaning. "I'm still a maid, if that's what yer asking. Even Aiden, fer all his arrogance, treated me with respect."

Graham sighed. "Though it could have solved yer dilemma with Drummond, I am relieved to hear it. I dinnae fancy having to challenge the MacTavish laird or his brother to atone fer yer dishonor."

"There has been no dishonor," Katherine replied. "Och, Graham, 'tis all such a quagmire. There has to be a way to escape from Hamish!"

Graham inhaled. "Well, Mother did have one idea that she passed along to me, though it's far-fetched and nigh impossible to accomplish."

"Tell me."

Graham reached out, took her hand, and looked directly into her eyes. "Sir Hamish cannae marry ye if ye are another man's wife."

Chapter Thirteen

There was an air of tense anticipation in the great hall as the McKenna retainers joined the MacTavish clan for the evening meal. Concerned that normally there was barely enough food to adequately feed the usual number who attended, Katherine had instructed her brother to relinquish whatever food stores they could spare and promptly brought those items to the kitchen.

Graham had raised a questioning brow at her odd request, but complied. Fortunately, his men had been successful in their hunt last night and earlier that morning. A grateful Lady Morag had overseen preparations of the fresh meat they provided and the result was an ample amount of simple, well-prepared food for all.

Katherine remained quiet throughout the meal, her mind consumed with thoughts of her future. 'Twas a relief to know that her brother—and mother—didn't expect her to be submissive and meekly comply with an unacceptable arrangement and marry Hamish Drummond.

Unfortunately, her father had other ideas and it

appeared Katherine would not be afforded the necessary time she needed to change his mind. Instead, she would need her wits and cunning to escape that fate.

Graham's remarks had firmly planted two seeds of ideas in her mind of how she could accomplish that task. The more she considered them, the faster they grew.

Lose her virginity or marry another before returning to McKenna Castle. Both were appalling in their own way, with challenges and consequence, yet each were surely a means to an end. There was little doubt Hamish would abandon her if either occurred.

If she returned home no longer a maid she could very well remain unmarried for the rest of her days. No self-respecting noble would eagerly take another's leavings, no matter how large her dowry.

'Twas the height of hypocrisy, of course, as men had the freedom to do whatever they wished with the opposite sex before and even after their marriages. Women, however, were judged differently. They were expected to remain pure until they married and faithful after they had spoken their vows.

Nay, the more she thought about it, the more Katherine realized that surrendering her virginity merely for the sake of escaping Hamish was too high a price to pay. Personal repercussions aside, she could not inflict that dishonor upon her family, her clan, or herself.

That left one other possibility. She would have to wed another and return home a married woman. But who would take her as his bride?

Her eyes instantly turned toward Lachlan. God's bones, he was magnificent. Her breath caught just looking at him. But she could not let attraction and desire rule her head. She must be careful and considered and look to all possibilities before making a choice.

To that end, Katherine's eyes drifted over the McKenna

retainers seated together at the trestle table closest to the door. She knew nearly all of them. Several were unmarried; two had lost wives to illness last year. If she married one of them, their lack of property would not be a hindrance—as a wedded couple they could live at her dower estate, a half day's ride from McKenna Castle.

Her estate was a prosperous fortification, with fertile farmland and a breathtaking view of the Scottish hills. Any man would be proud to call the place home, especially a landless one.

In theory it sounded so simple. Yet would any of these men be willing to stand strong and face her father's ire? She didn't doubt their courage, yet she feared they were too loyal to cross him and marry without his blessing.

Her gaze turned away from the McKenna men and came to rest at the others seated on the dais. That her eyes again fell first upon Lachlan was no surprise. 'Twas inevitable. Ever since she had awoken from her fevered sickness she had been drawn to him in a way she didn't completely understand.

'Twas more than his handsome face and impressive physique. More, too, than the fluttering of desire that washed over her when he looked at her in a certain way. There was honor and empathy in him, coupled with strength of character.

His life had been harsh, but his heart was pure, his sense of humor intact. Aye, he was poor. His clan had neither stature nor wealth, two things her father respected, two things her father would expect in any man who became her husband.

But she was not her father.

Katherine couldn't take her eyes off Lachlan as her mind started spinning. Most would regard it as a very bad bargain on her end, but this was hardly a conventional situation. The prospect of being his partner, sharing his life, his bed, and if God was merciful, one day mothering his children, filled her with restless excitement.

This *would* be a good match for her—and him. With Lachlan as her husband she would face whatever struggles they encountered with strength and hope. They could build a life together with meaning and laughter and love.

It was possible. Her heart thumped, her breath quickened. Truly.

All she need do was convince him.

Sleep was impossible for Katherine that night, despite the comfort of the bed and the warmth of the chamber. Graham had declared that they would depart at first light, leaving tonight the only time to speak with Lachlan and put forth her proposal of marriage.

By necessity it had to be a private conversation, one she wanted no one to hear or witness. That meant waiting until the household slumbered and then sneaking into the chamber where Lachlan slept.

Katherine sat on the edge of her bed and stared into the darkness, straining for sounds of the household. All was quiet, letting her know that everyone had taken to their beds and pallets. Graham and Hamish had left the keep and slept in tents with the rest of their men in the bailey, so thankfully she wouldn't have to worry about accidentally encountering either of them.

Taking a final deep breath for courage, Katherine resolutely opened her bedchamber door and carefully made her way into the corridor. Gripping a stubby tallow candle at the base, she moved slowly toward Lachlan's door.

Black shadows loomed all around her and Katherine's heartbeat quickened. The steady sound of a heavy rain pelted the roof. She cringed at a sudden clap of thunder and turned her head away from the flash of lightning that momentarily illuminated her path.

She was dressed in the thin night rail Lady Morag had lent her when she first arrived. Due to the differences in their height, the garment swirled around her calves, leaving her ankles and feet bare and chilled. She had hastily thrown a blanket over her shoulders, but it was worn and thin and offered little protection against the cold and dampness of the hallway.

Holding the flickering candle aloft, Katherine strained to see ahead. 'Twas not uncommon for a page or squire to sleep at the threshold of the laird's chamber. If she stumbled over an unsuspecting servant the household would immediately be roused, ending the chance for a private meeting.

Fortunately, the path was clear. As she was trying to decide the best way to enter—knock first or slowly lift the latch—the door swung open and a large, dark form appeared.

"God's blood, Katherine, I nearly skewered ye!" Lachlan hissed.

Katherine gasped. Looking down she saw the tense muscles of Lachlan's forearm and lethal dirk gripped tightly in his hand.

"I'm sorry," she answered softly. "I needed to speak with ye privately."

"Now?"

She nodded. Fearing he might refuse her, Katherine pushed past him and entered the chamber. She heard him sigh. Half expecting to be hauled away, Katherine was relieved to hear the door close.

The chamber was in near darkness. Lachlan took her candle and lit two others. Placing his hands on his hips, he took a deep breath and looked at her expectantly.

Katherine's fingers knotted into a tight ball. The intimacy of the moment and the arrangement she was about to propose reminded her of how odd her words would sound. Yet she refused to hesitate—their marriage could prove to be the salvation they both needed. Determined, she did her best to smooth away the uncertainty of her expression.

"Ye know that I cannae marry Hamish Drummond."

Lachlan nodded. "Aye. After meeting the man, I can see ye have cause to avoid a union with him."

"My brother agrees, but my father, well, by all accounts he willnae easily allow me to break the marriage contract." Heart racing, Katherine lifted her chin, hardly believing she was being so bold. "However, he'll not have a choice if I return to McKenna Castle a married woman."

Lachlan's brows drew together. "And just who will ye be wedding?"

"Ye." She cleared her throat. "That is, if ye'll have me."

A thick silence settled over the room. Katherine pressed her lips together to keep herself from begging as she tried to read Lachlan's reaction. He was studying her carefully, his expression impassive.

"Are ye jesting with me, Katherine?" he finally asked.

"Nay!" Katherine bit back a grimace. She had hoped for a more enthusiastic reaction. The kisses they had shared had been filled with passion and longing. Or so she believed. Had she misjudged his interest in her? If so, a different tactic was needed. "Marriages are used to build alliances, acquire wealth, and enhance a clan's position. Ye shall do all three if ye take me as yer wife."

"Perhaps." The corners of Lachlan's lips curved up in an ironic smile. "But I'll also be adding the Drummond clan to an ever-growing list of enemies. Of course, they'll have to battle the Frasers and the McKennas first fer a piece of my hide."

Katherine dipped her chin. "My father will make peace with the Drummonds and ye'll be bound to the McKennas through marriage, an alliance that will hold strong."

"I cannae image yer father taking kindly to a man who married his daughter without his knowledge or permission. He's just as likely to run me through with his broadsword than offer his blessing of our union."

"Aye, it could be viewed as an act of defiance to marry ye without my father's permission," Katherine acknowledged. "However, my mother extracted a promise from him when I was a wee lass, granting me the right to choose my own husband." She cleared the dryness from her throat. "I choose ye."

"Why me?"

Katherine felt the color spread across her cheeks. "'Tis a bold move that requires a man equal to the task."

Lachlan raised his brow. "Flattery, Katherine? Ye think that all ye need do is flutter yer eyelashes and point yer breasts in my direction and I'll come to heel like a well-trained hound?"

"I think nothing of the sort!"

Lachlan raked his fingers through his hair. "I cannae help but wonder if ye'd feel the same way if Hamish Drummond had not arrived, demanding that ye honor the marriage contract."

His words surprised her. She pondered their meaning

and her serious expression broke, bringing forth a mischievous smile. "Have I hurt yer pride because I dinnae ask ye sooner?"

Lachlan turned his head and grinned. "Damn it, lass, that teasing smile will land ye in a tub of hot water one day."

Katherine's smile widened. "Would it truly be so awful to marry me?" she whispered boldly, breathlessly. "Ye'll have to wed sometime. As laird, 'tis yer duty to take a wife. And I need a husband. It seems like a simple, mutually beneficial solution."

"'Tis a permanent solution." Lachlan scrubbed a hand across his face. "Ye see the condition of our keep. 'Tis old, and in need of extensive repairs. Our livestock are few and those we do have are thin and often sickly.

"The harvests are poor, no matter how hard our people work in the fields. The seeds are either washed away by rain or rot in the ground. In the lean months of winter, despite all my efforts, there are times my people go hungry. I have no business bringing a noblewoman of yer wealth and stature to live in such squalor."

Katherine bent close to him, placing her hand on his arm. She could feel the muscle tighten and tense, but she refused to remove her fingers. "My dowry includes rich, fertile land. The yields from these fields could feed the MacTavish through a long, hard winter. There is more, too, much more. I will bring household goods and other foodstuffs along with funds that can pay fer repairs to the keep and buy healthy livestock."

Lachlan scratched the side of his head. "A marriage could solve several problems. Fer both of us."

Excitement pricked her. "'Tis a sensible solution," she agreed.

Yet uncertainty glimmered in Lachlan's eyes. "Ye've

put forth all the judicious reasons fer our union. But what of love? Ye told me once how important it was to ye. I'll admit to having feelings fer ye—strong ones. But I'll not lie to ye—lust is not love. Are ye willing to pay such a steep price fer this marriage?" he asked, his voice laced with caution.

Katherine regarded him with a composure she didn't feel. "I must be practical, therefore I hope fer a man who will treat me with respect and dignity."

Lachlan nodded. "If we marry, that I can promise ye, lass."

Katherine's heart started beating wildly. Her answer had only been partially true. She had not abandoned her quest to one day share a deep and abiding love with her husband and she believed it could happen with Lachlan. An uncomfortable feeling of guilt settled in her stomach for not speaking of it to him, but she feared it might cause him to reject her.

"I understand yer concerns about my father and vow that my brothers and I will do all that we can to prevent a feud between our clans," she said. "I know that a conflict has the power to fuel itself, much like an unattended fire."

"Aye, and the blaze it ignites will consume us all in pain and grief." The furrow between Lachlan's brow eased. "Ye've no cause to be so fearful. Though I imagine he will delight in stringing my innards from the McKenna Castle battlements, I can hold my own with yer father."

Lachlan laid a comforting hand over hers. The sensation of his fingers on her flesh made Katherine shiver. He held her gaze and she could feel the tension sizzling between them, enveloping her senses. It felt good to confirm that she had not imagined the desire she had previously seen in his eyes.

If only he would kiss her! Then, he would feel a different sort of need for her. One that might sway his decision. She tilted her chin and gazed at him provocatively. His eyes narrowed and darkened for a moment, but disappointingly he made no move to accept her blatant invitation.

"Ye've given me much to consider," Lachlan said slowly. "My actions have consequences fer all the members of my clan. 'Tis my duty to provide fer and protect them. Yer dowry would be welcome—as long as I can wrestle it from yer father. But our marriage will make enemies of the Drummonds and further deepen the tension with the Frasers, placing a greater burden on all my people."

Katherine could feel a cold sweat break out on her brow. "I dinnae wish to be a burden to anyone."

His expression softened. "Any man would be proud and honored to have ye as his wife, but a decision this important should not be made in haste."

The pain of disappointment struck hard. Katherine pressed her hand against her chest and took a deep breath, trying to ease the pounding of her heart. 'Twas not the answer she had hoped to receive. The only small bit of comfort was that he had not rejected her outright.

"Alas, there is no time to weigh the merits of our union," she said sadly. "I will be leaving with Graham at first light."

Lachlan searched for her hand, slowly rubbing her fingers between his own. "I'm coming with ye. Graham suggested it would be best if I explained to yer father in person how ye came to be with us. I agreed."

A tiny frisson of hope surged in Katherine's chest. All was not yet lost. "Perhaps we will have more to tell my family when we arrive at McKenna Castle," Katherine suggested wistfully.

"Mayhap."

Lachlan's gaze remained fixed on her face. Katherine smiled, trying to appear unconcerned and carefree. Desperation was hardly an attractive quality.

"I need to return to my chamber before I am discovered," she admitted reluctantly.

As much as she wanted this marriage, she would not entrap Lachlan and embarrass them both by being discovered in his bedchamber.

"Wait. Let me make certain no one is about." Lachlan opened the chamber door and checked the hallway, then signaled it was clear.

Holding her candle high, Katherine exited. She walked slowly, carefully, her heart heavy with the realization that she had failed to receive the outcome she sought, leaving her future riddled with uncertainty.

Lachlan watched Katherine slowly make her way down the corridor. Once he was assured that she was safely back in her chamber, he shut the door and slumped against it.

Marry Katherine! Shit! The very notion had his head spinning in uncountable directions. The idea of having her by his side and in his bed was a temptation that cast all common sense aside.

In so many ways it was an unthinkably high-reaching match for him. She was the daughter of a rich and powerful man; he was the laird of a poor and disgraced clan. She had been raised among luxury and ease; he had fought each day for survival.

Was it the appeal of something he knew was forbidden to him that made it so tempting?

Nay, it was Katherine herself. Her teasing humor, her bravery and kindness, her gracious nobility, the friendship and regard that had begun to blossom between them.

Ever since he had kissed her, he had been unable to forget the sweet taste of her lips, the feel of her luscious body against his own, the heat and passion she had stirred so effortlessly within him.

She had the power to ignite a desire that burned hotter and fiercer than any he had ever known. But he was not a man who would allow himself to be ruled by passion or personal desire. He could not risk the future of his clan by allowing himself to be enraptured by a woman. Even one as beguiling as Katherine.

It had been torturous to deny her, to deny himself. The glimmer of hope in her eyes had nearly unmanned him. But he had to be measured and practical in this decision.

Lachlan admitted 'twas harder after meeting her betrothed. Drummond was a poor choice for many reasons. His temperament was unsteady, his countenance immature. Worst of all, there was no warmth in his gaze when he looked at Katherine. 'Twas obvious he held no genuine affection for her.

Drummond was merely intent on retrieving his wayward betrothed in order to impress his father and regain his pride. A situation that bespoke of an unhappy union if Katherine and Drummond married.

Lachlan knew it was dangerous to concern himself with Katherine's broken betrothal. Still, the impulse to be chivalrous, to rescue her from a fate she didn't deserve ran deep and strong within him. Along with the selfish desire to make her his own.

Yet as he returned to his bed and stretched out upon it, he vowed not to indulge either until he figured out a way to make certain it would bring no harm to his clan.

At daybreak, they prepared to ride.

Lady Morag and Aiden were among those who came to see them off. Lachlan spoke with his brother privately for several minutes, then embraced his stepmother. She whispered something in his ear. He nodded.

Several members of the clan crowded around Katherine to bid her farewell and she was surprised to feel a lump of emotion clog her throat. The couple whose cow she had rescued wished her well, as did the mother of the bairns she had helped.

Young Cameron sniffled, threw his arms around her waist, and hugged her tightly.

"I shall miss ye, too," Katherine said softly, kissing the top of his head.

"When will ye return?" Cameron asked, his voice muffled against her heavy cloak.

"Fate will decide," she whispered in his ear before breaking away.

"Godspeed, milady," Cameron's mother said.

The rest of the women surrounding her respectfully curtsied and bid her safe journey. During the exchange, Katherine could feel Lachlan's eyes upon her, yet he made no move to come to her side. 'Twas Graham who helped her mount her horse and secure the reins.

"I hope yer journey passes swiftly and uneventfully," Lady Morag called out to Katherine.

The older woman looked decidedly uncomfortable and Katherine could only imagine what she was thinking. No doubt she was pleased to see Katherine leave and in all likelihood praying this was the last time she would ever set eyes on any of the McKenna clan.

Aiden said nothing. His handsome features were taut, his shoulders visibly tense. He acknowledged her departure with a quick, short nod. Katherine gripped the reins tightly and answered his expression in kind.

Graham led the group out of the bailey. He drove them hard throughout the day, stopping only when necessary, to water the horses, see to personal needs, and eat sparingly of their food rations.

Following her brother's dictates, Katherine rode in the middle of the train, grateful for the McKenna soldiers who surrounded her, for they kept Hamish away. He was sulking like a spoiled lad, casting her sidelong glances filled with annoyance, clenching his jaw so tightly she wondered if his teeth would break.

To the consternation of the men protecting her, Drummond repeatedly tried to move close enough to engage her in conversation. Katherine ignored him. He was a distraction she had neither the time nor inclination to acknowledge. She had three, possibly four nights to convince Lachlan to wed her and she fully intended to concentrate her efforts on achieving that goal.

As the light faded with the setting sun, the moon rose to illuminate their path through the forest. They finally halted in front of a sprawling inn, where they were expected. Ever the planner, Graham had instructed one of his men to ride ahead and make the arrangements.

Katherine slowly dismounted, her legs wobbling

when she reached the ground. One of the McKenna retainers gallantly offered her his arm and she gratefully accepted his escort into the inn. It was a crude establishment, with a hard-packed dirt floor, long misshapen wooden tables and benches, and kegs of ale stacked in the corner of the common room, which was empty of other travelers. Katherine wondered if her brother had made those arrangements, too.

The chamber she was shown to was sparse and fitted with simple furnishings, but the rushes covering the wooden floor appeared fresh and free of vermin. At Katherine's request, a maid brought her hot water to wash along with her dinner.

After spending the entire day in the saddle, she felt almost too tired to chew, but Katherine's stomach rumbled when she caught a whiff of the delectable smells wafting from the tray.

Surprised at the quality of the stew, Katherine finished the meal quickly, brushing away the last of the crumbs when she was done. Moving her chair closer to the fire, she let herself relax. The pleasing warmth, along with her full stomach, caused her eyelids to grow heavy. Drowsy and content, she soon drifted off to sleep.

Roused by a sharp knock, Katherine was startled awake.

"Lachlan?"

She stumbled, nearly tripping in her haste to reach the door. Disappointment reigned when she saw the maid standing on the other side.

"I've come to help ye prepare fer bed, milady." The lass nervously chewed her bottom lip and waited. Fearing she must look like an ogress, Katherine smiled in a friendly manner and gestured for the maid to enter.

The lass was quick and efficient, helping Katherine unlace and remove her clothing. Since she had no night rail, Katherine elected to sleep in her chemise. Rummaging in the pocket of her cloak, she gave the maid one of the silver pennies Graham had gifted her with this morning. Eyes shining bright with gratitude, the lass left.

Katherine climbed into the bed, but her little nap had taken the edge off her exhaustion and left her mind far too alert.

Had Lachlan decided yet about their possible marriage? she wondered. Would he come to her when the inn was quiet and tell her of his intention? Or should she venture outside and try to find him? Indecision gripped her, but in the end Katherine reasoned that no matter how difficult, the sensible choice was to wait.

She drew the blanket off the bed and wrapped it around her shoulders. Then turning the chair toward the door, she sat, silently willing it to open and have Lachlan appear on the other side.

There were few private chambers in the inn. He would know where to find her.

Resolved, Katherine stayed awake in that chair for half the night, her ears straining to hear the sound of a knock on her door.

It never came.

Chapter Fourteen

By the start of the third day, Lachlan still had not given Katherine an answer and with each mile they rode, her hopes dwindled.

Just as darkness began falling on the evening of that third day, they rode into an abbey courtyard. A tall, slender man dressed in the simple brown robes of a monk came out to greet them. His hair, as well as the neatly trimmed beard that covered his jaw, was streaked with gray.

"I bid ye welcome, Sir Graham." The monk's eyes traveled swiftly over the large group, darkening with pleasure when he spied Katherine. "I see that ye have been successful in yer quest to locate yer sister."

"Aye, the Lord be praised." Graham dismounted, then offered his hand to assist Katherine from her horse. "Brother Gregory is the monastery's abbot. He provided us with shelter and a fine meal on our journey north to find ye."

"Brother Gregory." Though stiff from hours in the saddle, Katherine managed a dainty curtsy.

Hamish bullied his way forward, rudely interrupting the introductions. "Brother Gregory, I demand that ye take us to yer chapel immediately. Lady Katherine and I must wed without delay."

Brother Gregory's eyes widened. "I am a monk, not an ordained priest, sir. In the eyes of the church, I cannae marry anyone."

"Then summon a priest." The determination in Hamish's eyes was strong. "There must be at least one in residence."

"Father Joseph has been called away to minister to a pair of children who have taken ill in a nearby village. I dinnae know when he will return to us."

"Send someone to fetch him," Hamish ordered.

He reached beneath his tunic and brought forth a small leather pouch. "I will pay the messenger well fer his time. And ye and Father Joseph also."

Katherine's mouth dropped open and for a moment she found herself unable to breathe. The resolve in Hamish's expression along with his stubborn demeanor was most troubling. She turned a frantic eye toward Graham.

Help me, she mouthed in panic.

"I mean no offense, Sir Hamish, but I must refuse," Brother Gregory said in a dignified tone. "We are an order that embraces self-sacrifice and our commitment to the vows of obedience, chastity, and poverty willnae be abandoned. Father Joseph is doing the Lord's work by comforting the sick. I cannae take yer money and ask him to spurn his responsibilities."

"If Father Joseph is unavailable to wed us, then ye must make an exception in these unusual circumstances. Accept these coins and perform the ceremony yerself," Hamish bristled, his brows drawing together in an irritated frown.

"Put that money away, Drummond," Graham commanded, his voice laced with warning. "Ye're insulting the abbot by attempting to bribe him into forsaking his vows and embarrassing us all."

"I am merely extending charity to those less fortunate, as is my Christian duty," Hamish countered.

"The gesture is fer achieving yer own aims," Graham retorted. "If ye are so intent upon bestowing Christian charity, those coins are best served as alms fer the poor and destitute."

"Fine. I shall gladly donate the funds wherever my bride decrees. I shall make it her bridal gift," Hamish said with a sly smirk.

"Once again ye speak without thinking," Graham said sharply, regarding Hamish with undisguised scorn. "There will be no marriage ceremony. Even if the priest returns before we depart, I'll not allow my only sister to be wed without my parents in attendance."

Graham's curt refusal caught Hamish by surprise. For a few tense moments they stared at each other.

"She is my betrothed. 'Tis my right to marry her when and where I desire, as yer father decreed," Hamish insisted. The coins jingled obscenely as he pounded the purse into the palm of his left hand.

"'Tis my duty to see to the welfare of my sister," Graham replied, his voice stern and unyielding. "Ye shall wait. And I warn ye, dinnae push my ire any further, Drummond. I promise ye'll not be pleased with the results."

There was a flicker of uncertainty in Hamish's eyes. His face reddened, his eyes narrowed. After another long, tense moment, he reluctantly replaced the pouch beneath his tunic. Then refusing to look at anyone, Hamish stalked toward the entrance to the abbey.

Katherine slowly released her breath. Graham stepped beside her and placed a reassuring hand on her shoulder. He smiled kindly, yet she swore she could feel her brother's consternation. Whoever would have imagined that Hamish Drummond could cause her so much aggravation in such a short span of days?

The matter was dropped for the time being, but this was far from over. Katherine knew she was treading a thin line. Hamish was almost certain to demand they marry the moment they arrived at McKenna Castle. She would have little time to make her case for avoiding the marriage to her father.

Yet she clung to the notion that no matter what he believed, the McKenna would not allow her to be forced into the union against her will. Of course, all of that could be avoided if she arrived home married—to Lachlan.

She glanced over at the MacTavish laird. He had remained quiet during the exchange, yet curiously stood behind her brother as he argued with Hamish. A silent show of support and solidarity? Or merely a coincidence?

As the hour was late, the evening meal was immediately served to the weary travelers. Dinner was a quiet, awkward affair. The fare was simple, the portions generous. Most of the men, including Lachlan and Graham, ate heartily; Katherine was too distraught to do more than push her food from one side of her trencher to the other.

She was also careful not to drink too much of the surprisingly good wine the abbot served them, knowing she needed to keep her mind clear and alert.

Katherine sat as far away from Hamish as possible, wedging herself between her brother and one of the McKenna guard. The one time she did dare to glance in his direction, Hamish favored her with a belligerent look.

A most absurd impulse seized her and she had difficulty resisting the urge to stick her tongue out at him. God's teeth, it had been a long, exhausting, and tension-filled few days!

By meal's end, Hamish was slumped forward in his chair. He drained his goblet of wine, then signaled for the postulant to refill it, scowling at the nervous lad as he did his bidding. Katherine wrinkled her nose in disgust, amazed that she had once thought he would make a suitable husband.

When the meal ended, Brother Gregory escorted Katherine to her chamber. "Ye look a wee bit faint. Is there anything that I can bring ye, milady?" he asked kindly.

A husband? Katherine sighed and shook her head. She wasn't faint or dizzy; instead she felt as though a rock had settled in the bottom of her stomach. Lachlan had paid her no heed throughout the meal. Indeed, he seemed to make a concerted effort to avoid her. She could only speculate on the meaning of his behavior, and any of her assumptions did not bode well for her future or her heart.

Damnation!

She bid Brother Gregory good night, shut the door, and allowed her eyes to adjust to the gloom of the small, simple cell, telling herself that the quiet and solitude would serve to help her absorb her disappointment.

The silence however, didn't last. Katherine heard the sound of heavy boots in the hallway. The iron latch lifted and a cloaked figure slipped inside.

Lachlan!

"We need to talk," he said, closing the door firmly behind him.

He gave her that pensive, intense look that always made her heart skip a beat. Was he here to deliver good news or bad? Katherine's stomach curled with apprehension. She laced her fingers together, feigning a serenity that she was far from feeling.

"Have ye made a decision about my proposal?" she inquired.

"I've come to ask if ye are still determined to follow through with yer plan." Lachlan widened his stance and placed his hands on his hips. "To be sure, Drummond is an arse. However, do ye truly believe yer father will force ye to wed him? 'Tis obvious to anyone with sight that the two of ye are not at all suited."

"I dinnae want to believe that I'll be forced, but anything is possible," Katherine replied, wetting her suddenly dry lips. "I've given it considerable thought and have a strong inkling of how Hamish will approach the matter. He means to remind my father that the McKenna honor is at stake and it shall be a great blight upon it, if he allows the marriage contract to be broken. That might be enough."

"'Tis a good plan. One that I might also employ in similar circumstances. No Highland laird wants to be known as a man who reneges on his word." Lachlan walked slowly around her, his gaze fixed upon her face. "Nor will the McKenna want ye to form an alliance with few benefits. Yer father will not approve of me. He'll determine that I am an ambitious man, out to further my fortunes through marriage."

Katherine shrugged. "That is how many marriages are arranged."

"But not fer ye, Katherine. We both know that ye want something different, something more."

He looked so earnest, so sincere. Katherine felt a blast of guilt shiver down her spine. Lachlan had kept faith with her. He had found her when she was ill, saved her from Archibald Fraser, promised to return her home without a ransom.

He had treated her with kindness, respect, and dignity. Withholding the full truth about her hopes for their possible marriage made it feel like a betrayal of sorts.

"I must be honest, Lachlan. 'Tis not only the need to make certain I dinnae become Hamish Drummond's wife that prompted my proposal to ye." Katherine's heart started thumping in hard, irregular beats. "I've developed a strong attraction to ye that I dinnae understand, that I cannae fully explain. All I can do is feel it."

He favored her with a gentle smile. "'Tis bothersome, isn't it?"

Mortified, Katherine turned her head and bit her lip. "Och, there's no need to mock me."

"Ye misunderstand me, lass. Though I resisted, I feel it too." He took her hand and held it between his own. "My blood heats and my heart quickens whenever I glance at ye. I swear, at times the need to kiss ye is so strong it weakens my knees."

"Why do ye resist?" she whispered.

He raised his hand and lightly brushed her cheek with his knuckles. "I fear the spark I'm trying so hard to quell will ignite and the flames will scorch us both."

Katherine shivered. The sheer, solid strength of him nearly overwhelmed her. He was beautiful in a raw, rugged, masculine way that made her heart ache. There was no other man who could compare to him. Regardless of the circumstances, she was determined to have him. If not as a husband, at least as a lover.

Katherine sidled near and trailed her fingertips sensually down his arm. "This attraction between us need not remain unfulfilled," she said with a throaty voice.

Katherine leaned against him, brushing her lips against his, softly, tentatively. Lachlan groaned. Encouraged, Katherine deepened the kiss, pushing her tongue inside the warmth of his mouth. He placed his arm around her waist, holding her tightly in place.

Not that it was needed. Katherine doubted she could have moved away if the monastery suddenly caught on fire. Their kiss was filled with passion and honesty and she strained with the need to prove to him that he was the man she wanted. She would choose no other, accept no other.

The ardor of their kisses slowly grew and Katherine's need for him heightened with each stroke of their tongues. Lachlan's hand moved slowly up her ribs and she angled herself close to his heat.

Her breath caught when he cupped her breast, brushing across the sensitive nipple with his thumb. A tingle of intense pleasure bolted through her. She rocked her body against his, longing for more.

Lachlan's lips broke away from hers. His mouth glided down the curve of her neck, causing her body to shiver. Katherine's hands reached urgently for him but he stopped their progress.

"We must not."

"Why?" she cried in frustration.

"Ye know why."

He nuzzled her temple and Katherine struggled to clear her head. How could Lachlan be so practical, so levelheaded in this moment? Did he not sense her yearning, hear the rapid pounding of her heart, see the excitement and desire in her eyes?

"I've had three long, torturous days to consider our future," he said hoarsely. "I've had countless discussions with yer brother and called upon my years of experience dealing with the powerful Lowland lairds to aid me in devising a strategy that will allow me to take ye as my wife and still protect my clan."

Katherine's head reared. His wife? Did she hear him correctly? His words caused a riot of emotions within her, ranging from relief to excitement to concern.

"Are ye truly prepared to face my father?" Katherine asked breathlessly. "I warn ye, there is no other like him. He is every inch the stubborn, proud Highland laird."

"I'm counting upon it." Lachlan swallowed hard. "'Tis still a risk, but the odds are in my favor. Our favor. I've spoken with Graham and made all the arrangements with Brother Gregory and Father Joseph."

"Arrangements?"

"Aye. 'Twas important to me that at least one male member of yer family gives us his blessing and attends this most solemn and important event."

Lachlan went down on one knee. Katherine gasped. He raised his head, held out his hands, and took hold of hers. "Will ye marry me, Katherine?"

The chapel was small, with beautifully embroidered cloths adorning the altar and an intricately designed metal cross hanging above it. Someone had taken the time to add another touch of beauty by also placing a vase with a small bunch of snowdrops in the center of the altar.

Katherine smiled when she saw the delicate white flowers, an ironic reminder of the afternoon that she had left the safety of the MacTavish Keep with young Cameron and nearly been taken by the Fraser laird.

Lachlan had saved her that day. Just as he was doing now. She noted that there were a number of McKenna retainers crowded into the small church and Katherine was pleased that she would not be wed in secrecy. She nodded her thanks to them as she walked down the small aisle with Graham and accepted the hand Lachlan held out to her.

Brother Gregory assisted Father Joseph with the ceremony. Lachlan spoke his vows in a clear, strong voice and Katherine tried to do the same, pleased that her voice didn't waver when she repeated the words that bound her to Lachlan for all eternity.

As they knelt for the priest's blessing, Katherine glanced at her brother. His expression was solemn, but he smiled and nodded his head. His approval warmed her heart. She was glad to have someone from her family attending her nuptials, demonstrating that no matter how her father reacted, she could count on her brother's support.

After the priest finished his blessing, Brother Gregory presented Lachlan with a scroll.

"'Tis a record of the ceremony, signed by myself and Father Joseph. Despite the number of witnesses, Laird McKenna might require further proof of the validity of yer marriage and there are others who might challenge the union. Scores of men in the Highlands and Lowlands vied fer the hand of Lady Katherine and some will openly resent, mayhap even confront, the man who captured the prize."

Katherine appreciated Brother Gregory's tact by not specifically mentioning Hamish Drummond, though they all knew to whom he was referring.

"I shall hold and protect my wife at all costs," Lachlan proclaimed in a strong voice, accepting the document.

There was a rumble of noise as several of the men, led by Graham, started stomping their feet in approval.

"Aren't ye going to kiss yer bride, Laird?" one of the men called out.

Lachlan glanced at Katherine, raising his eyebrows

questioningly. She smiled. A kiss sounded like the perfect way to honor the vows they had just spoken.

Lachlan bent his head. His kiss was light, gentle, a caress with not only his lips, but his tongue. Katherine felt a trembling begin deep inside her, a tantalizing promise of what was to come. She savored the kiss, longing to explore the delightful cravings that had started swirling within her.

To that end, Katherine boldly slipped her tongue along Lachlan's lips, teasing him. He growled low in his throat and ran his hand down her back, cupping her bottom. She gasped at the intimate touch.

Dimly, she heard the sound of a cough. Lachlan broke away. She stared up at him with luminous eyes, her heart beating at an irregular rhythm. His fingers caressed her cheek and his thumb slowly traced her damp, swollen lips.

Her face flushed. Candlelight flickered in the chapel, bathing his features in an almost golden glow. He was a glorious male specimen—so strong, handsome, and powerful.

And he was all *hers!*

Katherine felt the ground give way beneath her at the realization and a nervous thrill shuddered through her body. There was so much to absorb in that moment that she had difficulty separating and understanding the myriad emotions swirling through her.

There was relief that she was free of Hamish Drummond and a feeling of triumph that she had managed to escape a marriage to him. There was a sense of excitement and pleasure at becoming Lachlan's wife. He possessed the courage and honor she most admired in a man and wanted in a husband.

However, there was also a twinge of apprehension

and uncertainty over their future. Lachlan's initial reluctance in committing to the union concerned her—would he soon come to regret his decision if she didn't please him? And what, precisely, did she need to do to make him happy?

'Twas almost sinful how good it felt to kiss him. Did he feel the same? His eyes told her that he desired her. Yet as he had so profoundly stated lust was not love. When a man's heated blood needed to be quenched any female would do, and above all, she did not want to be any wench to him.

She blushed at the feelings of desire Lachlan was able to evoke in her, even feeling a strange tremor when she heard the deep timbre of his voice. Always curious, she was excited at the prospect of greater intimacy with him.

In his arms she felt the stirrings of great passion, the type she had always hoped she would experience with her husband. From what she knew of him, she believed he was a man who would not just take from a woman, but also give in return.

But would he give her love?

She was a McKenna through and through, possessing a strong need to love and in turn be loved. Katherine knew that she would come to love her husband, yet was unsure how she would cope if he never came to love her in return. Would she turn bitter? Hateful? Or would she graciously learn to accept whatever joys they were fortunate to share, along with the sorrows and disappointments?

They turned together, preparing to leave the chapel, and the men all gave a heartfelt cheer. Katherine remained silent as Lachlan took her hand and led her outside. She flushed at the familiar, possessive way his hand held hers, enjoying the contact.

"I know that this was not the wedding ye always envisioned," Graham said as he embraced her.

"I've no regrets. Truly. I only hope that ye'll not suffer Father's wrath fer the role that ye played," Katherine said honestly, grateful for her younger brother's support.

"I look to yer husband's good sense and tact to keep us both in Father's good graces," Graham said with a smile.

"I dinnae wish to court disaster by mentioning his name, but I must know. Where is Sir Hamish?" Katherine inquired. "I half expected him to come charging down the chapel aisle during our wedding ceremony, brandishing a sword and cursing us all to Hades."

Graham and Lachlan shared a conspiring look. "Drummond is passed out drunk in one of the monks' cells. Brother Gregory was charitable enough to assign him a chamber with a door lock. Though 'tis doubtful he will regain his senses anytime soon, we locked Drummond in the cell, just in case he awakens before dawn."

"Ye've thought of everything," she remarked with a grin, heartened to witness her brother and Lachlan working together.

It boded well for future family relations, which were sure to be strained once her family—especially her father—learned of her marriage to the MacTavish laird.

A glint of satisfaction eased into Lachlan's eyes. "I'm glad that I've pleased ye."

Katherine nodded, but her joy was short-lived. "We cannae be together tonight," she regretfully whispered to Lachlan. "The abbey has strict rules about men and women sharing the same chamber, even if they are married."

"I respect Brother Gregory and wouldn't abuse his hospitality so blatantly," Lachlan replied. "However, I'll not be denied my bride so soon after our vows have been exchanged."

Her heart leapt with excitement. Intrigued, Katherine bowed her head and asked, "How can that be?"

"Do ye not know that ye've married a wise and capable man? In addition to the wedding ceremony, I made the appropriate arrangements fer our wedding night."

His lips curved up in a mischievous smile that made him look carefree and years younger. It brought such bliss to Katherine's heart to see his delight that she found she could not cease smiling back at him.

"Married less than five minutes and ye are already bringing me joy," she quipped, her smile widening. "I knew that where ye were concerned, Lachlan Mac-Tavish, I was right to trust my instincts."

Chapter Fifteen

Lachlan tightened his hold on Katherine's hand and led her through the courtyard and away from the monastery. The moon broke through the clouds, but the path was difficult to negotiate in the darkness and she had to squint to find her way. Her feet stumbled on the uneven ground. Instantly, Lachlan's arm curled around her waist, preventing a fall.

"Thank ye," Katherine muttered, before stumbling again.

"Bloody hell," Lachlan swore. "Fergive me. I should have brought a torch to light our way."

Katherine was about to tell him that she was fine when he stopped, reached down, slid his hand beneath her knees, and lifted her into his arms. Squeaking in surprise—and delight—she laced her fingers together behind his neck.

"Och, now that's much better," she teased. "When ye lose yer footing, we'll both take a tumble."

He laughed. "Aye, lass, we'll be tumbling fer hours, that I can promise ye."

His tone was sultry and intimate. Katherine could

almost feel her blood start to heat. Lowering her eyes, she joined in his amusement.

He walked through a dense copse of trees into a hidden clearing. In the distance, Katherine spied the fabric of a tent, nestled within the trees. They entered and Lachlan set her down. She heard the strike of a flint and soon the soft glow of candlelight filled the space.

"How on earth did ye manage to get a proper bed in here?" she asked, amazed at the sight.

"The MacTavish are resourceful men," he replied, gathering her again in his arms. "Only the finest will suffice fer my bride, so I made certain to provide it. I'm glad that it pleases ye."

"It does."

Katherine couldn't fully see his face in the dim shadows, but she could feel the heat of his body, hear the sounds of his breathing. He smelled of clean soap and fresh air and hungry male. 'Twas a heady mix.

Shivers of anticipation coursed through her. She felt cold all over, then flushed with heat. Taking a deep breath, Katherine willfully pushed any doubts about the future from her mind. This was her wedding night and she was going to open her heart, surrender her body, and find as much pleasure from it as possible.

Lachlan cradled her face in his hands and kissed her, his mouth moving restlessly against her lips. Katherine responded, parting her lips and sliding her tongue forward. Their kisses grew slowly in intensity until they were sending a restless, dizzy excitement through her. Lachlan's hands slid down her sides to her hips, then around to her bottom. Her pulse spiked as a trembling ache claimed her. His touch was gentle, soft, and infinitely arousing.

He broke their kisses and when she opened her

eyes, she was staring directly into his. "I like it when ye kiss me," she whispered.

"'Tis but the start," he promised. "We've all night, Katherine. No need to rush."

Lachlan moved to the small table near the bed. He poured two goblets of wine, handing one to her. She gazed into the dark liquid, then raised her vessel in a toast.

"To us," she said solemnly.

"Yer happiness," he replied, raising his goblet higher.

Only mine? What of yers? Trying not to read too much into his words, Katherine took a small sip. The wine was tasty, with a rich, smooth flavor that coated her tongue. She took another gulp, then placed her goblet on the table.

She had eaten little supper and did not want the wine to muddle her head. Nay, she wanted to be in possession of her full senses tonight.

"I wish that I could have worn a more suitable gown fer the ceremony," Katherine said, smoothing her hand over the dusty skirt of her dress. "I wanted to look pretty fer ye."

"Ye are beautiful." His lips parted in a rakish smile. "I'll let ye in on a little secret, lass. A man prefers his woman without her clothes."

His woman. Her heart quickened. She liked the way that sounded—very much.

"Do ye need my help?" Lachlan asked.

Katherine stared stupidly at him for a moment, then realized he meant removing her garments.

"Aye. Would ye unlace the section down the center of my back?"

She turned, showing him what she meant. He downed the remainder of his wine and reached for her. It took several moments to successfully untie the knot securing the laces at the top of her gown and even longer to pull them free. Katherine lowered her head and smiled, secretly pleased to discover Lachlan's fumbling unfamiliarity with women's clothing.

After he bared her back, he slowly ran his finger along her spine. The warm touch stormed her senses, making her shiver with anticipation. His fingers next threaded through her hair as he searched for the pins binding it tightly to her scalp.

Lachlan removed them carefully, unbraiding her locks until they were free of constraint. Unbound, Katherine's hair tumbled beyond her shoulders to her waist in a thick, glorious shower.

She could feel his fingers gliding through the silken strands. The sweet caress made her catch her breath and a bloom of warmth spread through her lower body. Eagerly, she tugged down her sleeves and chemise, baring her upper torso.

Lachlan released a low exclamation of pleasure. Encouraged, Katherine rubbed her damp palms on her skirt, then pushed the garment down past her hips. She pivoted on trembling legs and turned to face him. Lachlan's eyes skimmed over her naked flesh in quiet admiration, emboldened her to stand tall and proud, despite the nerves that fluttered in her stomach.

"Ye are quite lovely, Wife," he said in a husky, sultry tone that sent a pulse of desire rippling through her.

The heat of a blush warmed her cheeks and she lowered her head. But only for an instant.

"I should like to gaze upon my husband as well," she said softly. "Unclothed."

Lachlan favored her with a lazy, almost lopsided smile and reached for the collar of his tunic. He pulled it up and over his head, removed his shirt, and made quick work of divesting himself of his boots and trews.

Katherine sucked in a sharp breath at the sight of him. The candlelight shimmered over his muscular physique and the dusting of hair that sprinkled his chest. His waist was narrow, his arms and thighs heavy with muscles. His strength was daunting, masterful, thrilling.

She moved closer, drawn to his magnetism. He stroked the side of her face with his thumb, then tipped her chin. His eyes darkened and Katherine knew that he was going to kiss her. She circled her arms around his neck, raised herself up on her toes, and leaned closer, molding her body to his.

With a low growl of impatience, Lachlan's lips found hers. She gloried in the kiss—the sensual feeling of his soft lips moving over hers, the stroke of his tongue, the pleasing scent of fresh soap and sunshine. He tasted as wonderful as she remembered and she pressed forward, eager for more.

He held her in a tight, possessive embrace and she clung to him with equal fervor, raw emotion seeping out of every pore. She could feel the furious hammering of his heart against her own, delighted to discover his passion for her was equally consuming.

Their kisses grew deeper, stronger, almost frenzied. Katherine felt her control spiraling and slipping as she gave herself over to the bold, swirling feelings Lachlan so easily evoked inside her.

The ropes of the bed groaned beneath them. He rolled her onto her back, his heated weight pressing her into the straw mattress. She gazed into his eyes and felt her heart start to throb with a sweet, tender ache.

They were married, bound together for the rest of

their days. The wonder of it all was almost too impossible to believe.

"I want ye to find pleasure in our joining," he said softly. "Though I've heard the first time can be painful fer a maiden."

"I'll not break," Katherine promised, moving her legs restlessly.

Lachlan smiled. His muscles were taut, his eyes glazed with desire. Without warning, he pressed his open mouth to her throat and she was so startled by the caress that she cried out.

He seemed to enjoy her response, nipping playfully at her collarbone before moving across her chest. His mouth traveled temptingly over her breast and then suddenly he pulled her nipple into his mouth.

Katherine moaned, arching toward the pleasure he created as he suckled enthusiastically. Her hands reached for him, threading through his hair, holding him close. She could hear her rapid and uneven breathing, could feel the flush of desire rise from her chest. Lachlan overwhelmed her senses and she responded instinctively, allowing the passion between them to break free.

His hands and mouth seemed to be everywhere. He feathered kisses lower, down her ribs, across her stomach, coming to rest at the top of the curls between her thighs. Katherine lay utterly still, her breathing halted.

Nay, he couldn't mean to . . .

She cried out as she felt his tongue glide over the slick, aching bud of her womanhood. Good Lord, how could he know to do this to her? 'Twas indecent, immoral, depraved—and utterly glorious!

Her body seemed to come alive, the sensitive heat pulsing between her legs. It felt so wicked to have his mouth against her flesh. She was shocked and slightly embarrassed, but any protests of modesty died on her lips as the pleasure kept rolling over her, through her.

He cupped her bottom and lifted her to his lips. Stroke after stroke, his tongue curled against her in the most intimate, provocative kiss. Every nerve ending tingled and danced with excitement. She felt mindless in her need for him, in her cravings for the satisfaction his questing hands and tongue promised her.

She moved her hips closer to his teasing tongue, pressing against his mouth, desperately searching for a release from the exquisite torture. With each new caress, she could feel herself starting to lose control. Suddenly, Katherine shoved her fist in her mouth, stifling her screams of ecstasy as her body crested the peak.

When it ended, she felt boneless, contented, and completely spent. Slowly, she looked up, having only the strength to half open her eyelids. Lachlan loomed above her, his body tight, his breathing labored.

She could feel the evidence of his desire, thick, stiff, and heavy against her belly. His knee slipped between her thighs, nudging them apart, pressing his arousal against her still-throbbing womanhood. She reached out to him, hardly believing they could find even greater pleasure together.

"The pain might be sharp, but hopefully swift," he promised.

Their bodies merged. Shocked, Katherine bucked, barely managing to smother her cry of pain. Lachlan immediately stilled. He held her close, nuzzling her cheek with his forehead, pressing his lips against her hair. Wrapped in the circle of his arms, Katherine gradually felt her body start to relax.

"Is it over?" she whispered.

He groaned, his breath hot and moist against her ear. "I'm not yet fully inside ye."

"Oh." She chewed her lower lip. That was most unfortunate.

Lachlan pushed himself onto his elbows and gazed down at her. Katherine averted her eyes, unable to look at him. It had started so well. She'd felt his passion and it had intrigued her, excited her.

He had done wicked things to her body—kissing her in the most intimate places—and she had reveled in it. Their joining was the culmination of a carnal promise that began with their very first kiss. And instead of being the fulfillment she had so eagerly anticipated, it had cooled her ardor faster than a bucket of ice water.

"It takes time fer a couple to learn the best rhythm," he said gently, brushing a damp strand of hair off her brow. "We need not rush. We have all night. We have a lifetime."

The sudden shyness and embarrassment that gripped Katherine slowly eased. He wasn't angry or disappointed. Thank goodness.

"I do want ye, Lachlan," she insisted, raising her hips.

His cock pushed farther inside her and the discomfort returned, but she forced herself to ignore it. His fingers skimmed along her thighs, gently massaging her flesh, attempting to soothe her.

"Wrap yer legs around my waist," he instructed. "I promise ye willnae be disappointed."

Trustingly, Katherine did as he requested, wriggling her bottom to better position herself. Lachlan dipped his head toward her breast, capturing the nipple between his lips. He pulled hard, suckling her until a moist heat pooled between her thighs and the restless desire once again began to stir.

Katherine's breath grew erratic as he continued to arouse her with his hand and lips. Gradually, the flush of passion and yearning returned. Their eyes locked and held as Lachlan slowly slid inside her, inch by inch. The pain eased and her body yielded and Katherine felt herself once again trembling with desire.

Reaching out, she touched his chest and shoulders, marveling anew at his strength and magnetism.

"Better?" he muttered.

She nodded, hardly recognizing his voice, deep and hoarse with longing. His caring and concern touched her heart, spearing it with a fit of possessiveness.

Mine! He belongs to me just as I belong to him.

Gripping the taut cheeks of his buttocks, Katherine pulled him toward her. Understanding her need, Lachlan drove into her deeper. He had promised her greater delights and she fully intended to experience them.

The cool night air brushed against her face, but Lachlan's heat radiated through her. It was the most extraordinary feeling to be joined together thusly, but there was no time to think upon it. Every nerve ending in her body was alive with a growing excitement.

His thrusts increased in speed and intensity. Faster, harder, deeper, stirring her body into an almost wicked frenzy of want and need. She could feel the raw strength and power of his flesh pounding against her, reminding her that in this act they were equal participants, equal partners. They were no longer two, but one, joined together in mutual need, desire, and passion.

Lachlan wedged his hand between their bodies, placing his fingers at the juncture of her thighs. Pressing against her most sensitive spot, he rubbed the delicate nub and Katherine felt herself quickening again.

Her hand gripped the blanket, balling it between her fisting hands. The sweet spasm of another climax took her unexpectedly and this time she allowed herself to cry out her pleasure. This time she held nothing back as her body exploded.

Lachlan quickly joined her. She could feel his cock pulse and jerk within her as every muscle in his body strained and then went still. The warm rush of his seed bathed her womb. He fell forward, landing heavily atop her, his breath coming in short, loud pants.

Katherine's arms rose to cradle and embrace him. She kissed his neck and nuzzled against the scruff of whiskers along his jaw. Emotions she never imagined flowed through her, bringing tears to her eyes.

The connection, the feeling of belonging together, of being important and valued by her husband, was humbling. She had hoped consummating their marriage would be pleasant—and it had been—but she was surprised by the depths of joy that she felt.

Not wanting to break the physical contact, Katherine rested her head on Lachlan's shoulder, her cheek pressed against the strong bone. It was covered in a fine sheen of sweat and she breathed in the tangy scent of sex and intimacy, reveling in the moment.

He finally lifted his head, then took her fingers and brought them to his lips. "Are ye well?"

"Aye. Wonderful. Glorious. Awed, sated, and sticky," she said with a giddy laugh.

"Me too." Lachlan sat up and slipped out of the bed, returning with a basin filled with water and a small cloth. "Fer ye, milady."

"Thank ye." Grateful, and slightly embarrassed by Lachlan's forethought, Katherine stood, dipped the linen into the water, wrung it out, then turned her back and washed herself.

When she was finished, Katherine handed the cloth to Lachlan. She watched beneath lowered lids as he swirled the cloth over his chest, arms, and finally between his legs.

"I'm sorry the water is so cold," he said when he was finished.

"'Twas soothing," Katherine admitted, flashing him a sheepish grin.

"Wait!" Lachlan held up his hand to stop her from climbing back into the bed. "Our bodies are not the only thing that needs to be washed. I asked Brother Gregory to give me another sheet, so we may slumber in comfort."

'Twas then Katherine noticed the specs of red marring the white linen—her virgin's blood. Working together, they removed the stained linen and replaced it with the fresh one.

"We need to keep it," Katherine declared, folding the soiled linen and holding it close to her heart. "'Tis proof that we have consummated our marriage, proof that we have an unbreakable union."

Lachlan shook his head. "Sheets streaked with blood prove naught. On a wedding night they are easily fabricated using a cut on the body in a place not seen or a vial of animal blood." Lachlan gently removed the linen from Katherine's hands. "Yer family will believe we are in truth married and I shall attest to yer purity if Drummond or any of his kin dares to question our word."

"I want nothing to challenge the validity of our marriage," Katherine said.

Lachlan tilted her face to his. "One look at yer glowing, contented face and everyone will know exactly what has passed between us."

Katherine worried her bottom lip between her teeth. "Will it be enough? I confess to being pleased there were none here to conduct a bedding ceremony, but one would have provided the required proof that the marriage has been consummated. The few bedding ceremonies I have witnessed were torturous fer the couple, especially the bride, but they made certain the marriage could not be challenged."

Lachlan shrugged and climbed onto the newly made bed. "A bedding ceremony is mild compared to the English practice of consummating the marriage while others stay within the chamber, so they can testify the act has been completed."

"Nay!" Katherine exclaimed in horror. "What couple would allow such an embarrassing thing? And what sort of person would want to witness such an intimate, private act? Ye're jesting."

"'Tis the God's honest truth," Lachlan insisted. "The bed curtains are closed during the consummation, so the witnesses cannae gawk."

"Och, but they can hear." Katherine shuddered.

"Far more than one wants."

"Ye attended one of these?" she asked, her voice hitching in shock.

"Aye. Not by choice. The bride was English, the groom a Scotsman."

"And the English have the nerve to call the Scots barbarians," Katherine remarked with a cluck of her tongue.

Lachlan rose to his knees and extended his hand. "From this day forward, I vow that none shall be allowed to gawk at yer lovely naked form or listen to yer cries of passion except me."

With a smile, Katherine accepted his hand and climbed in beside him. "And none shall gaze upon yer splendid physique or hear yer groans and grunts of ecstasy except me."

"Groans and grunts of ecstasy?" Lachlan repeated, lifting a brow.

Katherine fought off a giggle. "Aye. They are most inspiring, Husband."

"Minx!" He swatted playfully at her rump, but she dodged his hand and instead landed a blow on his backside. With a mocking growl, he captured her in his arms and pulled her beneath the covers.

Katherine shrieked with laughter and struggled against his hold. His arms were like iron. She pushed against them with all her strength, yet was unable to free herself. Tiring from her efforts, she surrendered to the inevitable, and snuggled against his chest.

It felt heavenly to be in his arms. Safe, protected, cherished. The candlelight flickered against the fabric of the tent. The air was cool, but it was warm and cozy beneath the covers, with their mingled body heat.

Taking a deep breath, Katherine allowed her mind to rest and soon found herself falling into the safe, peaceful darkness of sleep.

Lachlan pressed his back against the rough headboard and pulled Katherine against him so that her head rested on his naked chest, over his heart. She draped herself over him like a luscious blanket, her right leg thrown carelessly over his thigh. Bathed in the soft glow of candlelight, her expression was one of pure contentedness and utter relaxation and her deep even breaths filled the tent.

Alas, an equally peaceful slumber eluded Lachlan. He curled his arm around her waist and attempted to shift her to his side. She moaned in protest and burrowed closer, tickling the hair on his chest with her nose. From this angle, he could see the soft, round side of her delicious plump breast peeking through the rough linen sheet, the nipple pink and tight.

Though so recently and thoroughly sated, Lachlan could feel his body stirring again with desire at the sight. Telling himself he was strong enough to resist the temptation, Lachlan stroked her naked back lightly, savoring the smooth, silken skin.

He shifted his body lower, placing his head on the pillow. With a sigh, Lachlan closed his eyes, removing the sight of her luscious sweetness, hoping that would cool his ardor.

It didn't work. In his mind's eye he recalled every detail of their lovemaking—the sounds of her moans of pleasure, the salty taste of her excitement, the feel of her muscles tightening around him as he thrust deeply inside her.

His body responded to the memories of their recent encounter with the speed of lightning. Lachlan's breath hitched, his cock pulsed. He rocked his hips in a slow rhythm, creating a smooth pressure against the top of her thighs that soon had his breath quickening.

How she had managed to so quickly and thoroughly spark his desire was a true puzzlement. Bloody hell, the woman was sound asleep, yet still she tempted him beyond measure!

'Twas true that before tonight it had been many months since he last bedded a woman. Their earlier coupling should have taken the sharp edges off his passion.

Instead, it had only increased it.

'Twould be cruel to wake her. She was exhausted from the days of hard riding, emotionally spent from today's life-altering events. He smiled in the darkness, remembering the hard riding they had just done together.

Nay, he would be a considerate husband and not break her slumber. However, if she awoke on her own . . .

Craning his neck, Lachlan found her lips and took them in a kiss. Soft, gentle, unrushed. Katherine moaned, the lovely sound coming from deep inside her throat and vibrating against his lips. Encouraged, Lachlan trailed his fingers over her breasts, grazing the nipple.

Katherine's breath hissed into his mouth and she deepened their kiss, thrusting her lower body enthusiastically toward him. His already stiff penis grew harder and the ache in his balls made him squeeze his eyes shut.

He'd worried that she might need coaxing to make love again, but her eagerness quickly dispensed that thought and heightened his craving.

Impatience thundering in his blood, Lachlan rolled Katherine onto her back. Her legs parted in invitation and her hips rocked back and forth against his groin. Nuzzling her neck, he slipped one finger inside her, pleased to find her passage slick and ready. Catching her hips between his hands, he lifted her.

She released a long, shuddering moan when he entered her, curling her arms around his shoulders.

"Are ye sore? Does it hurt?" he inquired in a concerned voice, wondering where he would find the strength to withdraw if she asked.

"Not as before. I'm a bit tender—nay, dinnae stop!"

This time he loved her slowly, drawing out the pleasure with long, deep strokes of his body. She stared up at him in wonder, arching beneath him with each thrust, bringing herself closer to him. Yet it was not just their flesh joining. There was a spiritual, emotional communication between them that transcended the physical.

Time and again they surged together, moving as one. Her sobbing cry of release spurred his passion to new heights. Lachlan felt his body seize and pulse and he lost his breath in the storm of his fulfillment. She held him tightly through the last lingering shudders. Thoroughly spent, he collapsed on top of her.

"I'm crushing ye," he murmured in apology, praying she wouldn't agree. For if she did, Lachlan would be obliged to move and the feeling had not yet returned to his limbs. Would it ever?

She laughed, deep and throaty in his ear. "Ye are still inside me. I forbid ye to move until *all* of ye leaves me."

"Ye are a wicked wench, Katherine MacTavish," he said with a delighted laugh, allowing his fingers to dance down her skin.

"Be honest. 'Tis one of the reasons ye married me," she said with a smug smile.

"'Tis true. I like wicked women."

"As I predicted, we are a well-suited pair," she declared.

Laughing again, Lachlan shifted to his side, bringing Katherine with him. She nuzzled close and he was pleased at how easily and trustingly she relaxed in his arms.

"Try to rest," he said, placing a kiss upon her brow. "Tomorrow we arrive at McKenna Castle. If I've learned anything about yer father from ye and Graham, it will be a difficult day. Fer all of us."

Chapter Sixteen

The sight that greeted them when they rode through the large village at the base of McKenna Castle caused Lachlan's brows to rise. It looked as though the entire clan had turned out to welcome Katherine home. They lined the streets, leaned out of second-story windows, and crowded onto the parapets, shouting and cheering, calling out blessings and thanks for her safe return.

Graham and Katherine rode at the head of the procession, weaving their way slowly through the sea of people until they reached the imposing castle gates. Katherine glanced over her shoulder at Lachlan, signaling him to move forward. He spurred his mount, pushing his way past a brooding Drummond and the McKenna guards that surrounded her.

Lachlan deftly placed himself at Katherine's side and they rode together into the bailey. He could almost feel the touch of hundreds of eyes staring curiously at him as they made their way toward the group gathered in front of the entrance to the great hall.

A tall, middle-aged, broad-shouldered warrior stood in the center. Clearly, he was Katherine's father. He carried an air of absolute control, leadership, and supremacy. Even at his advanced age, the man was a formidable, battle-hardened sight.

Laird McKenna was flanked on either side by a woman. The older female was easily identified as Katherine's mother—the resemblance was striking. The younger female, well, Lachlan was uncertain who she might be, though he conceded that her blond beauty was extraordinary and breathtaking.

Two children clung to her skirts, a lass and a younger lad. Both the women and children were smiling broadly, waving as the riders approached.

However, one look at Laird McKenna's thunderous expression told Lachlan that Katherine's father had a very different feeling about his daughter's return. He glared like an angry bull preparing to charge. Lachlan swore if he looked close enough he could see a rise of steam billowing from the laird's nostrils as he snorted in anger.

Lachlan glanced at Graham, wondering exactly what details Katherine's brother had included in the message he sent to his father announcing that Katherine had been found and was on her way home. All Lachlan did know was that her refusal to honor her betrothal to Hamish Drummond was to be mentioned—her marriage to Lachlan was to be excluded.

Despite Katherine's pleas to the contrary, Lachlan had insisted the marriage not be revealed. Laird McKenna was a man who respected honor. Marrying his daughter without his permission was hardly an honorable act and Lachlan felt the best course was to reveal the news in person.

However, when Laird McKenna crossed his arms over his broad chest and pointedly glared at him,

Lachlan wondered if somehow Katherine's father knew the truth. Knew, and was far from pleased about it.

The cheers grew louder when the group on horseback reached the family welcoming party. Lachlan dismounted quickly and turned to Katherine. Her fingers lingered on his chest when he assisted her down from her horse, a tactile reminder of the intimacy they had shared, the bond that now existed between them. It boosted his courage.

As they had agreed, Lachlan draped a shawl of Mac-Tavish plaid that he carried over Katherine's shoulders before she turned to face her sire. The McKenna's eyebrows rose when he spied the garment, his expression narrowing.

"Why are ye wearing that plaid, Daughter?" he demanded.

"Katherine is my wife," Lachlan answered, loud enough so that those around them could hear. "I am Laird Lachlan MacTavish and I'm proud and honored to have her wear our clan colors."

Lachlan felt the McKenna's critical stare sweep over him. "Yer wife?"

"Aye." Lachlan nodded his head twice for emphasis, boldly meeting the challenge of the McKenna's gaze.

Katherine also nodded, sliding her arm through Lachlan's and looking up at him with an expression of pride. The McKenna shifted his eyes to his daughter for a brief moment, then glared back at Lachlan.

"Daughter!" Lady Aileen caught Katherine's hand, leaned in, kissed each cheek, and then tightly hugged her. "Finally, ye are home. Many feared the worst, but I refused to accept that anything dire would befall ye."

A look of contrition bloomed on Katherine's face. "I'm deeply sorry fer causing ye worry."

"'Tis forgiven," Lady Aileen said with a sniffle and another hug.

"Father?" Katherine looked over at the McKenna. His mouth twitched, yet he remained unapproachable. Katherine sighed and lowered her gaze repentantly to the ground.

"We are all so relieved that ye are safely returned to us at last." Breaking the awkward tension, the stunning blond woman came forward and embraced Katherine. As she lifted her arms, the material of her gown stretched over her figure and Lachlan could see the distinct, tell-tale bulge of pregnancy.

"Thank ye, Joan," Katherine replied. "I am pleased to be here with my new husband."

Lachlan smiled at the dazzling woman who was introduced to him as Malcolm McKenna's wife. He had heard tales of the tart-tongued beauty who had captured the heart of Katherine's eldest brother and was surprised to discover the stories had not been an exaggeration. Lady Joan truly was breathtaking.

The children scampered excitedly toward Katherine. She knelt, threw her arms wide, and enfolded them both in a hug. They giggled and squirmed, showering her with kisses. Soon, the laughter of the many others witnessing the reunion surrounded them.

Except the McKenna's. He neither laughed nor smiled nor made any move to embrace his daughter and welcome her home.

Looking as though he might explode, Hamish Drummond pushed his way forward. "What's this I hear? Ye are married? 'Tis all a lie! Katherine cannae be married to MacTavish. She is betrothed to me!"

"Was betrothed." Lachlan reached inside his cloak and pulled out a scroll of parchment. "We were married at Clayton Abbey last evening, as this document will attest. 'Tis signed by both the priest who married us and Brother Gregory, the monastery's abbot. Graham stood as one of our witnesses."

"Impossible!" Drummond shouted. "Brother Gregory refused my request to arrange a marriage and Graham insisted that he wouldn't allow Katherine to be wed without her parents in attendance."

"When I proposed myself as the groom, Graham wisely altered his opinion on the matter," Lachlan revealed.

There were gasps of shock and surprise, along with a few chuckles of amusement as the revelation rippled through the crowd like a wave. Lachlan swore he could feel the bodies surging closer as everyone tried to overhear more of the titillating conversation.

Seeing the parchment agitated Drummond further and malicious intent sparked in his eyes. As Lachlan read the threat, his right hand moved to the handle of the sword slung over his back.

"This is an outrage! An insult!" Drummond shouted. "Ye are a thief, MacTavish! Ye have stolen my betrothed."

"I chose Lachlan to be my husband, as was my right," Katherine declared, throwing back her shoulders and raising her chin.

"Ye picked me first," Drummond bellowed, the pulse at the base of his neck ticking furiously. "Yer father—and mine—signed a binding contract of betrothal less than a fortnight ago."

"Aye, we did," the McKenna agreed with a disparaging look at Lachlan and Katherine. "A legal document."

Katherine's brows drew together in a distressed frown. Lachlan gently squeezed her hand encouragingly. "I'm not a scholar, versed in the finer legal points of marriage, Laird McKenna. Yet 'tis clear that vows exchanged in front of a priest have more validity than a betrothal contract."

"Hogwash!" Drummond exclaimed. "This marriage must be set aside so the union agreed upon between myself and Lady Katherine can take place."

"Never," Katherine declared passionately.

Drummond made a strangled noise in the back of his throat and reached out to touch Katherine's arm. She stiffened and moved away, pressing herself closer to Lachlan.

"I bear ye no grudge, Drummond, but that will quickly change if ye persist in upsetting my wife," Lachlan stated firmly, pinning his advisory with a warning glare. "Katherine broke the betrothal and fled. She refused to take ye as her husband and is now married to me. I've had her and I intend to hold and keep her."

It took but a moment for Hamish to grasp Lachlan's meaning that the union had been consummated. Drummond growled, his expression turning bitter. He took a menacing step toward them. Lachlan pushed Katherine from his side and pulled the sword off his back.

"Hold!" the McKenna bellowed.

Lachlan froze, yet kept his weapon at the ready. "Ye will cease accosting my wife, Drummond," Lachlan said in a deathly calm voice. "Is that clear?"

Graham also stepped forward. He stood in front of Hamish, his hand centered on the man's chest.

"How dare ye treat me in such a disrespectful manner," Drummond cried, shaking his fist. "My father will be furious when he hears of these insults."

"He shouldn't be," Lachlan answered. "A true Highland laird respects a man's right to guard and protect his woman."

"Lady Katherine is mine!" Drummond protested, beating his chest with his closed fist. "Ye stole her from me and I demand justice. Ye must stand trial fer thievery." Then he spat in the dirt and began to pace like a caged beast.

Lady Aileen let out an indignant huff. "Katherine is not yer chattel. Though it might be the more common way of thinking fer most men, I can assure ye, Sir Hamish, that my daughter is no man's possession. Not even her husband's."

"Aye. I honor and respect my wife, care fer and cherish her," Lachlan said. "I dinnae own her, therefore I could not have stolen her from ye."

These unconventional comments rendered Drummond speechless; however, judging by the expressions on the faces of Katherine's family, Lachlan knew he had made the correct response. Even Laird McKenna managed to soften his glare. A wee bit.

Unfortunately, that small bit of softening vanished the moment Lady Aileen suggested they all go inside. The McKenna refused, shaking his head, widening his stance and planting his feet. Lachlan wondered if there was any force on earth that had the power to move him.

Lady Aileen repeated her request. The McKenna again refused. The two locked eyes in combat, each assuming a nearly identical stubborn countenance.

Silent tension reigned. Then suddenly, the McKenna blinked. Releasing a loud grunt of frustration, he took a few steps toward the wide wooden doors that led to the great hall.

Those around them released a breath of relief, yet undercurrents of tensions swirled between the various members of the family—and Drummond—as they fell in line behind Laird McKenna and his lady.

As Lachlan walked the long length of the McKenna's great hall, he felt more like an itinerant knight and less like a laird of equal rank. He thought himself immune to the sight of wealth and comfort, but McKenna Hall was beyond anything he had ever seen, even in the richest holdings in the Lowlands.

In truth, 'twas fit for a king.

Massive tapestries embroidered with silk and gold threads hung along the gray stone walls. There was clear glass in the narrow windows and colored panes in others. The rushes under his feet were fresh and sweet smelling, the wooden trestle tables polished to a high shine.

There were a half dozen multitiered wrought iron chandeliers strategically hung from the high rafters throughout the massive chamber. The costly beeswax candles positioned in them gave off a warm glow and a pleasant odor.

The servants scurrying to and fro looked well-fed. Their garments were clean and tidy, their faces shining with good humor and health. Even the hounds sleeping in front of the hearth appeared content and well behaved.

"I have much to share with ye," Katherine announced to her family as they gathered around the table set upon the dais.

"We are anxious to hear everything," Lady Aileen answered. "It must be a fascinating tale."

Lady Joan motioned to one of the servants and within moments platters of cold meat, cheese, meat pies, dried fruit, and brown bread were set on the table, along with pitchers of wine and ale. Broodingly, Drummond poured himself a tankard of ale and began noisily drinking. No one else touched any of the offerings.

"Mistress Innes, please take Lileas and Callum upstairs," Lady Joan instructed, casting a wary eye toward Drummond, who had already downed a second tankard and was starting on a third.

"I want to stay," the lass whined. "I want to hear Aunt Katherine's story. Callum does too."

"Hush, Lileas, and do as yer bid," Lady Joan replied in a firm voice. "Aunt Katherine will speak with ye later in yer chamber."

"When? When will she come to see us?" Lileas asked, her voice rising anxiously. "If she waits too long, Callum will fall asleep. We'll have to wake him and he'll be cross. Aunt Katherine wouldn't want that to happen."

"If Callum is asleep when she arrives, she will leave him be and speak only with ye. After all, ye are the older sister and therefore entitled to a special privilege."

"But Mama—"

"Enough! If ye continue to argue, ye willnae see yer aunt until tomorrow."

Lachlan smiled at the uncanny resemblance between the lass's whining and Hamish Drummond's complaints. 'Twas remarkable, really, to note how much the man sounded like a spoiled, petulant babe when he protested the loss of his betrothed.

Lileas's mouth turned down in a mulish frown. She crossed her arms and huffed, but a stern glare from Lady Joan silenced any forthcoming protests. After a second, louder sigh, the lass nudged her younger brother with her elbow.

"Mama says we must go." Lileas suddenly brightened. "Prince will come with us and keep us company so we willnae be lonely while we wait."

One of the hounds lounging in front of the fire lifted its head. Lachlan assumed the mangy dog was the aforementioned Prince. Lady Joan beckoned the beast. Tail wagging, it lumbered over and obediently followed the children from the chamber.

"I will speak with ye, MacTavish," the McKenna demanded, standing toe-to-toe with Lachlan. "Alone."

Katherine's eyes widened in alarm and she clutched the sleeve of Lachlan's tunic. Lachlan smiled gently and placed a comforting hand on her shoulder.

"'Tis to be expected," he said, inflecting his voice with a reassurance he didn't entirely feel.

Head high Lachlan followed Katherine's father from the great hall, girding himself for whatever objections, disapproval, and veiled threats he fully expected the McKenna to spew at him. Yet no matter what was said— or threatened—Lachlan would not yield. Katherine would remain his wife.

They entered a chamber with several large windows. There was a desk, another table piled with scrolls, and a thick woven rug covering the stone floor.

Two finely carved high-back chairs were set by the fire blazing in the hearth. The McKenna settled himself in one, then indicated Lachlan should sit in the other. Did he dare take it as a good sign that he was at least offered a seat?

"I need to decide what's to be done with ye," the McKenna said without preamble. "Drummond's protests that ye are a thief are not far off the mark. Ye did take what belonged to him. But I'll not condemn a man to lose a hand or be hung by the neck until I hear his side of the story. Explain yerself."

Lachlan held his expression steady, ignoring the deliberate provocation in the McKenna's voice. The man might be spoiling for a fight, but Lachlan was determined not to give him one.

"I've shown ye proof of my marriage to Katherine. If ye want—"

"I'm not a lackwit," the McKenna interrupted sharply. "My daughter tied herself to ye to avoid wedding Drummond. I want to know why. Did ye force her? Seduce and compromise her before ye spoke the vows?"

"Nay!" Lachlan declared vehemently. "I would never take advantage of a woman, any woman, under my protection, least of all one as gentile and refined as Katherine."

The McKenna restlessly tapped his fingertip on the arm of his chair. "Not wanting to marry Drummond is far different from wanting to marry ye." He scowled. "Ye know that ye dinnae deserve her, don't ye?"

"Aye. But I'm a damn better choice than Drummond. He would have made her life a misery. Ye already know that's why she fled. Katherine feared that ye might force her to honor the betrothal."

"I still might," the McKenna retorted with a sniff.

Though tempted to loudly protest, Lachlan resisted the bait. "I can understand that you dinnae wish to throw fuel on the fire of a feud that ye are struggling to prevent. But the cost is yer daughter's future happiness."

The McKenna shrugged. "I'll allow that Drummond has revealed a lack of character. He's young. He'll mature in time and with Katherine as his wife, he has the chance to become a far better man and a choice leader."

"I'm already a leader," Lachlan said modestly. "I dinnae expect my wife to be saddled with the task of molding me into a worthier man."

The McKenna scoffed. "If she's anything like her mother, Katherine will relish the notion."

"I'm certain Katherine willnae have to look very hard

to find flaws within me that she can try to reform," Lachlan replied with a fond grin.

The remark elicited a small crack in the McKenna's stoic demeanor. There was less open antagonism in the chamber, but Lachlan dared not relax his guard. The McKenna was a law unto himself, his power insurmountable. His mood could just as easily turn combative again.

"How do ye answer Drummond's charge of thievery?" the McKenna asked.

"I dinnae steal anything. Katherine married me of her own free will. As fer the kidnapping, my brother Aiden was the man who seized the chance to take Katherine when the opportunity presented itself," Lachlan replied.

"Fer ransom? Yet sent no messages. Why dinnae ye demand any?"

"Aiden hoped to make an exchange."

The McKenna let out a grunt. "Fer what?"

"Our youngest brother is yer prisoner. He toils in yer quarry."

"Christ's blood!" The McKenna's expression of puzzlement slowly gave way to cold appraisal. "Tell me what happened to her from the moment Katherine was kidnapped," he demanded.

Lachlan paused, wondering if it was possible to save a conversation that was rapidly slipping out of his favor. He filtered the events through his mind, trying to present the sequence in the most favorable light until he realized only the full and unvarnished truth would satisfy a man like Katherine's father.

Still, he chose his words carefully, starting slowly and gradually picking up speed as he related all that caused Katherine to be brought into his life. The only thing Lachlan deliberately omitted was Katherine's proposal, as he wanted to make certain the McKenna understood how important retaining this marriage was to Lachlan.

"Bloody hell. Ye've one brother who's a brigand—and my prisoner—and another who's a kidnapper. 'Tis an exemplary bloodline." The McKenna's sarcasm turned into a sigh.

"We're not perfect," Lachlan conceded.

"In truth, I know nothing of yer people except that the MacTavish fought beside Longshanks, against the Bruce, against *me*, in the war fer Scottish independence," the McKenna added. "I believed yer clan had vanished when Robert became king."

"We survived. Barely." Lachlan took a deep breath, ignoring the jibe. "My grandmother was a Comyn. John the Red was her first cousin. I'm sure you can appreciate the need my grandfather felt to answer the call fer justice when the Bruce stabbed John the Red on the high altar at Greyfriars Kirk."

"Not our king's finest hour," the McKenna admitted, shaking his head.

"Mistakes were made on both sides during the war, but it is long over. The MacTavish fully support the Scottish crown and the Bruce's heirs," Lachlan insisted. "We have sworn our loyalty and have kept faith with that oath. I have no regard fer the English. Fer many years I've fought with the clans in the Lowlands to keep the enemy on their side of the border."

It was a risk offering this information. Little was thought of men who sought their fortunes and pledged their swords in the service of others for coin. Yet Lachlan reasoned that the McKenna would discover it at some point. Best that he hear it directly from Lachlan.

"Ye claim to support the Bruce's son and heir. Fer how long?"

"Fer as long as he rules justly and fairly." Lachlan smiled ruefully. "We are not the first Scottish clan to switch sides in a conflict. There are many others who are not adverse to the practice, including King Robert when he sought allies to support his claim to the throne."

The McKenna snorted in acknowledgment. He reached for his tankard, drained it, then slammed the empty vessel on the table.

"I'm not unsympathetic to yer circumstances, Mac-Tavish. I can appreciate how persuasive my daughter can be when she wants something and 'tis obvious that she wanted to avoid a marriage to Drummond." The McKenna cleared his throat. "I'd be willing to compensate ye if ye set the marriage aside."

"Ye want me to abandon Katherine?"

The McKenna shrugged his shoulders, yet Lachlan could see the eagerness glittering in the older man's eyes. "I want to make peace with Laird Drummond and that will happen much faster if ye disappear. I'll pay ye half as much as ye would have received with Katherine's dowry. If ye leave within the hour, I'll even consider granting yer brother his freedom so that he may go with ye."

This was unexpected. Lachlan assumed he might need to talk his way out of being tossed in the castle dungeons. He never anticipated being bribed to renounce the marriage.

Lachlan paused. It was a good offer. As laird it was his duty to ease the burdens of his clan, but he knew he could never weaken and consider it, for it would mean losing Katherine.

"Ye place far too little value upon yer daughter,

Laird. Katherine's true worth doesn't lie in her worldly goods, but in herself. She is a female with strength and character. She will make me a fine wife and be a good mother to our children."

The McKenna cast Lachlan a suspicious look. "Ye tell a pretty tale, MacTavish. Was it yer silver tongue that convinced my daughter to take ye as her husband?"

Lachlan ignored the sarcasm. "I am humbled by Katherine's regard, fer she is a most extraordinary woman. I believe we are a well-matched pair. Far better than Katherine and Drummond."

"Weddings in the Highlands are meant to settle feuds, not start them," the McKenna said bitterly. "Hamish's anger over the breaking of this betrothal contract is a mere pittance compared to the wrath of his father. The last thing I want is a feud with the clan that resides on my southern border."

"There must be some way to appease them. Aside from dissolving my marriage," Lachlan hastily added.

The McKenna's gaze held steady. "I'm not inclined to search for another solution. If ye insist on holding fast to the marriage, ye'll have to take Katherine with the clothes on her back and nothing more. I refuse to relinquish her dowry to ye."

The McKenna's expression was most serious. Lachlan struggled to read the motives behind the words. Was this a test? A way for him to prove that he did indeed care for Katherine?

"'Tis yer decision," Lachlan said cautiously. "I'll not lie and say it doesn't matter, for my people are in need of much, including food stores to get us through the rest of the winter. But I'll not renounce Katherine over a bit of coin and goods. Though I warn ye that I willnae be pleased to have my wife pained over the slight of not bringing her rightful dowry to her marriage. She is a proud woman."

"Where, exactly, do ye think she came by that pride?" the McKenna scoffed.

"I also have concerns about the clan on my southern borders," Lachlan answered honestly. "Archibald Fraser was most displeased when he learned that I had concealed Katherine's true identity from him. Fortunately, I was able to thwart his attempt to take her from me."

"Ye could have bartered her freedom to Fraser and earned some coin fer yerself."

Lachlan nodded. "He was certainly interested, but fer years I've heard enough rumors of his cruelty to believe them. I could never consign an innocent woman to such a fate."

"Graham tells me that ye fought Fraser to save her."

Lachlan nodded. "I took his sword." Lachlan stood and reached beneath his cloak, bringing forth the weapon. "Katherine told me of the bad blood between Fraser and yer eldest son, Malcolm. I thought he would appreciate having it in his possession."

The McKenna accepted the weapon with obvious reluctance, his face puffing with indignation. "A sword fer my only daughter? That hardly makes us even."

"'Tis a start. I am willing to compromise on almost anything—except my marriage. Katherine is my wife and will remain so until God calls one of us to his side."

"Perhaps 'tis my duty to make my daughter a widow."

Lachlan felt his determination tighten. "Ye can try," he answered softly. "I'll not raise my sword first against my wife's kin, fer she loves ye all, but I will defend myself if provoked."

The McKenna gave him the slightest of smiles. Yet the glimmer of respect Lachlan thought he saw in the other man's eyes must have been a delusion, as Katherine's father then made his position very clear.

"Ye've given me much to consider. However, I've not yet decided if I'll allow the marriage to stand. In the meantime, ye shall enjoy the hospitality of my dungeons."

Chapter Seventeen

Being reunited with her mother momentarily eclipsed Katherine's worry over the conversation her father was having with Lachlan. Graham had somehow managed to remove Hamish from the great hall, affording Katherine, her mother, and her sister-in-law some much needed privacy. Yet once she had relayed some of her adventures after fleeing Drummond Castle, Katherine's thoughts again returned to her husband.

The McKenna's anger usually flared quick and hot and burned out as rapidly. But today had been different. His wrath had been deep and quiet so much so that he had not welcomed her home nor embraced her. She had been greatly disturbed by the air of hostility emanating from him and felt uncertain how to combat it.

Still, Katherine stubbornly refused to believe the father who loved her so dearly would hold this anger toward her for too long. A day? Mayhap two? More troubling to her was the gaze he had cast upon Lachlan; the McKenna had stared at her husband as though he carried the plague.

Katherine knew her father showed little mercy to those who thwarted him and she feared his vengeance could fall on Lachlan. A challenge would be issued; in all likelihood a contest of swords. The McKenna would probably appoint a champion to fight; however, if his anger remained this strong he might decide to enter the fray and wield the sword himself.

If anything happened to either of them—Katherine clasped her hand over her heart. She'd never be able to live with herself.

Katherine stood abruptly, her chair scraping noisily through the rushes. "Father and Lachlan have been alone together too long," she declared, her voice unnaturally high. "What can they possibly be discussing? I need to go in and make certain they aren't about to do anything foolish."

"Sit down, Katherine, and divest yerself of those dire imaginings," Lady Aileen said calmly.

"'Tis difficult," Katherine admitted, struggling to contain her trepidation. "Father is furious with me and I fear he will unleash that fury upon my husband."

"Yer father has long treated ye as though ye walk upon water," Joan said with a smile. "He's angry with ye and Laird MacTavish, but he'll not forsake ye."

Lady Aileen clucked her tongue. "He thinks foremost of yer welfare, Katherine. Never forget yer father holds fast to the ideal that he must protect his women, no matter what they have done. Aye, ye've caused a great deal of turmoil, but the current distance ye feel from him will ease. Yer father will fergive ye in time."

"'Tis not me that I am most worried about, Mother," Katherine replied pointedly.

Lady Aileen reached out and pulled Katherine into the chair. "The McKenna will bluster and threaten and probably shout at yer husband, but he'll do no harm without first taking Lachlan's measure and listening to his explanations."

"How can ye be so certain? Father favors severe punishment when he is angered."

Lady Aileen shook her head. "Yer father will put aside his displeasure and listen to reason. Aye, his first instinct might be to tear yer husband from limb to limb, but he willnae."

"I wish I shared yer optimism," Katherine replied grimly. Her mother's words were hardly a comfort. From limb to limb, indeed.

"Yer father is no fool. He can see how much Lachlan means to ye," Lady Aileen insisted. "The feelings ye hold fer yer husband are easily reflected in yer every gesture."

Katherine stilled. "He is my husband. Of course I care fer him."

Her mother smiled. "Ye love him, Katherine."

"I . . . I . . ."

"Ye gaze at him with yer heart in yer eyes," Joan agreed.

Katherine brushed her palm across her brow. "I had not realized it was so obvious."

"I'm happy fer ye," Lady Aileen said. "I always knew ye had the capacity to love deeply, if ye found the right man."

Katherine felt as if the wind had been knocked from her body. She had no idea that her thoughts and feelings were so easily displayed. It made her feel exposed, vulnerable. Yet there was no denying they existed.

"It frightens me," she admitted. She touched her lips, recalling the sensations of Lachlan's kisses, the arousing heat and burning need that had the power to overwhelm her. "The tight, warm rush of feelings are sometimes so intense they almost hurt. They fill me completely, until I am close to bursting with emotions."

Lady Aileen and Joan exchanged a knowing look.

"There's nothing to compare to that first blush of love," Joan said. "It fades and changes over time, holding true and somehow getting stronger. It will steady ye through the difficult times, easing yer burdens and dulling the disappointments that we all must face in life."

"What of Lachlan's love fer me?" Katherine asked. "Do I dare to dream that one day he will gift me with it? And if he cannae, will I be able to bear the pain of longing fer what will never be?"

Lady Aileen took Katherine's hand and held it between her own. "Sometimes love needs time to grow and blossom. He married ye, knowing he'd need to fight to keep ye as his wife. 'Tis a good sign."

Katherine's eyes narrowed. "He's a Highland laird through and through. He'll battle anyone who dares to take what he believes is rightfully his."

"Lachlan declared most vehemently that ye are not his possession," Joan reminded her. "He is a man, and therefore hides his true feeling, but he gazes at ye with awe and treats ye with respect and deference. Ye could have done far worse in making this match."

Her sister-in-law's observations gave Katherine pause. Joan's tragic past had left deep scars of distrust and dislike of men. Though Malcolm's love had softened Joan's harsh edges, she rarely had anything good to say about any man, except when speaking of her own husband.

"Yer words bring me comfort, Joan. At times I fear my affection fer Lachlan might have distorted my good opinion of him," Katherine confessed in a soft whisper.

"Ye are a sensible woman," Joan replied. "Dinnae question or doubt the strength and validity of yer feelings. They are meant to be shared with the one ye love."

Katherine's stomach dipped. The very thought of sharing her love with Lachlan brought on a rush of warmth. Not just a physical connection—which was a delight and joy unto itself—but an emotional bond. All her life she had harbored such hopes for her marriage. Would they finally become real?

Lady Aileen's brows drew together. "There are some men who believe that love between a husband and wife is a foolish fantasy, a delusion of silly maidens too unworldly to know any better."

"Ye have described Hamish Drummond most accurately, Mother." The cloud of dread slowly lifted as Katherine realized how close she had come to calling that beastly man her husband. "Fortunately, Lachlan has a different opinion or else I would never have married him."

"Good." Lady Aileen nodded her head approvingly. "Mark my words well, Daughter. In time he will come to cherish ye."

Katherine took a steady breath, drawing calmness and faith from her mother and sister-in-law's support of her marriage and hope for her future. They both appeared certain that the love she craved so deeply was indeed within her reach.

The women grew silent, each caught up in their own thoughts. Their tranquil mood was soon shattered by the arrival of the McKenna. He stomped into the great hall as though he were laying siege to an enemy castle. Undaunted, Katherine seized the chance and approached her father.

"Good day," she said cautiously.

"Good?" The McKenna scowled. "I think not."

Instead of his usual smile for her, the McKenna snarled. It hurt. Tears gathered, but didn't fall. She needed to be strong if she was going to convince her father to see her side of things.

"Ye're still angry with me," she said, her voice low and mournful.

"I have the right," the McKenna stated. "A willful, disobedient, reckless daughter is a disappointment fer any father."

"'Tis obvious that I have fallen out of yer favor. Yet I make no apologies fer my actions, so please, let loose yer ire and chastise me as ye will. I'll not cower and hide. I'll face ye with my head held high."

Katherine threw back her shoulders. Her father still glowered, taut lines pulling grimly on his mouth, yet she sensed a small change. Was it her imagination or did he truly eye her with some respect?

"I hear no regret in yer voice fer the havoc ye've caused, the mistakes ye've made," the McKenna challenged.

"I regret that I worried ye and Mother," Katherine answered promptly. "I regret that some of the loyal McKenna men who sought to protect me when I had to flee were injured when I was captured and others suffered yer displeasure. I regret that I have placed ye in a difficult position with Laird Drummond. But ye gave me little choice, Father."

A muscle in the McKenna's cheek jumped. "Ye dare to make me the villain? The tyrant?"

"Nay! I was frightened, upset, and I acted upon those strong emotions. I'm not too witless to understand the enormity of my misdeeds and I take responsibility fer my foolish actions, but I would do the same again."

"Did ye not trust me, Katherine? Did ye truly believe that I would force the marriage with Hamish and allow ye to be so miserable?"

The hurt in her father's voice rattled her, the anguish on his face struck her like a slap. "I only knew that I needed to save myself," she confessed lamely.

"Ye've no idea how frantic I felt when Brochan told me that ye'd been taken. The weight that pressed down upon my chest made it hard to breathe. There was no ransom demand, no clue to where ye might be. My blood ran cold as I imagined yer possible fate. I felt powerless fer the first time in my life and it nearly unmanned me."

The McKenna's breath left his lungs in a low, tormented hiss. Katherine's eyes filled with tears.

"I am deeply sorry fer that pain." Swallowing hard, she asked humbly, "Fergive me?"

Gradually, the accusations in the McKenna's expression eased. He scowled, yet held out a hand toward her. With a cry, Katherine threw her arms around his neck and buried her face into his shoulder.

The McKenna placed his palm on her head and patted it awkwardly. "Enough tears. Yer mother willnae cease scolding me if she sees that I've made ye cry."

Katherine sniffled and burrowed her head deeper into her father's strength. "These are tears of happiness. I cannae bear to have such animosity between us."

The McKenna cleared his throat loudly. "All is not so easily settled between us, Daughter. What of this sudden marriage to MacTavish? Were ye so desperate to avoid Drummond that ye made a hasty, poor decision without considering fully what it means?"

Blushing, Katherine withdrew from her father's embrace. "The need to arrive home already married did exist, yet I made no compromise in my selection. Lachlan was my choice, the right choice."

"That remains to be seen," her father said grudgingly.

Katherine grinned. The father she had always known had returned. Powerful and in command, his emotions masked and hidden so as not to let any hint of weakness emerge.

"Speaking of Lachlan, where is my husband?" Katherine asked, casting her gaze around the great hall.

Her father's conciliatory mood diminished. He raised his chin and looked at her with eyes filled with strength and determination. "There is much more that I need to learn about him before I will sanction this marriage. Lachlan MacTavish awaits his fate in the most appropriate location I could think of—the dungeon."

Katherine felt her heart accelerate and knew it was not only due to the speed at which she ran through the great hall. The fear that was attacking her mind went beyond the dire imaginings her mother had so glibly told her to ignore.

Lachlan in chains, beaten and bloody, perhaps even unconscious. Her chest constricted and she struggled to breathe. Hoisting her skirts so she could run unimpeded, Katherine raced down the stone stairway, taking the steps two at a time. Darkness shrouded her way as she descended into the bowels of the castle, her heart thumping in such a sharp, frantic rhythm her entire body shook.

In her grandfather's time, prisoners were kept in the tower, since it was the strongest part of the castle and the area that could be best defended if they tried to escape. But when her father made changes and strengthened the dwelling's defenses, he decided to use the least desirable section of their home to imprison those who offended him and built a dank, dark vault in the cellar.

The stench hit her like a wall when she reached the middle of the staircase. Damp earth, putrid air, and stale urine assaulted her nostrils, but she never broke stride. Darkness enveloped her. The cold draft was all that told her she had reached the bottom of the stairs, but the fear pulsing through her urged her feet forward.

"Lachlan? Lachlan? Where are ye? Dear God, can ye hear me? Are ye injured?"

"I'm fine, Katherine."

Lachlan's voice came booming out of the darkness. Katherine lunged, then swore as her forward progress was halted by a wall of iron bars. Frustrated, she pushed her arm through, pressing in as far as the barrier would allow.

"Where are ye? In here? Lachlan? Damnation, I cannae see a damn thing. I need a torch."

Cursing loudly, she stomped back to the stairway, climbed to the top, and using both hands and a considerable amount of strength, yanked a heavy, lit torch from its holder. Swinging it wide, she managed to spread a sparse, eerie light that illuminated her way back down the stairs, and through the narrow passage to her husband.

Lachlan stood against the far wall of the small cell, feet spread, arms crossed. She saw defiance in his stance and the way he held his head high. The only sign of any agitation was the tightening of his fingers and the slight shifts of muscles along his jaw where his teeth were clenched.

The sight brought her the briefest moment of relief,

quickly replaced with shame and a heavy dose of guilt. This was all her fault. She had badly miscalculated her father's reaction to her defiance and Lachlan was paying the price. How misused by her he must feel!

"Och, Lachlan." Katherine reached through the bars, needing to feel close to him.

"Shh, Katherine, dinnae fuss. All will be well."

"I shall do far more than fuss," she cried, casting him a confused, frustrated look that earned her a gentle smile. "I shall box my father's ears. Or better still, tell my mother to do it!"

The cell was foul, damp, and filthy, reeking like a swine pen. Yet he smiled at her. Smiled? She wanted to weep and wail, to scream like a shrew and throw things, specifically at her father's head.

"The McKenna does not like to be challenged." Lachlan's expression grew solemn. "I understand his attitude and fully believe that with time it shall change. But anything that ye say or do at this moment might make this worse."

"What could possibly be worse than having ye locked away in this horrid place?" she lamented, distressed that she had been caught so off guard. If she were wiser, she would have prepared herself—and Lachlan—for this eventuality.

"I'm not in shackles. I have not been beaten or whipped. And I still draw breath." Lachlan moved away from the far wall. Katherine again reached through the bars and he took her hand. The connection of their flesh momentarily calmed and soothed her.

"'Tis all my fault. I gambled that we would be able to deflect his anger and avoid his harsh, judgmental nature. I am more sorry than I can say. Please, fergive me."

"I dinnae blame ye, Katherine. Indeed, I fully expected yer father to raise some objections to our marriage."

Objections! Saints preserve us, this imprisonment was far more than an objection. Her heart full of regret, Katherine squeezed Lachlan's hand.

"I shall put this to rights, I swear," she vowed. "My mother will support us once she learns of this injustice. Graham will help and I'm sure I can get James and Malcolm on our side, when they return. Father will be unable to stand against such a united onslaught."

"Hush, dearest, ye'll make yerself ill."

"I'm furious!" Katherine stomped her foot for emphasis, nearly crying out when her boot hit a jagged stone.

"So I see." Lachlan slowly stroked her hand. "'Tis wiser to wait until yer father's anger has cooled before ye say or do anything."

"What of my anger?" she countered.

"If these bars were not between us, I can think of several delightful ways to help it vanish."

Katherine nearly laughed out loud, grateful for his attempt to distract her. He was the one imprisoned, yet his attention was focused on casting aside her fears and misgivings.

"Unlike the McKenna I can control and channel my fury," she remarked daintily.

"Then I ask that ye hold yer tongue."

Frowning, Katherine shook her head. "Lachlan—"

"Fer now," he added hastily. "It will take time to smooth over this breach and have yer father accept our marriage."

Katherine shrugged, uncertain how to respond, unable to completely ease the sense of foreboding that gripped her. In her mind, the longer Lachlan was confined to the dungeon, the easier it would be for her father to keep him imprisoned.

Despite his bleak surroundings, Lachlan looked

magnificent, his powerful presence reaching beyond the bars that sought to contain him. Her gaze locked with his and something deep within her shifted as she realized she had committed herself to him heart, body, and soul.

It was a ridiculous time and place to declare it, but somehow the moment felt right. Even if she were alone in her feelings, they were too profound to keep hidden. He had captured her heart with so little effort and she wanted him, needed him, to know.

"I love ye, Lachlan MacTavish," Katherine whispered, feeling the wonders of the emotions encompassing her as she spoke the words.

Lachlan gently stroked her hand. "'Tis yer guilt talking, Katherine."

A faint flush mottled her cheeks. "Nay. The thoughts, feelings, sensations are unlike any I've ever experienced."

"These feelings could be an infatuation or a simple attraction made all the more appealing because yer father seeks to deny our union," he reasoned.

Katherine swallowed back the swell of emotion that nearly choked her. "There is nothing simple about what I feel fer ye. My heart beats faster, my breath hitches, fie, my whole body tingles when I am near ye."

Lachlan coughed nervously. "Are ye certain 'tis love? Sounds more like the flux."

Katherine's heart turned in her chest. What had she expected? A declaration of undying love and devotion from him?

All in good time. As Mother said, sometimes love needs time to grow and blossom.

"These emotions exist whether or not ye are willing to accept them," Katherine said forcefully. "And I swear that someday ye shall not only embrace them, but return them."

Then grasping his tunic with both hands, she pulled him toward her and covered her mouth with his. The iron bars were just wide enough for their lips to meet. Katherine poured all the intense emotion of the past few days into that kiss, leaving them both breathless and dazed.

Hope flooded Katherine's heart. Taking the risk and declaring her love had freed her spirit. She knew that she was strong enough to survive if Lachlan hurt or disappointed her, yet she would do all within her power— and beyond—to make certain that never happened.

"Hear me well, Lachlan. I shall hold my tongue and not yet speak to my father, as that is yer wish, but I willnae be an idle, docile female, a weak simpering maiden and do nothing while the man I love is in discomfort and danger."

Lachlan watched her storm away, momentarily mesmerized by her fire. His chest swelled with pride knowing this brazen, passionate woman loved him. Her declaration had been a shock, though not an unpleasant one. 'Twas an honor to be loved by Katherine McKenna; an honor he hoped he would do proud.

And what of his feelings for her?

'Twas difficult to decipher them. He could not ignore the intimate connection nor deny the passion between them. Fie, there were times when she tilted her head and gazed at him, it felt as though a fist of emotion had slammed into his chest.

She stirred a storm inside him that at times made him feel restless and insatiable. She made him laugh, made him think, made him consider his actions before he took them. His good opinion of her had continued to increase every time he learned something new about her.

He wanted to protect her from the evils and hardships of the world. Yet he was astute enough to see that she didn't always need it; Katherine McKenna—nay MacTavish now—had the spirit and courage to defend herself.

Was that love? The kind that she wanted, the kind that she deserved? Perhaps.

She had a generous nature and good heart. She was witty, intelligent, caring, and considerate of others. She had both strength of character and strength of conviction. She was the most determined woman he had ever known—the kind of woman he wanted to have by his side—hell, she *was* the only woman he wanted by his side.

Many would say he had gotten far more than he deserved. 'Twas certainly how Katherine's father viewed the marriage. And, aye, there was a part of Lachlan that feared he would fail her, especially after seeing the comfort and luxury of the castle where she had been raised. He could not offer her even half as fine a life—though if his petition to the crown was granted, some of his clan's financial burdens would be eased.

He wanted to please her, to make her happy. He looked forward to spending every day with her—even the days when there were struggles and challenges to overcome.

Bloody hell! The realization hit him like a physical blow. Aye, that was love.

He sprung to his feet, fidgeting restlessly. The need to see Katherine, to hold her in his arms, coursed through him. But he resisted the pull. He would not reveal his heart to her while he was a helpless prisoner.

Nay, he would wait until he was freed from this filthy dungeon.

Pray God that would be soon.

Lachlan's stomach rumbled and he wished he had partaken of some of the food and drink offered when they first arrived. He had been confined to this filthy cell for hours and there was no telling how much longer he would remain. Days? Weeks? His mouth turned bitter at the thought.

With a sigh, he looked for a section of the cell free from vermin droppings and sat, leaning his back against the wall. Eyes closed, his mind drifted, searching for the peace that was just beyond his reach.

A bustling noise broke through the quiet. Katherine had left the torch and he was able to clearly see his wife marching toward him. Three servants trailed dutifully behind her, their arms laden with all manner of goods.

"Are ye well?" she asked, her brow furrowing with concern.

"Ye've only been gone a few hours."

"I worry the dampness will give ye a chill."

It was on the tip of his tongue to tell her that he had slept in far worse places—under more trying conditions—than this, but Lachlan shifted the conversation.

"Did ye speak with yer father?"

"Nay, I heeded yer command and said nothing to him. But I did tell my mother what he's done. She had some rather choice words to share with him, yet he refused to relent. Mother said he'll likely stew in his anger all night. I swear his head is as thick as the stone walls that surround the castle."

"Give him some time," Lachlan replied with a slight smile. *So this is how it feels to have a champion.*

She nearly snorted at him and his smile widened. Lord, she was magnificent!

Katherine turned and spoke to those who stood behind her, "Where is Dougall?"

The servants looked nervously about, then pressed themselves against the wall, clearing a path. Katherine motioned, and a stout, heavily muscled man worked his way forward. She pinned him with an icy stare and demanded that he open the cell.

The man shuffled his feet, looking uneasy. "The laird dinnae give me permission to open it, Lady Katherine."

"Even a lowly prisoner deserves to be fed," Katherine replied. "What do ye propose that I do, push the meal through these bars?"

The guard's expression remained uncertain, yet he eventually wilted under Katherine's glare and unlocked the cell. Katherine sailed inside, the trio of servants following closely on her heels. There was hardly room for all of them in the crowded, small space, yet somehow they managed.

Fascinated, Lachlan watched as Katherine stood with her hands on her hips, taking stock of the grim surroundings. Finally, she reached for the thick pallet one of the servants held and laid it close to the bars. The servant then knelt and covered it with fresh linen and a thick fur, and finally placed a pillow upon it. A pillow!

Katherine instructed the second servant to set a low wooden table beside it. The third servant placed a tray of hot food upon it, along with a pitcher of wine and a goblet. Lastly, Katherine placed a brace of candles on the small table.

In the blink of an eye, Lachlan had a comfortable bed, a warm fur to ward off the chill, good food, wine, and light. Miraculous!

Katherine shooed the servants and they scrambled out of the cell. One soon returned, carrying a large tabby, who meowed in protest.

"I hope that I shall not be in here long enough to require the companionship of a pet," Lachlan joked.

"The cat is here to keep the rats away," Katherine explained, gathering the struggling feline in her arms. "The stable master assures me that she is a master hunter."

The cat continued squirming until she succeeded in releasing herself from Katherine's arms. Once on the ground, the animal sauntered over to Lachlan's pallet, sniffed it, and switched her tail. Then after turning in a circle several times, the tabby settled herself comfortably in the center of his pillow.

He raised a brow and smiled at Katherine. "I guess she needs time to settle in before beginning her duties as a rat catcher."

Katherine looked at the cat dubiously and Lachlan's smile broadened. He half expected his wife to begin lecturing the animal on her duties, but then Dougall stepped forward.

"'Tis time fer me to secure the bars, Lady Katherine," Dougall announced, staring at her expectantly.

"Then do so," Katherine replied boldly, snaking her arm around Lachlan's waist.

The soldier scratched his head in puzzlement. "Ye must come out. I cannae allow ye to stay inside with him, Lady Katherine."

"I willnae leave my husband's side," Katherine declared, tightening her grip. "If my father sees fit to imprison him, then he shall imprison me also."

"If ye dinnae come quietly, I'll have to remove ye by force," Dougall threatened.

"Ye can try." Katherine's lethal look of anger was so intense Lachlan almost felt sorry for the man.

'Twas obvious he didn't want to manhandle the laird's daughter—yet she clearly had no intention of cooperating.

"I think it best if ye do as Dougall asks," Lachlan interjected. "I feel certain that one of yer father's aims of putting me in here is to keep us separated."

"I'm only following the laird's orders, milady," the guard replied with a pleading look.

There was a long, tense moment. Then with her brow furrowing, Katherine stomped out of the cell. "Bring another pallet," she ordered one of the servants.

"Katherine, no," Lachlan protested, realizing it was for her. "I'll not condone having my wife sleeping in such filth."

"My place is at yer side," she insisted. "Fer better or fer worse, remember? And as long as ye are confined to this hellhole, I shall stay with ye."

She nodded her head for emphasis and he knew it would be useless to argue. Emotion gripped Lachlan's chest and he smiled. Aye, he did indeed love her. Very much.

Chapter Eighteen

The sounds of the household awakening to begin a new day pulled Katherine from a restless slumber. The torches and candles in Lachlan's cell had burnt out hours ago and the darkness of their confined space made it difficult to discern night from day. Yet the familiar sounds were unmistakable.

It tugged at her memory and heart. Who would have ever believed that her first night back home would be spent in the bowels of the castle?

She heard the cat pounce, then hiss and meow with pleasure, and was grateful that the lack of light hid the prize that it no doubt held in its mouth. At least the feline had not failed her.

Katherine sighed. Her sleep had been fitful, and filled with pressing fears over Lachlan's fate. How long would it take until her father saw reason and released her husband? A day? Two? Longer? Try as she might, Katherine could not understand what her father hoped to accomplish with this action beyond exerting his power and authority.

Perhaps that would be enough. Perhaps he would quickly grow tired of punishing them both.

Aye, perhaps pigs would fly, too.

She heard another noise—this time from the top of the stairwell. Footsteps approached and then a dim circle of light appeared.

Lachlan stirred. She reached through the bars and grasped his hand.

"So, 'tis true that ye spent the night down here," Graham muttered, his voice tinged with awe. "I thought Mother might have said it merely to anger Father."

Katherine lifted her chin. "My place is with my husband."

"Try as I might, I could not persuade her to leave," Lachlan said with a shrug.

"We need food, Graham. Hot water and clean towels, too." Katherine stretched, then rubbed her arms vigorously. "And tell the servants to bring wood fer a fire. 'Tis cold as ice down here."

Lachlan threaded his fingers through his hair and frowned at her. "There's no place to build a fire. Katherine, please, go abovestairs, so that you may have a proper bath and partake of a nourishing meal."

As lovely as that sounded, Katherine shook her head. "Nay. My father has proved himself to be unpredictable and unreasonable. I must stay to make certain no further harm befalls ye."

"Yer father might be angry, but he'll not act rashly and do something drastic. I am a laird. If he demands justice fer our marriage, he'll allow me to fight with my sword," Lachlan reasoned. "Do ye not agree, Graham?"

"Aye." Her brother nodded.

Katherine shuddered. "If yer aim is to steady my nerves, ye have both failed miserably."

Lachlan looked at Graham and shook his head.

"Katherine, please go with yer brother. Ye can return once ye've eaten and changed yer clothing. It will bring me no small measure of delight to see ye dressed in yer best finery."

Katherine glanced down at her disheveled appearance. Her gown was crushed and wrinkled, the hem streaked with mud and dirt. Her mouth felt dry, no doubt her breath was sour. She noticed several hairpins scattered on the sleeping pallet and realized her unconfined hair must look a fright.

Katherine wavered. A bath sounded like the most luxurious thing in the world right now. "If ye are certain . . ."

"Aye!" Lachlan immediately answered. "I'll be right here when ye return."

His attempt at a joke brought a tender smile to her lips. Wearily, she followed Graham as he lit the way out of the dungeon, shielding her eyes from the sunlight that painfully attacked her when she entered the great hall.

The family dais was empty, but many who were already in the hall turned from breaking their fast to look at her. She saw sympathy in some of those gazes, surprise and uncertainty in others. As usual, people were taking sides—some agreeing with the McKenna's treatment of Lachlan and others believing that Katherine was in the right.

Deciding she really needed the comforting soak of a hot bath, she crossed the great hall. She was nearly at the staircase when a loud commotion erupted in the bailey, diverting her attention.

Curious, Katherine looked out a nearby window and saw a contingent of mounted men riding into the courtyard. She immediately recognized the Drummond standard one of the men carried fluttering in the breeze.

Damnation! Why are they here now? Though she had

assumed they would appear at some point, Katherine had hoped to have her marriage to Lachlan acknowledged and accepted by her father when she next faced her former betrothed and his sire.

Laird Drummond was gesturing wildly at the lad who was trying to grab the bridle of his horse. The animal reared in protest, its lethal hooves pawing at the air, nearly striking the lad. Fortunately, one of the soldiers was close at hand. He was able to control the mount before the child—or anyone else—was injured.

Grimacing, Katherine watched the men dismount. Slithering like a snake through the tall grass, Hamish moved to his father's side. Reminding herself that she needed to keep her emotions under control, Katherine took a deep breath. Her first instinct was to flee, but she quelled it.

This was not going to be a pleasant exchange. Though her presence could incite further anger from Laird Drummond—and perhaps her father—she needed to be aware of what was being said so that she could defend herself.

Melting into the shadows, Katherine brushed away the worst of the dirt from her clothing and tucked a knotted section of hair behind her ear, knowing she must look a fright. Oh well, 'twas too late to do anything about her dirty and disheveled appearance. What mattered now was that she kept her wits about her.

Clearly disgruntled, Laird Drummond and Hamish strode into the hall, with over a dozen of their burly soldiers, hands noticeable on their sword hilts, trailing on their heels. Drummond's disrespectful show of strength in another laird's hall was a clear proclamation of his belief that he had been wronged and solid indication of his confidence that he would receive a satisfactory resolution to his grievance.

His attitude soured Katherine's already agitated mood.

"Where is the famous McKenna hospitality? Are ye not going to offer me a drink and invite me to sit by the fire and warm my bones?" Laird Drummond bellowed when he reached the middle of the great hall.

The iron chandeliers rattled noisily. Her parents had entered the chamber from the opposite side just as the Drummond party arrived. Lady Aileen raised a brow, advanced, then extended her hand regally. Still blustering, Laird Drummond had no choice but to grasp it and bow. Looking sheepish, the soldiers surrounding him also bowed.

"Our friends are always welcome in our hall," Lady Aileen said, her eyes gleaming with censure. "Had we known that ye were coming, I can assure ye that we would have prepared a more fitting greeting."

Laird Drummond's hands balled into fists so tight his knuckles turned white. Yet even he had the good sense to rein in his temper and present a more controlled façade.

Lady Aileen graciously indicated a chair in front of the large hearth, next to her husband, who had said naught since the arrival of their uninvited guests. Somewhat mollified, Laird Drummond sat while his son stood at his shoulder.

The rest of his soldiers gathered a few steps away, their eyes trained upon their laird. Katherine noted the McKenna retainers also had their eyes solidly trained on the Drummond soldiers. It seemed as though one false step would bring about a full-on battle in the middle of the great hall. Katherine held her breath and stepped from the shadows, barely able to comprehend the result of such a melee.

Nervous servants laid food and drink on the low table between the two lairds, and Katherine gazed about the suddenly crowded chamber. It appeared that every servant and retainer with a possible excuse to be in the great hall was lingering here, their curiosity obviously piqued.

Laird Drummond took a long swallow of his wine. When he finished, his shrew eyes scanned the occupants of the hall, coming to rest upon Katherine. He ran a measured gaze over her. She inhaled deeply and fought to keep from squirming.

"What the hell has happened to ye?" Laird Drummond asked, his nostrils flaring with disgust.

"I have spent the night beside my husband's cell in the dungeon," Katherine replied proudly, undisturbed by Laird Drummond's rudeness.

The older man's animosity visibly cooled as he shifted in his chair, turning to the McKenna. "Does this mean ye willnae allow the marriage to stand?"

The McKenna shrugged. "I've yet to decide what I am going to do with the upstart MacTavish laird."

"I have several suggestions," Hamish retorted tartly.

There was a ripple of laughter from the Drummond soldiers. Fists on her hips, Katherine glared at the men and they soon quieted. Logic told her 'twas folly to try to reason with Laird Drummond—and mayhap her own father—yet Katherine would have her say.

"Hamish knows full well why I made the decision to end our betrothal," Katherine said, barely restraining her annoyance. "I would hope that you also see the merit of my decision and would respect my honesty in this important matter. Barring that, I expect ye to abide by it. I am married to Lachlan MacTavish and shall remain his wife through this life and the next."

It felt good to stand up for herself, to show strength and purpose and address him as an equal. Unfortunately, Laird Drummond did not appear to appreciate either her words or her position. His face was molten red, his eyes wide and bulging. He tried to respond, yet succeeded only in sputtering a string of incoherent phrases.

Though her father looked none too pleased at her outburst, he refrained from comment, sitting silent and pensive. As for her former betrothed, well, Hamish favored her with a smirk that was clearly a threat.

"Ye dare to unbraid me with yer wicked tongue?" Laird Drummond bellowed when he finally found his voice. "I understand the high-strung nature of some females, but I'll not sanction it and allow one to make a fool of me and my son."

Katherine's mind spun quickly. Trying to keep her simmering temper under control, she stepped forward. "Yer son hardly appears heartbroken over the incident. And if he were, surely there are females eager and available to comfort him. Is Mistress Fenella no longer residing at Drummond Castle?"

Hamish actually snarled, while his father, looking stunned, sputtered again in outrage.

"I will not be ruled by the dictates of a headstrong, foolish lass!" Laird Drummond shouted. "Ye have broken an alliance between our clans and created a divide that establishes us as enemies."

"I remind ye, Drummond, 'tis customary to show respect and deference when sitting in another laird's hall." The McKenna spoke calmly, yet there was no mistaking that he was poised to inflict bodily harm if further provoked.

Laird Drummond looked none too pleased at the rebuke. Holding her breath, Katherine exchanged a worried look with her mother. Lady Aileen appeared perfectly serene and unconcerned at her husband's blunt retort. However, both women were very aware that this was the best opportunity to peacefully resolve this issue, if somehow the McKenna and Laird Drummond could manage to subvert their pride and hold on to their tempers.

Graham marched forward. "Fergive me, Laird Drummond, but ye are being too hasty with yer declaration of animosity between us. The union between our clans is a sensible and desirable alliance, yet it need not be made between Katherine and Hamish."

There was a flash of ire in the older man's eyes. "Hamish is my only unmarried son."

"I believe ye have an unmarried daughter?" Graham asked, lowering his voice to a most respectful tone. "Of marriageable age?"

Laird Drummond paused, scratching his chin thoughtfully. "Cordelia is in a convent. 'Twas her mother's wish that she serve the Lord."

"A commendable notion." Graham rocked back on his heels. "Tell me, has Lady Cordelia taken her vows and in truth pledged herself to our Savior?"

"She is a novitiate."

Graham lowered his head. "Then I propose to unite our families with a marriage between Cordelia and myself."

"Graham, nay!" Katherine grabbed her brother's sleeve. "There has to be another way. Ye need not sacrifice yerself."

Graham placed a hand over Katherine's and leaned close to whisper in her ear. "I am a third son," he said softly. "Father has been generous, as has Malcolm, but I understand that I need to make my own way in the world." He turned and faced Laird Drummond. "If ye agree, I will take yer daughter as my wife. I will protect and care for her and treat her with reverence and respect."

There was a long silence. Hamish bent down to speak with his father, but Laird Drummond shooed him off with a tight wave of his hand.

"As she was promised to the Church, Cordelia will bring no land and no dowry to the marriage," Laird Drummond declared cagily.

"That can be remedied," the McKenna interjected. "I will gift the newlywed couple with a parcel of land along my southern border, if ye will match the acreage. Even combined, it will not be an overly large holding, but one which will provide Graham and Cordelia a comfortable living and create a stronghold between our lands."

"I shall construct a suitable keep on the property and we will marry once it is completed," Graham concluded.

"I dinnae trust the McKennas to honor a betrothal contract," Laird Drummond announced with a hard stare at Katherine. "I'll not be taken in a second time, especially if I've pledged land and allowed ye to build a keep upon it."

"Then I shall forgo a betrothal and marry Cordelia by proxy," Graham replied.

"When?"

"Today."

There were several gasps of shock. Laird Drummond rubbed his chin again and gazed intensely at Graham, as though trying to judge his sincerity. He must have liked what he saw, as the disgruntled look of distrust on the laird's face abated.

"My daughter has many laudable traits. Among other things, she has been taught by the nuns to read and write and been given lessons in the healing arts."

Laird Drummond turned to the McKenna. "This union has yer blessing?"

"Aye. 'Tis a surprise to me as well, but my son shall marry whomever he chooses," the McKenna answered. "If this is what he wishes, then so be it."

Laird Drummond nodded. "Have someone fetch parchment and ink so that we may set the terms in writing."

"Nay!" A disgruntled snort rushed from Hamish's lips. "Ye cannae be serious, Father. 'Tis blasphemy to force Cordelia to wed. The only honorable alliance between our clans is fer me to marry Katherine. My mind is set upon it—I'll not give her up!"

"Ye already have, Hamish." Laird Drummond turned his back on his son. "Yer sister will marry Graham McKenna. Today."

The entire hall seemed to exhale at the pronouncement, but Katherine's heart sank. Despite Hamish's protests, it was an excellent way to keep the peace and finally unite the two clans, but the sacrifice was too great. She would never ask this of anyone she loved, especially her younger brother.

"Graham, please, ye must reconsider." Katherine pulled him aside, refusing to let him leave until he listened to reason. "Ye've never even set eyes upon the lass. Ye cannae marry a complete stranger."

"Many couples do. I am content with the decision. 'Tis the best solution to avoid a feud with the Drummonds," Graham insisted, trying to go around her.

Blocking his exit, Katherine blew out a frustrated breath. Why did her younger sibling have to be so pigheaded?

"What if she objects?" Katherine asked. "What if Cordelia has set her heart upon serving the Lord?

What if she hates ye fer arranging a marriage that she never expected and has no say in accepting? What sort of a life will ye have then?"

Graham stilled. "'Tis true that many women are at least granted an opinion in the selection of their husbands, though 'tis their fathers, brothers, or guardians who make the choice. In this circumstance, it is not possible or practical. Cordelia is a gently bred female. She knows her duty to her father and her clan and will graciously accept her fate."

"She believes her duty is to become a nun!" Katherine shouted, quickly lowering her voice when several others turned to stare at them. "Ye are cheating yerself, Graham, tossing away yer chance fer a loving marriage and 'tis all my fault."

"Yer guilt is misplaced, Sister," Graham said patiently. "I have never held with the notion of making a love match, but always knew that I would marry fer more practical reasons. I'm pleased with the arrangement and enter into it freely and without regret or reservation."

"Ye might not feel the same after ye meet yer wife," Katherine grumbled.

Graham waved his hand dismissively. "I have no home in which to bring my bride. Therefore, I willnae fetch her until a proper keep has been constructed upon the land gifted to us by our sires."

"That could take years."

"Precisely." He regarded her with an amused expression. "A lot can happen as the seasons change."

Her brother's cryptic words brought Katherine little comfort. A marriage by proxy was as legal as if the bride was standing beside the groom. The one piece that was missing from the event was the consummation of the union, yet that alone did not constitute grounds for an annulment.

Or did it? Had her brother already concocted a way to dissolve the union if necessary?

Graham walked away and Katherine allowed him. 'Twas clear that nothing she could say or do would change his mind. However, 'twas also true that this marriage would benefit her and Lachlan as well and neatly solve the sticky problem of the Drummond alliance. Her broken betrothal would be forgotten.

The conundrum of the situation twisted inside her. Katherine's worry over the wisdom of such a hastily arranged and considered marriage increased tenfold when the priest was summoned. Events were moving at lightning speed. She looked to her mother for a voice of reason and calm, hoping she would stop things before it was too late.

Lady Aileen was engaged in earnest conversation with Graham. When it ended, she hugged him tightly, then kissed his cheek, apparently giving him her blessing.

Biting her lip, Katherine ran her hand back and forth across her brow, trying to rub away the pain that was throbbing behind her eyes. She had to do something to stop this travesty—but what?

"Leave it be," a soft feminine voice commanded. "He has made his decision without prejudice or coercion."

Katherine cast her sister-in-law an incredulous look. "There has to be another way to make peace between our clans. I dinnae know how I shall live with the dark guilt that already begins to consume me."

"Ye had no part in this turn of events," Joan countered in her usual direct manner. "Becoming a martyr over it willnae serve any useful purpose except to make ye miserable."

"Perhaps 'tis what I deserve."

Joan regarded her with a jaundiced eye. "Or perhaps

the unthinkable will happen and Graham will be content in his marriage."

"The world truly has gone mad when ye are the one spouting words of matrimonial hope and happiness," Katherine groused.

Taking no offense, Joan laughed. "Exactly my point. I never believed that I would love any man, but Malcolm stole and keeps my heart. The impossible can happen. All ye need to have is faith."

If only it were so simple. Still, Katherine heeded Joan's advice and resisted the temptation to disrupt the proceedings. With a sharp huff of resignation, she joined the rest of her family as they stood together. Word quickly spread throughout the castle and beyond and clan members soon crowded their way into the great hall to witness the event.

"This is a dreadful idea."

Katherine looked over, startled to realize that it was Hamish who had spoken. "For once we are in total agreement," she replied, stepping toward him.

Hamish's expression turned eager. "Then let's stop it, Katherine. If we speak up now and declare our intention to marry, we will save our siblings from this fate."

Katherine slowly shook her head. He was like a dog with a bone, nay worse, for he seemed incapable of letting it drop. "Why, Hamish? Why is the notion of our marriage such an obsession fer ye?"

Hamish's shoulders slumped. "'Tis the most important task my father—and my clan—ever asked of me and I failed them."

"Not intentionally. Yer heart had other plans, as did mine." Katherine laid her fingertips gently on his arm. "What of Fenella?"

His eyes grew dim. "She is gone. Father sent her away. I know not where."

"Then find her. Prove yer love fer her and she will gladly be yer wife."

Hamish grimaced. "'Tis not as simple as ye make it sound, Katherine. Not everyone has the courage to defy their father and forsake their duty."

"Fie! No one can fault ye on how persistently ye tried to fulfill our betrothal," she remarked dryly. "I swear ye would have followed me to the ends of the earth to have yer way."

"Aye. And ye would have run even farther to avoid me."

Katherine's lips curled in an ironic grin at the truth of his words. "Search fer Fenella," she urged. "'Tis not too late to find the happiness ye seek."

Hamish's expression contorted with doubt. "I could have made ye happy, Katherine."

"Nay. My destiny lay with Lachlan. He is the man that I was meant to marry, just as Fenella is meant fer ye." She lowered her chin. "Ye dwell too much in the past, Hamish. Look toward the future instead."

Looking torn with conflicting emotions, Hamish shifted his weight from one foot to the next. "Fenella might not wish to see me. She was very upset the last time we spoke."

Katherine cleared her throat. She could well imagine how Fenella felt, yet she also believed that all was not lost. "If she cares fer ye as much as I think, her anger and hurt will abate."

"Truly?"

Surprised by the sudden glint of hope in his eyes, Katherine nodded. "Aye."

The dark scowl on Hamish's brow lightened. "Then

I shall be a bold and courageous fellow and follow yer advice."

"Good."

Shocking her utterly, he then graciously bowed. "Good-bye, Katherine."

"Farewell, Hamish," she replied, a genuine smile upon her lips.

Turning her attention back to the activities in the great hall, Katherine realized the wedding was about to take place. Joan was chosen to stand in for the bride. Her lovely smile lent an almost festive air to this most solemn ceremony. Graham remained relaxed, sounding very pleased with himself as he spoke his vows.

Katherine was still struggling to grasp the enormity of it all when Father John gave his final blessing. A hearty cheer went up from those in attendance, no doubt in anticipation of the celebratory meal that would be served later that night, which would include free-flowing ale and whiskey.

Mercifully, the Drummonds elected to depart the moment the ink had dried on the marriage documents, forgoing any celebrations in the hopes of returning to their land before full darkness descended. Graham dutifully escorted them outside, along with the McKenna, Lady Aileen, and Joan.

Still struggling to comprehend and accept all that had happened, Katherine stayed behind.

"Mistress Innes said there was a wedding and that Mama was the bride," a young voice intoned. "Who did she marry?"

Katherine glanced down at her young niece, Lileas. The child's face was ringed in curiosity along with a touch of annoyance, for Lileas always wanted to be included in everything.

"No one," Katherine answered. "She married no one, since she is already married to yer father."

"I heard Mistress Innes tell one of the maids that Mama married Uncle Graham. Is he my papa, too?" Lileas's expression brightened. "He always has treats fer me and Callum and takes us the farthest away from the castle when we ride our ponies. I think I shall like it very much having another papa."

Katherine could not contain her smile. Ever the opportunist, Lileas looked to find the best in every situation, especially when it benefited her. Perhaps Katherine could learn something from the lass's attitude?

"A child has one father and one mother. Malcolm, and only Malcolm, is yer father," Katherine explained.

"But Mama is my second mama. My first mother is in heaven," Lileas reminded her solemnly.

"Ye may only have one father and one mother at a time," Katherine clarified.

Lileas's brows knit together tightly. She was a bright, inquisitive child and Katherine assumed after digesting the information she would understand the difference.

"Callum has two fathers," Lileas said slowly. "I heard Papa speak of it once. He called him a bloody Fraser bastard, unfit to walk—"

"Honey cakes!" Katherine shouted, not wanting to be reminded of Joan's brief, disastrous marriage to Archibald Fraser. The only good that had ever come from the union was the birth of her son, Callum. A child that Fraser disowned, but Malcolm willingly adopted as his own.

"Honey cakes? Where?" Lileas's eyes widened with excitement.

"In the kitchen. Hurry now, before they are all eaten."

Lileas turned and started running across the great

hall. "I shall eat one and then take two," she called over her shoulder. "One fer me and one fer Callum."

Katherine felt a pang of guilt as she watched the lass scamper away. 'Twas a cowardly way to abruptly end the conversation, but the first thing she could think of to distract the lass. Her biggest hope was that Cook had in truth baked a large supply of Lileas's favorite treat or else the commotion in the kitchen would rival the upheaval that had just taken place in the great hall.

Katherine turned to leave just as the family returned. Her gut tightened when she caught sight of the dark, brooding expression on her father's face. Her brother had just married an unknown woman in order to secure the alliance he craved. Should he not finally look pleased? Or was his displeasure with her too strong to overcome any feelings of joy?

Every muscle in Katherine's body tensed as she struggled against the urge to burst into tears. The words she had just spoken to Lileas about having only one father echoed through her head.

And mine despises me. Stifling a sob, Katherine turned away.

"And just where do ye think ye're going, Katherine?"

The McKenna's voice boomed through the vast chamber, nearly rattling the glass in the windows.

Katherine turned back and met her father's gaze with one of defiance. "Below, to be with my husband."

Lady Aileen jabbed her husband in the side. The McKenna grimaced. "There is no need to go to the dungeon, Katherine. Yer husband is here."

Katherine turned and did indeed see Lachlan, standing in the shadows, flanked by two McKenna guards. His eyes were dulled from fatigue and lack of sleep, his jaw covered in a heavy blanket of stubble.

The urge to race to his side and embrace him was strong, yet Katherine held back. Instead, she cast a suspicious eye toward her father.

"Is he still yer prisoner?" she asked.

"Nay."

"Good." Katherine pressed her lips into a thin, flat line. "We shall retire to my chamber to bathe, rest, and eat our meals. Kindly send word when my dowry is ready to be transported. We shall then gladly take our leave of ye."

The McKenna stiffened, clearly laboring to control his temper. Katherine glared at him. She intended to make a point and it appeared to have boldly hit the mark.

"Ye must excuse Katherine's passionate ramblings, Laird McKenna. My wife is tired and distressed. We shall gladly join ye fer the evening meal, if ye so desire."

Katherine turned an astonished gaze upon her husband. He now stood at her side. She had been so unsettled, she hadn't even realized it.

"It would please Lady Aileen to have ye both at our table," the McKenna replied, somewhat mollified.

"Excellent. Until this evening."

Lachlan slid an arm around Katherine's waist and steered her toward the staircase. She opened her mouth to protest, but his pointed glare silenced her.

"I know that ye are angry—and hurt—Katherine, but I'll not be the cause of an estrangement between ye and yer father," Lachlan insisted. "We will stay here until the breach is mended."

"Och, well, unless the McKenna undergoes an epiphany and makes amends, then ye had best be prepared for a long siege," Katherine retorted.

Chapter Nineteen

"We've won, Katherine," Lachlan said as he shut her bedchamber door. "Ye must now be gracious in victory and allow yer father to retain his pride."

"If I live beyond a hundred years, I will never completely understand how honor and vengeance can mean so much to a man," Katherine remarked bitterly.

"'Tis a somewhat rigid, consuming emotion that often overrides good sense," Lachlan replied. "Yet I cannae fault yer father's actions. We are not blameless."

A pang of guilt needled Katherine. Her marriage to Lachlan had far greater repercussions than she had ever anticipated, for everyone. Yet even knowing the consequences, she would do the same again.

Would Lachlan?

The weariness around his eyes told her he hadn't slept any more than she had last night. Though she had done all within her power to make his cell comfortable, 'twas no surprise that he was unable to rest easy while in captivity.

"I am truly sorry fer all the grief that I've caused ye," she said.

His gaze narrowed. "Like most men, I have regrets

over things I've done in my life." His arm slid around her waist. "But marrying ye, isn't one of them."

She stared into his piercing blue eyes and her breath caught in her throat. He regarded her with raw hunger, an all-consuming intensity that made her tingle with need. She might not yet possess his love, but she most certainly aroused his desire.

Lachlan's lips claimed hers. A deep, passionate excitement pounded through Katherine's body, making it swell and tighten. Her lips parted and she felt herself melt against him. The welcome familiarity of his kiss, his caress, soothed her restless spirit as nothing else could.

His kisses were the most sensuous thing she had ever experienced. She returned them eagerly, feeling the passion flowing between them. Enthralled in his spell, Katherine pressed herself closer, the tension curling through her body. She was tired, hungry, and none too clean, yet all she could think about was getting naked and climbing into bed with her husband.

She splayed her hands across his chest, stroking the tense muscles of his torso, reveling in his strength.

"I want ye so badly it hurts," Lachlan whispered roughly. She could feel his penis, hard and urgent, jutting against her thigh, proof that he spoke the truth.

"'Tis but a few steps to yon bed," she muttered, smiling when she heard the rumble of his laughter.

A series of loud knocks, rapid and persistent, shattered the mood.

"Lady Katherine, 'tis David. May I enter?"

"David?" Lachlan asked.

"The castle steward," Katherine explained, slumping forward.

"I've brought food and drink," David called from

the other side of the closed door. "And yer lady mother has ordered baths prepared fer ye and Laird MacTavish."

Katherine heard Lachlan sigh deeply and felt him press his lips to her forehead. "As much as I would enjoy the delectable sight of ye in the bath, the pink tips of yer nipples lifted high enough through the water to grant me a most pleasing view, I have a far more pressing need. Fer God's sake, send the man away!"

Needing a moment to gather herself, Katherine cleared her throat. She stepped out of Lachlan's arms and crossed the chamber. Opening the door ever so slightly, she schooled her features into a calm expression and peered through the crack.

"We have no need of anything at the moment," she said breathlessly. "Thank ye, David."

"But Lady Katherine," the servant sputtered, looking indignant over her refusal.

Katherine shut the door. Firmly. Then barred it for good measure before turning to face her husband.

Lachlan had wisely used the time she was dispatching the steward to remove his clothing. He was now stretched out on her bed—naked—his arms raised and propped behind his head, his eyes half-lidded and provocative.

The sight disarmed her. Katherine felt her entire body dampen as desire spread between her legs. Pulling and tugging at her clothing, she freed herself of their constraints.

She lay down on the bed beside him. Close enough to feel the warmth of his body, yet not touching. She expected him to grab her and roll her onto her back the moment she settled at his side, but instead he remained still. Was he waiting for her to take the lead?

The very thought delighted her and she decided to take full advantage of the opportunity. With a sultry smile, Katherine slowly ran her hand from Lachlan's chest to his hip.

"Ye are the most beautiful man that I have ever seen, ever touched," she whispered in his ear.

He tilted his head toward her. "I should hope that I am the *only* man that ye have ever seen and touched so intimately, Katherine."

She laughed. "Jealous, Lachlan?"

He held her gaze. "Absolutely."

"Good."

Katherine wiggled close. She dipped her head and blew on his nipple, then her lips followed, blazing a hot, tantalizing trail down the flat plane of his belly. She could hear his breath hitch as his hips thrust upward, feel the tremors in his thighs. He slipped his hand around her neck, encouraging her explorations as she moved lower.

She willingly obliged him, dipping her tongue into his navel, then lifted her head so she could see his expression while she dragged her hand caressingly up and down the inside of his thigh. His breathing grew sharper as Katherine moved her fingertips in slow, tantalizing circles, drawing ever nearer to her prize.

When she cupped his balls, he startled. Then she curled her fingers over his shaft, rolling her thumb over the thick head. His eyes closed and his jaw tightened. Empowered and emboldened, Katherine dipped her chin and licked him from base to tip in one long, wet stroke, then took his hot, hard penis into her mouth.

Lachlan cried out and nearly leapt from the bed. His hands fisted in her hair. Katherine grabbed his buttocks to pull him closer. She licked and sucked with total abandon, relishing the taste and hardness of him. His chest was rising and falling in deep, shallow breaths and knowing the pleasure she was giving him made her feel closer, more connected to him.

The surge of power she felt being in control was intoxicating. Every sensation was heightened, every movement more sensual and exciting than the last. She felt bold and wicked as she touched him with her mouth, lips, and tongue.

A warm feeling ran through her and she continued to tease and arouse him until her body cried out with the insatiable need to connect with his.

She lifted herself, threw one leg over his hips, and straddled him. With a roar, Lachlan thrust upward at the same moment Katherine plunged down. Their bodies met and joined in a rising tide of desire that quickly pulled them both under.

She felt a pure, primal thrill at the way her womanhood gripped his penis so fiercely. She started slowly with a steady pace, pulling herself in and out in a sensuous rhythm that soon grew frantic.

Lachlan held her hips as she moved up and down, his sharp cries of release coming much faster than Katherine expected. She could feel her inner muscles clenching as his body shuddered and his seed spilled deep inside her.

Her body tightened and pulsed. Katherine arched her back and rocked against him, creating the friction she needed to push her own release. She moaned as her body moved of its own accord, gritting her teeth to prolong the pleasure that swirled and grew.

"Come fer me, lass."

The sound of his voice, so deep and intimate, broke her and she shattered, like glass fracturing into a thousand pieces.

She collapsed on top of him. Tears gathered in the

corners of her eyes and she blinked. The intensity of her feelings rattled her. Her heart was so full. Lachlan completed her in a way that no other man could. She knew, with certainty, that she could not live without him.

"Katherine."

"Hmmm." Keeping her eyes closed, she shifted to his side and gently rubbed her finger across his sweat-covered chest.

"I love ye." His words were a strained whisper. Plain, simple, direct—so like the man himself.

Katherine's eyes flew open. Her heart leapt as her throat closed with emotion. It felt as though she had waited a lifetime to hear those words.

"Truly?"

"With all my heart."

Swallowing hard, she felt a fresh trickle of tears slide down her cheeks. "'Tis glorious to hear ye say it."

"I waited too long to tell ye," he replied roughly. "But 'tis true. Ye've the ability to touch my heart and it brings me such joy at times I feel as though I could burst."

"Aye." Sniffling, Katherine snuggled closer. "I love ye, too, Lachlan MacTavish. Now and always."

Lachlan rose up on his elbow to look at her. His gaze was tender yet possessive, and it thrilled her. Relief, joy, and wonder rushed through her.

"'Tis an odd thing, these feelings of love," he admitted. "I've waited my whole life fer something that I never knew I was missing. And now that I've discovered it, I'll never let it—let ye—go."

"Ye are the faceless man that I've always dreamed of finding," Katherine replied. "Someone unique and special to hold within my heart. Someone who will love me as fiercely and completely as I love him."

"Aye, lass, we are a well-matched pair."

"A perfect pair," she insisted, her mouth twisting in a wry smile.

His arms wrapped around her waist and he pulled her closer. A surge of unmatched pleasure filled her and she savored the sensation of being held in his arms. The man she loved. The man who loved her. With a contented smile, Katherine closed her eyes and fell into a blissful slumber.

All was quiet when Lachlan entered the stables the following morning. As was his custom, he had risen before dawn, his body rested and sated, his mind in turmoil.

Yesterday had been most unusual, a day like no other he could recall. He and Katherine had stayed in her bedchamber, bathing together, eating, making love, sleeping, and then loving again.

They had talked, too. About their current predicament, their hopes for the future, and their determination to preserve and defend their newly discovered love, allowing nothing to come between them.

It had taken some persuasion, but Lachlan had eventually succeeded in convincing his stubborn wife to sit at her father's table for the evening meal. Once she had agreed, Katherine had taken extra care with her appearance, fussing over every detail, and the results had been astonishing.

Lachlan had always thought his wife was a beautiful woman, but seeing her garbed in her finery had stolen the breath from his lungs. The low, round neckline of the deep green gown that she had chosen was embroidered on the bodice, sleeves, and hem with a Scottish thistle design of golden thread.

When she moved and caught the candlelight just so,

the garment shimmered and sparkled, surrounding her in an ethereal glow. The luscious fabric clung to her upper torso, then fell smoothly from her waist, making her appear taller. The matching green slippers she wore on her dainty feet were barely visible when she walked—nay, glided—into a room.

A maid had been summoned to arrange her hair atop her head in an elegant twist. A gossamer veil of white silk held in place by a bejeweled gold circlet was added, completing her elegant transformation.

At the first sight of her, Lachlan had been struck dumb. Bathed in wealth and dignity, she looked every inch a royal princess.

"I am only doing this because ye have asked me," she had stated, holding out her hand to him.

The gems in the rings on her fingers winked at him. He had held himself awkwardly for a moment, feeling unworthy of claiming such an elegant, angelic female as his own. But then she had pulled her lower lip between her teeth—a sure sign of nerves and uncertainty. The vulnerable gesture had jarred him from his trance. She needed him, depended upon him.

He would not fail her.

A hush had fallen over the great hall when they had entered. She had started trembling and Lachlan had pressed his hand to Katherine's waist, offering comfort and support. Her parents were already at the table and Lachlan had intentionally moved his chair closer to Katherine's once they were seated on the dais.

Conversation had initially been stilted and awkward, but it appeared that both Katherine and her father were making an effort not to deliberately provoke each other. Lady Aileen, Graham, and Lachlan had all worked hard to ensure the discussions remained light-hearted and cordial and they had managed to survive the evening without a single disagreement between Katherine and her father.

Though far from ideal, it was a beginning. A beginning that Lachlan sincerely hoped would not suffer a setback today when he asked the McKenna for permission to see his brother Robbie. 'Twas hardly a conversation that Lachlan was keen to have, knowing a reminder of his brother's crimes against the clan would only serve to confirm the McKenna's already low opinion of his daughter's husband.

Ah, well, after that, there was naught to do but rise, Lachlan reasoned.

Fortunately, Katherine's opinion of him was far different. She loved him! 'Twas humbling knowing that she had given her heart to him, disbelieving, too, that such fortune had found him. He had never thought of himself as a particularly lucky fellow.

Until now.

Lachlan smiled, remembering the intensity of their coupling yesterday, last night—and this morning. He had turned to Katherine in the predawn hours, before the sun prepared to rise, and she had welcomed him openly, eagerly. Their joining had been slower and less frenzied, but no less intense.

He had never before experienced the like. Much more than physical pleasure and contentment, there was a poignancy, a feeling of pure and utter completeness that touched the deepest part of him when he was with Katherine. It baffled him. Aye, and even scared him a bit.

Yet he wouldn't change it for the world.

Lachlan was lost in these thoughts when a rustling sound at the entrance to the stable captured his attention. Instinctively, he drew his blade, swiveling to face the intruder. In all likelihood it was only a stable lad coming to feed the horses, but Lachlan's warrior instincts bade him to remain cautious and prepared in every circumstance.

Two children, hand in hand, carefully crept into the stables. He recognized the pair as Lady Joan's bairns. He had heard their names, yet couldn't recall them. Lily? Colin? Nay, that didn't sound right.

He searched his memory. Lileas, that was it. And the lad was Callum.

Lachlan looked over their shoulders for a nursemaid, yet saw none. Though he knew little of young children, it seemed odd that they were allowed to roam unsupervised at this early hour of the morning.

He stepped from the shadows and they froze, staring at him wide-eyed.

"Who are ye?" Lileas challenged, her eyes fixed on the knife in his hand.

Lachlan sheathed his blade and closed the gap between them in a few long strides. "I'm Lachlan MacTavish."

The lass tilted her head and narrowed her expression. "MacTavish? Och, now I know ye. Ye arrived the other day. Ye're the dishonorable, cowardly, faithless cur who stole my aunt Katherine."

"Cur," Callum repeated.

Lachlan grinned. Apparently, the lass had a talent for overhearing conversations and recalling them with biting accuracy.

"'Twas actually my brother who stole her," Lachlan replied casually. "I'm the one who brought her home."

"Grandfather doesn't like ye," Lileas said solemnly. "I heard him talking about ye to Uncle Graham, Mother, and Grandmother. He was shouting and stomping his feet. Then he started banging his fist on the table."

Lachlan bit back a smile. "It sounds as though he was angry."

"Aye. He kept shouting, but Mother covered my ears with her hands, so I dinnae hear the rest. Then she started yelling at Grandfather. Grandmother yelled at him, too." The lass sighed dramatically.

"Very loud," Callum echoed, placing his hands over his ears.

"It sounds most unpleasant," Lachlan said sympathetically.

Lileas shrugged. "We McKennas like to shout. A lot. Well, except fer Papa. When he's mad his voice gets quiet and controlled and that's when ye know that yer in big, big trouble. Be extra careful when that happens."

"I thank ye fer the warning." Lachlan smiled. She was certainly a font of information. He shifted his gaze to the lad, who was sucking his thumb. "Shouldn't the two of ye be in yer beds, asleep, instead of in the stables alone?"

Lileas's face contorted in guilt, then suddenly her expression brightened and she favored him with a smile that was hard to resist. "We aren't alone—ye're here with us!"

"Purely by accident." He gave them a thoughtful sideways glance. "Though I suppose 'tis all right, now that I'm yer uncle by marriage."

Lileas shook her head. "James and Graham are my uncles. They are Papa's brothers. How can ye be my uncle if ye aren't Papa's brother?"

"I married yer aunt Katherine."

"Married!" Lileas started hopping from one foot to the other in excitement. "Is she going to have a baby? Married ladies have babies. I love babies. Mother is going to have one, but it won't be here until summer, which is so, so far away. Aunt Davina had a baby. 'Tis a lad. She let me hold him and he never cried once when he was in my arms. His name is Brian, the same as Grandfather's.

"But I want Mother's baby to be a lass and the next one to be a lad and the next one to be another lad and then I want two baby lasses. At the same time! That's called twins."

Lachlan chuckled beneath his breath, wondering what the lovely Joan would think of Lileas's plans for such a large family.

Footsteps alerted them to someone approaching and they all spun around.

"Papa!" Lileas and Callum shrieked in unison, racing toward the tall, broad-shouldered man who stood at the front of the stable.

He knelt and caught one child in each arm as they launched themselves at him. Lifting the pair with ease, he smiled and hugged them tightly, shifting them in his arms so that he could look closely at their faces. They hugged and kissed him, then began peppering him with a rapid series of questions. His eyes flashed with warmth and affection as he answered each one patiently and with good cheer.

Lachlan used Malcolm's preoccupation with the children to study Katherine's eldest brother. His physical stature would overwhelm most and the air of authority he exuded proclaimed him a strong leader.

Yet it would appear that there was a soft side to the heir of the McKenna clan, a man whose reputation as a fearless, skilled fighter was well-known throughout the Highlands and beyond. Lileas's resemblance to Malcolm was marked, in both features and coloring, but the lad was fair-haired like his mother.

And his sire.

Callum was Archibald Fraser's natural son, a result of Joan's first unhappy marriage to the Fraser laird. Lachlan was surprised to see how easily Malcolm showed the same concern and affection for the lad as he did for his own daughter. One would never guess that McKenna blood did not flow through the lad's veins.

"I see that we are not alone," Malcolm said, his gaze traveling slowly over Lachlan.

"Aye, Papa, Callum and I know that we are not allowed to come to the stables on our own," Lileas promptly replied. "That's why Uncle Lachlan is here with us."

"Uncle?"

"He married Aunt Katherine."

"Aye, yer mother told me all when I returned home late last night."

Malcolm carefully set the children on their feet. He brushed the hair back from his daughter's forehead and gave her a kiss, then did the same with the lad.

"Will ye take us riding, Papa?" Lileas begged. "Our ponies feel sad staying in the stables all day."

"'Tis still dark out and far too early to ride beyond the castle walls, as ye well know, Lileas," he scolded. "Mistress Innes will be frantic when she finds that ye are missing from yer beds."

"Mistress Innes willnae be worried," Lileas assured her father. "She's sleeping. I heard her snoring before we left."

Malcolm gave his daughter a quelling look. "I will only take ye and yer brother fer a ride if ye return to yer chamber before she discovers that ye are gone."

Callum jabbed an elbow into Lileas's side. "Hurry!" he yelled.

Lileas's squeal of excitement pierced Lachlan's ears. She ran after her brother, quickly overtaking him, pausing once to look over her shoulder and wave at Lachlan.

"My wife tells me that ye've made quite the impression upon my father."

Lachlan turned and met Malcolm's unwavering stare with an equally intimidating one of his own.

"The McKenna looks at me as though he just realized he's stepped into a fresh pile of horse dung," Lachlan admitted wryly.

"Is he wrong?"

"Aye. Just ask yer sister." Lachlan looked directly at Malcolm. "I regret that I've been the cause of so much tension and strife within yer family, but Katherine is my wife. I will do anything to ensure her safety and happiness."

"According to my wife, this unpleasantness was not all yer doing," Malcolm conceded.

"I never realized that Katherine could be so fierce until I saw her tangle with yer father," Lachlan said with a slight grin.

"The McKennas are loyal and protective of those they love." Malcolm shrugged. "I suppose there are worse family traits."

Lachlan nodded and the tension between the two men lessened. "I can only hope that yer father will respect the loyalty I carry fer my family when I ask a great favor of him today."

"The McKenna can be persuaded, if ye present a reasonable argument. He enjoys having men in his debt," Malcolm revealed. "What will ye ask of him?"

"To see my youngest brother, Robbie. He's imprisoned at yer quarry."

"The quarry?" Malcolm's eyes flared and Lachlan could see his right hand tighten into a fist. "Yer brother's crime was against me—and my wife."

Lachlan looked at Malcolm quizzically, surprised at learning this detail. "Did Robbie act alone?"

"Nay, he was one of three other men who sought to profit from a misunderstanding between myself and the MacPhearson clan." Malcolm's expression softened slightly. "Fortunately, Joan managed to thwart their plans."

The answer was unexpected. Truthfully, Lachlan had not thought much about his brother's crime, only that he had been caught and was a prisoner. Though he was curious to learn more, Lachlan wisely decided not to press Malcolm for details, assuming recounting the event could dredge up memories best forgotten.

"Do ye think I'd be allowed to see him, to speak with him?" Lachlan asked.

Malcolm shot him a thoughtful gaze. Lachlan waited, daring to hope. Finally, the other man nodded. "Katherine will certainly champion yer cause. I shall too."

"I'm grateful."

"I do this fer my sister," Malcolm replied. "Joan tells me that she loves ye very much."

"Aye." Lachlan lowered his gaze, mortified to realize that he was starting to blush. "Nearly as much as I love her."

Malcolm stepped forward and extended his arm. Startled by the gesture, Lachlan hesitated only a moment before clasping it.

"'Tis good to find another warrior like myself—and my brother—who sees the value in allowing himself to follow his heart," Malcolm said with a grin. "Welcome to the family."

Chapter Twenty

Dawn was barely breaking when Lachlan returned to the bedchamber. He approached the bed just as Katherine was stirring from her slumber. Her eyes were half-lidded and inviting, her lips moist and parted with languid drowsiness. Lachlan reached for a lock of her tawny hair and slid it slowly through his fingers. It was smooth and silky, just like the rest of her.

"Good morning," he murmured.

"Aye, it looks as though it will be a lovely day." Her brow furrowed. "Why are ye dressed?"

"I was outside in the stables. The cool breeze helps clear my head."

She twitched her nose. "Aye, we both partook steadily of the wine and whiskey last night."

They had, but that was not the reason he needed the fresh air. He opened his mouth to mention his unexpected meeting with Malcolm, but the sight of Katherine's delectable sweetness sent those thoughts flying out of his head.

God's blood, she was irresistible.

As he held her gaze, Lachlan could feel the sizzling power of sexual tension stirring between them. For an instant it left him witless, robbed of any thought except fulfilling the driving need to sweep her into his arms and kiss her until they were both senseless.

How was she able to do this to him? What magical spell did she weave over him that made his senses sharper, his feelings run so deep and fierce?

"Ye're looking at me in a most enticing way," he remarked, moving closer.

"Am I?" She rolled onto her back. The thin linen shift she wore dropped off her shoulder, exposing the delicate, porcelain skin. "I hope that I have not caused any offense."

She was wanton and wicked and he admitted freely to himself that he adored it. Some men demanded piety and meekness from their wives. They were fools. Vibrant passion and confident enticement made life far more interesting and worthwhile.

Lachlan placed his knee on the edge of the bed and loomed over Katherine. With a sensual grin, he pushed the garment farther from her shoulder. She wriggled toward him and reached up, resting her palm against his cheek.

Delighted, he slowly ran the tip of his finger across her shoulder, down her arm, then lightly over the creamy expanse of her breast. Her breath hitched as the nipple tightened and she released a soft, almost feline-like purr.

"Ye know that ye'll need to answer fer those sultry glances ye keep sending my way," he said.

She caught his caressing hand and pulled it toward her face. Her pink tongue darted out and she ran it slowly over the pulse at his wrist. Desire shot straight to his groin and Lachlan felt his cock harden.

His breathing slowed as he tried to regain a measure

of control, but she threw her arms around his neck, digging her fingers deep into his shoulder and Lachlan's need overcame him. He cupped her buttocks and pulled her against his erection, the heat and passion driving them both to near madness.

She began rubbing her thigh up and down against him and Lachlan swore he could feel the thundering of his heart. He felt on fire for her with a desire so strong it made him shudder. He pulled her hair back and began kissing her neck.

"Why are ye wearing so many clothes?" she asked with a breathless voice.

"The barrier of cloth is all that keeps me from ravishing ye like a wild beast," he admitted, feeling almost dizzy from the strength of the yearning tearing through him.

A sensual, feminine smile curved up the corners of Katherine's sweet mouth. "Hmmm, that sounds most intriguing. Pray, remove yer tunic and trews and show me exactly what ye mean."

"Are ye certain?" he asked, not truly knowing how he would contain himself if she needed him to hold back. No doubt her body was sore and tender from their previous couplings and the last thing he wanted was to cause her pain.

"Come to me," Katherine rasped, arching her back and pressing herself closer. "Pleasure me."

His heart hammering in his chest, Lachlan somehow pulled off his clothing. Then with a strangled groan, he grasped Katherine's hips, lifted her off the mattress, and plunged inside her.

Her cry of excitement caused him to nearly spill his seed the moment the warm wetness clenched around his throbbing penis, but he was hell-bent on bringing her to her release before achieving his own.

He pushed his hand between their sweat-soaked bodies until he reached the juncture of her thighs, and pressed down with the tips of his fingers on her mons. Katherine arched, whimpering low in her throat.

"I love ye, Katherine," he whispered before claiming her mouth.

He delighted in the heat and excitement he tasted. Ablaze with hunger, he rocked against her, their bodies straining and twisting together. Harder, faster, deeper until he felt the tremors inside her beginning.

"Ye're mine," she said, holding his face between her hands.

Pulling himself forward, Lachlan rose above Katherine, surging one final time, spilling his seed just as her body shuddered in release. He held on to her tightly as the storm of pleasure subsided, his heart full.

He tried catching himself, but instead slumped forward, resting fully on her lushness. A rush of tenderness overwhelmed him. With each joining, he felt closer, more connected to her in ways that continued to confound him. Yet he gloried in every moment.

She resisted when he started moving off her. "Nay, stay with me, my love."

"I'm too heavy," he countered, knowing he should shift his weight to his elbows, yet lacking the strength. Or the will.

"I like it," Katherine insisted.

Lachlan smiled. She was strong, his precious wife. And willful. Opinionated. Often stubborn. Yet utterly his.

Basking in the completeness, the sense of peace invading his every limb, Lachlan closed his eyes and promptly fell asleep.

* * *

"I'm coming with ye," Katherine insisted when Lachlan told her of his plans to visit his brother.

"I dinnae know what I'll discover," Lachlan replied cautiously. "It could be very . . . disturbing."

Katherine's eyes glimmered with concern—and determination. "All the more reason why I should be with ye."

Lachlan hesitated. He recognized that look in Katherine's eyes. Protesting and arguing with his fiery wife could prove to be a waste of time. 'Twas far wiser to save his breath for negotiating with the McKenna if Robbie was desperate to be released.

They departed as soon as they had broken their fast. Once they cleared the castle gates, Katherine spurred her mount to a gallop and then a run. Lachlan and the half dozen soldiers who accompanied them had no choice but to follow suit and join the race. Shouts and laughter filled the air when Katherine pulled ahead of the pack, successfully beating them all.

They slowed to a more reasonable pace and Katherine began pointing out various landmarks. When the fields opened and there was nothing of interest to see, she regaled him with stories and the history of the McKenna clan.

He gazed at his lovely wife and smiled. He knew what she was doing. Distracting him in an attempt to ease his concerns over the impending meeting with Robbie. She was a marvel. Lachlan inhaled deeply, wondering how fate had been so kind as to gift him with such an extraordinary woman.

When they entered a small village of thatched cottages, a tall man of substantial girth, with thick, muscled arms and a crooked nose that had surely been broken more than once, greeted them. Recognizing

Katherine, the man bowed his head respectfully and listened intently to her instructions.

Having Malcolm's permission and the laird's daughter at his side made everything far easier. No one questioned or protested the unusual request to see a prisoner and one of the workers was promptly sent to fetch Robbie.

Lachlan's mouth grew dry as he waited, wondering if his brother would be shackled, hoping if that were the case he would be able to remain calm and stoic. 'Twas also possible that Robbie would be sickly, pale, and drawn, and near complete exhaustion from being underfed and overworked.

Lachlan was therefore astonished to see a strapping man walking out of the quarry gate unencumbered, conversing with the McKenna clansman at his side as though they were friends.

Robbie stood straight and proud. He appeared taller than Lachlan remembered, his chest broader, his arms more muscular. Days of swinging a heavy mallet and lifting man-sized stones into carts had made his brother lean, fit, and muscular.

The men marched their way. Katherine gave his hand a reassuring squeeze and Lachlan moved forward in greeting.

"Good day, Brother."

A muscle above Robbie's eye started twitching and he flushed red. "Lachlan? Is it truly ye?"

"Aye."

Lachlan grasped his brother's shoulders and hugged him. Instead of the stench of an unwashed body and torn, ragged clothes, Robbie was dressed in a clean, thick woolen tunic, wool hose, and padded leather half shoes.

"Ye seem fit," Lachlan said, glancing at the solid muscles on Robbie's forearms.

"We are well fed so that we can work hard. I break and carry the stone, yet sometimes work in the forge with the blacksmith, keeping the chisels sharp and making metal wedges for the quarrymen," Robbie explained. He reached out and touched Lachlan's sleeve, almost as though he were confirming that Lachlan was indeed real. "How were ye able to find me?"

"I have my ways." Lachlan's lips curled in a crafty smile. "And my wife's connections."

Robbie's eyes darted around, coming to rest upon Katherine. "Lady Katherine." He bowed respectfully.

Katherine met his inquisitive stare with a sweet smile. "Hello, Robbie. I am pleased to meet ye, though I prefer that it were under different circumstances."

"I heard a rumor that a MacTavish had married the laird's daughter. Then it's true?" Robbie asked, studying her with wide eyes.

"Aye." Lachlan nodded, pride filling his chest. "I've been blessed with a most exceptional wife."

"I'm pleased to discover that some good has finally come to our family." Robbie lowered his chin. "I've brought dishonor upon our clan, Brother. I pray that ye can forgive me."

Lachlan couldn't miss the sincere remorse in Robbie's voice. "'Tis true that ye acted foolishly and without thought. But ye're making amends fer yer deeds. I can ask no more of ye."

He saw Robbie's shoulders relax, as though a weight had been taken from them. "I swear that I shall make ye proud of me one day."

Lachlan squared his jaw and regarded his brother with a rising sense of respect. "I cannae make any promises, but I might be able to strike a bargain with the McKenna fer yer freedom."

Robbie's eyes shifted and he grumbled under his breath. "I'll not have ye begging fer my release and waste what little coin ye possess to save my hide. Not while the rest of our clan wants fer so much."

"I'm not foolish enough to believe the McKenna would give ye to me fer a price, even if I had the coin," Lachlan admitted.

Robbie's head twisted toward him. "My crimes against the clan are serious. I was one of four men that set upon Sir Malcolm and Lady Joan. Thankfully, they escaped with minor injuries, which is the only reason I still draw breath. By rights, I could have been executed."

Lachlan rubbed his hand over his jaw. "Aye, yer guilt is clear, but I might be able to convince the McKenna to allow me to make amends another way and have ye released sooner."

Robbie peered at him. "How? 'Tis far too late to request a trial by combat."

"Aye," Lachlan agreed. "But a Highlander appreciates sport and loves a contest. The McKenna might consider granting me the right to fight fer yer freedom."

Katherine clasped her hand over her heart. "With swords?"

Lachlan brushed her arm soothingly. "A contest of skill and stamina, Katherine. Not a battle to the death."

A nervous laugh rushed from Robbie's lips. "What if ye lose? Will I have to stay longer?"

Lachlan's brow rose. The possibility of being defeated honestly never crossed his mind. 'Twas not arrogance exactly—well, perhaps a bit.

"I willnae be defeated," Lachlan proclaimed.

"I thank ye fer yer offer of help, but I dinnae need it. My sentence was one year and I've already worked nine months of it. I'll stay until I pay my debt in full." Robbie cleared his throat. "Truth be told, I was hoping that after the year was reached, I'd be allowed to remain and continue working in the quarry fer a wage."

"Ye're a MacTavish," Lachlan protested. "If there's work to be given, it will go to a McKenna man."

"Perhaps ye could use yer influence with the laird and make the request on my behalf?" Robbie asked hopefully.

Lachlan snorted. "And break yer mother's heart? Nay! She'll be filled with grief if ye dinnae return home."

'Twas the most daft notion Lachlan had ever heard. Robbie was the son and brother of a laird, not a common laborer. He had been trained to be a warrior, to defend the honor and property of his clan. Lachlan braced himself for a heated argument, but Robbie pivoted away and was no longer paying him any mind.

What the bloody hell was going on? Had his brother worked out in the sun too long? Hit his head upon a large stone and addled his brain? Quirking his brow in puzzlement and frustration, Lachlan turned to Katherine.

She looped her arm through his and leaned close. "Look yonder and ye'll see what—or rather who—is distracting Robbie so completely."

Scratching his head, Lachlan first looked at his brother. Robbie was standing slack-jawed, his eyes fixed upon a lass who was walking near. She was a pretty creature, with long dark hair and clear, milky skin. Though fine-boned, she managed to carry a large wicker basket in her arms with ease.

"Who's that lass ye are searing with yer gaze?" Lachlan asked.

"Her name is Glynnis," Robbie replied in a voice tinged with awe. "She helps Cook make and serve our meals."

"She's a comely lass," Lachlan observed.

"She's beautiful, an angel in both looks and temperament," Robbie replied. "All the men stop working to watch her whenever she comes to the quarry."

"Including ye," Lachlan remarked dryly.

"Especially me." Robbie sighed. "A short, simple conversation between us leaves me joyful fer days."

"Och, so she's a natural flirt then," Lachlan countered.

"Nay, ye're wrong," Robbie insisted vehemently. "See how she keeps her gaze modestly lowered. She is a paragon, with a gentle voice, a quick wit, and a kind heart. There is no finer woman in all the land."

"Fie, he has it bad," Katherine whispered beneath her breath.

Damn, Katherine was right. His brother was clearly a lovesick fool. "If she means so much to ye, then ask her father fer her hand and bring her home as soon as ye are set free."

"Her mother is an invalid. Glynnis cares fer her and willnae leave. Besides, I've nothing to offer her at Mac-Tavish Keep."

The truth of that statement stung. Lachlan's plans to improve conditions for the clan had not yet reached fruition, yet he remained hopeful his petition to the crown would be considered soon—and granted. But until that time, he had nothing with which to tempt his brother to come home.

"'Tis time to return to work, MacTavish," a stern voice boomed from the quarry gates.

Robbie's eyes grew anxious. "I must hurry away."

"Aye." Lachlan pulled his cloak tight across his shoulders as he and Katherine prepared to leave. "I shall write to Mother and let her know that ye are well. As fer telling the rest, that I leave to ye, Brother."

* * *

Lachlan was silent on the journey back to the castle and Katherine also remained quiet, respecting his need to mull over all that they had learned.

"I need to write to Lady Morag," Lachlan said when they reached the courtyard, dismounted, and proceeded into the great hall. "She will be greatly relieved to hear that I have seen and spoken with Robbie and that he is well."

Katherine rested her head on Lachlan's shoulder. "What else will ye tell her?"

"Nothing. I meant it when I said 'twas Robbie's responsibility to tell her—and Aiden—the rest."

The irony of the situation was not lost on Katherine. Aiden had kidnapped her in hopes of exchanging her for Robbie's freedom. But Robbie had no desire to leave McKenna captivity and in all likelihood would not have left even if Lachlan had consented to the plan for an exchange.

"Damn it, Aileen! Stop pestering me or I swear I shall turn ye over my knee and spank ye like a bairn!"

"I dare ye to try, Brian McKenna!"

Katherine stopped short. She looked across the room and saw her mother standing guard over the McKenna, who was seated in a cushioned chair in front of one of the enormous fireplaces. The pair were glaring daggers at each other, locked in yet another of their famous battles of will.

"What's wrong?" Katherine asked her mother, momentarily forgetting her determination to avoid her sire.

"Yer father willnae drink the tincture I've prepared," Lady Aileen huffed, her face flushed with annoyance. "He's acting like a babe, mewling and protesting and carrying on worse than Callum when he's tired and needs a nap."

"Fer the last time, Aileen, I'm not ill," the McKenna shouted. But his voice cracked and he bent forward, succumbing to a fit of coughing.

"Och, well then, what's all that noise ye're making, Brian McKenna?" Lady Aileen folded her arms across her chest. "Ye kept me awake half the night, hacking and sputtering like a goose."

Concerned, Katherine drew closer. The noxious odor struck first. Her nose wrinkled in distaste and her eyes began to tear. 'Twas then she noticed the tankard that her father was holding gingerly away from his body.

"Ye've made him a cure, Mother?" Katherine asked.

"Aye. And I'll not leave his side until he drinks every last drop of it."

Oh, dear. Her mother's healing skills were legendary—for all the wrong reasons. Judging by the smell, this potion could do far more harm than good. Even if her father did manage to drink it, the contents would most likely not stay inside him for long.

Katherine exchanged a look with Lachlan. He nodded in understanding, then suddenly tripped himself forward, knocking the McKenna's hand and spilling the medicine on the floor. One of the castle hounds lounging nearby hurried over to investigate. The dog sniffed the puddle of liquid, then jerked up his head, turned tail, and ran.

"Fergive my clumsiness," Lachlan apologized as he righted himself.

"Dinnae fret," Lady Aileen replied. "I made a full pitcher of the brew. 'Tis best drunk when hot. It will take but a few moments to prepare another dose."

Muttering to herself, Lady Aileen departed. The

moment she was gone, the McKenna turned a pleading eye on Katherine.

"Fer God's sake, Daughter, take pity on me and stop her," he begged.

Katherine tossed her head. "My husband and I have already aided ye," she replied, stooping to wipe the foul-smelling liquid off the floor. Some of it had already seeped into the rushes and Katherine determined they would need to be replaced—as soon as possible.

"Saints preserve us, ye heard yer mother. She concocted an entire pitcher of this vile stuff. 'Tis more likely to kill than cure me, as ye well know."

The McKenna broke into another fit of coughs. Hearing her father struggle for breath brought on a tumble of emotions inside Katherine, chief among them worry. Her father's cough sounded nasty, maybe even serious. He might truly be ill.

Flushed with concern, she knelt at his side. "Mother is right. Ye must take some medicine to ease the tightness in yer chest and prevent the cough from overtaking yer lungs and stealing yer breath."

"I should have known ye'd take yer mother's side against me," the McKenna lamented. "Neither of ye have any respect fer my authority."

Katherine lowered her head to hide her grin. He *was* acting like a bairn. "We only want ye to get well."

"I'm not ill!" the McKenna shouted before doubling over.

Deep, rumbling coughs echoed through the hall, even as the McKenna fought to contain them from escaping his throat. Katherine placed her hand on her father's back and rubbed, her concern deepening.

"Katherine is recently recovered from a similar ailment. She could show Lady Aileen a more palatable recipe to ease yer cough," Lachlan suggested.

The McKenna's nostrils flared and he sat upright.

"I promise that I'll drink whatever Katherine prepares fer me."

Katherine cast her father a skeptical look, fighting against being pleased at his faith in her. "Me? Ye'll trust me to such a task?"

"Have I cause to worry? Is yer anger still so great that ye would mix a tincture that could do me harm, Daughter?"

A tight emotion constricted Katherine's chest. "I hold my anger so that I may fight fer what I am owed, as ye have taught me. Ye refused to accept my marriage, refuse to bequeath my dowry to my husband, as is right and proper. And so I'll ask ye again to reconsider—seriously—paying my dowry."

The McKenna knitted his brow and leveled a hard stare at her. "Och, so ye think to strike at me while I'm at my weakest?"

"I will use any advantage that presents itself."

The McKenna remained still. Katherine tilted her head to see him better. She was prepared for more anger and protest, but his features were oddly calm.

"Three wagons filled with sacks of grain, winter vegetables, and other foodstuffs were dispatched north to the MacTavish Keep this very morning," the McKenna said quietly.

Katherine's heart stilled. "Part of my dowry?"

"Aye. Yer husband told me that his people were hungry. I couldn't let them starve, could I?"

Her chest swelled with emotion. Did she dare to hope that her father was finally starting to see reason? Was the riff between them beginning to mend?

"What of my dower lands?" she asked.

She felt Lachlan's tender touch on her shoulder. "We should save any further discussions about yer dowry until yer father is feeling better."

Katherine nodded. Lachlan was right. This was a significant gesture from her prideful father, a sure sign that he was softening his stance over her marriage. 'Twould be best to graciously accept this victory and bide her time until the next opportunity presented itself to press her suit.

"I'll steep mint leaves and willow bark, then add honey and whiskey to a mixture that should ease yer coughing," Katherine said.

"It sounds like the nectar of the gods," the McKenna said wistfully.

"I shall also convince Mother to allow ye to drink my tincture instead of hers," Katherine added.

"I am grateful to ye, Daughter."

"There is no need, Father," she replied truthfully. "The McKennas care fer their own."

"Aye." The McKenna sniffed. "Now hurry and catch yer mother before she returns with more of her evil brew. If she does, I shall be forced to spill it upon myself and I've no doubt the foul odor will forever linger, even if this garment is washed a hundred times."

Chapter Twenty-One

"May we ride beyond the large boulder near the loch today, Aunt Katherine?" Lileas asked excitedly. "That's where all the birds go to build their nests. I want to look and see if we can find one with eggs inside."

"'Tis much farther than we usually go," Katherine replied. "Ye and Callum will get tired and so will yer ponies."

"But we did it last summer with Uncle Graham and we never got tired," Lileas protested. "Not even once. Uncle Graham always agreed it was the best place of all to ride. Please, please will ye and Uncle Lachlan take us."

Lachlan bit back his smile. Barely six years old and Lileas McKenna was most assuredly the boldest lass in all the Highlands. He didn't envy Malcolm and Joan's job of raising—and controlling—such a free-spirited lass.

"'Tis not summertime now, 'tis the cold winter and I dinnae think yer father would approve of such a long outing," Katherine replied.

"Papa willnae mind," Lileas insisted. "He likes it when Callum and I are happy."

Katherine's brow rose. "Does he now?"

"Aye." Lileas nodded her head enthusiastically. "So does Mama."

Katherine blew out her breath and Lachlan's smile broke free. These morning rides with the children had quickly become part of their daily routine and Lachlan was surprised by how much he enjoyed them. Callum was a good-natured lad, thoughtful and intelligent, and Lileas never ceased to provide a challenge to everyone's patience.

He started toward them, preparing to lend Katherine assistance, when his attention was diverted by a rider thundering into the bailey.

There was no mistaking the distinct colors of the MacTavish plaid the man wore. His horse was frothing at the mouth, evidence of a long, hard, swift ride. Two stable lads ran out to meet him. One held the horse while the other reached out to steady the rider as he dismounted.

"I must see Laird MacTavish at once," the rider demanded as he struggled to catch his breath. "Do ye know where I can find him?"

Apprehension shivered down Lachlan's spine as he stepped forward, realizing the man looked familiar.

"Jamie?" he asked, recognizing one of Aiden's men.

"Aye, Laird." Jamie bent forward and placed his hands on his knees, attempting to steady his breathing. "I've an urgent message fer ye."

Straightening, Jamie reached beneath his tunic and pulled out a rumpled parchment. Apparently, it had been written in such haste a seal had not been employed to close it.

Lachlan quickly read the brief note. "Do ye know what this says?" he asked the exhausted messenger.

Jamie nodded. "Mostly. 'Tis about yer brother Aiden.

Three days ago he was captured by the Frasers. Ye must come at once."

Katherine was suddenly at Lachlan's side, her face wide with anxiety. "Who sent this message?"

"Lady Morag," Jamie replied.

"What does she say?" Katherine asked, peering over Lachlan's shoulder.

Hastily, he crumbled the letter in his hands. "Aiden is being held by Archibald Fraser. He demands that I come to his castle and meet with him or else he shall torture my brother until he no longer breathes."

"Dear God!" Eyes wide with fright, Katherine squeezed Lachlan's arm. "What will ye do?"

"I must go."

Lachlan stole a glance at Katherine. Her lips were pursed so tightly with fear they had turned white. He hated causing her such distress, but his duty was clear.

Katherine grabbed his hand and held it against her breast. "This could be a trick, Lachlan, a ruse that will put both ye and Aiden in the Fraser dungeons."

"That thought has certainly crossed my mind," Lachlan admitted, lowering his voice so he would not be overheard.

"As well it should," Katherine hissed. "And there is more to consider. Who knows if this is indeed true? They could all be conspiring against ye—Lady Morag, Aiden, and Fraser. 'Tis no secret that Aiden wants to be laird. And ye cannae have forgotten that 'twas Lady Morag who sent Fraser the message about me."

"I've forgotten nothing, Katherine," he replied, almost wishing he hadn't told Katherine about Lady Morag's lapse in judgment. "But if this is true and Aiden is indeed in Fraser's clutches . . ."

Katherine's eyes grew rounder. "Christ's bones."

Lachlan lowered his lips to her ear. "Say no more

until we are inside. I dinnae want Lileas and Callum to become frightened."

The curious pair had wandered close. Katherine distracted them with the promise of sweets and a long ride to look for a bird's nest. The two happily scampered off to the kitchen for their treats. Meanwhile, he and Katherine escorted Jamie into the castle.

"Mary, fetch food and ale fer Laird MacTavish's man," Katherine ordered the servant. "Then send someone to find my brothers."

"What can ye tell us, Jamie?" Lachlan asked as soon as Malcolm and Graham arrived.

The messenger shrugged helplessly. "Aiden was hunting with a group of his men when the Frasers attacked. They wounded several of the others and took Aiden with them. A missive arrived a few hours later from Laird Fraser, stating his demands. Lady Morag bade me to come find ye with all due haste."

"How is Lady Morag?" Lachlan inquired.

"Frantic with worry," Jamie replied.

"That fear is not misplaced," Malcolm muttered under his breath. "Fraser is not a man known fer his mercy."

Lachlan silently agreed. Jamie shoved a meat pie into his mouth and drained his tankard of ale and Lachlan wondered how long it had been since the messenger had eaten.

"Ye've ridden hard," Graham observed.

"Steadily fer two days and two nights," Jamie acknowledged. "Fraser is not a patient man. I had to reach Lachlan quickly if Aiden is to have any chance of surviving."

Lachlan noticed that Lady Joan had joined them. She stood beside her husband, her expression grim.

"We need yer help, dearest." Malcolm tenderly cupped her chin and she looked directly into his eyes.

"Fraser has captured Lachlan's brother. We need to devise a rescue plan. Ye lived at the castle fer several years. What can ye tell us about its defenses?"

Joan shuddered. "Archibald takes great pride in making the castle impenetrable. Though a miser at heart, he does part with his coin to pay fer the defense of his property. His soldiers are well trained and ruthless and always fight to kill."

"We have no time to plan a frontal attack," Lachlan said. "Do ye think we can bribe our way inside, Joan?"

"Nay. The clan's fear of Archibald is too great. He is hardly beloved, in truth most hate him, yet none would dare to cross him. They know his retribution would be swift and harsh."

"Then we'll have to find another way," Lachlan conceded.

"A rescue?" Graham suggested.

"Aye." Lachlan rubbed his hand over his jaw. "'Twould be a great help if we knew the castle layout. Can ye tell us where the dungeon is located, Joan?"

Joan's eyes clouded. "There are two, each placed in opposite ends of the main keep."

Lachlan turned to Jamie. "We'll need more men so that we can divide into two groups and search each dungeon at the same time once we gain entrance to the castle."

Joan shook her head. "In all likelihood, yer brother is being held in the high south tower. 'Tis Archibald's preferred location when he has a *special* prisoner."

Her lovely face creased with sorrow and sympathy. No doubt she believed Aiden already dead or close to it. 'Twas the same bitter outcome Lachlan contemplated himself, but even though 'twas only a slight chance, he had to try to free his brother.

Lachlan hardened his jaw. "Then it must be a small

rescue party, consisting of a few men. Disguised, we shall steal into the castle, free Aiden, and make good our escape before Fraser even knows we have come."

"I shall be one of those men," Malcolm stated.

Joan's eyes flashed with fear. "Nay! 'Tis far too dangerous. Archibald shall take even greater delight in capturing ye, Malcolm."

Lachlan reluctantly agreed. "Though I am grateful fer the offer, I could not ask such a sacrifice from ye, Malcolm."

"Ye dinnae ask. I volunteered." Malcolm turned to his wife. "Fraser remains a threat to us all. He needs to know that he has strong, powerful enemies who willnae allow him to exact unwarranted vengeance."

"I will come also," Graham said.

Lachlan glanced at Malcolm. "Jamie shall come, too, which means we need one more man. I would like my brother Robbie to ride with us. Will ye allow it?"

Malcolm nodded. "I'll speak with my father."

Jamie gulped down the rest of his food and jumped to his feet. "How soon can we leave?"

Lachlan rested a hand on Jamie's shoulder. "It will take us a few hours to get everything ready. In the meantime, ye need to rest."

The others departed, and once they were alone, Lachlan could feel his wife's eyes upon him.

"Ye must be very careful. Fraser will take great pleasure in making ye look the fool," Katherine said, her voice quavering with emotion.

Lachlan's heart twisted in knots. "Trap or no, I cannae ignore the threat. We all know what Fraser is capable of doing. Aiden's life could very well hang in the balance."

"And what of yer life?" Katherine choked, her eyes filling with tears.

"With Robbie, Malcolm, Graham, and Jamie at my side, I know that we can defeat Fraser." Lachlan clasped Katherine's shoulders and pulled her close, pressing his lips against her forehead. It tore at his heart to see her so distressed. "Try not to worry so, my dearest. I vow that I shall allow nothing to shatter the love we have and the life we are so eager to build together."

She hugged him tightly. "I shall hold ye to that promise, Lachlan MacTavish. Now make haste and return to me swiftly, fer I vow that I shall not rest a moment until I am once again in yer arms."

They purchased fresh horses along the route and took turns sleeping while they rode, arriving on Fraser land in two days' time. Over the course of their travels, the men discussed and discarded various plans, eventually agreeing on one. 'Twas bold, reckless, and just mad enough to succeed, as long as each man did his part at precisely the correct moment.

The time had come. Lachlan squinted into the midday sun and gave the signal. Robbie and Graham suddenly appeared, striding boldly toward the Fraser castle.

As he approached the outer gate, Robbie began staggering like a drunkard, merrily singing a bawdy tune while swinging a full tankard of ale. When he drew near, he generously offered to share his brew with the two guards at the gate.

The taller one glared at him in disgust, but the shorter fellow reached for the vessel and took a long swallow. The moment he was distracted by the drink, Robbie cracked him on the head. The other guard lunged, but Graham was in position and quickly knocked him out.

Each man dragged an unconscious guard behind the gatehouse and soon emerged wearing a Fraser tunic. They quickly assumed the same stance and exact positions as the guards before anyone noticed the exchange.

"Let's go."

Lachlan nudged Malcolm. The two men emerged from their hiding place. Each pulled the cowl of their monk's robes over their heads, hiding their faces. Walking slowly, as to not rattle the weapons strapped to their torsos, they slipped through the outer gate.

To avoid attracting any undue attention, they kept their heads bowed. Following Joan's directions once they reached the courtyard, they were able to quickly locate the outside tower doorway. As it was hidden from the parapet, they were able to approach the entrance unchallenged.

However, Lachlan's initial elation at their success faltered when he noticed the heavy metal lock securing the door.

"We can force it open if we strike it at the same time," Malcolm predicted.

Lachlan agreed. He turned and hunched his shoulders. Malcolm did the same. At Malcolm's signal, they struck the door with full force. It shook, yet held. Lachlan took a deep breath and nodded at Malcolm. They gave it a second and then a third lunge and finally the wooden door splintered off its hinges.

Lachlan peered inside. He motioned to the left, to alert Malcolm where the guards stood.

"The staircase is on the right. I'll take care of these two while ye climb to the tower," Malcolm whispered.

The men parted. Lachlan inched his way around the corner, then flattened himself against the wall when he heard voices. Breath held, Lachlan waited until the pair of serving women he spied coming his way reversed their course, their footsteps disappearing in the distance.

Lachlan's thick leather boots were silent on the stone steps as he climbed the staircase to the tower. He rotated his shoulder and prepared to burst through the door, but when he reached for the handle, he found it unlocked.

A trap?

Slowly, Lachlan cracked open the door, watching warily for signs of an ambush. Angling his head, he peered through the opening, disappointed to see a barren, empty chamber. Cursing beneath his breath, he opened the door wider and stepped inside.

The chamber was freezing. The leather coverings had been removed from two large window openings and the cold wind howled through the room with a keening cry.

Reaching beneath his robe, he slowly unsheathed his dirk and moved farther into the chamber. A slight rustling noise on his left drew his attention. Lachlan swung around and caught sight of a body on the floor in the corner.

"Aiden?"

No response.

Cautiously, Lachlan approached. He could see movement and realized it was the rise and fall of a breathing chest. Whoever it was, they were alive. Lachlan knelt down and carefully turned the body over.

He froze. 'Twas so swollen and bruised he barely recognized Aiden's handsome face. There were streaks of blood on his cheek and Lachlan realized that a swath of his brother's hair on the right side had been cleaved from his head. The scalp was raw and crusted—a sickening sight.

"Christ Almighty, what's he done to ye?" Lachlan choked out.

Aiden's eyelids fluttered. "Have ye come to give me last rights, Father?" Aiden croaked.

"I've come to set ye free, Brother."

Aiden's left eye opened to a slit, as the right was swollen completely shut. "Lachlan? God does indeed have a wicked sense of humor if a vision of ye is the final thing I see before I die."

"I'm no vision," Lachlan replied, slicing through the ropes that secured Aiden's wrists. They too were raw and bleeding, most likely from many unsuccessful attempts to break free.

Aiden grasped Lachlan's forearm and squeezed. "Ye're real," he exclaimed in wonder.

"Aye. Can ye stand?"

Aiden grimaced and shook his head. "My legs are broken."

Lachlan clenched his hand into a tight fist of rage. Fraser was every bit the monster they all said. However, now was not the time to dwell upon it—he had to get Aiden to safety. But how? His brother was unable to walk.

Flummoxed, Lachlan looked out one of the windows, wondering if it would be possible to secure a rope around Aiden's waist and lower him to freedom. But as he scanned the ramparts he realized it would be far too easy for one of the soldiers patrolling them to see the descent.

"Ah, so ye have finally come!" a male voice boomed in a cheerful tone. "I'm pleased to learn that ye received my invitation and acted so quickly to comply. Though ye should have announced yerself in my hall instead of sneaking in here like a thief."

Lachlan turned. Archibald Fraser stood in the

doorway. His face was flushed with wine or cold, his eyes watchful and alert, his hand tightly gripping a long-bladed dirk.

Lachlan kept his expression blank, swallowing back his disgust, tempering his response. Fraser was alone. If he could somehow maneuver him closer, there was a good chance he could slit his throat before the guards were summoned.

"I can see by yer treatment of my brother that yer hatred fer the MacTavish runs deep," Lachlan said, refusing to allow Fraser to see how shaken he felt discovering Aiden in such a state.

"Aye. I've much to be angry about." Though he spoke calmly, Fraser's eyes were seething with a violent fury. "Ye lied to me about the McKenna bitch and ye took my family's sword in an unfair fight."

"Yer feud was with me, Fraser, not Aiden," Lachlan said tightly.

"Are ye distressed by what has happened to yer brother, MacTavish? Well, ye've only yerself to blame. He would have been in far less pain if ye had arrived sooner," Fraser taunted.

"I thought it would be amusing to send him back to his family in pieces," Fraser continued, tossing the weapon he held from one hand to the other. "'Twas so difficult to decide where to start. An ear? A finger? Pity he wore no ring that his mother could easily recognize and thus know the finger belonged to her son. So instead I decided to start with a section of his golden hair. Do ye think she screamed or retched when she beheld it? I should like to believe that she did both."

Lachlan's stomach roiled. The bastard had *scalped* his brother. His fingers itched to reach for the dirk he had used to cut Aiden's bonds that now lay beside his brother, but he knew he would only have one chance to throw it. His timing needed to be perfect or else both he and Aiden would die at Fraser's hand. Of that there was little doubt.

"What are ye planning to do now?" Lachlan asked, inching toward the wall.

If he could position himself out of Archibald's direct line of sight, it should give him enough of a surprise advantage to make a lethal strike. If there was any justice in this world, Fraser would have a blade protruding from his black heart before he even realized he had been attacked.

"I've yet to decide my next move." Fraser laughed merrily, but there was no mistaking the murder in his eyes. "Shall I be merciful? Make certain yer death is swift and sure? Well, perhaps fer one of ye. But not fer both. Fer honor to be served, one of ye must die a slow and agonizing death."

The venom and pure malice in Fraser's eyes made Lachlan's blood run cold. Then suddenly, Aiden shouted a warning as Fraser lunged toward them. Lachlan's hand reached out fer the dirk, but came up empty.

Cursing, he crouched low, shielding his brother with his body. He could hear Fraser approaching. Somehow, Lachlan was able to raise his arm as Fraser struck, blocking the blow. The unexpected move surprised his enemy, knocking him off balance.

Fraser fell backward, staggering toward the large window. With a growl of anger, Lachlan ran toward him, slamming into Fraser's chest with enough force to send him through the opening.

There was a look of horror and pure fear on Archibald's face as he disappeared from view. Lachlan held his breath until he heard the dull thud of a body smashing against the hard earth below. The sound jolted through him.

He glanced at Aiden, waiting for the shouts of horror and outrage to start outside, yet all was silent.

Had no one witnessed Fraser fall? The window faced away from the courtyard, but it was the middle of the afternoon. Surely someone would have seen such a horrific sight.

"Why is it so quiet?" Aiden asked.

"I dinnae know. Fraser made no sound as he fell to his death. Is it possible none saw it happen?"

The quiet remained and hope began to flourish inside Lachlan. Was it possible that he and Aiden could flee the tower before the body was found?

"Malcolm McKenna is somewhere belowstairs. I'm going to find him. Between the two of us we should be able to carry ye out," Lachlan told Aiden.

"Without being seen?" Aiden shook his head. "Impossible. The Fraser guards will be here any minute. Go quickly. Save yerself, Lachlan, before they arrive."

"Nay. I came here to bring ye home and I'm not leaving without ye."

"Dinnae be a fool, Lachlan. Ye've a wife, a clan to lead, important responsibilities." Aiden released a shuddering sigh as he strained to continue speaking. "Ye've got far more to live fer than I do. Than I ever will."

Lachlan's gut twisted with pity. His proud, arrogant, defiant brother was a broken man.

"I'm not leaving ye here," Lachlan repeated, with a confidence he was far from feeling.

Heavy footsteps sounded on the stairs. "They must have found Fraser," Aiden rasped through clenched teeth. "Do ye have a dirk fer me?"

Lachlan pulled the weapon from his boot, pleased that for all his lamentations, Aiden did not intend to die without a fight. However, Lachlan had every intention making certain they both lived.

"Hide it fer now," he directed, placing the dirk in Aiden's hand. "I have an idea. If it works, ye willnae need it."

Lachlan retrieved his other blade from the floor and waited. It took but a moment for three soldiers, swords drawn, to burst into the room.

"Thank the saints ye've arrived," Lachlan exclaimed. "Is Laird Fraser all right?"

Startled by the greeting, the trio exchanged puzzled glances.

"He's dead," one of them said bluntly.

"Ah, 'tis as we feared. He lost his balance and fell from the window. It all happened so quickly there was no chance to save him." Lachlan slowly crossed himself. "Pity."

"Are ye claiming that his death was an accident?" the same soldier asked.

"Aye, a terrible, tragic accident," Lachlan repeated.

The men blinked in surprise, then two of them turned to the third. "William?"

"I know who ye are, Lachlan MacTavish. This was no accident. Ye killed our laird," William said with a cold look of accusation in his eyes.

"Nay! 'Twas an unfortunate mishap. A stroke of fate, the unexplainable will of God." Lachlan sighed with theatrical exaggeration. "However, now that Archibald is gone, the most important question is who will replace him as laird? He has no direct heir. I happen to know that in such cases Scottish law allows fer the clansmen to vote and decide amongst themselves who will next lead them."

A clammy sweat covered Lachlan's brow. Archibald had been a cruel tyrant to his people. Most, if not all, would be happy to be freed from his yoke of abuse.

Lachlan was counting on using that misery to aid him in bargaining for his and Aiden's lives.

William's eyes narrowed in suspicion. "Yer lying. The crown willnae allow us to choose our laird."

"They will," Lachlan insisted. "Especially if yer new laird has the support of the MacTavish clan."

"And the McKennas." Malcolm stepped into the chamber.

The three soldiers pivoted, lifting their swords and assuming a fighting stance.

"The MacTavish and the McKenna are our enemies," William cried.

"No longer," Lachlan insisted. "Ye have my word, and that of Malcolm McKenna. The feud between us died with Archibald. Accidentally, died."

Their eyes met briefly, and Lachlan knew William was fully aware that he was lying about Fraser's death. He held his breath, assessing their chances if the man refused to seize this opportunity.

He and Malcolm should be able to defeat these three. As for escaping from the tower with Aiden, och, well that would prove far more challenging.

"A most tragic accident," William said finally, taking a deep breath. He turned to the other men. "I shall inform the rest of our men of this tragedy. Ye two will have splints and a stretcher brought here at once. Laird MacTavish wishes to take his brother home."

Chapter Twenty-Two

Katherine spent all her waking hours in her mother's solar since it overlooked the gate where she could easily watch for any sign of her husband and brothers. It had been nearly a fortnight and still no word. When would they return?

Katherine paced, stopped, stared out the window, and paced again until she feared she might go mad. In contrast, Joan sat serenely, her hands occupied embroidering an infant skullcap for her yet-to-be-born babe, her head turning only occasionally to glance out the window.

"How do ye stay so calm?" Katherine asked, blowing out a frustrated breath.

"Ye must have faith in yer husband," Joan replied quietly, as she knotted her stitch and snipped the thread. "And mine."

"I dinnae lack faith in either Lachlan's or Malcolm's abilities," Katherine said, hugging herself. "'Tis the possibility of betrayal that frightens me. From Fraser. Or far worse, from Lachlan's kin."

Joan laid the tiny hat in her lap and stretched. "Our

husbands are far too clever to be caught in a trap. They are seasoned warriors with the wits and the will to best Archibald."

Katherine huffed and put her hand on her hip. She knew that Joan spoke the truth, but her worries would not ease. A warning horn blared and Katherine swiveled excitedly to the window.

"Riders on the horizon!" she yelled in glee.

Katherine lifted her skirts and ran from the solar. She paused at the bottom of the staircase and Joan nearly bumped into her, as she was following so close on Katherine's heels.

Katherine smiled. Apparently, Joan's outward appearance of calm and serenity was not nearly as deep as her sister-in-law proclaimed.

Yet all other thoughts vanished the moment Katherine entered the courtyard and saw a familiar figure riding toward her. The moment he dismounted, she threw her arms around Lachlan, laughing and sobbing at the same time.

"Thank the Lord ye've returned to me," she cried. "I've been out of my mind with worry."

"A part of me feels insulted at yer lack of conviction in my skills," Lachlan quipped, brushing his hand along her cheek. "But a far greater part is thankful to be once again holding ye in my arms, lass."

His voice was tender and loving. His strength and power surrounded her causing the fears and worries of the last days to vanish. Katherine lifted her head and rained a volley of kisses along his jaw, cheeks, and lips.

"Christ's blood, Katherine, give the poor man a moment to catch his breath!"

She drew back slightly and caught her father's eye. The McKenna came forward and slapped Lachlan on the back. "I'm glad that ye've all returned safely. Were ye successful?"

"Aye. Aiden was rescued, though badly injured." A bleak cloud swept over Lachlan's expression. "We brought him to MacTavish Keep to recover. Robbie and Lady Morag are anxious to care fer him and vow to bring him back to full health."

"Can they?" Katherine asked.

A darkness settled in Lachlan's eyes. "Aiden will live. As fer the rest, 'tis in God's hands."

"We shall all pray fer his recovery," the McKenna announced. "Come inside. Ye have much to tell us and we are eager to hear all."

Lady Aileen gave Malcolm, Graham, and Lachlan a quick hug and then, pulling Graham to her side, followed her husband. Malcolm, his arms wrapped tightly around Joan, fell in step beside Katherine and Lachlan.

To ensure complete privacy, the family congregated in the McKenna's private solar. A protesting Lileas and a wide-eyed Callum were whisked away by their nursemaid, quieting only after Malcolm promised his children a special surprise.

"Well?" Lady Aileen asked.

Lachlan and Malcolm exchanged a glance.

"Archibald Fraser is dead," Malcolm said flatly.

Joan gasped and grabbed Malcolm's hand. "How did he die?"

"I pushed him out a tower window," Lachlan replied.

She closed her eyes and pinched the bridge of her nose. "That sounds swift. And painless."

"Aye, 'twas quicker than I would have liked," Lachlan replied. "But I can assure ye, Fraser knew what was happening. And it terrified him."

"Good." Joan shuddered and placed her hand

protectively over her womb. "Never again will he haunt my dreams or threaten the peace of our family."

"We must prepare fer a clan war," the McKenna declared. "The Frasers will be out fer blood over their laird's death."

Katherine rubbed her forehead. "'Twas Lachlan who killed him. They will seek vengeance upon the MacTavish, not the McKenna."

"We stand with the MacTavish," her father said defiantly. "They are our kin."

Katherine blinked and a tear slid down her cheek. Hearing her father's vow to stand with her husband was the final proof that he had fully accepted their marriage and forgiven her.

Malcolm leaned forward. "Thanks to Lachlan's quick thinking there will be no calls for retribution against any of us, as long as we agree to acknowledge the legitimacy of the next Fraser laird."

The McKenna stroked his chin thoughtfully. "Is he an honorable man?"

Lachlan and Malcolm exchanged another look. "We have no idea. The men of the clan have yet to decide. Truthfully, whoever they pick has to be better than Archibald."

Everyone nodded in agreement. The room grew silent and the crackling of the fire in the hearth filled the chamber. Katherine leaned into Lachlan. All she wanted to do was to rest her head against his strong chest and listen to the steady beat of his heart.

"Damn, in all the excitement I forgot!" The McKenna rose from his chair and rummaged through the papers scattered on his desk. "A missive was delivered fer Lachlan."

Katherine's head snapped up from Lachlan's shoulder. "When? I never saw any messengers."

"Aye, 'tis astonishing ye missed him considering how ye gazed out yer mother's solar window fer days on end." The McKenna handed Lachlan a rolled parchment. "It arrived two days ago. It bears the royal seal."

Heart pounding, Katherine watched Lachlan break through the wax and read the letter. He lifted his eyes from the missive and his solemn expression turned to one of amazement. "My petition to the crown to restore the MacTavish lands has been considered—and awarded."

"What?" Katherine snatched the parchment from her husband's hands and quickly scanned the letter. "'Tis not the same parcel of land that once belonged to yer family, but rather a tract of property equal in size, not far from the McKenna borders."

All eyes turned toward the McKenna and Katherine swore she saw her father blush. "I might have expressed my preference to the crown fer having a friend rather than a foe on my eastern border."

"Is the property adjacent to my dower lands?" Katherine asked excitedly. "We can expand that holding and create a new home fer all the MacTavish clan."

Lachlan's brow furrowed as he gazed down at the simple map drawn on the deed. "Nay, there appear to be many miles between the two."

"However, yer land borders my quarry." The McKenna cleared his throat. "I propose that we exchange Katherine's dower estate fer the quarry and several hundred acres surrounding it."

"'Tis hardly a fair exchange," Katherine protested. "The dower estate produces goods that generate money fer our coffers."

"The quarry will provide an even better income. And I will double the amount of seed and livestock that is part of yer dowry," the McKenna countered. "However, ye must provide me with the stones I require to make repairs to my curtain wall and castle at no charge."

"And ye shall sell me the material that I will need to build my castle at a very low price," Graham interjected.

Lachlan's eyes lit up with interest. Katherine leaned in and whispered in her husband's ear, "'Tis a much better offer."

Lachlan stood and extended his hand. "I agree. I am anxious to give my clan a better life in a more hospitable location and I find that I, too, would be pleased to have a friend rather than a foe on my border."

The next day, after a vigorous morning on the training field with the McKenna brothers, Lachlan entered their bedchamber and found Katherine peering down at a large parchment unfurled on the table.

She turned and smiled, motioning him forward. "Come and look. 'Tis the map of the new MacTavish holdings. Father had it drawn fer us. I've marked three different building sites we should consider fer the keep, but I'm sure there are others. The property is vast. It will take us weeks to view it all."

She leaned forward and Lachlan took a moment to simply stare at her, admiring the view. His lovely wife did have a most delicious arse. Unable to resist the temptation she posed, he came to her and drew his arm around her waist. Molding his chest against her back, Lachlan bent forward and began nibbling on her earlobe.

The exhaustion and emotions he felt from the grueling pace of the past few days vanished. Holding Katherine in his arms had the power to bring forth a peace and contentment unlike any other. 'Twas a soothing balm to his soul.

"Are ye certain ye have no regrets about giving up yer dower estate?" he asked.

"Not a one," she assured him, nuzzling her cheek into the palm of his hand. "We are blessed to have the good fortune of building a home fer ourselves and our clan. 'Tis where we will raise our children and grow old together."

"Bairns. Well, Wife, ye know what we must do if ye wish to have them." He caressed her thigh, sliding her gown up so he could touch the tender flesh beneath.

She wiggled suggestively against him, expelling a throaty sigh. "We must begin our search fer a master builder soon so that we can start construction the moment the ground is no longer frozen."

Lachlan groaned. "God's teeth, Katherine, I'm trying to seduce ye and all ye can speak of is building a keep."

"Not just a keep, Lachlan. We need a moat and curtain wall, stables, mews, an alehouse, a dairy, a chapel, and many other outbuildings I'm sure."

"Damn, I should have bargained fer more coin from yer father," he muttered.

"We'll make up the difference by charging Graham more fer his quarry stones," Katherine said as she loosened the ties of her bodice.

Lachlan took immediate advantage of the invitation, filling his hands with her naked breasts. "Clever, lass."

He made love to her then, sweet and slow, until she cried out, exploding in pleasure as his seed bathed her womb. After, as the vestiges of their passion ebbed, Lachlan held Katherine close to his heart and contemplated the years ahead of them.

"Ye are very quiet, Lachlan." She turned to face him, her smile lighting up his heart. "Do ye have an idea fer our new home?"

He could feel his chest rumbling with laughter. "I

have several, though I suspect most will be overruled by my headstrong wife."

"Well, not all of them." She traced her finger lovingly over his face. "We'll find our way together, Lachlan."

He kissed her tenderly. "Aye, lass, we will."

Epilogue

Three years later

Lachlan watched Katherine carefully make her way across the bailey, his brow furrowed with concern. She was so heavily burdened with child that he worried about her entering the great hall and climbing the stone steps to their bedchamber alone. He started toward her, then hesitated, debating the best way to approach his wife.

She was prickly as a thistle these days. Smiling one moment, shouting the next, holding him tight, then pushing him away. The midwife insisted 'twas a sign that the babe was strong and healthy and that he need not worry.

Lachlan could only pray that she was correct. A miscarriage the year before had left Katherine heartbroken and depressed. Though at the time she had not even known her womb had quickened with life, the subsequent loss of the child had been hard on both of them.

Mercifully, their shared grief and the distraction of

building a home had eased their sorrow and strengthened their bond. It had taken two full years to complete the main tower and thick curtain wall surrounding the modest-sized castle Lachlan had commissioned on the land granted him by the crown. They had moved in as soon as it was finished and Katherine had gradually transformed the dwelling into a comfortable, welcoming home.

The village at the base of the castle was also nearing completion. Most of the MacTavish clan had moved south, lured by the fertile land and the chance for a better life for themselves and their children. They tilled the soil, proud to grow crops that bloomed and flourished, while others worked the quarry, earning a small wage for themselves and a steady income of coin for the clan.

As predicted, Graham had been the quarry's best customer. The fortress he constructed on the land given to him by the McKenna and Laird Drummond required massive amounts of stone and Graham sheepishly admitted 'twas growing to a size that could eventually rival McKenna Castle.

Katherine insisted that her brother kept building merely as an excuse to avoid the proxy marriage he had undertaken to secure peace with the Drummond clan. For when his castle was completed, Graham would no longer have an excuse for keeping his bride languishing in a convent. He would be obliged to bring her home and begin their marriage in truth.

A fact that Hamish Drummond loudly mentioned to Graham—and all the McKennas—at every opportunity.

Robbie had taken charge of the quarry and shown an interest in learning the building trade. He had demonstrated a true talent for the task, proving himself to be a tremendous asset. In thanks, Lachlan had given his brother his own cottage.

Filled with confidence, purpose, and self-worth, Robbie had finally persuaded the lovely Glynnis to marry him. He had brought her parents to live in a cottage next to theirs, so his bride could continue to care for her mother. 'Twas an arrangement that suited them well and the young couple seemed very happy.

Lachlan's garrison had swelled in numbers; the many soldiers were housed comfortably in a large barracks designed by Robbie and constructed in the inner courtyard. Lachlan trained his men hard, confident in their fighting skills, knowing they would be ready if they were called into service by the crown.

Not all the MacTavish clan had moved here, though. Aiden and a few of his loyal men had elected to stay in the north. He had recovered from his injuries, though he walked with a slight limp that became more pronounced when the weather was especially damp. At his mother's suggestion, he also grew his hair longer on the left side to compensate for what was missing on the right.

Aiden had pledged his loyalty and sword to Lachlan as the MacTavish laird in a public ceremony with uncharacteristic humility and sincerity. Though Lachlan prayed often that he would never have a need, he was confident that if he called upon his brother, Aiden would willingly fight at his side.

Lady Morag had decided to remain in the north with Aiden during the warmer months of the year, but she spent the late fall, winter, and early spring with Lachlan and Katherine. Lady Morag wrote often, expressing her desire to visit as soon as her first grandchild arrived no matter what the weather.

A grandchild. His child.

An unmistakable emotion tugged at Lachlan's heart, tightening his throat and squeezing his chest until he could hardly take a breath. Enduring Katherine's pregnancy had put his patience to the most extreme test. He had worried daily over her health and that of the child, constantly battling his fears.

Far too many women—and their babes—perished in childbirth. If anything happened to her . . . he shook his head sharply, unable to even consider the thought.

"Ye should be off yer feet, Katherine," he called to her as he crossed the bailey, drawing near his waddling wife.

"Cease fussing at me," she snapped, swatting his hand away. Then suddenly she sighed, lowering her head in contrition. "Och, my tongue seems to have a will of its own these days. A nasty one, too. I dinnae know how ye can endure my company."

"I love ye, Katherine, with all my heart."

The soft expression in her eyes lasted only for a moment and then the tears started. "This has been torturous fer ye, Lachlan. Admit it. No man can gladly suffer a wife so ruled by her emotions that her mood changes with the hour. Ye must be counting the minutes until it ends."

"If ye are asking me if I'm happy that our child will soon be born, then I'll say aye," Lachlan answered.

Katherine fisted her hand on the small of her aching back and frowned. Oh, how she wished she could be more agreeable! But she was unable to sleep for more than an hour at a time, her bladder always felt full, and her feet were so swollen she hobbled more than she walked.

Frustratingly, her emotions were beyond her control and she marveled constantly that Lachlan never ceased to be anything but kind, patient, and loving toward her.

He held her arm and she leaned heavily upon him as they climbed the stairs to their bedchamber. Once there, she allowed Lachlan to assist her into bed. The brief slumber she achieved was soon interrupted by a sharp, constant pain that spread across her entire back. The midwife was summoned and a messenger rode hard to McKenna Castle to fetch her mother.

And thus Katherine's long struggle to bring her child into the world began. Her labor lasted well into the next day, but the sound of her child's lusty cries chased away Katherine's exhaustion.

Tears filled Katherine's eyes as she accepted the small, squirming bundle from her mother. Lady Aileen's eyes misted too. She placed her arms around Katherine and her newest grandchild and recited a prayer of joy and thanks.

Cradling the babe close to her breast, Katherine called for Lachlan. He appeared almost immediately, his eyes red-rimmed from lack of sleep—and possibly several drams of whiskey—his hair rumpled, his jaw covered with dark stubble.

Lady Aileen shooed the midwife and the other women from the chamber, casting a happy smile upon the new family as she shut the door behind her.

"Come and meet yer daughter," Katherine said.

She placed the infant on her lap and carefully unwrapped the swaddling. Lachlan leaned closer and the two marveled over the babe's tiny features. Her sweet, delicate face and rosebud mouth, her small, perfectly shaped limbs and the tuffs of downy hair covering her head.

"She's so tiny," Lachlan whispered, brushing Katherine's cheek with his lips. "So perfect."

He set his finger against the bairn's palm and the wee one gripped it tightly. Seeing the two joined hands—one so new and delicate, the other hard and battle-scared—brought a fresh batch of tears to Katherine's eyes.

Lachlan was going to be a wonderful father—kind, loving, caring. A true protector, who would give his life to keep them all safe.

"Some men would be disappointed to have a female fer a firstborn child," Katherine ventured, voicing a nagging fear.

"Witless fools." Lachlan tickled the infant's chin with the tip of his nose. "She is the most amazing creature ever born. My heart is near to bursting with love fer her—and her mother."

"Here, take her," Katherine choked, lifting the babe. "Hold yer daughter."

Lachlan's expression grew horrified. "I fear I might crush the sweet angel. Or drop her."

"Ye shall do no such thing." Katherine sniffled. "Yet, if it makes ye more at ease, sit beside me on the bed. If she falls, she'll not have far to land."

A visibly nervous Lachlan took the newborn babe in his arms, holding her close to his chest as Katherine instructed. For a moment stark silence engulfed the room and then the babe opened her mouth and yawned.

Lachlan and Katherine broke into proud smiles, cooing and laughing at their daughter.

"Isn't she incredible?" Lachlan gushed.

"A superior lass in all ways," Katherine agreed.

Two hours later, Katherine lay enfolded in Lachlan's arms, too happy and excited to sleep. The new parents could not stop peering down at the cradle next to their bed, which held their sleeping daughter.

"She's perfect, isn't she?" Lachlan said for easily the tenth time.

"Aye. We shall cosset and spoil her until she becomes

an unholy terror," Katherine jested. "A lass who will put Lileas's willful ways to shame."

Lachlan rolled his eyes. "Heaven forbid."

"I need ye to promise me something," Katherine said, looking deep into her beloved's eyes. "When the time comes, and our daughter must marry, ye will allow her to choose her husband."

Lachlan squirmed uncomfortably, setting his jaw in a hard line. "Fie, Katherine, ye've only just brought her into this world and ye're already asking me to give her to another."

"We will have many, many years with her until that happens," Katherine said soothingly. "I want her to have a marriage such as ours—filled with hope and trust and love. Promise me?"

The chamber was bathed in silence for a long time. Katherine opened her mouth to ask again and Lachlan let out a long-suffering sigh.

"Aye. If it means so much to ye, then I'll promise." He moved his hand protectively over the cradle and sighed again. "I suddenly understand how yer father felt when ye brought me to him. 'Tis a miracle he ever allowed me out of his dungeon."

Katherine traced a finger over Lachlan's chest. It seemed impossible, but the love she had for him once again grew stronger and deeper. He was the only man she ever could have called husband. The other half of her soul, the one who completed her.

"It took him some time, but in the end my father realized that he could not deny me my heart's true desire," she said boldly. "I chose ye, Lachlan MacTavish. Ye are mine."

"Now and always, my love," Lachlan agreed, as he pulled her close and kissed her deeply.